INDEPENDENCE BLUES

INDEPENDENCE BLUES

W. B. GARVEY

Jonkro Books
Phoenix, Arizona

First printing 2021

ISBN 9780982229477
LCCN 2020919334

Independence Blues is published by Jonkro Books, LLC, 1008 W. Allen St., Phoenix, AZ 85041.

For information please email info@jonkrobooks.com

Cover design by Sheer Design and Typsetting

Printed and bound in the United States of America

www.jonkrobooks.com

For my son

INDEPENDENCE BLUES

On a hot New Mexico desert in 1963 I discovered my mother was a champion fighter. I was nine that scorching midsummer day, stuck on a patch of black asphalt, sipping a cold orange pop alongside my father, watching the world turn cockeyed. It had not yet dawned on me, as we pulled off the highway and up to the bright pink motel in our pale-green push-button Valiant my father claims he bought so my mother would have a fancy new car to drive back home on their island, that we had crossed into hostile territory.

"Roll, I said! You're not kneading dough for Mr. Chen-Lee's bullah!"

Maddy cut her eyes at the hated ruler confiding its menace like a schoolmate's grin or the dreaded tamarind switch. Thwack! Her stung fingers went skating; blind feet on a startled crab, but her thumb kept hold of the violin.

"No jerking the wrist! Tuck in that elbow!"

A harsh tooth drew blood, moistening her pouting lip. Too late.

"Stop with the crocodile tears! Try again!"

Rebel eye-water clouding her eyes, Maddy took a second stab at the impossible scale. Out squeaked more spine-shrinking notes.

"Jehovah! Yuh deaf or what? Look—yuh even have poor Charlie runnin' from yuh!"

The frail girl sucked up her sniffles in time to see the small green lizard scoot from his favorite sun-drenched spot on the windowsill.

The despised ruler flashed, landing another stinger.

"Pay attention! How yuh expect to learn if yuh can't even concentrate?"

"Yuh de one seh look 'pon Charlie!"

"No back-talking the teacher!"

"Yunnot a teacha—yuh jus' mi bruddah!" Ten-year-old Maddy taunted her tormentor with a spearing pink tongue.

The older boy smiled in contempt. "Better drop that quashie rudeness—Little Miss Big Head!"

"Don't *you* call me that!"

The ruler sliced down with quickened vengeance but instead of flesh it encountered a stick that promptly struck the floor with a heart-stopping *crick!* His grown-man's face creasing in horror, her brother stooped to rescue the injured bow, his breath stopped as he stood and gingerly unwound its silver screw. The black frog sank from the drooping horsehairs like bait on a fishing-rod.

"You crazy stupid gal—you broke my bow!"

"Not me break it—you the one hit it with your ruler!" There would be hell to pay and Madeline wanted the record set straight.

"I never should try teach a nincompoop!" her distraught brother huffed. "This is a fine musician's bow—it cost plenty!"

"Then yuh shuddena bruck it," she countered logically, before ducking a reproachful fist.

"Liar! You tryin' to make like it's not you break it?"

"Is de truit!"

"Is not!"

"Is so!"

The teenaged bean-pole drew up like an offended country constable. "We'll see about this when Miss Dora gets home."

The surprise threat tore through Maddy's vaunted resistance. Her assurance snuffed out, she stood forlorn as Mason snatched his violin and haughtily set it inside its case. She had fought her fears from those first stressful lessons when her best friend suddenly mutated into a sadistic dictator—smack! if her thumb was too high, whack! if her hand wasn't cupped like an umbrella. She was fed up with him and his blasted ruler. Not that the slaps hurt all that much—it was just so frustrating! She would finally manage to tuck the violin the right way under her chin, point her full-sized head at the music, then spot the hated ruler and feel her mind go blank. Her brother claimed he only slapped her hand to help her remember.

Well, she remembered all right—every unjust blow!

"Mason—" she whispered, "I'm really sorry about your bow." Her voice was earnest because it was true. She hadn't meant to flinch, any more than she expected her fingers to be so clumsy. If she had known he would make her feel so hopelessly incompetent, she never would have begged him to teach her to play the rotten violin. "It was an accident," she persisted weakly, the thunder in her eardrums rising as he continued to ignore her. "What? Yuh leavin' it there—like that?" she cried, as her brother arranged the loose-haired bow on the balsawood stand with a lawyer's cold-eyed care—Exhibit A for the prosecution. "Yuh not gonna try fix it?"

Mason's disdain cut like a razor. "That's not some limb off a breadfruit tree, you ninny. It takes special wood from Brazil to make a bow like that."

"It's just a little split along the top. Maybe we could glue it back—"

"Of course! Why didn't I think of that?" Mason sneered at her from under the crown of black curly hair he took pride in parting down the middle then pomading flat against his large square skull. "You don't have a clue, do you? We can't 'glue it back.' That bow was made in *Italy*," he explained, sniffing the air to remind his little sister of her burdensome ignorance. "You need an expert to fix it properly. How many experts do you expect we'll find on our Lilliputian island?"

Madeline chewed inside her lip and tasted blood. She hated being ridiculed and especially her brother's recent delight in confounding her with words like 'Lilliputian.' "You sure an expert made it? Maybe somebody was just foolin' you!"

Mason threw up his hands. "I give up. You can't enlighten a nitwit."

"I'm not a nitwit!"

"Then stop behaving like one!"

Maddy rethought her strategy. Normally, after the hour of mutual torment, all would be forgiven; Mason would take her to the nearby Chinese shop and buy them each a half-penny bullah and a packet of new sugar. Best friends again, they would hike down to Stinking-Toe Gully then sit touching knees on the tumor bulging from the trunk of a jackfruit tree while she complained about her latest ordeal with the mean girls at school, her patient brother nodding in sympathy while he cut holes in the semi-sweet buns and squeezed in the thick black syrup. The comforting ritual never varied. Mason was a stickler for regularity.

"Are we still going to Mr. Chen-Lee's?" No sooner had the plea escaped her lips than Maddy squirmed, knowing that the words she hoped would magically set things right only made her sound like an even bigger saphead.

"You're really something else, you know that? You think you're getting off scot free for this? You're getting a whipping for sure!"

Fleeing through tears, Maddy rushed out to the sunken front porch and plopped down on the bottom step, her frail chest heaving. She could not believe her brother was being so horrid. The perilous number of times she risked a hiding for answering back or acting uncouth, Mason had always stepped in to save her. Not like her laba-laba sister, who never failed to seize her most vulnerable moments to remind Miss Dora of the scars she had imprinted on her older daughter for far less abominable conduct. She sulked, her tight throat convulsed with hiccups, watching Charlie Chaplin hop from the porch's rain-stripped railing and light on her shoulder. "You'd never call me that hurtful name, would you, Charlie?" she grumbled, running a sullen finger across her playmate's bumped skin. Mason's betrayal had shaken her deeply. She could bear the dreaded tamarind switch. What she never could bear was her brother's contempt.

For all the attention and rare tenderness she sensed in her earliest memories of Miss Dora, Mason was the one she remembered always being there when she opened her eyes. Precisely when the sickness took over her body she had been too little to recall. Little enough that Miss Dora, at four-foot-ten, could wrap her in a blanket and carry her through the miles-long shades of Golgotha to rouse Dr. Joseph who took one look at the motionless child with flesh hot as fire and grimly prescribed an ice-cooled bath and a bracing passage from Job.

Precious monies tucked away for special occasions were spent on a custom-made coffin, but while the tiny silk-lined box gathered dust, Maddy's red and white army mobilized every cell and corpuscle. The battle expected to last scarcely a week dragged on into months. Her stagnant days shrouded in a fog made memory an incomplete quilt of lucid patches her mind clung to like bursts of cheering sunshine. It was then, during those reviving moments, that her eyes would draw open and find Mason, his face pained as he whispered, "fight on, Maddy, fight!"

Month after month they prayed, the good Christian ladies who came each Sunday afternoon to lay on hands and softly press the tiny struggling chest; their voices, restored by Miss Dora's pineapple cake and mint tea, grown thick with hymns and bombastic devotion—'sweet Jesus, heavenly Father! See how this innocent child is fighting! Do, Lord, grant us our miracle!' An anguished year passed and, as faith gave ground to bush-teas and fruitless elixirs, the visits receded along with Miss Dora's dwindling stock of butter and flour. Then, just when they had closed the book on Kings and turned back to stoic Job, little Maddy began to recover. Amazed, but loath to seem apostate, the re-gathered faithful claimed never to have wavered. They had known all along their intercessions would find His Favor once the Good Lord saw fit. But when the three-year-old's fickle consciousness no longer faded inside flaring fevers, it was Mason's big grin that Madeline recognized and smiled at peacefully through her sweat-cooled cheeks.

"Look, I'm sorry—I rully am—it ain't up to us—"

"But your sign says 'vacancy' ..."

The redhead with the fake eyelashes made her spearmint gum go pop! and avoided my mother's glare to wink down at me with a phony grin. "Aren't you a cute little goober," she cooed. "I'd take you in a heartbeat, only my boss would fire me fer shure." She snapped the Wrigley's with a shrug poised between chagrin and self-pity. "Like I said—it's motel policy."

Picture a volcano, looming about five foot two, erupting. "That's unacceptable!"

Two frozen stares and a snap-free gum.

"Do you have any notion as to whom you are speaking?"

My mother's verbal brimstone was like a bath in molten lava.

The gum-chewer's sidekick, a jittery snow-white brunette, summoned her nerve and joined the cause. "Listen, lady—"

"No, you listen!" Returning fire, Mom kept the two of them locked in her sights while she called for backup. "Tell them, Emerson. What they're doing is against the law." She ignored my father's nudge as he muttered, "it's all right, Madeline, let's just go—"

"No. It's not all right!"

My father turned from the desk with a weary look and tugged my elbow.

"You thirsty? I saw a Coke machine out in the parking lot."

Trust my dad to drag me away just as the standoff was coming to a head. It baffled me that he wanted to retreat and I decided his brain must be fogged from all the driving because a sugar-laden pop was not something he would let me drink were he in charge of his faculties. My throat could be as parched as the New Mexico desert, but no matter how hard I pleaded that the water at those rest-stops tasted like *cat pee,* and besides it wasn't even *cold,* he would calmly reply that there was only one cure for thirst and it was plain old H two O. I knew that dehydration could make you crazy, so as we turned to leave the air-conditioned office and wander back out to bake at a hundred and fourteen degrees, I feared that before the day was over the three of us would be stark-mad, sunstruck zombies. He changed his mind and sent me back inside while he went to the car to hunt up some change. I remember staring across the parking lot of that crummy motel past the deserted highway and perceiving nothing but miles and miles of sand.

To be honest, my dad seemed less confused than defeated. We had been on the road since daybreak, but I sensed he wished we had kept on going. I could hear his brain-wheels straining for a peaceful solution and bumping against my mother's lust for combat. The way he viewed things, lecturing two dim-witted motel clerks about President Kennedy's civil rights bill was not going to get us a shower and beds for the night. Weary travelers stuck in a hostile land don't call for war, they seek appeasement.

I felt as if I'd stumbled into one of those Western reruns; the part where the hero has just been exiled to the badlands on account of a crime he did not commit. And then it hit me—how I saw myself was actually a mirage. It made no difference that my teachers thought I was 'gifted;' it did not matter that I was proficient on two instruments and a minor hero at my cross-town school for replacing the Christmas program's typical piano-student offering of *Für Elise* or *Jingle Bells* with Leroy Anderson's jaunty *Sleigh Ride*. No one cared that I was leaving my best friends forever, even Shayla, the strong honey-brown girl I had planned to marry until my father explained 'becoming winsome' meant my oldest playmate was too grown-up to wrestle. In a world that unfair, it amounted to less than a hill of beans that my throat was coated with half the dust in Arizona and I was starving and sore from eleven hours cramped in the back of a Plymouth Valiant beside my parents' piled-up possessions. I was stuck on a desert in Las Cruces, New Mexico, and worth less than a savage.

My mother was still blasting the poor receptionists. Having set their ears on fire with a salvo that ranged from Executive Orders to Interstate Commerce, she shifted her attack, and with a look used for a small disobedient child, told the one anxiously smacking her Wrigley's that she wished to speak with the motel's owner. "Fine. If he's not here, I suggest you call him. Now!"

The redhead, her green eyes hopping from Snow White then back to the telephone, blushed the color of her French-rolled hair and nearly choked on her gum. She had clearly never gone nose to nose with a woman like my mother and from the look on her face seemed to be trying to decide if this primly-dressed gal tying her brain up in knots practiced hoodoo. She cast my mother a timid glance and grabbed for the receiver.

My dad held up two bottled orange pops and like a lily-livered traitor I shuffled out to join him. Thirst and my mother's tirade had left me shell-shocked, so I said not a word as we leaned against the Valiant's bug-splashed fender to drink it all in. Slurping the ice cold soda, I tried to imagine what would happen if we were stranded here at sundown. All I could think was either none of this was real, or my parents had both gone loopy. I mean, who in their right minds would leave their friends and a perfectly good house in L.A. to be outcasts in the desert? I felt a glimmer of hope seeing my mother stride out of the motel door, only for it to fade when she ignored my dad's feeble pleas and stalked to the payphone by the soda machine.

If, at the time, I was conscious of the mesas in the forsaken distance waiting to reveal themselves in the blood-light I don't recall. Eventually, those immovable shrines for displaced gods would help mend my perspective, but back then what tore at my gut was how bad I felt for my father. I found it pretty pitiful of him to leave my mother to fight our battle. It was the journey's first lesson and while I had just begun to grasp bits and pieces of this puzzling new existence, all I knew was that my father, the esteemed Emerson Gardner, who could explain Kepler's Law and expound on Gandhi, Socrates and Tirhakah, was a coward.

Seeing Adrianna's glee as she dashed to cut their mother a whip, Maddy told herself that no matter how much it hurt, she was not going to cry. Two years had passed since the day she had fended off Mason's ruler and ended up breaking his bow, and although that was not the last time Miss Dora had warned her about her behavior, she had always escaped the dreaded switch, her bout with death having earned her a lifetime of saving bells.

"It wasn't really her fault ... the way it broke was just bad lucky ..."

Miss Dora had already gripped the branch from her well-pruned tamarind tree when Mason glimpsed the terror on his sister's face and changed his tune. That he was lying to save her skin had been as plain as the remorse filming his eyes, but the costly bow had been broken and their mother firmly believed that a child who suffers for youthful mistakes will have fewer regrets when grown. After reminding her children it was a sin to bear false witness, Miss Dora had ordered Mason to drop his trousers and touch his toes. Maddy had bawled the whole time she salved his shredded bottom with beeswax and plantain-leaf, then banished herself to bed without supper to weep into her pillow.

Adrianna returned with a branch so green it quivered and Maddy could hear her smirking sister thinking, 'Mason isn't here to save Little Miss Big Head this time!' She firmed her back, urging her knees not to fail her.

"You mean you're not gonna beat her—again?" Adrianna's eager look turned to rage seeing Miss Dora grasp the quivering switch and set it aside.

"With all the rumpus, I wasn't watching the time. I need you to help me in the kitchen. Mr. Jans will be here shortly."

"She *never* gets punished!" Adrianna pointed to the soiled blouse slopping out of Maddy's ripped skirt. "You'd tear the skin off my legs if I came home looking like that!"

"That's enough! We'll deal with your sister after dinner."

Crouching behind Miss Dora, Maddy stuck a thumb in her ear and waggled her fingers at Adrianna who aimed her a glare that declared if a look could kill she'd be dead.

"That's what you always say! You know Mr. Jans will let the disgusting little monkey off with just a talking-to!"

"Curb that tongue, young lady, or I'll save you some licks! Now march yourself into the kitchen and grate me some coconut."

Her short-lived happiness now a salted wound, Adrianna stamped off in a rage and Dora turned wearily towards her youngest. "Maddy, you can't be brawling with boys."

"Potty is the one who—"

"Not one word!" Miss Dora's glower stifled all excuses. "Go wash up yuhself, then set the table. We'll finish this when Mr. Jans gets here."

Now that Mason's apprenticeship with the railway had him living halfway across the island, Mr. Jans' bimonthly visits seemed fated to leave serious carnage in their wake. The custom had gone on peacefully for years, but with puberty's onset finally rousing little Maddy's dormant hormones, Dora feared that the contest for Mr. Jans' affections was on the verge of turning her daughters' verbal snipes into family-rending eruptions.

"Madeline seems to think she can hide behind that innocent look to run roughshod over people and get her own way—and I know the samfie charmer she gets it from."

If instead of halting his fork at Miss Dora's jibe with a contrite look Mr. Jans had detected the sparkle in her hard gray eyes, he would have waited until the girls were asleep and swept her into his arms. So many times she had wished he would read her mind and slip through her defenses, more than that once since her desperate pact with God. The Lord had kept His bargain and spared her child, but that old devil temptation still churned inside whenever she drew close to the man her body and soul never stopped loving.

"Don't tell me our Little Miss Big Head has been up to more trouble."

Maddy shied from Mr. Jans' blithe smile and gazed stonily down at her plate.

"Trouble?" blurted Adrianna, her knife and fork gripped with rage. "That's all she's ever been! Trouble and boderation!"

Miss Dora glared at her outraged daughter. "Excuse me, Mr. Jans and I were conversing! Do you need a whipping to remember that children are to be seen and not heard unless spoken to?"

"I'm not a child, I'm almost sixteen!"

"Then it's time you set your sister a better example."

Maddy hid her face with her hand and squashed her snigger. No matter how hard she tried to get her into hot water, Adrianna was always the one who ended up getting scalded.

"Yuh find something funny?"

The ice in her mother's tone chilled her amusement. "No'm."

"Good. Now tell Mr. Jans what you've done. I'll let him decide on your punishment."

Even though their neighbors rightly presumed that Mr. Jans had fathered Miss Dora's three children, his place in the household was ambiguous. In Maddy's eyes he was more a benevolent uncle than a father. With Mason away in the country, she would be lost if her only advocate sided with the prosecution.

"Right then, let's hear it," Mr. Jans coaxed her kindly. "What mischief has made my little Maddy want to bury her head?"

"She's upset about her stupid lizard," Adrianna finally broke in when her sister sat in silent misery.

"One more word and you'll be tasting that switch!" hissed Miss Dora, shifting her annoyance with Mr. Jans onto her daughter who flung down her serviette and rushed from the table. Dora gave the fifteen-year-old's departing back a glower that said, 'you'll pay for this later' then calmly continued. "Maddy went next door looking for Charlie and caught the Pottinger boy trying to stone him. Instead of just telling him to stop, your little hellion butts the poor boy in his stomach and was grabbing up a rock to hit him. Thank goodness Mrs. Pottinger was looking out her window and called her off. The child is growing too wild—she needs a man to manage her."

"What happened to Charlie?" asked Mr. Jans, gliding past the implication.

Miss Dora gave a shrug. "We haven't seen him since. Madeline thought she found a piece of his tail.

"What she did was wrong, but we can't really blame it all on Maddy, now can we? That Pottinger boy had no business stoning an innocent lizard."

Maddy felt a rush of relief. She judged Mr. Jans' dissent as meaning to let her mother know that if he was to be the one meting out justice, his verdicts would be fair.

"Here I'm trying to raise a Christian young lady and you make excuses for her behavior. What if she had badly hurt that boy? You need to take her in hand. Me one can't manage two warring hard-ears hellions."

Maddy quailed inside. It would defile their bond if Mr. Jans whipped her for protecting Charlie. Her only pet had barely been born when she found him on her bedroom floor, dazed from a fall. When the teeny lizard did not move at her cautious poke, she hid him inside a shoe-box and fed him bugs and torn up leaves fetched from the garden. Even after he had recovered and jumped for his freedom they remained companions. When she and Mason could not agree on what to call him she had asked Mr. Jans and he had said, 'how about Charlie?' Her silly eight-year-old brain had forgotten all about their secret and with Miss Dora sitting right there exclaimed, 'Oh yes! Let's call him Charlie Chaplin—like that funny little man at the moving pictures!' Mr. Jans had absorbed chapter and verse of Miss Dora's Old Testament fury and won a place in Maddy's heart forever and ever.

As soon as she stepped back out of our car with her brushed-up hair and fresh lipstick I knew my mother was ready to rumble. Though she was only two spins around the sun short of fifty, as she stood smoothing her light cotton dress around her hourglass frame she could pass for a deeply tanned movie star.

My father cast her a tired look as he returned with our empty pop bottles, having failed to charm the redhead into giving us water. "You're not going to change them."

"Emerson, they're breaking the law."

"No they're not. We may find it reprehensible, but what they're doing is perfectly legal."

"Wrong, Dr. Gardner!" my mother crowed, as if announcing 'checkmate.' "Didn't you see where they hung their sign?"

I followed her finger to the giant billboard that said BUY AMERICAN in blue and red letters, then noticed the pink-lettered green sign right beside it urging travelers to the Amity Motel. "That's on an interstate highway, which means it's on federal property. They are flouting the President."

I could tell my dad was losing his cool to the point where if any hairs remained on his sweat-shined head he would be pulling at every strand. "Are we to lounge out here until darkness is upon us so you can debate legal niceties with a couple of high school drop-outs? Just get back in the car and let's move on—your son and I are tired and hungry!"

Big mistake. Even at nine, I had sense enough to know that was not the tone to take when Mom was on the warpath.

"Typical. You're worried about your stomach while these people treat you like scum. Well, I won't stand for it!"

Before my dad could get hold of himself for a reasoned comeback, a sun-scarred Volkswagen bug put-putted into the parking lot. A limber young man in a blue Hawaiian shirt and chino shorts hopped out.

"Mrs. Gardner?"

My mother stroked her brushed up hair as she turned to greet him. "That's me."

"Kip Rothschild, Southwestern News."

While she flashed us a 'told-you-so' grin, I had my eyes on the reporter's cool, collected face and wondered what a sun-bronzed surfer was doing living out in the desert.

"So good of you to come. This is my husband, Dr. Gardner, and our son."

My father shook the eager copper-toned hand, looking less than impressed.

"On the telephone you said you were with the L.A. Times—"

Madeline fluttered a pair of bashful eyelashes. "I'm sorry I wasn't more clear. I'm sure you can understand, considering our stressful situation."

A frown nettled the mellow beachcomber look and I sensed the young reporter losing interest.

"So, you're *not* with the Times?"

"Not me *personally*. I have a friend who covers regional news—we met when Governor Brown honored me for my work with California's Blue Ribbon Commission on improving public education—" She waited until her slightly inflated bona-fides sank in. "In fact, I called Max right after we spoke and he's *very* interested in letting his readers know what travelers can expect in your town." Having dropped her bait in neatly, she paused for a meek smile before landing her fish. "Of course, the Times would love it to be your own story, Mr. Rothschild. Max said that way no one can accuse them of being unbalanced."

Kip snatched the pencil from above his ear and flipped out his notepad. "I got a handle on the scene over the phone. How about we fill in some more background?"

Egged on by Kip's solicitous nods, my mother was sharing another highlight of her adapted life story when a dark sedan came roaring up in a cloud of dust and lurched to a stop. The powerful engine went dead and the entire desert seemed to fall silent. No one made a move and, caught in the suspense, I stared at the gold-tipped rattlesnake boots, then the bulging torso straining inside stiff-pressed khakis, and finally the glinting badge that matched the sedan door star and left me shivering. Dad was right—we were going to jail!

"I'll be right back," my mother simpered, abandoning Kip with an affectionate hand-pat.

I could see Snow White and Ginger peeking nervously out the office window as I searched for my father and saw that he had gone to sit inside our car. I could tell he was stewing in his juices by the way he was staring through the windshield with both arms locked across his chest. He did not budge as the lawman confronted my mother.

"What seems to be the trouble?"

"I'm *so* relieved to see you, Officer!" she said compliantly, not batting an eye when the sheriff turned out to be a six-foot-tall Mexican-American with a weightlifter's build. "This establishment needs to be enlightened about the law."

I glanced in time to see the redhead race from the window to unbolt the lock and call out through the half-open door. "In here, Sheriff Gomez!"

The thirty-year-old lawman stuck a thick hand on his hip and slid the other across a spikey crewcut. He peered at me then across to my father still stewing inside our Valiant. "Has a crime been committed here?" As his broad head swivelled between my calm collected mother and the angry receptionists, he sounded mystified.

"Hey there, Georgie. I see Mrs. Gardner called in the marines."

"Kip?" The sheriff squinted across the lot in surprise as Rothschild ambled back from the pay phone. "*Que pasa*, buddy? What brings you here?"

"Same as you, George. Mrs. Gardner here is stirring up some dust."

"Sheriff Gomez!" shouted the redhead, her tone clipped and demanding. "Inform that woman that they are trespassing on private property!"

My mother's eyes sparkled in delight. "You hear that, Officer? She openly defies the law! Look for yourself! That sign right there clearly says 'vacancy'!"

The sheriff's meaty shoulders constricted and my Nancy Drew-trained nose sniffed out his dilemma. Like most men around his age, seeing my attractive mother gazing up into his face like Miss Wide-Eyed and Helpless had the poor man melting faster than a midday ice cream bar at Venice Beach. Reassured by his courteous reaction, my fear gave way to a thrill—I was standing next to a real-life sheriff slinging a Colt .38 trooper revolver in a black-leather holster dotted with honest-to-God .38 caliber bullets. And he was Mexican!

"The Gardners just want a place to spend the night," Kip explained, sounding matter of fact. "I'm not sure she's right on the technicalities, but she knows some pretty high-up folks in California. I'll give it to you straight, Georgie—" the reporter stopped with a contrite look, "my boss thinks there's a story."

The lawman scratched his jaw and studied the tips of his rattleskin boots. I was pretty sure his heart was on our side, but he still had to live with these people.

"Well, Sheriff, what's it gonna be?" Snow White had ventured out to back up her partner.

His shoulders bending at the challenge, the lawman stood up to my mother's bristling five foot two like a cornered truant hunting for an alibi.

"Ma'am, look—" he said, facing her uneasily, "I got nothing against it. I mean … we're all pe—" He kept himself from saying 'people,' at a loss as to how to proceed until he regained his footing and promptly stumbled. "Heck—you-all ain't so bad—take Joe Louis—great boxer—maybe the greatest—"

For a millisecond, my mother looked as if she'd been cold-cocked by a stealthy uppercut. "I need to speak with the mayor," she cut him off.

Bedlam was inducing panic inside the stone-walled dumb cell. Inflamed by the tortured prophet's screams, those on the loose had bolted blindly down the compound's inner passageway and into a cul-de-sac. Trapped by the alerted guards, the men were fighting back out through a barrage of vengeful bludgeons, while inside the hated dumb cell, the victim continued to struggle.

"Damn it, Bolden, I told yuh, keep still!" the corporal urged as a second merciless boot rammed the prone man's side.

"Not Bolden—" the injured man gurgled through a froth of

blood and bits of teeth, "I am Prince Zephaniah called to warn God's people!"

Corporal Winters leered at his obstinate prisoner—the bungohead definitely belonged in the madhouse. "Beg pardon, your Majesty, but would his Highness kindly stay still so we can fasten his royal shackles?"

Moved back into the yard, the skirmish swelled into a fractious contest. Intoxicated by the resilience granted by superior numbers, the inmates were committing skin and bone to the battle. Inspired by their pluck but doubtful of victory, their comrades stuck behind bars heightened the protest, striking up an artful chant. "Young Doc! We—want—young—Doc!"

Private Campbell gave a frightened look as the cries grew more raucous. "Why yuh don't jus' shoot him, Corpie? That would quiet those naiggahs."

The corporal kneaded his thick, sweaty black neck. "No," he said ruefully, "that might just stir them up more. Anyway, my pistol is up in the superintendent's office. Let's hope he has the sense to have the army send us men or our goose may be cooked."

"Corpie!" the second guard cried. "Look!"

Two sightless milk-white eyes stared up at the terror-struck guards who took two nervous steps in retreat, their gaping stares transfixed, seeing the prisoner's dark pupils completely vanished. Outside, the chants and fury were rising to deafening pitch when, suddenly, they were eclipsed by the sound of banging metal then bursts of applause and whistling cheers. Just as the tempest seemed set to roar into a deadly crisis it subsided, the source of the calm now rapping at the dumb cell door.

"It's Emerson Gardner. Open up at once!"

The cell bolt loosened and the corporal stiffened to greet the chubby young man in a rumpled white smock. Gardner glanced at the prisoner on the blood-stained floor with Campbell's knee pressing his windpipe. "Get off him this instant!"

"All right, that's enough," Winters commanded, seeing the intern fixing to yank the frightened guard off by his neck. "Madman fight like lion, Doc," he explained as Gardner knelt to inspect the marks from a savage beating.

"So that gave you the right to try and end his life?"

"Dammit, Doc—" Winters started to spout then checked his tone. "The man cause too much problems. It wasn't much, just a little touch up."

Gardner was about to say a broken collarbone was far from 'a little touch up' when the victim began jerking with spasms. He hurriedly stripped off his smock and folded it under the inmate's head.

"Corporal, tell Dr. Coombs I need fifty CCs of phenobarbital—go!" Ignoring the guards, the intern cupped Bolden's woolly head in his palm and turned it gently as if caressing an egg. "And get them out of here!" he bellowed, nodding past his shoulder to the privates hovering behind him.

Winters cast a wary eye at the cell-door's narrow sight-hole. "Not certain that's a good idea—" he started to hedge then gave in to Doc's scowl. "Campbell, stand guard outside—but listen up sharp!" he barked on his way to alert the surgeon.

Inside, the prisoner's spasms had turned into frantic thrashing. Gardner gripped the tight locked jaw, prying it open to blow air down the inmate's throat, hoping to trigger the pharynx's failing reflex. The lungs responding on instinct, Bolden retched up a blood-seeped sliver of fat then lay limp and began breathing freely.

At no time had anyone other than Emerson Gardner and the three prison guards been inside the dumb cell that notorious day, but one-upmanship being a jailhouse staple and embellishment its natural spice, within the week the episode spawned over twenty versions. A particular guard favorite claimed that Winters had ordered his men not to shoot before battling Bolden's demon with his two bare hands, managing to drain enough of its superhuman strength that Doc could blow the evil spirit out of the madman's earhole. The inmates, on the other hand, were partial to a more biblical retelling. Here, Moses had appeared to Bolden in solitary to remind him that he bore the seed of King Solomon's line returned to free the oppressed from Babylon, just as prophesied. But Bolden's brain could not take the strain so it was left to Doc Gardner to save him and chasten their tormentors. If few of the inventive parables

were actually swallowed, one judgment would remain unanimous—
Young Doc had saved everyone's bacon.

From the day he showed up inside the eighteenth century
fortress crowned with embrasures and British merlons, the
residents of Yallas Prison had tried to decide which of the night sky's
distant planets the new intern would point to as home. With its
underpaid guards and overpacked cells, the island's main
penitentiary was not a place sensible earthlings entered cheerfully,
yet here came this fat-cheeked young chemist day after day bearing
the same soothing smile and courteous manner. For Midas
Coombs, who took pride in leaving his eager-to-get-out-and-get-
ahead assignees scarred by their mandated stint in Hades, Emerson
Gardner turned out to be a provoking challenge. Not only was he
foiling the surgeon's secret joy in life, the twenty-one-year-old had
the gall to play dumb when staff and prisoners alike took to calling
him 'Young Doc,' despite Coombs' stern objection.

Intent to destroy the neophyte's infuriating self-assurance and
also avoid leaving the peaceful confines of the second-floor hospital,
Coombs had sent him off to manage the rounds on his own,
expecting to sit back and enjoy watching Gardner get eaten alive by
the cell block's bully-boys. But his new charge proved more than a
match even for the prison's infamous 'Big-D' gang. Whether he was
ferreting out the ones with syphilis and tricking them into
quarantine or deciding between a coincident case of diarrhea and a
potential outbreak of dysentery, Young Doc approached every
threat with the same unflappable aplomb. 'Small wonder,' Coombs
grumbled, seeing his attempted subterfuge blow up in his face, 'the
cocky bastard's marks had been tops on the island.'

That's not to say the young intern was never tested. When the
seasoned malingerers discovered that the sick were now getting sent
to hospital instead of the mine, they brushed up their formidable
skills to mimic every ailment and disability known to contemporary
medicine. But while Emerson was saddened to see the amount of
native ingenuity being wasted in incarceration, even the finest actors
failed to escape a single day's hard labor. Perversely, the fact that he
was impossible to fool only worked to inflate his stock with the
stymied inmates and left their grateful guards in awe.

His most daunting test had been the enigma the guards called Buster Bolden but who insisted he was Prince Zephaniah. Bolden's stubborn refusal to have his unkempt hair cut or touch food 'defiled by swine' had vaulted Corporal Winters into an unbending rage. When a week in solitary living on crackers and water failed to break the self-proclaimed prince, Winters appealed for the intern's help in getting the nuisance transferred.

"Careful 'round him, Doc," he warned as they came inside and found Bolden pacing the cell spouting dire prophesies and poetic damnation. "The boy not right in the head."

After dismissing the corporal and speaking with the prisoner at length, Gardner announced that not only was the half-starved man not insane, he should be allowed to rejoin the general population and granted his request for a pork-free diet. This was a bridge too far for Corporal Winters who swore that before he granted 'that nut-case' any special privileges, the boy would have to get down off his 'high horses' and let the barber chop that 'dirty naiggah bush' off his head. When Gardner maintained that there was more to be gained in suspending the rule, so long as the prince kept his hair properly washed and combed, Winters waited until the intern was safely upstairs in the dispensary to thwart this threat to his authority.

It was Prince Zephaniah's consequent screams that had touched off the riot and provided Midas Coombs his long-awaited opening just as Gardner was being marked for sainthood. According to Winters, Bolden's bad attitude had caused the 'whole darn-fool thing.' He was sorry Young Doc was disappointed, but he and his men had been 'perfectly calm and reasonable' as they explained why the stew-peas could not be cooked separately and it was only after the madman spat in his face that they felt forced to teach him some manners.

"You know, Gardner," said Coombs, seemingly amused by his assistant's outrage, "you would have saved that boy a beating and the rest of us a host of trouble had you taken Winters' advice. The idiot would be happier strapped in the asylum."

"What makes you say that? He may not be descended from Solomon but the man is as sane as you and I."

The seventy-year-old surgeon looked tickled. "A Jamaican quashie fancies himself a Hebrew prince reborn in the 1930s—what is possibly insane about that?"

"And those we entrust with this country's future believe God ordained them to be rich at our expense. Unless God is an imbecile, we should *all* be locked up."

"Ah, a noble egalitarian, defender of the righteous rabble. What are you, Gardner? A dew-eyed Communist?"

He was tempted to say that the man they took for a fool understood more about what ailed their island than the lot of them, but it had been a long trying day and Coombs would be less than impressed to learn that his assistant shared a quashie's views on a healthy diet. "No, sir, just a simple scientist," he finally replied, making a show of trailing his eyes across the makeshift lab with his stacking notes on the prison's outdated stock and exhausted supplies. "We all cope with the intolerable as best we can. It's a trait of human intelligence."

Coombs' beige features flamed, sensing the moment ripe to put the smart-aleck in his place. *"Mister* Gardner, when you're less the simpleton and more the scientist, you will learn that when it comes to primitives like your woolly-headed prince, arrogant self-regard is not a sign of intelligence, it is self-delusion."

"It's not such a bad idea, Georgie."

The Doña Ana County sheriff's face was a globe of confusion.

"You serious, Kip? You think I should get the mayor tied up with this?"

The redhead was fiercely working a fresh stick of gum as she tottered across the pebbles by the motel entrance on her high-heeled shoes. She stopped a safe distance from where the four of us stood in back of the patrol car and her flushed-pink face seemed to fuse with the hot-pink motel.

"Now see here, Sheriff—you gonna let them stand here bending your ear or you gonna do your job? My boss says either move-em on or arrest-em, lickety-split! They're scaring off good customers."

Smiling, my mother held up her delicate wrists. "Do you want to cuff me, Officer Gomez? Perhaps Mr. Rothschild would like to take our picture—"

Kip was focusing his camera when I heard my father slam our Valiant's driver-side door before stomping up to end the showdown. "Maddy, enough! We're getting way off schedule."

"We can't leave, Emerson," she objected, her arms still raised to the sheriff. "I'm being arrested!"

If the weight of his sigh could make up for losing face, my father's honor might not have felt so slight in the balance. I had grown up respecting his cool philosophical head, but after watching my mother in action, I knew that logic would no more dampen her spirit than a night in jail would sap her convictions.

The redhead popped her gum with a grin. "You heard her, Sheriff, slap her in cuffs."

My father shoved himself in front of my mother. "My apologies, Officer Gomez. Our presence should not have placed you in this predicament."

"Emerson!" My mother pushed at his shielding arm but my dad stood strong and overrode her crafty half-protests.

"Sheriff, we've had a tiring day's travel—perhaps you can recommend an alternative nearby that would prove more amenable."

The big Mexican rocked on his heels in a way that made me think of a circus bear wobbling on a tightrope. "Gee—can't say off the top my head—maybe try the next town over—"

My mother evaded my father's arm and tilted her head at the copper-toned lawman. "You disappoint me, Officer Gomez. Come take our picture, Mr. Rothschild. We'll call your mayor from jail."

The sheriff seemed to be searching for a hole to hide in and again my father tried jumping to his rescue.

"No, Emerson, I won't just come along!" my mother cried, squirming from his clutch. "Right is right and the law is the law!"

The redhead stormed off to dial her boss and as Kip directed the four of us to stand by the motel's green neon sign reading 'vacancy,' a tan and brown station wagon pulled up beside us. Oatmeal streaks from dust and caked-on sand slathered the car's fake wood panels and a set of bulging suitcases filled half of its rear compartment.

On her way back to confront us, the receptionist stopped midstride and clapped a hand to her mouth blurting, "oh, my God!" before scurrying inside. The sheriff stared helplessly across at Kip who laughed as he caught sight of my mother's face.

Stiffly unfolding from the sand-smudged wagon was a middle-aged black couple.

"Potty, you rascal! I told you to drop me off at the gully!"

The teenager cupped a hand to his ear, pretending not to hear. Maddy released her grip on the handlebar and fastened both arms around his torso.

"Stop this minute or I swear I'll break your ribs."

"Oooh! harder—I like the feeling!" Potty yelled into the rushing wind, revving his engine.

"Last chance."

"I'm trembling!" the strapping teenager joked, then gasped when the slender arms dug cruelly into his sides. He righted his balance in time to curve the bike around a deaf-eared donkey. "Jesus Christ—you trying to get us killed?"

"I'm as good as dead if some laba-laba sees us," Maddy hollered, easing her hold but preserving its threat.

Potty gunned the motorbike, sending some antsy pedestrians scattering as he zoomed off the main road to a plunging path riddled with stones. He down-geared to a bumpy stop and Madeline slipped from the wooden back seat, the hem of her loose skirt bunched inside her fist. It rankled her that it was crass to be seen exposing her legs when a girl in trousers was considered lewd. So while she had leapt for the chance to ride Potty Pottinger's dreamy new motorcycle, she had made sure to keep her knees covered.

Potty shook his head watching her struggle to straighten her skirts. "You'll be of age next year, you're done with school—what's the worst that can happen?"

"You don't know Miss Dora. She whipped Adrianna for trying

to sneak out to her own graduation party. I don't want her scarring my legs."

"That *would* be a crime," Potty agreed, stealing a peek at Maddy's perfect ankles. "No disrespect, but your mum's a bit barmy. It's 1931 not the bloody Dark Ages."

"She's never whipped *me*, thank God! I don't intend to give her a reason to now! But thanks for the spin—it was jumping good fun!"

"That's it? I'd say you at least owe me a kiss!" Potty proposed impishly, undoing the chinstrap on his leather helmet.

"Potty Pottinger—you sleazy cad!" she scolded, feigning disgust. "Is that why you offered me a ride, you—you—quashie Quasimodo!"

The lanky eighteen-year-old swung a fashionably shod leg across the shiny black Rudge and slithered close, miming the smoldering gaze of Rudolf Valentino. "Now don't be coy, my pretty. Admit you were yearning for an excuse to encircle those delightful arms around this chest."

Maddy neatly eluded his teasing grab. "Behave, you ogre, or I'll give you another slug in the stomach! I still owe you a smack for stoning Charlie."

Emboldened by the streamlined, post-adolescent good looks that had won him both a surfeit of female attention and a rare good job downtown, Potty fell to his knees then made her jump when he reached as if to fondle her feet. "What penance does the beauty demand of this unfortunate beast?" He let one eyelid droop and humped his spine like the notorious hunchback.

"Oh, just stop," said Maddy, sniggering. "You're a beastly fool."

"Yes, but look!" Jumping to his feet, Potty pulled out the gift hiding in his pocket. "I bear new sugar ... although I assure you my lips are even sweeter!"

Madeline laughed, shaking her head of wavy black hair. "Honestly, you're such a clown!"

"See!" he exulted. "You can't stay mad at me the rest of your life—I was just a fat lonely child craving your attention. So, whaddaya say? Meet me at the pictures on Saturday? It's Chaplin and Fairbanks!"

Her face enlivened at the proposal then sagged. There was no way she could sneak out to a matinee on the Sabbath. "I've got to go—"

"See you tomorrow?" Potty called out after her, his look far from hopeful as his untouchable heartthrob disappeared down the goat walk across Stinking-Toe Gully.

Her mother was sitting in wait as she stepped through the door. Maddy stalled, spotting the switch.

"Have I slaved all these years to raise godless tramps?" Shards recalled from raw wounds pinched Miss Dora's voice. "I thought you had more sense than to hop on that boy's infernal motorcycle. How dare you clasp yourself to him in public, like you're his succubus?"

Maddy's pulse, which had been speeding with anticipation the whole walk home, raced faster. She had hoped her news would lift her mother out of her funk, if just for a day or two. "Who's the nosy parker that came and upset you?"

"Never you mind! I won't stand for you bringing more shame upon us."

"Shame?" Madeline cried, looking mystified. "What shame are you talking about?" She never understood why her mother put stock in gossip. She only had to listen to those pious hypocrites flap their gums to know that the truth was never strong enough to spoil a good scandal.

Miss Dora's resolve seemed to waver, then, drawing a breath, she rose from her chair, her conviction rebounded. "Stop give me chat and drop those drawers! You'll not disgrace this house."

"You're going to beat me? For what? Accepting a lift from a friend to save my feet?"

Her mother flicked the switch, stinging Maddy's ankles and making her skip. "Looks to me those feet work just fine," she said coldly. "It's my fault for never correcting you. This whipping is long overdue."

A rush of compassion suddenly overtook Maddy's temper. Having suffered along with her mother's latest miseries, she had begun to see through that layered husk to the stunted woman inside. As a child, she had taken it as simply the hollow platitude that mothers say, but she realized now that Miss Dora's rod served as more than a painful correction meant to spare her offspring; it was a cleansing blade aimed to crop the filthy stubborn weed plaguing a husbandless woman with desires sure to ruin her time on earth and bar her from the peace of heaven. Although she did not know why her parents had always lived apart, as she grew to perceive the root of her mother's ill temper, she understood that while Miss Dora had gladly exhausted herself to provide for her children, some early wound had drawn the blood from her reserve of love and the strength to trust. Navigating the straight and narrow demanded vigilance, for somewhere near respectability's precipice, Satan was lurking.

Madeline steeled her back and faced up to her mother's wrath. "Before you whip me, I want you to know the nursing board says my exam score guarantees me a full scholarship. So go ahead. Beat me if you think that will solve your problems, but if you do I'll leave this house and never come back. You'll lose me just like you've lost Adrianna."

The purging switch rose, ready to lash the defiance Dora was grieved to see on her daughter's face. The threat, chafing on its redemptive thread, hung through blood and eternity between mother and child, destined to cut either way. As Madeline stood firm, Dora's toil-roughed hand let the cruel rod fall and contrite tears spilled down two pairs of burning cheeks.

No one said a word as the weary couple scrunched out of the sand-streaked station wagon. Even my mom stood lost for words as they tested their blood-swelled legs and stretched to the relative heights of Mutt and Jeff. They smiled at our dumbstruck gathering with relief.

"Greetings, fellow travelers! Care to join me in getting arrested?"

Mr. Mutt, dressed all in gray except for a red St. Louis Cardinals baseball cap, took a long step back, in case my mom was a dangerous lunatic. "We're not looking to stir up any trouble, Officer," he declared respectfully, wisely ignoring my mother to address the person in uniform. He nodded to his dumpling-shaped partner whose head barely reached above his shoulder. "Connie here spotted these folks out in the parking lot," he shot my dad a questioning frown as my mom flashed him her practiced movie-star smile, "so we figured this place might be amenable." He paused with the same baffled look coming from the sheriff. "We actually passed by earlier but the couple motels we tried said they were already booked up, so we doubled on back."

The redhead came tottering back while Snow-White stood guard at the motel entrance. "What is this ... a convention?" She stopped a safe distance away but close enough that I could hear her hectic jaw make her chewing gum snap. "Now see here, Sheriff. My boss is lookin' to blow his stack. Do your dad-blame job! They can't camp here all night."

"Welcome to Las Cruces," my mother said tartly, as the redhead tiptoed off in a huff and Connie squeezed up her face, shaping to cry.

"If I have to get back in that stinking-hot car, why, I think I'll just die!" she whimpered. She aimed her pinched mug at Mr. Mutt. "I told you we shouldn't drive this way."

"You got a better way to get from El Cajon to Tuscaloosa?" her husband snapped as his ramrod bearing wobbled with a passing knee-buckle.

"And this is just New Mexico—" Connie wailed. She took two petulant steps towards their car and stumbled on her three-inch heels. My father swooped in time to keep her dumpling rump from frying on the asphalt. "Why, thank you much, kind sir!" she simpered, leaning on his arm like some fainting southern belle. "I get so terribly clumsy when I'm overtired."

She batted her long eyelashes at him while my dad held on until her legs had steadied and Mr. Mutt stiffened. I made a quick check on my mother but she did not seem bothered. No doubt she was busy figuring that, with potential reinforcements, it was time to revise her battle plan.

"Don't you worry, charming Connie," she said, smiling as she came to greet her. "I'm Dr. Gardner's wife by the way—can I call you Connie?" she asked, taking a dig at her little flirtation with my father. "We are all going to have beds to sleep in tonight. If not here, then the county jail, isn't that right, Officer?"

Gomez stuck his thumbs inside the gun-belt hugging his waist and stood peering into space as if confused by her question. It was clear he would sooner bite the head off a rattler than tangle with my mother. When he stayed mute she gestured familiarly across to Kip.

"My contact at the Los Angeles Times is anxious to read Mr. Rothschild's column. Who knows, Officer Gomez? Your town may become famous."

Right on cue, Kip asked the mismatched couple if they cared to join the group picture. Mr. Mutt bristled under his baseball cap, a convincing replica of a menacing statue. Connie managed to balance on her own two feet as she minced her way back to her car fussing about her mussed up hair until my father suggested that before we all said 'cheese' and spent the night in the sheriff's 'chapel for freedom,' it would be nice to know the names of his cell-mates.

His curt injection of humor seemed to scale back the tension. The drafted martyrs relaxed and went about glad-handing the three of us with shamefaced grins, "pleased to meet you, Doctor—and this is your boy?—hello, young man, I'm Captain Angell—that's okay, just call me Delroy—you've both met Connie—"

My mom, shrewdly observant as ever, had taken note of the station wagon's faded bumper-sticker. "You're a veteran, Captain Angell?"

Delroy stuck two fingers to the brim of his cap with a diffident pose. "Double-U double-U Two, United States Army Air Force."

For a second I thought Kip's jaw had locked on open.

"You were in the Air Force?" For the first time that afternoon the laid-back reporter was not shockproof.

Delroy Angell faced him resentfully. "Does that surprise you? I was with the 332nd."

"No kidding ... "

"*Santa María!* A real life war pilot!" Sheriff Gomez clicked his heels with a snappy salute. "It's an honor, Captain! I've seen *Twelve O'Clock High* must have been at least a dozen times—"

My mother lost no time drawing him aside. "Officer, here's the thing," she whispered, checking to make sure the redhead was still out of earshot. "I think there's a way to work this out without anyone losing their job. This is a big country with a lot of important people starting to pay attention. You were right about Captain Angell being a hero. I'm willing to bet your mayor would appreciate the person who helped him avoid bad publicity—"

The sheriff paused, one eye on the pilot being quizzed by Kip. Doubt still shadowing his indigenous features, he told my mom to give him a minute and left to sit in his patrol car. He sat there for a while, keeping us in suspense, then stepped out to announce that, before he was obliged to take them into custody, Mrs. Gardner could make one last call. "That's the mayor's home number," he whispered, spotting the redhead stalking his moves through the motel window and pretending to hand my mother a summons, "just don't tell those *chismosas* how you got it."

"Officer," she beamed, touching her hand to the somber Mexican-American's impressive biceps, "you're a champ!"

Emerson Gardner struggled to read the painstaking scrawl:

Dear Doc,

Greetings from prison. The situashon here has gotten very bad. Since you gone no body treat the suffering. I had a next attack but Doctor Coombs still send me back down to the Chalk Hole. Thanks to you Corpie no let the guards ruff us up bad like first time but since I Prince Zephaniah speak out against the ill treatment them whisper that one day them gonna mark me. I try tell them we is all bredren stuck servin' liars in Babylon but them dont have eyes to see. I's trust in Corpie to give you this as I know you and him talk sometime. Please come help me. Before is too late.

your honest and faithful friend,

Prince Zephaniah

p.s. Read Psalm 64 to understand.

Gardner took a moment to master himself then held the letter up to the grim-faced corporal. "When did you get this?"

Winters paused from twisting his kerchief to swipe dots of

perspiration seeping from his forehead. "Couple weeks back—maybe more—"

"Now you come to tell me the man is dead. Did you kill him before or after you read his letter?"

The corporal flinched. "Don't do me like that, Doc. The man was off his head. Nobody kill him."

"You knew he felt his life was in danger and yet you said nothing, even after I asked you to look out for him?"

When Winters stayed silent Gardner did not need to consult the psalm's lament to grasp its plea. The arrow of God the precocious young prophet had hoped would save him had turned to pierce his own chest. To think that the guards he exchanged pleasantries with for almost two years were capable of beating a man to death made him sick. Having come to know Prince Zephaniah over the weeks he spent treating his injuries, he had never understood how it was that reed-thin epileptic had been sentenced to ten years hard labor.

"Doc, yuh ever watch a spider weave its web?" he replied when Gardner asked how he had ended up in Yallas Prison. "It start off like it jus' decide to try fly in the air fuh fun till yuh notice it done shoot out this tiny-tiny thread yuh gots to squint yuh eye to see it. Somehow that spider knows when that little thread is ready to hold cause it walk careful 'cross it then back to the middle before it fly off again. Then, after it done and the light strike it right, you see this big beautiful web, so perfect yuh wonder how an insect so little bit could create such a miracle. But next mahnin when you wake up and see all the other bugs that get snagged inside it you realize that's just how the cunning operate: they build a web you can't see to trap poor people."

Midas Coombs had scoffed at his intern's proposed solution.

"This is a prison, Gardner, not a spa for the ladies' tea club. I'm not about to start handing out barbiturates to an erratic hooligan."

"I understand that, sir, but the Luminal would help us manage both the seizures and these invidious superstitions. The guards get spooked every time he has an attack."

"Oh, well, if the guards are getting spooked—" Coombs had responded with biting sarcasm, "but why stop there? I'll prescribe a good sedative and have them meet with a psychiatrist. I'm sure the prison's lavish funds will cover it. Honestly, Gardner, come down from the clouds."

The letter proved he had missed what the Prince originally tried to tell him and now the man was dead. He turned to press Winters further only to be called off by an arriving customer.

"Good morning to you, Miss Leguerre. How have we been keeping?" he suppressed his anger and welcomed the starchy old woman with a caring look.

"Well as can be expected, I suppose," she answered grumpily, "seeing that my hands are paining me something terrible. I hope this time you have my order, Doc. I'm finding it hard to demonstrate."

He viewed the steel-haired spinster with genuine sympathy. He sensed that, even more than teaching her students, the comfort she derived playing her cherished instruments was what made her constricted life bearable. "Now don't be cross with me, but I'm afraid it has still not arrived," he admitted evasively. "Have you been using the emulsion I gave you?"

Her weak eyes crimping, Gloria Leguerre snooped past his shoulder to the shelves of emollients, powders and aphrodisia, then across to the bottled elixirs for overindulgence before investigating a sinister row of brown-glass vials with handwritten labels. "Tchuh!" she said, sucking her teeth when she failed to satisfy her suspicions. "I thought a smart young pharmacist with a nice new store would carry the latest treatments. I need something stronger than that so-so fish oil! Don't you read the papers? They say arthritis can be cured with rattlesnake venom."

"Now, Miss Leguerre, I know you don't believe every word in the newspaper—or you'd have me rubbing my bald head every night with gingered bay rum," he teased her gently, alluding to an unfortunately worded ad for a hair-growth remedy.

The old woman's wheat-colored face went pale and Winters made a brisk retreat from the counter, stifling his laughter. In Kingston, even straitlaced spinsters knew that a bald head was slang for male circumcision.

"I'd love to have back my full head of hair," Emerson Gardner went on wistfully, "but if wishes were horses beggars would ride. As a wise woman once told me—what the young chasing the latest trend reject as old-fashioned is often the tried and true."

"All right, Doc, you win," Miss Leguerre relented, her embarrassment diffused by the compliment. "I'll give your fish oil another try."

After she had left, her feelings mollified with some discounted menthol and liniment, Winters stepped back to the counter with a mirthful cackle. "Still got the soft touch, eh, Doc?"

Even for a reluctant businessman, charming customers was a compulsory habit, but Emerson was not in a charming mood. "Don't even start! You still haven't told me what happened. If your men didn't kill him, explain how the Prince died?"

The corporal looked offended. "How me supposed to know? I wasn't there when it happened. All I can tell you is that the man didn't die from any beating. The coroner didn't find a bruise on his body. Go ask old Coombs if you don't believe me."

Although he wanted to believe that Winters told him the truth, Gardner was far from relieved. Even in a place as horrendous as Yallas Prison, a violent death can lead to a host of awkward questions, questions Midas Coombs would bargain with the Devil himself to avoid. Coombs made it easy for people to despise him because he always chose to expect the worst from others. And yet, even though the man never displayed an ounce of compassion, Emerson appreciated the skill with which the surgeon was able to maintain his infirmary on paltry resources, resources that relied heavily on the prisoners' diligence in breaking rocks in the hated Chalk Hole. In such a dubious system, it was not hard to envision someone as disruptive as Prince Zephaniah being usefully worked to death.

Kip Rothschild broke off interviewing Captain Angell and raced to catch my mother who was on her way back to the payphone with the breezy stride of a numbers winner. Sheriff Gomez had gone to cool down the riled-up receptionists, leaving Dad and me alone with our new companions.

The retired fighter pilot spoke up first. "So what's the deal, Doctor? Is your wife angling to get us a place to stay or her picture in the papers?"

You could tell he meant it as a friendly jab, but my dad's sore look said he took it as a punch below the belt. "My wife does what she thinks is right," he hit back smoothly and I felt the knot in my gut unbind—maybe my father still had some fight in him! "She's hoping to shame them. Who knows how far she'll get, but if you think you have a better idea, let me know."

My pride up off the floor, I fancied my dad and Delroy Angell going at it toe to toe when Connie rushed to call 'time!' "I apologize, Dr. Gardner. That's just Delroy poking fun. We appreciate what Madeline is trying to do."

The captain reached out an arm as if offering the peace pipe. "Easy, Doctor, I was just messin' with you. I have to hand it to your wife. She's quite a little spitfire."

My father chuckled, as if to say 'no hard feelings.' "You're telling me?"

The pilot became abruptly serious. "Thing is, I don't cotton to that pretty-boy's questions. Where does he get off asking am I willing to spend the night in jail on principle? Hell no! I don't want my woman sleeping in some honky-tonk cell. What was I supposed to say? I know there are kids getting their heads split open over crap like this. But Christ! A man shouldn't have to turn his life inside out just to get a room for the night."

As he and my dad discussed what to do next, I was trying to figure out whose side Delroy Angell was on. I figured a WWII pilot was nobody's coward but he didn't seem any more eager than my father to back my mother. Maybe he had lost his nerve, like that hard-nosed General Savage in *Twelve O'Clock High*. Or maybe he thought her mission was impossible.

"Nothing is impossible," my mom reminded me when I told her I had been kicked out of my new school's choir and there was no way I was getting back in. "I'm going to speak with Miss Finch. You can count on me to defend you—as long as you tell me the truth."

The truth is, the Japanese kid spat on me first. The problem Truth had was that Miss Finch did not see it. Mom tried talking to the principal. It didn't help. But it taught me one thing: you could be right and still wronged.

With the desert temperature no longer set on broiling, I noticed that, as my dad and Delroy grew at ease in each other's company, the pilot began drawling his speech, spicing it with mild profanities and folksy similes in a way I would come to recognize as a male bonding code that was routine in our old neighborhood, but a habit my father somehow never acquired.

"No need to let Rothschild get under your skin, Captain. He's just fishing for a front page story. You should be proud. After all, like the sheriff said, you're a war hero."

Delroy sent a bead of saliva sizzling onto the asphalt. "War hero, my butt."

"Don't you be making this fine boy sour on earning his stripes," Connie scolded, before smiling my way. "Honey, don't you pay Captain Angell no mind," she said, wiggling in her high-heeled shoes, "he's just being crotchety. Mercy me, my poor feet are about to quit! I'd go wait in the car but it's gotta be an oven sitting out in this heat."

"You could try running the air conditioning for a spell," my father suggested. "It shouldn't take that long to cool now that the sun's not overhead."

The captain shook his head. "Nope. We got a long ways to go and I don't plan on ending up a parched stray dog in the middle of Texas."

"Please, Delroy. I'm feeling a little faint—"

"Dammit, woman, didn't I just say no?"

Unlike my mother who, in spite of her wish-fulfilling dimensions, had a 'look-but-don't-touch' caution sign, Connie was the fleshy sort who drew men like flies. It did not help her husband's obvious jealous streak that along with her Shirley Temple nose and forty-inch chest she had a child's open nature.

"If it's heat stroke, she really needs to cool down. It shouldn't do any harm letting her run it with the engine on—"

My dad's concern for his wife knocked Delroy's nose back out of joint. "Thanks for your concern, Doctor, but I'll decide what she needs," he said bluntly. "It'll take a good half hour to cool that car enough for her to sit in there without griping and my tank's already on low. Who the hell knows where we'll end up spending the night. The last thing I need is to be stuck here outta gas because her feet hurt."

My father glanced towards our Valiant and I could see what he was thinking before he changed his mind and decided against more gallant gestures; Connie's husband surely knew better than he if his wife was exaggerating.

"You think we might have to sleep in our cars? Please, Lord, no," Connie murmured, searching through her purse, "I need a nice cool bath—I'm all grit and itches." She pulled out a tissue and dabbed her cheeks. "Forgive me, Dr. Gardner. I must look a sight. I told Delroy we shouldn't risk coming this way, but he never listens to me." Her plump face crinkled behind a mess of purple eye-shadow and melting mascara. "My husband would quicker cut off his leg than credit me with a thimble of sense."

She went on whining to my father and Delroy looked just about ready to smack her when Kip Rothschild came galloping back.

"Well, we tracked down the mayor. Your wife sure is letting him have it!" he crowed to my dad before cornering Delroy. "So, Captain, shall we continue? It's gonna be a while—"

Madeline was suffocating inside her mother's silence. Even now that she seemed to have made peace with Adrianna's reckless marriage, Miss Dora rarely spoke except to command, as if sharing her feelings would only sharpen her grief. Considering how Adrianna had tormented her to the point that she sometimes feared she would do her harm, Madeline was surprised by how imprisoned she felt at home with her sister gone. She was even more surprised by a joyous sense of reprieve as she held her niece. Holding that tiny new being, so needy and trusting, feeling the petal-soft infant mold her warm defenseless body to Madeline's breast and shoulder, she felt empowered. Uplifted by the sudden awareness of her own value, she took to stopping by every day after her nursing-school classes, eager to kiss her niece's nose and watch her giggle at her aunt's silly faces.

Although the baby's healthy arrival had engendered enough good feelings to see the runaway couple welcomed back into the family fold, Madeline was not ready to accept Adrianna's claim that she regretted having labeled her Little Miss Big Head. That she was now confident enough to make allowances for her sister's cruelty did not make forgiving and forgetting any easier. It had not helped that, by the time she was strong enough to sit all day in class, she was two years behind. And while her long illness had yielded the slender compensation that she still looked six when, in fact, she was almost ten, thanks to Adrianna her one advantage had been turned into a curse. In her defense, her sister had learned that cruelty from a grown-up.

"She might as well dedicate her life to the Lord," one of the church ladies had observed in all kindness, unaware that Miss Dora's elder daughter was in earshot. "Such a shame," she said, clucking her tongue. "With that big head that little miss will never find a husband."

Even Dr. Joseph, who reminded her after each of her check-ups that she was God's special miracle, thought it tragically unfair that, after fighting so fiercely for life, this intelligent, active child faced the fate of an ostracized dwarf. Those childhood scars had failed to heal, even after hormones saw her transformed from a half-bald gnome to a sixteen-year-old black-haired beauty. As much as the devotion she felt for her niece urged her to forgive, she could never forget how her sister had sided with the schoolyard bullies, telling them that if she had been born a sick little freak, she would have asked God to let her live with Him in Heaven. So while Adrianna might truly regret having done all she could to make her younger sister feel hideous, Madeline still did not trust her.

It did not take long for her mistrust to prove justified. As the elation over a quick second child crashed under scarcity's hard reality, her sister took to using her visits as a chance to recount every nursed slight. She resisted taking the bait when Adrianna grew determined to extract her confession, blaming Maddy for it all: she was the reason Miss Dora refused to let her attend her own graduation party; it was her fault Mr. Jans had left; it was her atrocious behavior why people looked down on their family and made her have to settle for marrying a barber. After each inquisition, Adrianna would promptly spring tears, denouncing her own stupid pride and wailing for God to forgive her, leaving Madeline enraged and bewildered as she strained to soothe her terrified nieces. Had her classes covered psychotherapy, she would have recognized that her sister was suffering from a serious bout of depression, but it was 1933, and no one believed that poor people suffered unconsciously.

Though she had not classified the symptoms, Madeline was fairly sure of their cause. More than the normal childhood she and her sister felt had been denied them, it was the fervor with which Miss Dora tried to protect them that drove Adrianna to flee with the first turned head who came with the promise of a home and a reliable income. Even had they known their mother had taken up her own rough cross hoping to spare her children the same lifelong sentence, after absorbing her unshed tears for far too long, the time was destined to come when they must either swim free or drown.

Maddy never knew why Mr. Jans left to work in Sierra Leone except that he had come to tell them exactly a week after the one time she ever heard him return their mother's anger. As he promised to write and send her pocket money, she had been too distraught to cry or ask him why, even while he bent and sadly kissed her good-bye. Her nieces helped to fill the void and pushed her to spend her free afternoons helping her sister around the house. Seeing how every chore became an imposition amplified by Adrianna's constant sense of persecution, she took an inward measure of wicked pleasure in singing cheerfully while she went about the washing and cleaning. More charitably, when her sister moped that motherhood had made her fat and ugly, she assured her that, with their father's caramel complexion and those pretty freckles, she would always draw admirers. Finally, when she whined that there was no point getting back in shape just to be stuck inside changing diapers, Madeline promised that after this third child was born and Adrianna was back to her old self, she would take the children home so she and Mr. Smalls could see *It Happened One Night* and enjoy an evening to themselves.

"What the hell do you know, Little Miss Big Head?" her sister sneered. "All that man wants to do is to lie on top of me. I'd have been better off marrying Dracula!"

"Hush! You'll hurt the baby," she cautioned when Adrianna started pounding her bloated belly then stopped to stare with shining eyes as if seized by a harrowing insight.

"Mother was right. Sorrows are what a pure woman reaps from a soiled man's seed."

My mother came sashaying up, smiling like a new Miss America. "We won!"

"Won what, exactly?" asked my dad.

"What do you think?" she airily replied, waltzing on by. "Officer Gomez?" she called out abruptly, stopping halfway between the patrol car and where I stood sharing a cloud of hopeful confusion with my father and Connie. "The mayor wants to speak with you. Don't worry, he's really sorry about what happened."

The way she stressed her words sent me flashing back in time.

"Hey, wait up!" Justin Ito caught up with me as we were leaving school. "I'm *really* sorry I got you kicked out of choir."

"Why'd you spit on me?"

Justin shrugged and kicked a pebble along the sidewalk, as if to say he had no idea. "Listen—you wanna come over? I got a basketball for Christmas."

"Nah," I said, "my mom will have a fit." That was probably an exaggeration, but why risk it? I had talked my dad into letting me stop taking the school bus using a sure-fire tactic—I reminded him of all the money he'd be saving—but the deal was that I would walk straight home. The one time I was late my mother 'just happened' to be cruising crosstown in our old Studebaker. Luckily, I had my hands full with the nine books I'd borrowed from the Bookmobile, so she took pity on me and I got off easy.

"Aw, c'mon. Just for a little while. We can shoot hoops."

When his house turned out to be sort of on the way I said okay. Justin had just started attending our school that September, and since he never got picked to play kickball, I figured he was having a hard time making friends. "You sure your parents won't mind?" I asked as we got to his street and I saw it was one of the tonier ones where the houses were all fenced off with giant evergreens and sculpted hedges and you never saw kids out playing on the sidewalks.

"Naw, they're at work. They don't get home till half past five."

"Wow!" I said, "that gives you two whole hours to watch TV!" I thought Justin had it made. Except during the summer, an hour on Friday night and a couple on Saturdays were the only times I was allowed to watch television.

Justin gazed down at his P.F. Flyer sneakers I'd been coveting. "My mom doesn't want me being alone inside. My dad put up a hoop in the driveway but it gets pretty boring."

As an only child myself, I knew just how he felt, even if he did have the prettiest basketball I'd ever seen. It was smooth and solid gold. Not like the puckered dark-orange ones my friends and I were used to.

My mind was still on Justin Ito when my father asked if I'd like another orange pop. What I really wanted was a cold glass of water, but an admission like that was liable to buy me no more soda until I started college. It wasn't every day my dad gets heat stroke and loses his senses so I said, "sure."

"Did you say you spoke with the mayor and he's willing to help us?" The captain hurried to join my mother at a hop-step canter. From his gait and the gleam on his face, I guessed he had jumped at the chance to stave off Kip's questions.

"You heard right," she told him, beaming like a prom queen at a high school reunion. "Even better, the mayor *apologized.*"

The sun was turning red and sinking fast and my father was in no mood for pyrrhic victories. "We don't need his apology, we need somewhere to sleep."

"Hold your horses, Doctor," Delroy protested, "let's hear her out."

"Humph!" Connie grumbled, "glad you want to listen to *somebody.*"

My mother smiled at her. "I see we have the same problem."

"Maddy, no more martyrdom, please—?"

She ignored my dad and glanced to make sure Kip had arrived with his notepad before launching into her story. She said the mayor had hemmed and hawed at her 'perfectly legitimate argument' that their interstate sign made the motel's color code illegal then started to soften when she mentioned her friend at the Los Angeles Times and put Kip on the line to talk about Captain Angell. "By the time I got through telling him that my next call would be to the British Consulate he'd turned sweet as a custard pie."

"Why the heck would you call the Brits?" asked Delroy.

"I wanted him to know that Dr. Gardner and I were British citizens. Boy, did he sing a whole different tune after that! He said it was a shame we had to suffer such an ill-convenience and that he would see personally to rectifying the situation."

Delroy looked like he was itching to sweep her up into his arms, and from her laser beam glare, I reckoned Connie did not put it past him to try it. "Ain't *that* the berries! You sure know how to pull a fast one past these flour bags."

"It wasn't a ploy," my mother corrected him, resurrecting her superior pose. "We're naturalized Americans, but Emerson and I are still British subjects."

My dad gave a caustic chuckle and grunted 'not any more' while Delroy grinned and cast her a bow. "I don't care if y'all are from Uranus! Not having to choose between a night in jail and sleeping out in the desert just made this humble Negro happier than a dead hog in the New Mexico sunshine!"

"I'm sorry. Am I interrupting an examination?"

Emerson bounced up from his stool, dumping the teenaged nymph who had brazenly nested herself on his lap. The girl hid her face with her hand and feigned a kiss before fleeing like a tender promise. As he fumbled to button up his smock, he saw that the young woman waiting there patiently was relishing the egg on his face.

"Affectionate little thing—a second cousin—fresh from country—" As he blundered his way to an alibi, Emerson was not sure if his accelerated heart-rate was due to his discomfort or his new customer's sable-haired loveliness.

Madeline hounded him with mocking eyes. "How gallant! Why it's like a scene from an American movie. Or am I thinking of a song? *Kissing Cousins*—or was it *Little White Lies*?"

"I'm not that devoted to American taste," he parried, keen to rescue the remains of his self-respect. "One needs to be kind—the poor thing's not fully socialized—no father, you see—girls her age can get themselves in a muddle—hormones, you see—makes them over-stimulated ..."

"Really? How interesting! And here I thought she merely had a throat infection."

Seeing that his bumbling was only adding to her amusement, he gave up trying to repair his honor. "How can I help you, Miss—"

"I'm Madeline Jans," she pronounced gravely. "I wanted to ask you if there was something that could be done about my sister's strange behavior. She's not been herself."

"Have you consulted a doctor?"

Madeline looked annoyed. "Naturally I have. I'm a nurse in training. Unfortunately, Dr. Joseph does not think she's treatable. I suppose it's understandable a woman coping alone with three restless toddlers would be chronically exhausted, but she gets in these terrible black moods. No matter what I say, she refuses to set foot outside of her house. She just mopes in bed, sucking plums and reading lewd novels. It's 1935, surely there's something we can do—"

Gloria Leguerre came clipping inside and Madeline clammed up abruptly. There was a bristling stare-down and Emerson felt his pores continue to warm as the women exchanged terse good-afternoons. Apparently sensing his discomfort, Miss Jans suggested he attend to the one with more pressing needs.

With the barest of nods, Miss Leguerre acknowledged the concession, then waited to address the druggist until Madeline had gone to peruse the drugstore's pamphlet display titled *Attaining Good Health and Higher Consciousness*. She leaned across the counter as if to speak in confidence, but made no effort to lower her voice.

"Doc, you're a well-bred young man with a promising future so I hope you'll appreciate my offering you some constructive advice." Miss Leguerre's sharp eyes aimed to where Madeline stood absorbed by a brochure on metaphysics. "Beware. As it says in Proverbs, can a man take fire in his bosom, and his clothes not be burned?"

Emerson smiled to himself. Despite Gloria Leguerre's pleasure in finding fault, her impulses flowed from her view of compassion. Like so many colonials whose off-white color and liberal education befuddled their prospects, young Gloria had been convinced that the blooms of her musical talent would attract the ideal English gentleman, or at worst, a cultured facsimile. Now that the years had passed without providing her anything close, she had dedicated her final days on earth to preserving the island's entrenched pretensions.

"I'm sure you're right," he answered her carefully, trying not to sound snide, "but we must remember that when those wise words were written it was virtuous to believe that the Sun circled the Earth. When we humans can get something so obvious wrong it goes to show how hard that tricky devil is to recognize."

Madeline snickered inside her booklet as Gloria Leguerre scowled and snatched up her package.

"Fine, Doc," she grumbled, "have it your way. I expected better from a man with your pedigree."

"I despise that old troll!" Madeline swore after the spinster quick-stepped outside. "When that mouth of hers finally finds its rest, half of Kingston will throw a party."

"I wouldn't be so hard on Miss Leguerre. The woman may be an incorrigible gossip, but she can teach a block of stone to play a stringed instrument. I thought my best buddy was out of his mind when he said she could have me playing the bass within a year but there it is—I've come far enough in ten months he wants me to join his new band."

Madeline looked perplexed. "Mason didn't tell me he was starting a band—"

"My word, I am slow sometimes!" Emerson suddenly grasped what he had missed in his initial embarrassment. "Madeline Jans! Of course, you're Mason's baby sister—" he stared at the change in her features, "not that you're a baby anymore—" His dark skin burned all over again sensing her annoyance. "Sorry—but it's been years since I last saw you."

Madeline brushed past his astonishment. "When did you talk with my brother about starting a band?" she demanded. "Mason only just got transferred back to Kingston."

"We kept in touch while he was working out in country. He'd been talking about forming a combo since our school days. Forgive me for not recognizing you—I had thought you were much younger—" he stopped short again, "there I go, inserting foot back in mouth. You must think I'm a complete donkey."

"Why? Perhaps I should be flattered—after all, you do like them young."

"There's where you and Miss Leguerre have something in common," he hit back adroitly. "Judging on mere observation has left you both badly mistaken."

Her mocking eyes sparkled. "Since my brother approves of you, I'll take your word that you're not King Kong or a disgusting child molester."

Emerson struggled not to stare at the full sepal lips, curling lusciously even as they teased him. "Most tolerant of you, Miss Jans. Rest assured, I'd make a very poor monster. I'm a pacifist and actually quite chaste."

She shrugged off his efforts to charm her. "If we're through dissecting your licentious tendencies, can we return to discussing my sister? I came to ask your opinion on insulin shock treatment."

"Saddle up, *amigos*, we're hitting the road."

"What?" Connie wailed, alarmed as the sheriff came loping back from the payphone. "To where?"

The slammer, I figured.

Captain Angell stepped in front of his wife, sinews coiled like a spring. "What's the deal, Sheriff?"

"My guess is the mayor told him to usher us quietly out of town," my dad suggested.

"No, no, no!" shouted my mother, stamping her foot. "Did none of you hear a word I said? The mayor was asking Officer Gomez if he would kindly escort us to another motel."

The look on my father's face said something smells fishy. "What motel? Is he even sure they'll take us? Or are we to hang around for a repeat performance?"

My mother simply stared at him. None of us dared budge.

"Suit yourself." The sheriff shrugged then turned to head back to his patrol car.

Kip rushed to try and clear the air. "I know you're all skeptical. In your shoes, I would be too—but I know the man. He's on the level."

"Trust me," my mother urged Connie who again looked ready to cry, "the mayor doesn't want to hear any more from me. He knows I have his number."

Connie wiped her nose and strained a tiny smile as she swept up the strands of processed chestnut hair clinging limply to her clammy brow.

"Relax, *compadres*," said Sheriff Gomez, waiting patiently by his dark sedan with one rattleskin boot cocked on the running-board. "You're getting the best motel in town."

"And what's that going to cost us?"

Yep, I thought, Dad's back to his normal self.

"Don't worry," my mother snapped, "it won't cost you a dime. He's putting us up."

"What do you mean, 'putting us up'?"

"What do you think? The mayor is having us spend the night as his guests—compliments of his fair city!"

The veteran pilot's coiled stance relaxed. "Well, how-do-you-do! That's one heckuva gal you got there, Doctor. C'mon, Connie, you heard the lady, let's giddy-on up!"

As we trailed the sheriff's flashing amber lights, I could hear my mother's inward crowing feeding on my father's silence. Pride had my chest splitting its seams but I wasn't dumb enough to start singing her praises. Besides, my dad knew without my saying it that, no matter how this whole nutty thing panned out, I would still take her side. I might have fallen for the honey-hued girl next door, but my heart would always belong to my mother, the one who taught me how to read and write and to remember Every Good Boy Does Fine, who took a second job to pay for my music lessons and patiently transcribed her four-year-old's stab at composing, a piece I named *Dreams of Hawaii* after the Mickey Mouse Club held a luau on TV starring a black-haired Italian cherub destined to rile the sleep of every budding American boy.

Our deep attachment was totally predictable, seeing that once I could walk hours without being carried I became my mother's constant companion on her wanderings across half of L.A. I especially enjoyed the times we would board the funicular at Bunker Hill and ride down the thrilling steep slope to the farmers' market and buy fresh apricots and the sugar-sweet red persimmons we both adored, then, if the day was pleasant, board another bus and cross to the park where we'd sit by the olive-green lake and toss the crusts from our homemade sandwiches to the scrambling ducks. But our most memorable adventure started late one night when she came to my bedroom to gently shake me awake and help me get dressed. I remember how silent and still everything seemed as we walked through the shadows and how she held my hand tight and never said a word. Even though I was not quite five, I remember being surprisingly calm considering that, not only had we never gone out that late, as far as I can tell, that was my first time inside a moviehouse and sitting in the dark surrounded by strangers seemed a little creepy. To my great disappointment, I couldn't make heads or tails of the story, except that the heroine spent most of it crying. At least, that's all I managed to recall from before my Good and Plenty box was empty and I promptly fell asleep. What I will never forget is how proud I felt escorting my mother in the dead of night to a grown-up movie.

Once my father finished attending night school, the few times we did go out to have fun we went as the Gardner Trinity. After our worry-free trips to San Diego and San Francisco I was sure that, like the Three Musketeers, we were one for all and all for one. But that was then. Now, as our anxious caravan rolled on, leaving the Amity Motel behind us, I kept thinking that either I had been wrong all along or something had changed. There was more to what went on between my parents out on that parking lot than a spat over tactics. As I stared out wishfully to the end of the desert and just made out the remote red rocks setting the sky on fire, I feared the price the three of us would pay for my mother's triumph.

Stationed at the wrought iron gate with stern arms crossed, the pale-robed form appeared like a bloodless icon shining in the moonlit night.

"Look at my worthless children—walking the street at this unholy hour!"

"Mother? Why are you out here all alone?"

Mason dashed to Miss Dora's side and Madeline trembled. Only calamity could have urged their mother outside on New Year's Night when country hoodlums were known to take advantage of an expired plantation tradition to mask like ghouls and remind their citified brethren there were still sleep-stealing terrors left over from slavery.

Shivering, Miss Dora aimed them a rebuking forefinger. "'Test not the Lord lest He destroy thee with serpents!'"

And the night had started so well, Madeline rued guiltily.

There were balloons—red, white and blue ones—and treat-laden tables prettied with scarlet poinsettia and plaited palm leaves. Lower Kingston's respectable young, done up to the nines, stuck like pins on opposite walls, their giddy feet rooted to the floor while their torsos swayed to Jimmy Lunceford's emancipating, rampaging swing, supple as two by fours.

"My, don't we look luscious!"

Madeline flinched from the hot breath striking her ear. "What exactly are you up to, Mr. Pottinger?"

"Enjoying myself immensely," he replied, assailing her with his film-star looks when she turned to berate him. "Isn't that what we're here for?"

"This is the ladies side. Go back and join the other ruffians."

"So!" Potty exclaimed, feigning hurt, "not only am I no longer a worthy escort, I am to be scorned as an oaf!"

Madeline played a gloved hand across her slinky peach gown. "And just how was I supposed to mount a motorbike in this?" she protested, drawing more glares from the wall's shapeless yards of silk and lace and feeling her insides again warm with pleasure.

"Fair enough. But as your oldest friend and guardian, I demand the top spot on your dance card!"

"Potty Pottinger! Such an idea! This is a church."

Someone changed the record to Erskine Tate's *Cutie Blues* and a pair of brave souls ventured into the gulf between the sexes.

"Honestly, Maddy, you're such a prude! We're not in the sanctuary." Potty nodded across the long draped tables spread with assorted pastries and fruit preserves to the hawk-eyed vicar camped by the punch-bowl. "Old Felcher doesn't mind us dancing if we keep it decent so we make sure to start off prim as postulants." He bent in closer. "The codger's got a flask of whites stashed in his cassock," he confided with a grin. "In an hour the old coot will be so snockered he won't care if we're doing the jitterbug."

Maddy shrank. Here was her hoped-for moment again crossed with despair. She had never been to a social that permitted jazz music, much less dancing and alcohol, the two slippery steps into hell Miss Dora had warned against from the day her late-blooming body betrayed her. Sneaking out with Mason's lively new wife to see *The Dancing Lady* had felt wicked enough. To cavort with the opposite sex at a church-sanctioned function she might as well be an Egyptian trying to cross the Red Sea. "I really can't stay," she whispered miserably.

"Oh, come on—live a little. Don't you at least want to hear your brother's new band?"

Mason was now a married man with a home and a baby son, but it still annoyed her that, while he obediently refrained from dancing or joining his free-minded wife at the movies, their mother never condemned him for playing 'that devil music.' "You know Miss Dora—she'll put me out in the street if she hears I was jitterbugging."

"Now see here, Mrs. Grundy," said Potty, pressing her aside, "she's not going to risk losing another daughter. Besides, what's the harm in dancing? Good heavens, Maddy, it's about to be 1936.

You're twenty-one years of age. Miss Dora knows you came to enjoy yourself." He pointed to her Chanel-inspired dress. "Or did you slink out in those stunning rags without her noticing?"

Their mother's knees began to give way and Mason rushed to hold her up. Casting her son an ashen look, she started to speak but the words stopped in her throat. After a slow painful gulp, she garbled, "g-go fetch Doc. It's Adrianna—she—she—dear God, forgive me!"

While Mason raced off to summon his friend, Madeline stifled her alarm and led their mother inside to find Adrianna peacefully asleep in bed, her left wrist wrapped in binding.

Emerged from her stuttering distress, Miss Dora explained that Adrianna had shown up around ten with her three children in tow to announce she was leaving her husband.

"Why? What happened?" Madeline demanded.

"God only knows," her mother murmured, collapsing into the chair at her daughter's bedside. "I should have known better than to mention you had gone to that New Year's party. She must have found Mr. Jans' old razor and cut herself while I was putting the girls to bed. Thank the Lord I found her in time."

Despondent, Miss Dora stood to undo the constant scarf hiding her mane of lustrous black hair then vented her sudden ire towards Madeline's gown. "Look at you in your devil finery! That's how you use your hard-earned money? So you can traipse around looking like Jezebel?"

Freedom. That was the place she had made it to tonight. She had almost not gone after Mason's wife took sick on Christmas, but she was eager to hear her brother's band and show off the dress she had labored on for weeks. She had come determined that this New Year's Night would not find her worrying that all those worthwhile girls itching inside their corsets, smiling her way, were softly cutting her to pieces, or bored and alone shooting envious glances at the boys miles away across the room slapping dominoes and arguing about cricket. No, tonight she had found out that, contrary to what Miss Dora claimed, male and female could spend hours within kissing distance and still make it home with their futures intact. The rebel in her had dared and to her delight and relief, Potty's feet were as liquid as Bill Bojangles' and considerate enough for her sorry plodders to follow. She had even braved a Lindbergh stomp and been rescued when, just as she was starting to struggle for breath, her brother stilled the music and sent his violin soaring for the heavenly alto sax line from *Have a Little Faith in Me*.

"Do you mind, old boy? You've been monopolizing the loveliest girl here all night."

The confidence in the deep familiar voice gave Madeline's stomach a startling flutter.

"Doc!" Potty greeted his usurper cheerfully then drew back in surprise. "Wait—shouldn't you be up there playing your bass?"

"This set is only ballads," Emerson explained, his steady gaze on Madeline. "You don't want to know what I'm capable of with a bow in my hand."

"There, you monster, we have something in common," she hinted, smiling coyly as she recalled her great misdeed.

"Good enough then, Doc," Potty conceded, sounding peeved. "Since you two seem acquainted, you may borrow her—but just for this dance."

"Ignore him," Madeline scoffed. "I can neither be bought nor borrowed."

"I was pleased to see you got up the nerve to dance, it becomes you," Emerson said when his rival left to find solace with a congenial female.

"Save the flattery, Doc, I'm no longer sixteen," she teased as they danced at arm's length.

"And thank our star-angels for it! But let's not tread that old road. How is your sister? I'm glad you agreed not to pursue that shock therapy. I believe such radical measures should be an absolute last resort."

Madeline frowned. "I wonder. I mean it's no use my guarding her diet if she refuses proper food. I'm worried about her, Doc. I try my best, but it's never enough."

Emerson gave her a serious look, his droll tone grim. "I quite understand, Nurse Jans, but it is only New Year's Night. There'll be a whole year left to fret off all the hairs on that lovely head. As you can see, I speak from experience."

Madeline laughed along with the admired young druggist unfazed to be going bald at the age of twenty-six; he was not proving to be the stuck-up reprobate she first imagined. "All right, Doc, I confess," she ceded pertly, "you make a charming ogre."

Back inside our Valiant the silence was bruising. From the day we packed up to leave L.A., my warm loving family had seemed under a strain. It was as if a chill wind had swept in to uproot our lives and blown us into a parallel world at war. Although my brain rejected the idea as illogical, I sensed a strange deep freeze setting in between the Father and the Holy Spirit and that, while I might not have started it, the frost building up between them was also my fault. I kept wishing there was a travel machine that could whisk the three of us back in time so I could stop it from happening, but unlike my brain, at this point my stomach did not care either way. It was busy pondering how long it took for a nine-year-old to die of starvation. I told myself that hunger was making things look a whole lot worse than they were, that once we found a motel willing to take us, my father would get over his anger, my mother would smile, and the universe would go back to feeling normal. And like magic, at that very instant, the knot loosened inside my gut as the sheriff signaled my dad to exit the highway. The past shoved out of my mind, I sprang up excited by the sight of leaved trees for the first time in eight hundred miles.

The bleeding sun was reddening the desert in its dying light as we maneuvered through the gate's concrete columns and towards a two-story white building with forest-green awnings that blended attractively with the transplanted foliage. Scooting onto my knees to peek through the luggage taking up half of the Valiant's rear seat, I saw the Angell's dirt-streaked station wagon roll to a stop beside us in the well-lit parking lot. Praying to spy the tiniest hint of a thaw that would warrant my happier mood, I snapped back in time to see my father relax his knuckle-popping grip on the steering-wheel then drooped in despair as he still refused to look at my mother. I was ready to tug at my dad's cold shoulder and ask when he thought we might round up some grub when the sheriff came and rested his beefy arm on our car roof. He grinned through my mom's open window as if he had arranged this whole thing.

"You folks can go right on in. They're expecting you."

"We can't thank you enough, Officer Gomez," she said, accepting his hand when he gallantly opened her door. "You've been a life saver."

The sheriff avoided my father's stare. "Really, no, *Señora*—you just gotta know how to mesh with the lay of the land."

"Not that I question your word, Sheriff Gomez, but would you mind waiting until these arrangements you speak of are confirmed?" Although my dad asked him nicely, I could tell it was an effort. To me, it simply sounded like he still had his doubts about the setup, but my mother's retort told me she thought he was more concerned about his wallet.

"I'm sorry, Officer. *Mi marido puede ser un poco tacaño.*"

The sheriff tried hiding his grin and my dad looked stunned to hear her address him in Spanish. It surprised me too but I kept thinking I had heard her use that phrase before.

"Such faith, my dear," my father said acidly, "but that's not what concerns me. I'm sure that, having devoted all this time to us, the sheriff would agree it doesn't hurt to be judicious."

As I suspected, Gomez was in no great hurry. "I guess a couple more minutes won't hurt none."

"Officer, you're a kind and patient man," my mom said softly, bending to straighten the hem of her dress.

"Nice view ... huh, Sheriff?" Delroy Angell came ambling up and the lawman quickly lifted his gaze from my mother's ankles.

Gomez hid his embarrassment inside a thumbs-in-belt pose. "Yeah? What view is that?"

"Forget it ..." Delroy muttered, "you're a fabulous American."

"You folks enjoy your stay," the sheriff said sarcastically, casting my mother a curt salute before roaring off in his patrol car.

"Happy now?" my mother barked at my dad as we mustered at the entrance, but both he and Delroy looked too drained and disheveled to draw comfort from their patched up pride. Connie, meanwhile, had finally finished combing her hair inside the station wagon and slipped back into her high heeled shoes.

"I thought you'd want me looking decent," she said, catching her husband's impatient look as she tiptoed to join us.

The blood felt cold inside in my veins as we escaped the sweltering heat and stepped into the air-conditioned lobby.

"Welcome to Sunnyvale Lodge." A slim blue-eyed blond in a two piece green suit greeted us cheerily. Opposite our sun-drunk appearance, her cool peach-skinned look suggested that perspiring should be made illegal.

Even I could see the place was a big step up from the Amity Motel. Instead of vinyl floors and cement-board, there was plush wool carpeting and glossy papered walls patterned with little silver-spurred boots painted red, white and blue. The very air was enthralling—so much so that my memory of it was like stepping into Disneyland and feeling your senses drool as the smell of fried funnel cakes and hot-popped corn conjured back the first time you set eyes on a life-sized cartoon princess and spent the whole day spellbound inside an immaculate make-believe world.

"We got you-all nice and set!" Our hostess's voice was cloying, even as she shied from our wary faces. "Two doubles, just for tonight—that includes our buffet dinner for five—do I have that right?"

My stomach gurgled as I grinned at the miraculous Holy Spirit and she beamed and rubbed my scalp while Connie murmured 'praise Jesus!' Even the Father looked grimly pleased. I was no longer playing a role in some cornball Western. I was back to myself—a living breathing part of the human race.

Emerson felt the accustomed stab of misgiving seeing Officer Winters show up for his weekend packet. He had tried to convince the prison corporal turned sergeant of police that while it was useful for toothaches, cocaine was no more a boost to his 'one-eyed soldier' than a carrot or a cup of peppermint tea.

"I know what you're saying, Doc, but the spirit needs a little pick-me-up after dealing all week with the dregs. Ain't much of a line between me and them. A man does what he's got to do."

Emerson had to admit there was more than a pinch of truth in Winters' cynicism. Still, there was no ignoring the irony that the 'little pick-me-up' the sergeant requested in return for his services was the very thing that made his drugstore a target for those on the wrong side of that fickle line. The policeman's habit was not the only thing gnawing his conscience as he watched Winters slink out happily into the night. He had toured the countryside hoping to discover how an indigent epileptic born Buster Bolden came to see himself as a reincarnated prophet and had left horrified by what he'd seen on the big plantations. Not only did their ramshackle barracks leak, they lacked running water. Most had only a single outhouse and the nearest stream served as the latrine for hundreds of men. The ones brave enough to complain explained that they simply ended up owing triple for the coffee and bread that comprised their keep. It was easy to appreciate how someone as thoughtful as the Prince had responded to such inhuman conditions.

He had returned from the sugar estates fired up to advocate for a livable wage and basic hygienic practices. Three years on, his zealous campaign had earned wide praise, a petition with close to a thousand signatures, and gotten nowhere. Setting aside the words his anger urged him to employ, he penned the English governor a dispassionate appeal, warning that if the planters did not improve conditions, not only was the island risking a deadly epidemic, the workers' bottled rage was sure to explode.

All told, it was a terrible time to be falling in love, but here he was. Madeline Jans had burst into his life like a flame—effervescent, irrepressible, unworldly, yet game for any wholesome fun—impressing him that, for all her troubles, she unequivocally loved living. And yet, it was Maddy's zest for life's pleasures that gave him pause. He knew there would come a time when the thrills, like the tiny grains in Winter's packet, would no longer excite her caresses and muffle his frustrations inside the velvet fog of contentment. Always wanting more, that was the snare in the human brain, except the more he secretly wished for was not found in the material world. Had he been Catholic he might have withdrawn to the priesthood, or blessed with talent grasped the road of the starving artist. But as distant as he viewed the redemption of a world hooked on malice, ignorance and greed, he felt genuinely called to heal.

By the time my mother and Connie had freshened up, the restaurant was empty save for a silver-haired couple whose jeweled attire dripped wealth as did their golf-earned tans which blended with the angry red glare on the room's giant reproduction of the Petrified Forest at sunset. They paused seeing the five of us straggle inside, then quietly continued eating, shaking their heads as if wondering what the world was coming to. To my innards' distress, the Sunnyvale supper buffet turned out to be a tureen of pork and potato stew and platters of cold cuts and sliced white bread.

She smiled while my mother explained, but our hostess's indulgent front looked just about ready to crack. "Ah'm sorry, ma'am, that's all we have."

"I understand. You must find it an impossible task, trying to please all of your guests—" even when her voice was like syrup my mom could make an ice cube sweat, "but if it's at *all* possible, we would be happy with any odds and ends your chef could rustle up."

The peach skin blushed. "I'll speak with the kitchen and see what we can do."

It felt like eating a second breakfast, but when the food finally arrived I made short work of the Mexican omelette. By then the silver hairs were gone, the Angells had polished off their stew, and Connie had begged off to bed. Seeing that the four of us were the only ones left, Delroy ordered a third cold beer and stayed to get under our skin.

"So, what's the deal with you Gardners? You like them scrawny Hindus who won't kill to eat?"

I could already hear my father's spiel about our reasons being ethical and dietary, more than religious, but my mother beat him to it.

"I was raised Seventh-day Adventist, though you could probably tempt me with some fried chicken and watermelon. They say scorned habits die hard," she said, eyeing his beer.

Delroy laughed at the joke I did not get and lowered his sights to me. "How about you, Sonny? Don't tell me you've never tasted a good American hot-dog."

My mouth was full of the strawberry sherbet, so I just shook my head.

"That's too bad," he said, shaking his head in pity. "Just promise you won't start hating your parents once you're grown and find out what you've been missing."

"That's enough, Captain, lay off my son. People make fun, but we humans who love to boast about our great civilizations would be a lot more advanced if we followed Gandhi's teachings. Violence is an uncivil habit."

Dad's mention of the Great Soul appeared to anger Delroy. "Don't start with that Martin King turn-the-other-cheek crap. I don't know what it's like where you come from, but this is the U.S. of A. That non-violent baloney will just get you killed."

"I'll grant you it's not easy—" my father admitted, "and I question some of King's tactics, but if you hope to share this country in peace, I don't see how an eye for an eye gets you there. Someone's got to bury the hatchet, as you Americans like to say."

"You think the folks who slaughtered the Creeks worry about living in peace? I don't want a bunch of brainwashed kids getting their skulls bashed in thinking they're Hindus and this is India. There's only one thing the white man respects and that's a man with a gun who's willing to shoot. I joined the Air Force because since I was your boy's age I'd been dying to fly. But I was also dying to show those ofays I could match any dark, dirty deed they came up with. Musta scared 'em too, seeing that tin coffin they gave me to fly." Delroy stared at the blown up photo of the badlands at sunset. "Shame is—I never really got to show them. When my leg finally mended, the war was over."

My mother looked ready to puke her sherbet. "But you told Kip you'd flown combat!"

The pilot shrugged. "No call to fret. Even if they do decide to print it, ain't nobody gonna give a damn about it anyway."

"But I got the mayor to stick his neck out. Suppose someone checks?"

"They ain't gonna check." Delroy lingered inside his thoughts then chuckled, crumpling the empty beer can. "If they do, they'll just end up mixing me up with my brother."

"You had a brother in your squadron?"

"Sure enough," he muttered. "Lucky got his chance to fly— came home a man and got a silver star pinned on his chest—then they clipped his wings." He flipped the squashed can on the table. "The kid kept pestering me for a story so I gave him one. I figured, what the heck—if somebody *does* give a damn about knowing the truth, *then* I'll come clean."

His frustration reminded me of how I felt after I told my dad that Miss Finch had banned me from the choir without hearing my side. He said it might feel as though she was being unfair, but two wrongs don't make a right, and spitting was unsanitary. What made it so hard to take was that Justin didn't even like singing in the choir that much. He was just happy to have one less hour to burn by himself after school. My mother was the only one who seemed to care that Justin Ito spat on me for no reason. They say it's wrong, telling a lie, but listening to Delroy, I was starting to think grown-ups weren't all that concerned about knowing the truth.

The thought must have flicked a switch in my head, because I suddenly knew what had been bugging me since last year when Jennifer Cahill invited me to her birthday party. I had been surprised because she and I hardly spoke and Jennifer was the kind of doll-like blonde in fuzzy pink sweaters who always sat in the very first row and got Valentine cards from all the other girls in class. That, and the way Miss Finch used to fawn all over her, made me want to keep my distance, but to be fair, Jennifer Cahill was incredibly nice.

"You will come, won't you?" she whispered, running to catch me as we left the classroom. "I just love how you play the piano."

I showed my parents the invitation I knew most of the kids at my cross-town school would die for and after checking the address and sharing a couple of queer looks they said I could go. Since I had no idea what an eleven-year-old girl would like, my mother helped me pick out a present, a wind-up clock that played music and had pictures of Peter Pan and Tinkerbell. At last, the grand day arrived and my father left work early to take me. It was quite a long drive and as we made it to Jennifer's neighborhood I remember being struck by how far the golf-course-smooth lawns stretched between the houses and wondered why there were patches of Creeping Charlie where there should have been sidewalks. The tall sequoias were starry with Christmas lights and with the sun almost gone, it felt as if we were driving through a dark enchanted forest.

Her house stood a good way in from the road and I was shocked when my father pulled right up the driveway and instead of just dropping me off got out to come with me. I rang the chiming bell and Jennifer opened the door followed by a man I assumed was her father. He gave us a shrinking look and told Jenny to go back inside where I could hear the other kids busy playing. Jennifer smiled and thanked me for coming then left to rejoin her friends. As I watched her go, my dad put his hand on my shoulder and told me to wait for him out in the car.

When he came back a minute later telling me not to worry, I had done nothing wrong, I had no idea what he was talking about. I had pretty much forgotten all about it until we were stranded on that motel parking lot and I remembered sitting in the front seat of our old Studebaker with Jennifer's present on the floor at my feet, unable to enjoy the ice cream cone my dad stopped to buy me on the drive back home. Jenny never showed up in school after the holidays, so I never got to ask her what was the big misunderstanding. After listening to Delroy's story, I reckoned I would have left that party a lot less sick to my stomach had my father just told me the truth.

"How dare you propose to my mother before seeking my say on the matter?"

Madeline was annoyed when Emerson looked so pleased with himself, as if somehow her indignance served his plan.

"I thought it better to start with the lesser challenge," he responded glibly and did not flinch when she glared at him across the drugstore counter.

"Well, going behind my back certainly does more credit to your presumption than your bravery!"

If his ploy was to induce her to betray some mutual burning desire she was about to disappoint him. Although they had met up with friends and gone dancing several times since that unforgettable New Year's Night, and she liked how discreetly he held her close then shivered at the lightest touch of her breath, her feelings towards him had never risen above lukewarm. Not in a million years would the girl shunned as an ugly tomboy have imagined herself possessing the kind of delicate feminine airs needed to land the likes of Emerson Gardner. It was one thing to be playfully romanced by Potty Pottinger—they had grown up poor together—but it was quite another to be courted by the man the neighborhood's designing mothers with daughters hungered after as 'The Catch.' Mindful of their drugstore encounter, she had guarded against getting swept up by Doc's attentions, sure she was merely one of the many he chose to pursue because he found her pretty. So while the shock proposal had briefly stirred a jubilant heart-shimmer, her sister's disastrous marriage provided enough warning that a pleasing face was no guarantee that a wife would be honored and cherished.

Her practical mind did not ask if she loved him. She had never understood girls like Adrianna who, from the day they welcomed the 'change,' could describe the man they wanted to marry, as if he was sitting on a shelf in a Kingston department store beside the chubby pink dolls they dressed up in the home-sewn designs they had copied from fashion magazines. Considering her sister had wept for two straight days after seeing *Grand Hotel*, then admitted that part of why she eloped was to be finally free to visit the moving pictures, she was almost moved to agree with Miss Dora that the cinema was just another of Satan's devices meant to draw trusting girls into his clutches.

Perhaps their mother had treated her more leniently because she judged her too level-headed to find silver screen affairs anything other than frothy distractions from life's more pertinent intrigues. Far more exhilarating was venturing out to a Palace Theater dance. Nothing spurred her fantasies like being guided onto the floor by Potty Pottinger and hearing the admiring gasps as he grasped her by the waist and twirled her twice before striking a perfect Fred Astaire pose. But to her sensible side's disquiet it was when she was dancing with Doc, feeling the burn from her enemies' eyes, that her complexes vanished. Why then, with him standing there anxiously awaiting her answer, did she feel less eager than annoyed and embarrassed?

She had been surprised by her mother's hand, rough from forty years making ends meet scrubbing floors and washing clothes, grasping hers with a feeble touch she did not recognize. Who is this timid woman? Maddy wondered, searching to explain why her mother had felt elated, then terrified, when Doc asked for her daughter's hand in marriage.

"You need to understand," Miss Dora implored when her daughter jumped up angrily. "Doc comes from a respected, well-off family. He's going to be an important somebody." She averted her eyes to evade the head-on force of Madeline's fury. "So before you say 'yes,' it's best he hears this from you and not some laba-laba out to cause you more crosses." Again she paused and inhaled deeply. "Your father and I never married."

Her brain still spinning from Doc's surprise proposal, Madeline feared it was either a dream or some scurrilous power had warped her perceptions. If years fending off the slurs and murmurs had felt like skirting the edge of an inferno, hearing hateful rumor turn to truth in her mother's mouth felt like being thrown naked into a pit to be roasted by her accusers. Living on an island where good jobs were as scarce as hen's teeth, it seemed natural that, like so many fathers, Mr. Jans had been forced to spend long stretches apart from his family. Now she wondered if the reason she never asked why her mother was Miss Dora and not Mrs. Jans, or why her parents almost never went places together, was because she dreaded the answer. The question remained, as her confidence wavered and Emerson stood there waiting with maddening patience, how much did he actually deserve to know? For her own sake, or for her mother's, should she start from before fate's stream got shunted from its proper course? Would it change anything if he knew that her grandmother had died the day Miss Dora was born causing her grandfather to waste himself in grief and drink? That little Dora had, for years, carried the blame and as a result her siblings had removed her from school and trained her for work on her hands and knees? Should he know that the handsome soldier who would become Madeline's father had seduced a fifteen-year-old who welcomed his love like a lonesome fugitive? Did she dare tell him that on the day her mother was due to be wed, the magistrate had cast her a pitying look and threatened to arrest the groom?

How, she demanded to know, did you forgive him? He forgot?! What kind of man forgets getting married? When, after a flood of accusations and furious tears, she had calmed, her temper spent, her mother shared his half of the story.

"Your father admitted he had been a fool to enlist but his family desperately needed the money and the recruiter told him that if he paid a gal to get married, he could double his pay and have it annulled once the war was over. Except that Mr. Jans came home from the fighting with an inch of metal stuck in his head and half of his memory. He couldn't remember the woman's name or where to find her. 'Dora,' he swore on his knees, 'the marriage was a sham. I thought she had gone on with her life. I never dreamt she would turn up to lie and say I gave her that pickney.'"

"And you believed him?"

Miss Dora laughed scornfully. "That woman's child looks nothing like your father."

"So he could have divorced her!"

"He could have, but I wouldn't let him."

"You wouldn't *let* him?"

"Marriage is not something you play with," her mother said firmly, "and by the time the hussy showed up I was pregnant. I felt like a fool, but I wasn't going to have my innocent child tainted with scandal. When he saw I wasn't going to budge, Mr. Jans insisted that Mason be baptized with his name and agreed when I said I wanted him raised as a Seventh-day Adventist because they care about young people and, most of all, Satan's liquor is forbidden. Once your brother was born, he had us move to Kingston and promised to respect me as if I were his lawful wife." And then her mother truly shocked her. "Your father is the most decent man I have ever known. He never touched that woman a day in his life, but he took care of both her and her bastard child. The Good Lord punished us for our mistakes but I'll love that man till God sees fit to take me. Your father saw great abominations fighting in Africa, horrors that tore at his Christian soul. He kept his anger deep, but it was righteous, and that righteousness sustained me when our enemies were out to bury me. That war gave him his strength, strength to provide for two homes and to love me when I was too worn down to love him back. Without his strength, that rock to cling to, I would have cursed God years ago."

Madeline reflected on all the sacrifices her mother had made to keep their secret; there was nothing she need explain. For better or worse, she told her hopeful suitor, the answer is yes.

I was not a happy wanderer as I slouched through the gloom behind my parents and sulked inside our cold Valiant. The mayor had called late last night, inviting us to breakfast but, incredibly, my mother had thanked him and politely declined, explaining that we'd be leaving at dawn to make up for lost time. So while the mayor was facing a plate of hot waffles or maybe a stack of buttermilk pancakes, I'd be chomping on a tough green apple and half of a leftover peanut butter sandwich my dad thought should tide me over until restaurants were open. As we trailed the Angells out of the Sunnyvale parking lot, I was a stewing cross between sleepy and grumpy.

Slumped in back as we drove through the dark reminded me of when I was little and I'd wake up suddenly and be surprised that I was moving. The first two times, for a second, my heart beat faster, thinking I'd been kidnapped, then I'd remember my father wrapping me up in my blanket and carrying me out into the brisk night air, and me drifting back to sleep as he laid me across the backseat of our old Studebaker. I had stopped waking up on those nighttime drives except once, just as the sky was beginning to brighten, I was startled by my mother's voice. It was tight and raspy, as if she had a really bad stomachache.

'Face it, Emerson. It's not helping.'

'Why do you say that? You won't even give it a chance.'

'I did give it a chance.'

I had jumped to ask what was the matter and been confused by the pain in her smile as she faced me and said she was fine. That was the last of my midnight car-rides. Only later did I learn that my father had been driving her to and from her graveyard shift at the hospital. It took several months for my four-year-old brain to grasp that she had been delivering babies and not digging up corpses.

My second scare came later that year, not long after I started kindergarten. As usual, I was up before dawn to practice when I heard her yell from my parents' bedroom. I slipped from the piano stool to stick my ear against their door and felt my heart slowly stop throbbing when there were no more screams. I never believed my dad would ever hurt her. So seeing how pleased she looked when she came out and patted my head then left to make breakfast, I did not fret the following Saturday morning when my keen ears picked up her moans. Parents did mysterious things with their doors locked and at the time our Trinity still seemed perfect. How could I think otherwise when hours before, just like every other Friday night, the three of us had bunched close on the couch in our den to watch Perry Mason and eat pineapple upside-down cake warm from the oven. Those days my parents were careful to guard each other's feelings, but as our journey was about to expose, the good times were never as perfect as they seemed on TV back when the innocent were never found guilty and the guilty always confessed.

The sun had started glaring through our windshield and shielding my eyes I felt a trickle of relief spotting the sign that read, 'You Are Leaving the State of New Mexico.' The trickle dried to dust soon after we crossed into the wide lonesome sweep of Texas. Where were the mountains, the orange groves, the glimpse of houses? I missed California and I missed my friends. My waking brain was full as precious memories came flooding in to fill the barren landscape. Recalling those happy days, I wondered if my parents were also getting homesick and right then it struck me that almost all of our friends we'd left in L.A. were from someplace else. Anu was from Romania; Mr. Batori, my second piano-teacher, came from Hungary; my Aunt Gwen (not my real aunt, my mother's best friend and taller look-alike) was raised in New Orleans but met my

Uncle Cy, her Liberian husband, in New York City; Happy Molina had come from Cuba, and dear Mrs. Walters was born in Panama. Even Shayla, that winsome heartbreaker had moved to L.A. from Baltimore. Clearly my hometown was a worldwide magnet, so why were we leaving?

There is a clarity that comes with crossing the desert and while it would take me years to get the whole picture, the more I thought about it, the more I started to see what I had missed. Something had been a long time rotting in my L.A. paradise and, as the weather-man warned, the smog was most lethal when you could not see it. Even on those bad-air days that burned your eyes and made you squint, you didn't worry about the brown haze that hugged the freeways and put snot in your lungs because you knew the winds would shift and the wonderful life would come back into focus, for there was Hollywood, on its perch beneath a cleared blue sky, promising a new happy ending. The desert was much too stark and straightforward; no smog, no stench, no traffic. It was clearly no place for people.

My father had not turned on the air-conditioning even though the sun was already charring our Valiant like toast. As I watched him hunkered at the wheel trying to keep up with the Angells, my mother silent beside him in a sleeveless blue dress, her shining black hair half-hidden in a turquoise silk scarf, I knew I had a lot left to learn, so I did not cringe when the same heartsick song came twanging from the radio. After one-hundred-degree miles of nothing but creosote and yucca rushing past our windows I reckoned our brains were too dulled for meaningful conversation. That didn't mean my father hated country music any less.

"You could at least tune in another station," he grumbled, his eyes locked on the endless open road.

"There *are* no other stations. You didn't want to spend the money and get FM like I asked you to, remember? It's Vinton or Skeeter. Your choice."

"You call that a choice? How about plain silence?"

"I'm not going to sit here bored stiff—I already did three puzzles. Anyway, I like this song."

"Fine," my father spat, "corrupt the boy's ears."

Uh-oh, here we go, I thought wearily—time to play 'persecuted child in the middle.' Of late, no matter the contention, I was the shuttlecock to be whacked back and forth until the server felt confident they had shown the greater concern for my well being. I was not dumb enough to expose the one I was rooting for, but I cheered inside hearing my mother score first.

"So now you're concerned about his talent."

"What are you talking about? I've always wanted him to develop all of his abilities."

"Forgive me—I thought *I* was the one who paid for his music lessons."

"Let's just drop it."

My mother huffed in victory. "I bet you don't want to talk about it."

And so it went, back and forth, off and on, with the lovelorn weeping from the radio, over and over, past Canutillo, El Paso and Socorro. It was a good thing I wasn't one of those kids who gets carsick or those sappy pop songs might have had me puking my guts. They were all so sad and the same, like this sorry stretch of Texas. This was far from being the trip I had hoped for. One of my favorite pastimes back home was to pore over the globe in my bedroom and imagine traveling through those wild far-out places on my Aunt Gwen's postcards from Free Africa. I used to think the reason countries like Liberia were called free was because over there even the lions were not fenced in cages. I had started to get excited about us leaving when I asked my dad what Jamaica was like and he said it was a lot like Hawaii. But gazing out at the desolate wasteland, listening to another glum voice sing *The End of the World*, all I could think of was our school siren blaring and me diving under my desk in case the nuclear war had started.

The desert taught me one thing—happy endings are a mirage once you leave the field of dreams.

GLASGOW EMPIRE EXHIBITION OPENS IN TRIUMPH. Emerson nearly laughed out loud as he read the headline. Leave it to the Scots, he mused with a chuckle, to celebrate a whited sepulcher. A moment's reflection told him otherwise—for the richly privileged, the fact that Europe's colonies were falling apart and workers the world over were up in arms and raising hell offered a chance to profit. With Law under siege by Justice, 1938 promised to be a very dangerous year. He abhorred the violence, but having made plain where his sympathies lay left him in an awkward position with his steadfast protector now that the riots had spread to Kingston.

"So, Doc—if I catch one of those 'honorable demonstrators,' as yuh call them, settin' fire to your store, should I clap my hands or shoot him?"

Emerson shied from the sergeant's smirk. "I trust you'll be sensible," he answered weakly. He had hoped the strikes would replicate Gandhi's non-violent strategy in India, but peaceful non-cooperation had proved a bust in Jamaica. Until blood was shed, the governor had not acceded to a single demand. Now, suddenly, there was talk of elections and a new Constitution. It was a cynical gambit, for as Winters' needling implied, new clothes cannot be cut from old cloth; a browbeaten people don't turn magically into enlightened democrats. So with the planets all aligned for disaster, before daring the leap of his life, he had sought out his alter ego.

While classmates nicknamed him The Placid One, having found no insult pointed enough to bait Emerson's anger, Mason Jans had been dubbed Sir Calm. As earnest dissidents schooled by English reformists, the two were so in tune and had been friends for so long, they would argue for hours just to end up agreeing. Seeing the Old World combust, they debated whether passive resistance could still be noble once morality gave way to evil. When he wondered if it was right to be fretting about Spain when the poor were fighting for their lives right here at home Mason replied that the one unforgivable sin was willful ignorance.

"Your sister insists on getting married in May. What if we're at war?"

"What will be, will be, Doc," his friend replied. "All you can do is be true to yourself."

He never discussed his doubts with Madeline, afraid she would give them short shrift. His instincts proved right, for when he ventured to pose the stoic's question that had haunted him since his clash with Midas Coombs, she had dismissed it with contempt: "I'm a nurse. Ask the woman who scrubs your toilet why she works for so little." And despite his annoyance, he sensed she was right. Philosophers had bread and free time.

"Emerson! You need to come home with me this minute!"

A woman of unnerving girth and stature, Mildred Gardner was not inclined to move swiftly, so seeing her come galloping inside as if chased by wild animals made Emerson jump and drop his newspaper. "Mother? What on earth?"

"I knew you'd be here with your ears stopped and your eyes shut!" She slapped his hand away when he tried nudging her onto the stool to pause and catch her breath. "You didn't notice? Hardly a soul is walking the street. They're rioting downtown. I hear an innocent boy just got shot."

His first thoughts ran to Madeline but he hid his dread. "If the streets up here are empty you should go on home and not worry about me."

"Stop flapping your gums and listen! I just ran into Sergeant Winters. Thugs from Back-O-Wall joined with those country hooligans and their blinking protest. They're using the march as an excuse to smash store windows and start looting. You need to lock up right now and come home!"

"Mommy, please! Get hold of yourself." In light of her weight and blood pressure he feared seeing his mother in such a frenzy. "Nobody's going to trouble me."

"How you come so hardheaded, eh? You think a bunch of hungry vandals are going to discriminate? The police have their hands full. They won't be running up here to save you."

"If there are bystanders getting hurt, I need to stay open."

Mildred raised her hand to slap him then glimpsed the scar her ring-hand had left perilously close to her son's right eye. The years she spent bribing her son with indulgent amounts of ice cream and cake had still not salved her regret for beating him bloody the day his father wrote to say he was never coming back. So she softened, and instead jabbed a gloved finger at his temple. "Since I can't knock more sense into that thick bald head, promise you'll make it home before night?"

Emerson caught hold of the finger mid-jab. "I'll close early, I promise. If I'm late it's only because I had to wait at child services for Maddy. She could be out who knows where in the city. I need to see her home safe."

She tried to thwart it, but the mere mention of Madeline Jans made Mildred grimace. Though far too proud to admit it, she respected the fact that the girl had earned herself a profession and bent her knee to nobody, including her prospective mother-in-law. But while those were admirable qualities for an unmarried woman, they were dangerous for a wife. She could not dismiss the enraging sense that, once again, her brilliant son was coming out second best. She had lost a husband after twenty hard but rewarding years because Jamaica was too small and narrow-minded to suit his ambition and long distance marriage proved no obstacle for a conniving little trollop in Cuba. She had managed her bitterness buying properties with the extra allowance extracted from her husband's conscience and those rental incomes had paid for Emerson's drugstore. With its success she hoped that, even if her son ended up as frustrated as his father, he would be wealthy enough to darken a higher rung on the colony's social ladder. But no—rather than heed her advice and invest the profits, he had insisted on paying her back, then squandered what was left on his paupered fiancée who had the gall to declare that she intended to keep on working. Even worse, she was in no great hurry to have Mildred's grandchildren.

"Emerson, I hope you're not being a fool and letting that girl wrap you around her finger. You know there are even prettier ones out there. You could have your pick—"

"Mother, stop!" he implored, letting go of her finger. "I've made my choice. I don't want us at loggerheads over this my entire life."

"I would never get between you and the woman you chose," Mildred protested. "I just want you to be happy."

"Then can't you like her just for my sake?"

"Who says I don't like her?" she demanded, looking hurt. "You can like a person without liking what they do. She's out risking her life, flitting across town on that confounded bicycle, making people believe you cannot provide for her properly. I just pray she doesn't embarrass you."

"Embarrass me?" he echoed indignantly. "Mother, nothing Maddy does would ever embarrass me. She makes me proud."

There is a certain dignity, call it significance, that grows easily inside a child who knows that his parents had planned him. Even before his first fully-laid memory, the wanted child senses that he has landed safely in the right loving tribe. But dignity, while it may lessen the urge to steal or cheat, does not grant immunity to shame and insecurity.

"Enough! I can't take it any longer."

My father snapped off the dial with such force it set my heart pounding, all the more because the drive had been peaceful for the past half-hour.

"What's come over you?" my mother demanded, flipping the radio back on. "You've been in a funk since Las Cruces."

"I don't know how you can stand it. The same maudlin song over and over. Now you've got our son cheeping along."

Had I known then what they meant by surrealism I would have been better able to describe my thoughts at that moment. Here were my parents who got me hooked on the New York Philharmonic with the record-player they bought for my third birthday, fighting over a pop tune. The crazy thing was, after listening to *Blue on Blue* for what felt like at least a hundred times, I had become a Bobby Vinton addict. This from the kid who used to insist on falling asleep to the slow movement from Beethoven's Fifth Symphony. If it was true that I had been captivated by a corny love song, it could only mean that standing hours on that scalding parking lot had scrambled my brain. In my mother's case, it might not have been sunstroke so much as revenge. Seeing that my father's taste in music tended towards the heavy side—meaning Wagner—she was probably just out to torture him.

"Why must everything always be your way? So he was singing along—it won't damage his talent. Besides, he's heard us listen to Nat King Cole."

"So now you're comparing Nat King Cole to this drivel? And here I thought your pretensions were meant to show you had taste."

"My pretensions? How is this song any worse than *Ramblin' Rose*? I think it's heartfelt."

"It's depressing, and *Ramblin' Rose* is far from *Unforgettable*."

"What a surprise—I married a stick-in-the-mud who shares taste with a fascist—"

Even from the back seat I could feel the rising body heat. I needed a quick diversion.

"Dad, look!" Leaning across the front seat, I pointed towards the tiny dot flashing further up the sizzling highway, "the Angells want us to pull over."

He peered through the kamikaze bugs splashing our windshield. "You sure? How can you tell?"

The gambit worked as my mother dropped her tirade and squinted into the blazing desert sunshine. "He's right," she said, using her flat hand as a visor. "Flash the headlights so they'll know we saw them signal."

"Now you're telling me how to drive—"

"Honestly, Emerson, get a grip." She leaned in and clicked off the radio before the other Bobby could finish singing how lost he'd be without the one that he loved.

Delroy Angell stood waiting outside of his car, fanning his face with his Cardinals baseball cap. He bent down to the driver's window as my father parked next to the skinny white pole holding the giant orange ball with the number 76 in dark blue letters. "What's up? You folks finally want to grab some grub?" Behind him, a six-wheeler with a yellow rose emblem on the side of its van sat idle beside a rusted pickup truck.

My father stared at me over his shoulder then back at Delroy. "We thought this was your idea."

I tensed then relaxed as Delroy shot me a wink. "Sure thing. I'm a mite peckish myself."

"I'll go get Connie," my mother announced pushing out through her door. "She probably needs to powder her nose as well."

Delroy grinned at the obvious code. "Yeah, you sure look like hell."

"You watch that charming mouth, Captain Angell," she scolded him, smiling.

My father stopped as he stood up from the car and assessed our surroundings. He looked none too pleased. "Where are we anyway? This can't be Fort Stockton already."

"Naw, that's still an hour away. I don't know about you, Doc, but by then the rest of us could be meaner than a bunch of alley cats." Delroy nodded towards the discrepant stream out by the road that seemed to spring from nowhere. "Man, it's good to see some running water. I reckon these truck stops should be able to whip up some decent ham and eggs."

A freckled-faced boy with bleached straw hair came out of the service station's adjacent metal-framed diner hopping his way on one leg. He looked about twelve and it was plain that he was just showing off.

"You folks be wantin' gas?" he asked, his Texas twang cheerful.

"Yep, that and some of your grub," Delroy told him. "You're still servin' breakfast I hope."

The blond boy stalled on his two good legs with a worried frown. "Mama says we can give you gas and water but that's all."

"Not even some eggs? It's barely 11 o'clock—"

Connie reappeared followed by my mother, handkerchiefs clasped to their mouths, squeezing their eyes and shaking their heads. "Mercy! Somebody must've died inside that restroom. I almost went and hiked my haunches up over that stream."

The freckle-face scrunched with a look I had never seen, but would later recognize as sheer twelve-year-old panic. "You weren't s'pose to use the terlet!"

Before I could ask him why, the boy took off, this time making normal use of healthy legs. Delroy shrugged, then waved for the rest of us to plow on behind him. Inside, a lazy ceiling fan shifted flies and hot air around the hash house someone with a sense of humor had named The Oasis. Its three plastic-covered tables sat empty and as we chose our seats the boy scampered past us and back outside without a glance. Behind the counter, a thick-armed woman in a gray waitress uniform stood scraping meat off the griddle. Tufts of damp yellow hair had stuck to her cheeks flushed red from the heat.

She had her body half-turned but I could see her watching us from the corner of her eye as she scrubbed the stove with such ferocity the sinews bulged on her forearm.

None of the tables was large enough for five and as we started to split my mother chirped, boys at one table, girls at the other. The waitress had still not moved to greet us so Delroy raised his voice to get her attention. When she ignored his cheerful good morning he picked up the single-sheet menu sealed in plastic. From the looks of it, The Oasis fare card had spent a long career dabbled with Tabasco and corn oil.

The air was thick with the reek of fried meat and after more minutes went by my mother was annoyed to see that the waitress had turned to cleaning the floor. "Excuse me, miss—should we come to the counter? We'd like to order."

The waitress kept her back turned, mopping the same spot over and over, but making no headway on what looked to be a year's worth of spills and ground-in sand. Visualizing my picture book on the human body, I guessed that the big muscle pressing out her uniform was the trapezius. I would have asked my dad for confirmation, but reckoned this was one of those times when it was smarter to keep my mouth shut.

"Miss, it says here you serve breakfast all day," said Delroy, lifting his voice a few more decibels in case she was hard of hearing or just plain slow. "I'll have me some country-style eggs, bacon and coffee."

Connie leaned towards my mother to speak in a whisper. "Ain't it obvious? She doesn't want to serve us."

"Well, I'm in no hurry!" my mom declared, loud enough you'd have to be clear across the desert not to hear her. "We can sit here and chat until she has a mind to."

That brought the vigorous scrubbing to a halt. As the waitress turned towards us, the look on her face made me think of my classmates who returned to school after Christmas complaining that Santa Claus was a fraud and a lying cheapskate. Her hangdog look hardened and as she stood gripping the mop in her fist I noticed the band of pale white skin where a ring was missing from her finger. She just stood there staring, as if expecting my mother to finally get the message or simply wither away.

My father made a play for her pity. "See here, miss? I take it that boy who greeted us outside is your son, so as a mother you'll understand—we've been driving since sunup and our boy here is near faint from hunger."

After feeling whacked like a birdie for half the morning I had forgotten I was hungry, but I was pleased when his soft approach seemed to work. The waitress blew off the wisp of yellow hair that had fallen in front of her nose and answered not unkindly. "I can't be seen serving niggers, but if y'all go-on back outside I'll have Toby bring your boy some fixins."

I thought I heard a rattler's castanets shiver from the distant tumbleweeds. That's how quiet it got inside The Oasis.

Delroy was quick onto his feet. "Lady, you must be out of your cotton-pickin' mind! C'mon, people, let's go—this place ain't nothin' but a dump!"

Connie moved to follow but my mother grabbed her by the wrist and held her down. "No! I'm hungry. We're staying right here until she serves us."

"Madeline, for God's sake ... " My father looked about to fall on his knees. "We'll just be wasting more time and we've got some heavy driving to do if you want us to make New Orleans by morning."

"So we get there an hour late. People have to learn—this is *nineteen*-sixty-three!"

A blast of fiery desert air rushed in and I edged close to my father seeing two lank-haired men loom behind him. The way they lingered by the door, thumbs stuck in their belt loops, slit-eyes drawing a slow bead around the diner, I thought I was back inside that seedy Western—only this time I was the *chico* bandit on the 'Wanted' poster about to fall into the hands of ruthless bounty hunters. From the black oil drips on the front of their undershirts it seemed a safe bet that they had just crawled out from under the six-wheeler's engine. The mean-eyed dude in grimy blue jeans spoke up first.

"Toby says you got trouble, Martha?" The growth on his chin suggested he had not shaved in days, while the green and blue tattoos running the length of his arms somehow made me think of a jigsaw puzzle.

Martha tipped her head in our direction. She seemed less bothered than plum tuckered out. "These folks don't seem to get plain English. I told 'em we don't serve their kind inside."

I could see my father's shoulders tighten as he joined Delroy's side. "Look—we're not out to raise any hackles. We get the picture."

His consoling tone threw the truckers off balance. They stuck out their chests and tried to look threatening while they thought about what to say next. The one with arms covered with hair instead of tattoos frowned at his partner as if to say he was taking too long to give his instructions.

"Come, let's go ... " Delroy repeated softly.

The men parted with slit-eyed slowness, leaving just enough room for us to squeeze through one at a time. Connie was the first one out the door and I was about to tag behind her when I saw that my mother was still at her table, as cool as could be. I lurched to rescue her, but my dad held me back looking ready to blow his lid when, in response to his call, she calmly took a dollar bill out of her purse and smoothed it flat on the greasy table. Getting to her feet once it stuck, she ignored the two truckers and addressed the dank-haired waitress. "That's for the use of your restroom. I suggest you use it to buy some soap."

Spewing curses, the tattooed enforcer lunged, but as my mom spun to face him, her composure seemed to block his roundhouse. Then I saw the gun pressing his side.

"Be cool, Charlie," Delroy murmured pleasantly, poking the trucker with the snub-nosed revolver. "I *said,* we're leaving."

My mom was shaking as she slipped out to hold me and in my fear and surprise it crossed my mind, seeing my dad with the same dazed look he'd had in Las Cruces, that if one of us passed out now, this could really get ugly.

Young Toby came pressing inside and stopped in his tracks, spying the gun. He glanced at his mother clenching her mop as if to wring out its life, her face, like the dead-still trucker's, a sheet of white anger. All eyes were on the aimed revolver as Delroy shielded the three of us and we edged out backwards. Safely outside, we shouted to Connie off in the sunshine fixing her makeup and she hustled to join the mad dash back to our cars. I could finally feel myself breathing as my dad cranked the engine and sped for the highway.

It was 1939 and mortal enemies were sinking the world by pretending to be friends but for sweethearts eager to be wed the future looked as promising as a sunshiny day in May; everywhere hibiscus was blooming, spring birds were singing and tender thoughts were feeding dreams, making everything possible. And a good thing too, because the Gardners' perfect day was off to a disastrous start.

While custom dictates that the bride must add suspense by delaying her entrance, it was not required that her driver get lost on his way to fetch her or forget that he'd been warned when he borrowed the car that the tank was low on petrol. Happily, brides are known to be singularly blessed by Good Fortune and so it was that sunny May afternoon; that is, until good fortune led to a scandal, but of course that all came later. As fate would have it, Potty Pottinger was speeding to the church after a late night tryst meant to bury dead hopes when what should appear in his path but his dear lost love, stranded beside a disabled Vauxhall.

Twenty-five minutes of cold groom sweat and organ improvisations were dribbling into ever-after when the sound of a sixty horsepower, V-cylinder engine came roaring inside the walls of All Saints Church. Rubbernecks with a view through the doors gasped at the chiffon-white cloud breezing up from the back of a Jubilee racer and Gloria Leguerre returned to facing the altar with a tiny smile, flush with vindication. The grateful organist launched into his German fanfare, the ritual pairing of Wagner and Mendelssohn inspired by the empire's beloved dead queen earning neither a smirk nor a second thought, despite the newspapers' unholy headlines. The more sensitive eyes, the well-meaning, as well as the green, were already getting misty, no tears being more prized than those that streamed at the very moment the lucky bride came floating by.

As if to make up for the dream wedding she had missed, Adrianna had gone out of her way and created a bridal masterpiece complete with matching lace-sleeved silk dresses for her eldest daughters who wandered behind their aunt's white train like two awestruck cherubs. After the choir's opening anthem, Mason brought out his violin for a moving Ave Maria that left Gloria Leguerre dabbing her eyes, grieving for Europe and her own aspirations. To everyone's relief, Father Felcher managed to make it through the ceremony without a stumble and would have retired free of ridicule had he not suffered a nasty gash during the reception when he struck his head on the punch bowl as he stooped to retrieve the flask that had slipped from his cassock. A more damaging scandal had been averted as Gloria Leguerre came to compliment the bride with her firm hand clamped on Potty Pottinger.

"Congratulations. That was quite an entrance!" Her narrow face smug beneath a flat green hat, Gloria Leguerre's sardonic praise drew every eye within earshot. "You do have a weakness for motorcyclists. Don't tell me this gallant young man just happened along in time to pluck you from the wayside."

Madeline glared past the old woman to shoot daggers at Potty who shrugged and rolled his eyes. Fortunately, Mason was right nearby and waded in before there was bloodshed.

"Indeed he did, and I'm afraid the blame for my sister's misfortune is entirely mine." He cast his music teacher a repentant smile, embracing her while he loosened the death grip on Potty's elbow. "I had arranged for a car and driver to deliver the bride but forgot when I wrote him the address that our rulers had felt it necessary to consecrate Napoleon's final defeat on two disparate streets. As a result, the poor man was deterred by their second Waterloo. Our friend Pottinger here showing up when he did was clearly Heaven sent."

Forced to choose between admitting she had jumped to unsavory conclusions, or accusing her most highly praised student of being an unconscionable fibber, Gloria was left to splutter, "well—so it would appear—" before fleeing along with her annoyance.

"Thank you," Madeline whispered, squeezing her brother's arm. "You spared me from committing murder. Unlike this blabbermouth!" She scowled at Potty who kept himself from bursting with laughter.

"Water off the duck's back," he assured her casually. "Now that the record's straight, the old snoop can't libel you with some made-up story."

"I wouldn't be so sure," she muttered. "But you're right—why do I care?"

Crisis avoided, the rest of the evening proved a resounding success, despite old Felcher's mishap; great tubfuls of curried goat and rice scraped clean, the monumental wedding-cake devoured hours before the last of the pimento wine and hog-plum brandy sent inebriated toasts drifting to their merciful end. Mildred Gardner's profligacy had produced a banquet fit for kings, complete with monogrammed serviettes and Italian linen; each guest sent home with a tiny tin of sweets and a set of sterling silver commemorative coasters. But while Mason's vital intercession had spared his sister's meltdown on the happiest day of her life, it failed to keep her nemesis from feeding the mouths of Madeline's enemies.

The public's self-appointed guardians could only cluck their jealous tongues as Gloria Leguerre described the orgy of food and the three-level cake 'just *soaked* through with rum.'

"Now, I ask you," the paragon submitted, "what respectable Christian girl shows up for her wedding on the back of a motorcycle? Behavior like that is why this country is backsliding!"

Hearing Gloria Leguerre's hateful gossip spread like gospel, Mildred took comfort in the fact that, while the article did question if such a lavish affair was conscionable with the empire on the verge of war, her son's wedding had taken up two full columns in the city's main paper. As for the newlyweds, after standing on their feet for nine hours, they were simply relieved to have the day behind them. Emerson wanted nothing more than to preserve forever the look on his new bride's face at what came later.

"You built me a *house?*" she exclaimed, after he steered her inside and drew his palms from across her eyes. "Scoundrel!" she cried, slapping the hat from her effulgent husband's bald head. "You hinted not a peep the whole time you had me agonizing about having to live under Mildred's roof. I should brain you!"

"My poor mother," he chuckled, joining her childish glee as she laughed and hugged him close. "We're *such* disappointments!"

"It's so lovely," Madeline whispered, awed as she wandered through the three bedrooms reveling in the copper-plated fixtures, the colorfully contrasting tiles, the bathroom big enough to sleep in—and with the toilet inside! "How did you know my taste?" she asked, eyeing the dining room's handcrafted mahogany furniture.

"I hired a contractor who knows you a bit. Can you guess?"

Her mouth fell open. "You mean Mason did all this?"

"Well, most of it. Drew the plans, oversaw the workers, chose the fixtures. He even sketched some of the furniture. Not bad for an architect's first project."

"You two are cads. Plotting behind my back. I can't believe you kept it a secret."

"I wanted to surprise you."

"You've certainly made a habit of that, Doc Gardner," she responded dryly. "What else are you waiting to spring on me?"

Emerson grinned, "You're about to see, if you have the energy."

"Men—so obsessed with that ugly thing between their legs," she mocked him scornfully. "Hate to break this to you, but I'm a nurse, I've seen more than enough of them already."

"Oh, but mine is different."

Madeline escaped his pleading clutch. "Just stop!"

"Are you disappointed we did this instead of a honeymoon?"

"Don't be silly. What could beat not having to live with your mother?" She turned to lovingly caress the kitchen's smooth soapstone counter. "Seriously, Emerson, I adore the house—it's perfect—but I don't want us to start out keeping secrets." After a pause, she shifted to face him. "What were you and Dr. Joseph whispering about at the reception?"

Emerson grew quiet recalling the odd turn that followed the doctor's good wishes.

"I appreciate it's no longer in your plans. Just, please, think it over. Everyone knows you were cheated."

"That's gratifying to hear, Dr. Joseph, but I'm not a bachelor anymore. I have a wife to consider."

"I understand you're probably anxious to start a family, but who knows what will happen with this war. We *need* men with your abilities who care about our country—"

"Which of my husband's abilities are you after? He has many!" Madeline's face glowed with pride as she joined them.

"I'll let him tell you," Dr. Joseph demurred and was about to leave when he paused to take hold of her hand. "My little fighter— how beautiful you look, all grown up. I can't tell you how pleased I am you've found yourself a man like Emerson. He has the chance to be a great asset to this island. Take care of him—and his dreams."

"Well?" she persisted when her husband stayed silent, "what dreams were the two of you discussing?"

He gazed achingly at her questioning eyes, yearning to hold her tight, safe from the slights and tumult of a changing world sure to seek catastrophe. "I'll tell you later," he promised, kissing her forehead. "It was nothing pressing."

The flat, empty desert was zooming by outside my window as I peered to check the Valiant's speedometer and saw that we were doing over ninety. After years spent watching every car on the freeway leave our clunky old Studebaker behind in the dust, I was thrilled to be going that fast except with the sun peaking close to noon it seemed that at any moment we would plunge straight off the road into a lake of shimmering hot tar.

"Can you believe that Delroy?" My father's shoulders hunched as he clutched the steering wheel. "Suppose the gun had gone off?"

My mother ignored him and switched the radio on full blast. Out poured the singer with tears in his voice, sighing, *Hopeless...*

"I'm serious!" he cried, flipping off Andy Williams. "You realize what just happened back there?" He checked the Valiant's rear-view mirror for the fifteenth time. "Suppose they called the highway patrol?"

My mother had not said a word since we escaped from the

cruddy hash house and the silent pressure was getting unbearable. She slouched in her seat and shut her eyes. For a child praying for peace before my dad lost his temper and we all drowned in boiling asphalt, that was not a good sign.

"So now you're going to fake sleep and pretend not to hear me!"

When she did not stir he shook her roughly by the shoulder. "Answer me! Don't you think we should say something? Or just go our separate ways?"

I was beginning to believe that the Father and the Holy Spirit had sworn a pact that they would never let a sleeping dog lie. It made sense in a cockeyed way, if it was true what my father said—that eternal vigilance was the price of safety. But that was the thing about trouble, it had a habit of sneaking up on you.

"All right, all right," she grumbled, sitting up straight. "I'll talk to Delroy. He should not have gone off half-cocked, but it's over. Take a breath. Be glad nothing happened."

"Less than nothing would have happened had you not been so set on provoking them. You're lucky that lunkhead didn't break your nose."

My mother snickered. "That yokel was just showing off for the waitress. And so what if he did?" She gave him a loaded look. "I can take a punch, or have you forgotten—"

Her point gave me chills.

"So now you're Sugar Ray Robinson. You think you can cow folks with their mindset? Maybe next time you'll try a little suasion instead of escalation."

Rats! I thought, here it comes.

"You really are ungrateful, you know that? Would my rolling over like a helpless puppy have gotten you a bed last night? *Au contraire*, Dr. Pangloss! I showed them we West Indians have class."

"How? By pretending to be British? Day before yesterday you were Mrs. America, now we're back to being slavish colonials."

"For God's sake, Emerson—it was a ploy. It worked though, didn't it?"

"Yes, it worked, and I *am* grateful. You were magnificent!" he commended her, almost sincerely. "Just don't count hoodwinking a rookie reporter and a small town mayor as some moral victory."

I could not see her face, but I was picturing the steam flaring from her nostrils.

"I'm starting to envy Connie. At least she married a man with some backbone. You would have stood there soiling yourself and let that lout punch out my eye."

"And you and Delroy might have gotten us hanged!"

"Don't exaggerate."

"Exaggerate? Have you forgotten the state we're in? This is not New Mexico."

I could feel my mother wince.

"Right. So we're in Texas. It's also 1963. If nobody ever dares to say anything, when will it change?"

"You don't change folks like that."

"If you stand your ground they're forced to respect you."

"It wasn't you they respected, it was that gun in Delroy's hand."

From the grip on her lip I knew my mom was gearing up to land a haymaker. She stayed that way for several seconds and it struck me that she was having a hard time deciding where to aim. "You know what?" she retorted abruptly. "I'm glad he did it!"

My dad's new demon must have awakened because he jerked towards her, his eyes shooting fire, then stalled as I let out a scream seeing us about to run off the road and into the desert. He swung the Valiant's power-assisted steering, sending its tires squealing as we swerved back onto the shoulder, leaving two stripes of black burnt rubber and me in a heap amid the scattered luggage. Seconds of chest-thumping panic transformed into a comic adventure, I grinned and gave the thumbs up from the back-seat floor when my parents turned to check on me, their frightened faces gray. Sometimes a brush with disaster is a welcome diversion.

An hour later our nerves had settled and we arrived in Fort Stockton without a catastrophe. The Angells had not seen us veer off the road and were waiting at the first gas station looking both impatient and relieved to see our Valiant show up with the three of us in one piece. My father cut the engine by the pumps, then jumped out, slamming his door. I was keen to witness the showdown but my dad's sudden unpredictable anger held me in my seat. I could not get over how much of a stranger he had become these last two days.

He had always been a bit of a mystery to me compared to my mother, but something had changed the man who would always patiently answer my questions from I was just big enough to look down on a lawn jockey. I remember him telling me that those little black men crouching at the head of people's driveways were there for good luck, like the green-haired leprechauns guarding pots of gold at the end of rainbows, but now that I had seen more of the world I was having my doubts. Those hunched-over jockeys looked lost, like they didn't really belong there.

My dad and Delroy were speaking too softly for me to catch their words, but I could tell by the way Connie turned and walked off that they were arguing. The captain was staring at my father as if he had dropped from outer space. He finally threw up his hands.

"How many times do I have to say it? I had the safety on. It could not have gone off by accident!"

"That's not the issue!" my father countered, his voice raised to match Delroy's. "That cowboy act could have bought us a heap of trouble. I'm *still* sweating bullets!"

I thought my mother would have gone to join in, but she just sat in the car looking disgusted.

"Fine, Doctor. Next time I'll let that chump slug your wife." Delroy stabbed his finger into my father's chest. "But let's get one thing straight. If it's *my* wife, I'm doing it again."

Their standoff came to a halt as a uniformed attendant strode up from the Angell's station wagon wiping oil from his hands, with a look that said he was ready to get paid.

Delroy counted out three dollar bills from his wallet and shot the mechanic a wink when he looked surprised and said, 'thanks, pal.' The pilot squinted at the red script sewn on the breast of the attendant's gray overalls. "Roy is it—?" he asked, sounding amused. "Well, Mr. Roy, any idea where we might get us some good old bacon 'n' eggs and maybe a bowl of lettuce for my friend here?"

Roy thought it over as he slipped the generous tip in his pocket. "There's Mumbo-Jumbo's—first exit, then left at the light about a mile—you can't miss it."

"They'll serve us inside there, right?"

"Mumbo-Jumbo's?" Roy looked tickled by my father's question. "Sure thing, pardner. They'll take green from a coon."

"Ugh! You'd spend your money at a place called Mumbo-Jumbo's?" my father hissed once Roy had left.

"I don't care what effin' name they call it," Delroy barked. "I'm ready to eat my spare tire."

It turned out the diner was called plain Mumbo's and the bright orange and yellow formica looked so familiar I thought we were back in California. Inside, the scalding Texas air was chilled a good thirty degrees so the pony-tailed waitresses in their snug white skirts and orange-trimmed yellow aprons could bounce about perky as bunny-rabbits. We started for the first free table and discovered just how fast a Mumbo hostess could hop. She was on us in a blur.

"I'm sorry," she said, screwing up her brow for a sad-faced pout, "this section is reserved, but we have plenty of seats at our counter," she added brightly, beaming as if she expected the five of us to clap and jump with joy.

While Delroy tried making eye contact with my father, my mother did not miss a beat. "Young lady, we've been traveling your state since early this morning and a stool will not support my aching back. How long do you estimate the wait is for a table?"

Either the steel in her eyes or the clipped English accent knocked our sunny teenybopper off her game. She froze then started to stammer. "I-I'll go talk to the manager."

"You do that," my mother said crisply. "You can tell him we're traveling on official government business."

The pink lips parted and our greeter scampered off like a bunny at the dog-races.

"Official government business?" my father echoed, looking bemused.

"We are going back because an official asked you to—I just never said which government," she retorted, defending her integrity.

"I hope we can sit down soon—my blood sugar's so low my legs are going right back to sleep," Connie complained, squeezing her feet inside another pair of three-inch heels.

"Don't you fret, my little babycakes," said Delroy, shocking us all, Connie included, with his quaint note of affection, "while the

Gardners are here trying to take Iwo Jima, we'll be sinking our teeth into a couple of juicy steaks at that counter."

"Wow! Babycakes, huh?" my mother chortled, grinning at Connie. "I guess you two kissed and made up."

Delroy glowered at her coldly. "You don't know the first thing about it."

"You're right, it's none of my business."

As Connie gently massaged my mother's taut shoulder, a young man wearing a shirt patterned in blocks of orange and yellow approached, followed by our perky waitress. An iron-on patch on his pocket bore a tiny bushy-haired figure above the logo *Have a Jumbo at Mumbo's.*

"How can I help you folks?" he asked politely, his bespectacled face marred by a bad case of acne.

"We'd like a table," my mom said bluntly, directing his attention to the spacious ones in front sitting empty.

After a furtive survey of his customer-to-table ratio the manager's rutted features relaxed. He pushed the horn-rimmed glasses higher up on his nose and used the same finger to make a head count. "There're five of you, but I think we can do this," he said brightly. "Mindy, please show these folks to table twelve."

Trying bravely to ignore the ripple of heads that followed our entrance, Mindy marched us through the open dining area to a booth in back set across from a Middle-Eastern-looking couple and their well-dressed twins. The identical boys watched me with mouths and eyes open wide, like five-year-olds do when they're mystified.

Twenty minutes went by before we realized we'd seen the last of Mindy. While I mooned over the thought of a grilled cheese sandwich, the attractive young family had finished their meal. As they stood, the olive-skinned couple glanced us friendly, embarrassed smiles and tried to keep the twins from staring over their shoulders as they left to pay the cashier. Only later, as we departed, did I realize the kids had been staring at me and then back to the image I'd missed in the middle of the diner. Though I failed to see the resemblance, I guessed that the frizzy-haired black boy with blubber lips like a fish sucking on ketchup was Mumbo.

Fed up with waiting, Delroy swaggered off for the counter and my mother tagged behind him in search of the manager. I don't know what she told him, but by the time Delroy came strutting back boasting two plates of steak and eggs, the rest of us were halfway through four stacks of buttermilk pancakes (Connie's with bacon on the side) and the pockmarked supervisor was on his way back to our booth with five complimentary Mumbo sundaes.

The pilot braked mid-stride, crushed by the sight of his banana split. "What the hell did you say to that flourbag?" he muttered when the manager left.

My mother savored the maple syrup sweetening her tongue before responding with airy insouciance, "I told him we were with the Department of Health."

Europe's imperialist chickens had come home to roost, but for newlyweds an ocean away from Hitler's mayhem, married life remained a diverting bauble shining brightly as ever. And who could blame them? The happy Gardners had a home of their own and were free to live as they pleased. Unfortunately, happiness is not allowed to flaunt itself for long before some blinking observer decides it's time for the facade to be cracked.

"I've tried—I really have tried! I just cannot countenance your wife's behavior."

As should all wise sons with overbearing mothers, Emerson went on working behind the drugstore counter and held his tongue.

"With all the violence going on, how can she be riding through Back-O-Wall like a madwoman? A proper wife would be managing her home, not giving every self-righteous busybody license to smear our name!"

"Smear our name? Maddy agreed when you pressed her to be baptized in our church," he said slyly. "She does just as the Holy Spirit guides her—"

"Don't get cheeky with me," Mildred warned, her accusing finger aimed at his chest. "You told me she promised to stop riding that disgusting bicycle. It's unbecoming for a decent woman, much less your own wife."

"It's not her fault we Jamaicans are such a loving people," he deflected, pulling swabs from a wad of cotton then sticking them inside his vials to soak up damaging moisture. "What is a busy midwife to do? She can't very well reach those slums on the tram-car."

Mildred scowled, repulsed by the thought. "Why is she still working? You spent your last quatty building her that house and she can't even spare the time to take care of it. Better the two of you had come to live with me and saved all that money she makes you waste on a maid."

"Maddy's too much like you, I suppose. Her hand prefers the feel of cash to a sponge or a fry-pan," he quipped, smiling inside. His mother had always been a better businesswoman than a homemaker, which was one of the reasons he suspected his father was still in Cuba.

The cut proved pointed enough to draw Mildred's rare defensiveness. "It's one thing for a lady to manage a few income properties but quite something else to pedal a bicycle through Kingston with her skirts hiked up to her knees. Instead of worrying about hopeless girls whose children will never amount to anything—I'm sorry to say it, but it's true," she insisted when Emerson looked horrified, "she should be at home making herself attractive. Madeline is still not pregnant, is she—"

"Mother, really—we've barely been married two years."

Mildred puffed up her chest like an armored matron still eager to preen about her youthful conquests. "You think I just fell-out the mango tree? I know how healthy young couples normally carry on."

"Of course you do, Mother." Realizing it was not the ground he wished to fight on, he smiled inside and stayed mum until she finished speaking her piece. Lamentably, he would choose the worst possible moment to share her piece with his wife.

Madeline had made it home early and collapsed onto the drawing-room settee shortly before her husband arrived, densely unaware that she was fighting back tears. One of her young mothers, a willowy seventeen-year-old struggling to fend for herself in the city, had been found dead in her West End shack, her two infants bawling beside her body. She had warned the girl not to have intercourse too soon after her laparotomy: 'this is serious, Naomi. You were lucky Dr. Joseph was there on call.'

The way the girl's face would bloom like a diaphanous flower the second her two-year-old spotted Madeline on her bicycle and rushed to greet her crying, 'Nurse!' had affected her deeply. Naomi had made saucers of her eyes and tried to look mindful while she begged her not to get pregnant again, but just as she feared, the girl had been listening with half of her brain and calculating with the other. Now, two innocent children were lost to the mercy of strangers.

When she learned that Naomi had died, she had immediately thought of Adrianna, realizing it was only a matter of degree that separated her sister from that lovelorn child. For once a needy girl in Kingston made her first small wish a baby her man would love, the struggle to live became a stream of bad choices. When her milk went dry and her arms grew too weak for hugs, the love she craved turned out to be just another hungry mouth, her last consoling asset the softness between her legs.

Having watched girls like Naomi time after time bet their luck on some charming ne'er-do-well with a few loose coins jingling inside his pocket, Madeline was angry with herself for feeling defeated. What that short, unhappy life made so acute was her own steadily surging frustration. The frustration of knowing that, while a girl could watch a flying machine wing into the wondrous horizon, a woman stuck on a backward island had best dream small if she wanted something to live for.

"Is this all our lives are going to add up to—?" she demanded, sharply cutting her husband off when he went jabbering on and on, mocking his mother's coital disquisition, "—me killing myself, worrying about hard-ears girls who don't have the sense to mark a calendar, while you fritter the time away soft-soaping spiteful harpies so you can sell more cough drops and Gimpy's tonic?"

"Shall I get rid of the store?" he suggested lightly, stupidly misreading her mood. "Of course, we'd have to sell the house and move in with my mother—"

Madeline slipped off one of her flat-heeled shoes and chucked it at his head, but could not stop a chuckle when he took a dramatic fall and played dead. "Don't even joke! I'm serious. I fear I'm going to end up an insufferable, disgruntled scold, like your mother—or mine—God help me!" she amended, gasping at the thought. "Don't laugh! —it will be your own fault. I get criticized if I'm seen out without you, but I know the movies I like tend to bore you. Before we were married you used to pester me to go out dancing."

Emerson sprang to his feet, stunned to his senses. "Fine—let's go dancing! I'm not the reason you insist on coming home late every night, looking like something the cat dragged in."

Madeline kicked off her other shoe and stretched her sore legs across the elegant Windsor settee. She knew she was being unfair, but she just could not get past the pointlessness of it all. Because it wounded her to see children suffer, she ended up abetting the same damning cycle: more children bearing more babies for the island's scrap-heap. And if that was not enough to depress her, she had to bear Mildred's incessant reminder that she was a failure at what these reckless girls all seemed to manage at the drop of a hat. She felt like the butt of a cosmic joke, and there her placid husband sat with his no longer romantic hands folded in his lap. "Are you contented, Emerson ... day after day, treading the same old rut?"

Still in the dark, it baffled him to hear his unfailingly positive wife sound discouraged. This whole time he had thought that, despite her challenging work, she was genuinely happy. Why just last night, hadn't she thrown her arms around him and declared how lucky she was to have married a man willing to invite his mother's wrath and help her in the kitchen on Violet's days off? She had certainly looked happy when she saw the Queen Anne turntable he bought for her birthday sitting on its imported oak console, but apparently he had been silly to think that after a long hard day she would rather be snuggling on a cushioned divan listening to Ella than out jitterbugging like a carefree juvenile. No, it was something else—something he had never expected. Until she was ready to share it, all he could do was tell her how he felt.

"Maddy, the only time my life will feel in a rut will be the day I can't make you hap—" he stopped short, hearing the words mock his lips as the dam was breached and his wife's distress spilled out in sobs.

"And what will that happiness be like, if I can never give you a son?"

He moved in close, dying to comfort her but, try as he might, he had no comforting answer.

After Mumbo's, the grown-ups decided to pair up by sex. Given the choice of cars to ride in, I went with my father and Delroy. It wasn't my true preference but I was afraid Captain Angell would label me a momma's boy which, given my feelings back then, would have been a totally fair assessment. After we 'men' had settled inside the Valiant and taken the lead for the three hundred mile leg to San Antonio, something told me my father was the one who suggested the split. He broke the built-up ice with care.

"Captain, despite our butting heads back there, you should know that Madeline and I are grateful for what you did. But I'm curious—have you always felt the need to carry a gun?"

Delroy pushed his Cardinals cap back and cocked his head to the side to study my father, like a rooster trying to decide if that thing on the ground was a worm. "We're crossing the South on the way to Alabama and you want to know why I carry a gun?"

"I'm not a fool, I know the reason. It just strikes me as asking for trouble."

"You ever been to war, Dr. Gardner?"

"We already went over that. I do not sanction war. I'm a pacifist."

"You see? That right there explains your problem. I know what it means to kill or be killed."

My father's lips parted as if he was about to ask Delroy a question, but instead he finished his thoughts. "Madeline and I made friends with a colored G.I. while we were living in New Orleans. He told me it took years after the war was over to realize that he had walled off his feelings to the point where he had lost touch with his truer self. Violence is about destruction. To me, it's not something a thoughtful citizen chooses. Especially not when he's outnumbered."

"Outnumbered?" Delroy expelled his breath with scorn and stared out his window at another head-bobbing pumpjack sipping up fortunes from the desert's dead and buried. From the way he shifted his body it was clear he suspected my father was two cans short of a six pack. "You just don't get it," he said, sounding repulsed. "I know—you're a proper black Brit—probably went to a top notch school dressed in a shirt and tie and attended church every Sunday with your wing-tip shoes all nice and shiny. You never had to scrap for all you got. You get kicked enough times in the gut, you'll spew up that blessed are the peacemakers rot. Go back and ask the Zulus and the Apaches and the Incas—heck, ask the Jews if they wished they had guns when they came across those peace-loving Christians and see what they'd tell you."

My dad gave a tired sigh. "So I guess we're doomed to kill each other."

"If God is white, I'm the Devil. Ask that Darwin fellow. The future belongs to those who do the burying. It's the rule of the jungle."

"Only for those who've already buried their conscience."

Delroy gave him a pitying look and the two of them retreated behind ironclad silence. My dad's stress on 'conscience' reminded me of what I'd overheard my mother saying not long before we left L.A. She and my Aunt Gwen both sounded upset but what made my ears perk up was her mention of my winsome crush. 'That brave girl is younger than Shayla, but Mundy is right, she made them look small. It takes a soul with no conscience to swear at a child. I tell you, Gwennie, when I saw her picture in the paper with all those grown people screaming in her face, I wanted to go and hug her!' That night I asked my mother if something bad had happened to Shayla and she smiled and said not to worry, Shayla was fine. They were talking about a different girl, a far way away, who was not happy at her new school.

At the time I thought I knew just how she felt. I had not been happy either when my parents told me I would be changing schools in January. I was six, so I cried. I knew that made me a crybaby, but thanks to the chicken pox I had already missed my class's Halloween party. Now I'd probably have to wait for summer vacation to see my second best friend. Elan had joined our first grade class that September and since he was also an oddball whose mother made him oil his legs so he wouldn't show up for school with ashy knees, we hit it off from the start. I knew we would always stay friends because Elan agreed to try a meatless hot dog the first time he came over. He never said, but seeing that he ate the whole thing, I guess he liked it.

The good part of changing schools was getting to ride in the school bus. And as the first kid the driver picked up, I got first dibs on the back seat cushion above the shock absorbers, so shot that they'd bounce you in the air every time we ran over a bump. But as good as it felt, skipping the rest of first grade, second grade had me quaking in terror. None of my new classmates looked like me, or even at me, except to stare. And while Mrs. Calhoun had treated us like a doting grandmother, Mrs. Bernard seemed afraid that we all had contagious diseases. When I finally managed to stop shaking, listening to the kid sitting in back beside me stumble over simple words, I realized second grade was either going to give me a heart attack or bore me to death.

Since my whole life was changing, and the boys in my class had taken to calling me a stinky black sissy, I figured it was time to dump Nancy Drew and stick with the Hardy Boys. Although I was old enough to know that her detective adventures were meant for girls, giving them up turned out to be harder than I thought. Unlike Frank and Joe, I saw Nancy's smarts as making her more of a misfit; like the time she had a whole town thinking she was a witch. And after being banned from wrestling with Shayla, my mind's eye had begun to imagine Nancy Drew with dark curly hair and silky brown skin. So getting stuck with Dick and Jane's boring *Friends and Neighbors* just as I was trying to fit in and outgrow my fantasies felt like a rotten double-cross.

I would have dug in my heels and refused to get back on the bus that first week had I not discovered that my new school had its own orchestra. From before I knew myself I had wanted to play the violin. My mother traces it to when I was sixteen months and she took me to hear a twelve-year-old prodigy. If that seems a tender age to set the plans for one's life, credit the mesmerizing bow-strokes of a boy my color, and not supremely far from my size, reproducing the sound of my mother's voice. The story goes that I had become so obsessed with the violin that upon being offered a guitar to strum I promptly tried to hoist it up under my chin. Unappeased by the plastic one they gave me for Christmas, I went on begging my parents for lessons, but my father thought that at four years old starting on the piano was far more sensible, a decision I later suspected owed less to his musical acumen than the fact that my Aunt Gwen was a first-class pianist and would teach me for free.

My new school's music teacher helped me finally realize my undimmed hope. Twice a week, I would slip into the auditorium at the start of orchestra practice and sit with my eyes glued on the first violinist. When I shook my head at the glockenspiel then shoved back his cymbals, the music teacher rang my mother. 'Mrs. Gardner, you need to give your son violin lessons.'

The possibility that your life is not perfect hits a happy child like a brick. When we moved into our house on Elmwood, after living in a two-room apartment over a one-car garage, I thought the three of us had struck it rich. So I could not understand why my father said he could not afford both a violin *and* private lessons. That was the day my mother won my undying loyalty. 'Don't you worry, sweetheart,' she whispered as she tucked me into bed that night. 'Mom will find us the money.'

Back inside the Valiant my leg was pins and needles and I was starting to wish I had gone with Connie and my mother in the Angell's station wagon. There might have been room to lie down and take a load off instead of sitting here jammed beside the luggage. As I shook the tingles out of my leg, I heard Delroy snap on the car radio. Out spilled more *Blue on Blue* and after switching the dial and picking up nothing but static he grunted and snapped it back off.

"You'd think they'd play Ray Charles at least *some* of the time."

My father sympathized. "I know just how you feel. Maddy claims she likes Bobby Vinton but she only keeps the radio on to punish me for not ordering FM. I can't get it through her head that it wouldn't do us any good way out here."

That seemed to clear the air and the two of them proceeded to joke lightheartedly about their headstrong wives. We were still speeding across the vast nothingness of Pecos County when Delroy leered at my dad with an eager look.

"Speaking of pains in the neck—you know what would do me right good, Doc? Some of those new painkillers they've started selling. My busted knee is sore as a cat stuck out in the rain from all this sittin'. You think you could write me up a prescription when we get to San Antone?"

"Sorry—can't help you. I'm not that kind of doctor."

The captain's hopeful look sagged. "What kind are you?"

"I treat the nervous system. I'm what you'd call a back-cracker."

"A back-cracker?" Delroy repeated in half-disbelief. "Well, whaddya know—" he said, slapping his knee with a hearty chuckle, "the good doctor is a quack."

As she watched them lay her sister inside the earth, Madeline pictured Naomi's little children howling inside their dirt-floored shack, prodding their mother trying to wake her. She thought about how good it had felt hearing Adrianna thank her for saving her life, how she had hoped, after helping her through a difficult birth, that they had knit the breach between them. It had felt like a blessing having a big sister to confide in, so she refused to accept Dr. Joseph's diagnosis of a malignant brain tumor. Her family could preach forgiveness, she would still blame the man dripping his tawdry tears on her sister's coffin. Every cruel word, every absent night, every precious penny splurged on another infidelity had ravaged Adrianna's life as surely as any cancer. Neediness may have pressed her sister into his clutches, but as far as Madeline was concerned, a faithless husband was the reason four beautiful girls were going to grow up without their mother.

When it became clear that Adrianna would lose her battle, she had wanted to adopt the two youngest, but her sister was adamant:

'No! Promise me, Maddy. Promise you won't let him separate my children. If they're to suffer, let them suffer together. I don't want them envying each other.'

Remembering her sister's beseeching look as she made her promise, Madeline was shaken by all the trauma behind it. She never paid much shrift in guilt, but the rub of shame and resentment inflamed how badly bruised she had felt after she called to say their sister was dead and Mason took that grief-filled moment to unburden his conscience. Contrary to what Miss Dora had said, he told her that their parents had lived for years as husband and wife. "Before you were born they used to take me and little Adrianna to a church concert every Sunday. I wept when he left but I felt I had to be strong after Mother told me that, since I was now the man of the house, I should call her Miss Dora. I was already in school and wrapped up in my violin, so I pretty much took it in stride, but poor Adrianna kept asking, 'where is Dada? I want Dada.'" Mason stopped and drew in a snuffle. "You don't remember because it was before you got sick and you were still a baby."

For a moment, Madeline feared her heart had stopped beating. She thought the flashback was a mere figment of grief until the panic returned as she felt the unshakeable strength clamping her nose and mouth, and the echo of her mother screaming, 'Adrianna, stop! Oh, sweet Jesus—'

"Mother told you why she's not Mrs. Jans—Maddy? Are you there?" Mason waited while she reclaimed her breath and was able to mumble 'yes' before he continued. "It's a shame. No one would have been the wiser had the woman not shown up at our church talking loud, threatening a big scandal if Father dared to divorce her. I never heard what happened next except that we ended up moving again just before you were born and, for years, Mr. Jans was no longer part of our lives."

"What brought him back?" she snapped, fighting waves of shame and rage. "One wife wasn't enough to satisfy him?"

"Don't be loathsome, Maddy. He came back because he heard you might die."

She had not voiced her anger listening to her brother blithely forgive their father's cowardly dereliction. She did not doubt Mr.

Jans had returned to comfort them. She had loved him too, but as a pediatric nurse she understood that a toddler does not make her closest connections through sentiment. She uses concrete impressions; the voice she hears, the hands she feels, the body she smells. So she could imagine their father's sudden reappearance, just when all attentions were on poor sick baby Maddy, convinced six-year-old Adrianna that puking bundle of trouble was why her Dada had abandoned them. More than Miss Dora's unsparing rod, Maddy's very existence had been the bitter fruit nourishing her sister's hatred.

Listening to the minister intone 'ashes to ashes' and 'dust to dust,' she hoped the dead were allowed to rest in peace and her sister's spirit would not be haunted by their father's absence to the very end. She felt Emerson gently squeeze her hand, as if tuned to her inner turmoil, then joined in throwing dirt on the wreath-strewn coffin. She steadied her emotions and cast him a grateful look. She had been lucky; the man she married would not respond to the bitterness roiling inside her by running away and disgracing her with other women.

When he balked at adopting all four of her nieces she had not pressed him. Since he never asked how she spent her money, she was free to make sure they never went hungry or had their mother's memory blotted by hand-me-downs. She had hoped that using her spare time to sew them pretty dresses or take them on weekly outings would distract from her anxiety. Instead, she shuddered each time she hugged them good-bye and heard their giggling laughter echo inside her empty house that felt bigger and emptier each time they left. She had planned to wait before getting pregnant, but now that wait was about to outlive a five-year-old war. She had even begun fretting that Mildred was right, that riding a bicycle had left her sterile. She knew the notion was absurd but she had never been fully at ease in her grown-up body. And there was no denying the pain, no matter how carefully Emerson tried to ease himself inside her. Just to be safe, she ditched her bicycle and took to crossing the slums on foot, but when the cramps began lasting days instead of hours, she knew the time had come to share her fears with Dr. Joseph.

"Does Emerson know?"

Madeline gave a tormented look and drooped her head. "It would sound like I'm making excuses."

"Nonsense! Doc, of all people, will understand."

"I know that, Doctor, but understanding is not the same as feeling. Mason is like his own brother and his wife has already given him two sons. You know how useless that makes me look?"

Dr. Joseph reproached her sternly. "Now see here, Maddy, you're not some harebrained ninny, you're a seasoned midwife. You know these things are not that uncommon."

"Truthfully?" she whispered disconsolately, "it's his mother. She never wanted her wonderful son to marry me. You know the busy tongues in this town. I'll be a pariah the rest of my life."

"Truthfully?" he mimicked as her distressed face lifted, "you've overcome a lot more than hurtful words. So unless you intend to avoid your husband for the rest of your life—which I guarantee will ruin your marriage—you're going to have to put wishes aside and have the surgery."

Madeline lurched up on the examining table. "I can't! I won't!" she exclaimed, her chin set fiercely.

His demeanor unchanged, Dr. Joseph paused, deep in thought, the tips of his joined forefingers touched to his lips. "There is another option," he said cautiously, "it would not be permanent, but it would be less invasive … "

Before he could finish Madeline leapt to embrace him. "You darling wizard!" she cried, planting a loud smack on his forehead. "I knew you'd think of something!"

"I'm not promising miracles, mind you, " he warned, looking mildly flustered by her impetuous kiss.

"Oh, pooh! You're a genius, you'll find a way!" She clasped the diminutive surgeon in another bear-hug, grinning like a defendant just declared 'not guilty.'

"We must not let our hopes go overboard—" he chided, flustered all over again as he slipped from her crushing embrace, "there's still a risk. Now I must ask you to grant me a favor—"

"Anything, Doctor. You've already saved my life twice."

"Did Emerson ever tell you what we spoke about at your wedding?"

She gave a guarded frown. "He mentioned something about your wanting him to study abroad, and that he'd turned you down."

"And that's all he said?"

"Yes. Why? Was there more?"

"Before the war your husband earned the highest marks on the annual examination given by the Royal College of Physicians and Surgeons. Normally, that would have earned him a scholarship to study medicine in England, but for political reasons, that year they decided to award it to the chap who came second. I was appalled, as were his Jesuit professors. It's not just his intellect—Emerson wants to help his country and we both know Jamaica desperately needs doctors." He smiled at her gently. "I'm not saying you should give up hope, but it's possible you haven't been blessed with a child for a reason."

Madeline stared speechlessly at the elderly black physician. "What are you saying?" she asked in astonishment. "You want Emerson to sell the drugstore and traipse off to England? For how long? Am I supposed to go with him? How would we afford it?"

"I and the other trustees at the Health and Welfare Society are prepared to fund his pre-med studies in the United States. If need be, we can lend him the money for medical school. I know Doc dearly wants a son but he'll never be satisfied filling prescriptions and peddling liniments. He refused because of his love for you. No, don't answer me now," he interrupted when in bewilderment she started to shake her head. "Think it over. Perhaps you'll decide to exchange one dream for another."

From the slant of their bodies, my dad and Delroy appeared to be seething in their separate corners, like two boxers whose bout had been called on a technicality. I was engrossed in *The Story of Hannibal and Rome* so I wasn't sure what had ended the sparring. The tension continued to thicken until the captain tired of the suffocating silence and switched the radio back on to resume his search for a *Blue*-free station. Hannibal was in the middle of addressing his troops when a thundering voice broke in to declare that the daughter of Babylon had sipped the wine of fornication. Fascinated by the way the intense voice trembled, I stopped reading to listen. Growing rapturous, it warned that America had tempted the fires of eternal damnation and that all of her science and technological might would not spare us from the yoke of Satan's whore.

Delroy cursed and spun the dial. "Those doomsday pulpiteers make a fortune slinging that bunk," he muttered, then gave up hunting and snapped off the radio. "I swear, if they think you're rich, you can convince half the folks in this country that God wants them to murder their children. You'd think the saps would ask why these frauds keep begging donations if the damned world is about to end."

Delroy's logic made me think of the line in *Charlotte's Web* where Charlotte tells Wilbur the pig that people are very gullible. When I asked my dad what gullible meant, as usual, he told me to look it up in the dictionary, but then Charlotte explained that people will believe anything and I realized I didn't need to. My dad was right: you can figure out a lot, if you know the context.

"Works both ways, Captain," my father responded with an amiable chuckle. "They're hoping they'll get credit in heaven."

"You may be right, but I've known a few preachers. If there's a hell, they'll be in it."

"Sure, but the bastards will still die rich."

Delroy gave my father a long hard look then guffawed, clearing the air.

"Dad?" I asked softly, testing my courage, "are we still going to stop and see the Alamo?"

"I don't know, son. We'll see. We're a bit behind schedule."

I had fretted the whole dull slog to Fredericksburg that we would end up missing what I had been looking forward to the most on this lousy trip. Pick out any boy at my school and ask him what his first thought was when you said Texas, and the answer would be the Alamo. Asked why, he would take you for an imbecile then explain that it was every red-blooded American's duty to remember the Alamo because, even though the Mexicans had them badly outnumbered, every man, woman and child surrounded in that fort would rather have died than surrender to tyranny. Ask him who his favorite hero was among those martyred patriots and you might think you'd met up with a pint-sized historian. He'd tell you how at the tender age of three his idol had killed a full-grown bear, then by the time he was grown whipped an Injun tribe single-handedly and patched the big cracked bell that stood for America's honor, goodness, and liberty. If your scrubby mentor happened to be an official member of the Davy Crockett Fan Club, chances are he knew by heart every word to every song praising his hero and went to bed each night in his genuine coonskin cap clutching his plastic Davy Crockett flintlock. He could not care less if some lousy turncoat claimed that Davy Crockett had gone yellow and surrendered, he knew the truth having seen it for himself in living Technicolor. And besides, only a commie skunk would contradict John Wayne.

'I don't care what your teacher said—he's not a hero to me. And I'm not a commie skunk—so there!' Elan was the closest I had to a brother, so I dropped it. His mother was part Comanche so it seemed natural that he might carry a grudge. Still, knowing Elan, I had my doubts.

"Dad, it's part of history. I should see it. You promised—"

Delroy Angell slung an arm across the front seat and twisted to face me. "You're a right sharp kid, so I'm going to give it to you straight. The Alamo is nothing for folks like us to celebrate. Bowie and Crockett were fighting to keep us slaves."

Once again I could barely breathe. My brain was racing a mile a minute. What did he mean, they were fighting to keep us slaves? I knew grown-ups well enough now to know they made things up. No way was I taking Delroy's word for it!

"Miss Finch says Jim Bowie and Colonel Crockett died defending our way of life. They didn't fight to keep slaves!"

"It's all right, son," my father said in his logical, calming voice. "Captain Angell only wants you to know that there are two sides to every story—especially when it comes to war."

"But he's saying that if Davy Crockett had won they would have kept us slaves. Is that true?"

Delroy leered at my father. "Well, Doctor, is that true?"

As I waited for him to answer I got to thinking that nothing was true anymore. My teachers said God had blessed America because she was special but the preacher on the radio said our country would burn in hell. My mom called Delroy a war hero but the captain denied it and now he said neither was Davy Crockett.

"Son, those were different times and a long time ago," he tried to explain but I persisted.

"I know—but is it true Davy Crockett wanted us to be slaves?"

"We would certainly *not* be slaves now," he said firmly, ignoring Delroy's disgusted head-shake. "But yes, there were those who fought at the Alamo who supported slavery."

"Were all of us somebody's slave back then?"

"No, of course not."

"Did the Mexicans keep slaves?"

Delroy was quick to answer. "No, they did not."

"Not *lawfully*," my dad corrected him, "but some of them did."

"Listen here, Sonny. Your daddy's trying to sugarcoat it, but if you're ready for junior high school then you're ready to take it. Trading colored folks like we were cattle is how Bowie and his boys made their money, and plenty of it. Men like that don't think twice about risking their lives for that kind of profit," Delroy insisted. "If you doubt me, look it up for yourself. Once your teacher's great patriots got through beating Mexico, it was illegal to free a slave in Texas. To guys like Davy Crockett, we were nothing but niggers."

At that moment I hated Delroy Angell with all my heart. I had only seen three movies my entire life—not counting the one I fell asleep on—and *The Alamo* was by far my favorite. Now Delroy had me despising Davy Crockett. I remembered when I was reading *Huckleberry Finn* and saw the word my friends and I hated, my mom said it meant someone crude and ignorant and could be any color. But when I looked it up in the dictionary it just said, 'a black person.' Thanks to Delroy, I was putting two and two together. I always thought that catching a tiger by the toe never made any sense. Now I knew why. Tigers roar. A slave would holler.

I knew from reading Mark Twain that there was something shameful about being a nigger, but until today, I had never thought that much about slavery. The little I did know was from the Bible; something terrible the Israelites had escaped from in Egypt, back when men fought with spears and slingshots. None of my teachers ever talked about it, or how it was right for an American who believed in freedom and justice for all to buy and sell people like cattle. I hated to admit it but it seemed my buddy Elan had been right. And from the sound of my father's voice, that same squeezed voice he used on the drive home from Jennifer's party, it sounded like he was scared to hear Delroy Angell tell me the truth.

"Disgraceful, simply disgraceful. Ten shillings for a half-pound of saltfish? War may be mankind's fatal disease, but it reaps our ruling scoundrels a tidy profit."

Emerson was surprised to find himself agreeing with his former nemesis. "There's no money to be made rationing the rich. With all the fish in our tropical waters, we should not be feeding the poor with cod from Newfoundland, but the government is promising subsidies."

Coombs snorted. "Naturally, once the merchants have quadrupled prices and our elected thieves take their cut. Be thankful you're leaving for America. If I were you, I'd get that degree and never come back."

"And leave you all our good mangoes and white sand beaches? Not on your life!" He laughed off the suggestion but Coombs' contempt for his own country never failed to annoy him. He had shown him the Prince's letter and while the surgeon conceded that the implication was 'troubling,' he dismissed Emerson's outrage. 'Use your noggin, Gardner. Any numbskull could have identified a pneumothorax. Do you honestly think the colonial board was going to discharge an English coroner over some dead black quashie?'

It's that 'so what?' attitude, Emerson grumbled inside, that keeps our island corrupt and backward.

A second customer appeared and Coombs offered to amuse himself while Emerson completed his transaction. Wandering off, he sauntered to the drugstore's anomalous printed display and perused a booklet on Ethics and Prophecy with twinkle-eyed bemusement. Setting it down with a supercilious grin, Coombs cast a discouraged look at the pharmacy's half-empty shelves. "How have you been making out with the embargo?" he asked as Emerson returned. "I don't imagine these fripperies are in great demand." He fondled the silver perfume box shaped like a grand piano. "Have you tried the black market?"

"No luck. Tried getting some of that new wonder drug—not a drop of penicillin to be had. As for aspirin tablets—sheer robbery, so I've contrived a non-addictive analgesic as a substitute."

"You see?" Coombs exclaimed triumphantly. "You griped about the shortages, but I taught you how to adapt! I swear some of our illiterate countrywomen know more about the art of medicine than the nincompoop they hired to take my place. He's all agog about these German synthetics. Well, he's in for a rude awakening if he thinks they'll fit in a prison budget."

"I confess I'm a bit astonished that you've decided to stay. I thought once you retired you'd be joining your daughter in Edinburgh."

"I'm a bigger fool than I imagined," the surgeon grumbled, tracing a brooding beige finger across the black and white keys on the perfume box. "I've reaped my reward for having sent her to study in Scotland." He rolled his eyes and replaced the trifle. "I thought they would make her a gentleman's fitting companion. Instead, they sabotaged any chance of her becoming a contented wife by having her read Madame Bovary and some Norwegian nitwit! Now my dear half-English daughter is thirty-four years old and set on coming back home a husbandless poet. A poet! Here, in our glorious jungle Fontainebleau! I have a mind to ask the bastards for my money back."

"Knowledge is never a waste," Emerson dissented. "She'll be welcomed with open arms if she decides to teach."

Coombs studied him through constricted eyelids. "Teach what to whom?" he queried, his dour look settling just short of incredulity. "I'm sure our future banana pickers and cane-hole diggers are pining to learn their place in the world from Alice in Wonderland."

"That's a rather dark view of Jamaica's future," Emerson objected.

"No point shirking reality. Our masters can't wait to doom us to the sophistries of their precocious monkeys who think what this destitute island needs are more black barristers and moral philosophers—three cheers for Independence!"

Emerson guessed that the mordant dig was aimed at him, but even though he found Coombs' attitude offensive, it was not irrational. The war had made governing half of the world not worth the trouble. King Sugar no longer built palaces. The future was speeding westward, and as the atomic bomb made plain, lifetimes beyond Wordsworth's idylls. Jamaica might be many untouched splendors behind the twentieth century, but with her fruits rotting in her warehouses, more farmers would not be a cure-all. The cure was self-sufficiency, which relied on know-how, and know-how in an uneven, dog-eat-dog world took access—and a great deal of money.

Coombs' cynicism reminded him that, as much as he wanted to help his country heal and meet its potential, charting an entirely new course at this stage in his life was a risky venture. But his wife was eager and the stars appeared to be aligned in her favor: the Catholic sisters had already secured him lodgings up in New Orleans, and now Midas Coombs had just staggered him twice; first by revealing his role in procuring Emerson's scholarship and then by his less than miserly bid to buy the drugstore and 'take its burden off his hands.'

For Madeline, the final peace had been far too long coming. Her waning faith in a brighter tomorrow restored by Japan's abrupt surrender, she dared to picture herself as a doctor's wife, taking her seat in Kingston's boardrooms and seeing her ideas on reproductive education and early childhood nutrition debated in the press. She told herself it was all God's plan: Doc would honor his talent, Little Miss Big Head would silence her critics, and Mildred's reproaches would not cut so deeply.

She had made up her mind walking home from Dr. Joseph's and refused to give in when Emerson tried to deny what they both knew were his true desires. "I don't want you turning down this chance on account of me. I know the scholarship won't cover everything, but it's worth the sacrifice. Darling, let's be honest—I may never give you a son—let me help you with this."

Now, with her husband away in New Orleans, she filled her quiet evenings poring through fashion magazines for inspiration as she went about replenishing the skirts and frocks her nieces insisted on outgrowing. After the oft-failed challenge of trying to persuade another love-starved girl that the sweet-faced boy she feared would abandon her was more likely to stay if she told him no and stuck to her rhythm, coming up with patterns of her own helped to placate her emotions. What banished her frustrations the most was being able to replace the next ruined Sunday best and evade the lash of Miss Dora's tongue when she ushered her granddaughters home from another grass-staining romp at the Public Gardens. Regrettably, her mother-in-law remained as fearsome as ever.

"Listen here, daughter—is it true that sickness you had as an infant left you with some kind of deformity?"

Madeline had hoped that with her husband abroad there would be a break in hostilities, only to discover that his mother was determined to escalate their battle. "Deformity? How ridiculous. I'm surprised, I did not take you as someone so easily affected by vulgar gossip."

The Gardner matriarch quietly absorbed the jab of faint praise and poised her majestic frame on the Windsor settee. "My concern is not for me," she sniffed. "People are going to speculate, seeing that you're more interested in caring for these urchins crowding into Kingston than pleasing your husband!"

Madeline rushed to her feet, swallowing the retort she was sure to regret. "I'll go make us some tea and we can converse civilly."

"No, we'll sort this out now. Sit down!" Mildred commanded, patting the seat for Madeline to sit beside her. "Dear, I wish you would find it in your heart to confide in me. It's not a criticism—I just need to know—are you afraid of men? I'm told that there are unfortunate women like that."

"Afraid? Of Emerson? How could you even think that?"

"I know my son," Mildred stated proudly. "He would not have gone off to America alone if he was happy at home."

Madeline fiercely bit the flesh inside her lip. She wanted to order the woman out of her house but Mildred was not one to be cowed and the fallout would be ten times worse than hearing her out. She grasped for a path that might lead to a truce then realized that no matter what she said, a wall of resentment would stand between them until she managed to give her a grandchild. Seeing her turmoil reflected in Mildred's eyes, she realized that, despite her denial, the sniping tongues had finally penetrated the thick skin her mother-in-law had grown to deflect her own marital failures. That she could sympathize did not mean she had to let Mildred rule inside her bedroom. Was it not enough for his mother to know that Emerson loved her? The reminder brought Madeline enough comfort to restore her courage.

"You claim you know your son, but if you did, you'd know that Doc's soul died a little each day he sat in that drugstore not using his talent. Emerson was born to be a doctor. A dutiful wife does not put her wishes ahead of her husband's."

It was Mildred's turn to glare and stand abruptly. "Fine, then get yourself up to New Orleans and do your duty!"

'I will either find a way or I will make one.'

Daylight was fading as I reread Hannibal's words. They had set me thinking about how my mother had refused to back down in Las Cruces and risked her skin to protect me. Though the thought made me sick, it seemed a pretty sure bet that before this lousy trip was over we would face another gut-churning showdown. I reckoned that if Hannibal could march an army and thirty-eight African elephants across ice-capped mountains, I should at least have the stomach to make it through Texas.

The Battle at Cannae had saved me from going loopy over the longest, dullest stretch of road on the day's long, dull drive, and as it grew too dark for me to read, I was excited to see the glints of a city beaming in the eastern twilight. I shut the book and sat up to get my bearings. Shifting around and onto my knees, I was happy to see the station wagon with my mother and Connie safely trailing our Valiant. My eagerness increased as we left the highway and after wandering a while in circles parked on a cobblestone street that looked as far behind the times as the ones in Disneyland's fake frontier town. As the five of us set off on foot, the cypress-covered canal with its lamplit wraparound boardwalk and arching pedestrian bridges had me convinced that we had entered a fairy-tale theme park.

Night was settling in swiftly, floating a soft mist up from the river, bringing a refreshing coolness to our desert-baked skin. We roamed on to the core of the city and after the promenade's nostalgic welcome saw that it shared none of the canalway's entrancing harmony. Its buildings, like its people, appeared at odds; some slanting to a peak, some tall and straight, others low to the ground and generously curved. Red and green pennants, like the ones strung over a used-car parking lot, stretched above a bustling plaza lit with colorful lights that made me wonder if we had stumbled upon some festive occasion. My mother and Connie insisted on touring the outdoor market and as we pressed through the crawling hubbub, I felt cornered by hats and wrangling tongues, some hard but sluggish as mud, others liquid and lightning hot. My first thought as we were engulfed by the grating sounds and smells was that I was back strolling the open air stalls downtown in old L.A., except the sheer vibrancy of the motley crowd left me thinking this is what it must have been like shopping in Carthage. Someone bumped me roughly aside and after pushing blindly through the jam-packed bodies, I ended up facing an old Spanish church snagged in the jaws of a hulking department store, like a lifeboat being gobbled up by a whale. I was still standing there staring when a hand snatched my wrist. I started to scream then saw that it was just my mother.

"Son, you've got to keep up!" she snapped, nearly yanking my arm off.

It was only after she finished dragging me back to the others that I realized my father was the one she was mad at.

"If you're cheap, you get treated cheaply!" she finally exploded when he got around to explaining that the hotel Cy Helger had recommended was much too expensive.

To my surprise, Delroy jumped in to defend him. "Now don't go crucifyin' Emerson. Money ain't no guarantee. If they're going to bleed me dry I want to know what I'm paying for ahead of time."

"My poor feet," Connie grumbled when the grown-ups stopped bickering and agreed to keep looking.

We must have rambled for an hour before it sank in that we were right back up the creek without a paddle. At inn after inn we got the same distrustful looks; *ach, lo siento*, sorry, there are no more vacancies. It was as if we were a pack of stray dogs, covered in fleas and infected with rabies. The more we trudged from one place to another the more strangely passive my mother became. When she finally spoke up, I got the feeling she had been biding her time to get even.

"You all must be getting hungry," she said as we stopped beneath the overhang of the Morgan Hotel. "Why don't you see if there's a place we can eat close by and I'll reserve two rooms in the meantime."

A pearl necklace followed by matching pearl earrings magically appeared from inside her handbag and my dad looked ready to blow a gasket. "What makes you so sure you'll be able to?"

She snubbed his question and angled her mirrored compact to catch the light while she powdered her forehead and cheeks. "I vote for Mexican," she said casually when she got through blotting her ruby-painted lips. She still had not looked at my father. "That café down by the river looked promising—the one with the brass steer out front. I'll meet you there in twenty minutes?"

"Maybe I should go with you—" Connie snuck a worried glance at Delroy who looked as riled as my dad.

My mom reacted first. "No. They may need you to get a table."

Maybe it was her tone, or maybe the ten-hour drive had drastically shortened their fuses; whatever it was, it set my dad and Delroy off like firecrackers bursting in rapid succession.

"For pity's sake, Maddy, we're not children!"

"With all due respect, Mrs. Gardner, who put you in charge?"

She snapped the compact shut with a lofty look and went about straightening the pearls around her neck. "It's not about who's in charge. It's about finding the right approach."

My father snickered. "What approach are you proposing—that the four of us sneak in at midnight under your skirts?"

"Don't play the ass! I know what I'm doing, trust me."

"Trust you? Trust you to chide the victim? Be patient, Emerson—be more cagey. I've had it with all your pretense! I won't beg for respect."

"I never beg," she retorted coldly.

It was back—the wish that I could become invisible.

The captain reached for the olive branch. "Come on, you two. We can't let the enemy glimpse dissension in the ranks."

"I guess we'll have to sleep in the street, since your chief thinks changing tactics means defeat!" Her snarl earned a nasty look from a leathery old woman passing by with a basket of green and yellow gourds balanced on her sand-whipped fedora.

That night, as I stood outside the Morgan Hotel shrinking inside my skin, I realized just how ruthless my mother really was. Nothing we faced came close to touching her. At each new obstacle barring our way she more closely resembled a warrior who had crossed the frost-slicked Alps with Hannibal and become so hardened just trying to survive that it took only a look for the enemy to know he was the one who should be frightened.

Connie rested a soft, fleshy palm on my father's arm. "Why not let her try? I bet before she's through your wife will have them convinced she's Brazilian or an Egyptian princess."

"Right," he muttered, "anything but a Negro."

Delroy shook his head with a grimace, as if someone had just jammed a stick up his britches. "Forget it! I'm not going through that whole rigamarole all over again. I say we grab some of that Mexican grub like Madeline suggested then drive all night. That's what I planned on anyway. It's not that far to New Orleans. We can switch off the driving."

My mother silently removed her pearls and tucked them back inside her purse. "My husband doesn't trust me driving at night," she said bluntly, then shifted her annoyance my way. "Sorry, son— you'll have to try and sleep sitting up."

"Don't fret, sonny boy. I'll make room in our wagon so you can stretch out for the night."

My feelings about Delroy changed, hearing him rush to my rescue. Space inside our car had been a source of contention from the very beginning. Apparently, my dad had failed to tell my mother that since we were driving the Valiant right onboard ship we could not use a roof rack, which meant that the backseat was the only place left for our extra clothes and her sacred belongings. And that was even after my dad had to dump a brand new cooler.

We were barely inside the Res Café when the fat-nosed maitre d' hustled to block our way. He was as tall as Captain Angell and dressed in the skintight black pants, white shirt and *rebozo* you'd see on prosperous TV Mexicans. His plump round face and crew-cut had me dreaming up a wacky schoolyard rumor: *Zorro unmasked as Curly from The Three Stooges!*

"Yes?"

Delroy spoke up first. "Table for five, please."

The foyer's only illumination came from amethyst hurricane lamps set on shelves against the brick wall leading to the bartender's station and, as my eyes began to adjust, I noticed there were several old bullfighting posters framed in between them. At the restaurant's more brightly lit center were eight white-clothed tables, while a line of five-foot-high wooden booths hugged the far left wall. My rising curiosity halted at the table with four elderly women, their faces flamed with pink splotches as if a hot iron had been touched to their brows and cheeks. I gazed with envy at the furry tails dangling from their coonskin caps then glimpsed Delroy watching me and quickly looked away.

The maitre d' took his time sizing us up. "You part of them communists?"

"Actually, we're Baptist."

Connie's witty comeback surprised the rest of us and left the fat-nosed *caballero* off balance. He avoided her toothy smile and turned to Delroy. "I don't stand for no antics so I'll make myself plain. There's a free booth by the kitchen. You-all can take it or try someplace else."

Delroy gave my father a look that said what do you think?

"We'll take it."

My dad's quick decision seemed to please everyone except my

mother who promptly asked for the ladies' room. The maitre d' stood stiff for what felt like a lifetime while my mother sweetly smirked at his face. After more seconds passed, he gave the ceiling a glance that asked, 'why me?' then nodded for us to follow. We were nearly at the kitchen's swing-doors when my mother spotted the restroom and vanished inside before Curly had time to stop her.

When we had settled in the booth farthest in back and our host left us to study the menus, Connie hunched down to whisper. "What was all that stuff about us being communists?"

Delroy gave a disinterested grunt. "The man's wacko. Where does he get off dressing like a Mexican?"

"That's just part of the restaurant's motif," my father explained. "He was worried we were looking to stage a sit-in."

"You're jivin'! Do we look like a bunch of college kids?"

"It's not just college kids." My mother came strutting in from the bathroom, the smirk in her eyes migrated to her lips. "These days even grandmothers are joining them in jail."

"God bless 'em!" Connie exclaimed, winning a look from Delroy that made my gut hurt.

"Asinine. Pushing old women to get their brains bashed in." He sat back in the booth with a savage look. "Pacifism is for suckers. It won't buy justice because allegiance ain't even skin deep. The crackers taught me that when I put on their uniform."

"Jesus, Delroy!" pleaded Connie. "Let it go. It's our country too and the law is coming over to our side."

"Talk to Hitler about the goddamn law!" Having silenced the four of us, the pilot hopped to his feet. "If I have to drive all night, I need to get a load off—"

My father whispered to his wife when he left. "I don't get it. Your husband keeps harping about the war, but says he lied about seeing combat."

Connie looked confused. "Lied? Lied about what combat?"

"He told us he'd busted his knee during training and that whole story he fed Rothschild was really about his brother Lucky."

"Bless his heart," Connie said, smiling. "Delroy doesn't have a brother. His buddies called him Lucky because the bombers his squadron escorted never took a hit."

"So what he told Kip was actually true?" my mother asked hopefully.

"I don't know what he told him. What I *do* know is that Delroy would just as soon forget about our time in Alabama. But don't let him fool you—he's proud as punch about what he and his buddies accomplished, flying those dangerous missions. It's what went with it that left him pissin' vinegar."

"Who's pissin' vinegar?" Delroy came light-stepping back and his wife quickly buttoned her lip. "What did I miss?"

"Apparently the truth," my mother replied and paid Connie no mind when she tried curling up into a ball.

Delroy glared at his wife. "Woman, what have you been spilling?"

"Relax, Captain," my mother cajoled. "She was just bragging about the man she married. Why did you give us that cock and bull story about a brother? You ashamed of being a hero?"

"Now see here, Miss Madeline, I'm tickled to have made your acquaintance but what went on in my life is *my* business."

"I'm not prying into your business. I just don't appreciate being played for a fool."

"Fair enough. If that's how you feel, I'll beg your pardon." He met my mom's warrior look with a tiny chuckle. "Trust me, you're the last person I'd pick to mess with. The truth is, there are things a man wants to be proud of, but the reality just won't let him."

Dad's eyes were on my mother. "Captain," he said, "I know *just* what you mean."

She had been warned more times than she cared to remember. Still, seeing it writ plain and bold as life, Madeline's spine wobbled. **Whites Only**. That is the sign, she thought, firming her back; welcome to the United States of America.

It was a balmy midsummer, two years since Dresden and Hiroshima signaled the last traumatizing tremors of a war that should end all wars, so it halted her steps to see the train station overrun with young bloods in their green army uniforms. The glow of conquest still bright on their faces gave her spine a second shudder as she pondered traveling alone from Biloxi to New Orleans with a libidinous battalion.

Her suitcases surrendered to the stoop-shouldered porter, she obeyed the Colored Only sign and boarded the car third from the back, relieved when she managed to slip unseen past a group of huddling soldiers and into a free compartment. As she stowed her makeup bag on the overhead rack, she thanked her lucky stars for the open window. Army wool was thick and the summer heat's ripe odors were making her nauseous.

"Whee-ee-whoo-oo!"

Madeline glowered at the black G.I. stalled just inside the cabin door running a slow reverent gaze from her head to her toes. "Excuse me. Have you lost your dog?"

The whistling lips parted, revealing a mouthful of blinding white teeth. "No, gorgeous, but you make it mighty hard to control him."

"Well, I don't wish to have any dogs in here with me."

"Don't worry, he don't bite and he's awful friendly, Miss—"

"*Mrs.* Gardner," she answered curtly, wondering if it was enough to shed her glove and display her ring or wiser to flee.

The coffee-dark soldier grew contrite. "Beg yer pardon, ma'am. Guess such a purdy sight done dashed my manners—Private Edmund Peters, engineer, United States Army, at your service!" He rose up to salute just as the train lurched to a start, flinging him headfirst against the luggage rack. Peters hauled off his two-cornered hat and clapped a hand on his scalp with a goofy pose. "Nine months fighting the Jerries, not a scratch—first day back and an angel knocks me flat!"

Madeline firmly squelched a titter. Just because a handsome soldier knew how to lay on the charm, good looks and an army uniform did not make him harmless. "Seems to me your opponent was that bag rack."

"Now don't you talk sweet!" the G.I. exclaimed, hearing her accent. "You ain't been in Uncle Sam's country but a minute, have you?"

"Sailed in this morning to join my husband—he's at university in New Orleans," she stressed proudly.

"College boy, huh? *Très bon, ma chérie*—as they say in Paree! He's one lucky fella." Peters wistfully shook his head as he hoisted his duffel bag onto the rack then squeezed in beside her.

"You know, Private—" Madeline shrank from the big white grin closing within breathing distance and pointed to the opposite seat, "we would both be more comfortable if you sat over there."

"I'm not doggin' you, gorgeous, but here in the U. S. of A, a soldier back from war is in his rights to ask a pretty girl for a kiss."

She forcefully shoved him back. "I'm not a girl, so you'll have to find someone else to give you that kiss."

"Okay, I get the message—" Peters grumbled when she made a point of turning her face to the window. "I suppose it's natural— being in a new country and all—"

Her nervous breaths slowed when he sincerely apologized and retreated to his seat only to quicken again moments later as it became clear that traveling in silence appeared to offend him.

"Let me guess—you're from one of those islands down in the Caribbean. Is it as lovely down there as they say? How long has your husband been in New Orleans—?"

When she ignored him and refused to answer, the private suspended his persistent questions and instead began to regale her with his overseas escapades, offering up self-amusing, thigh-slapping accounts of his early mishaps with the foreign lingo. When that tack proved no more successful, he rambled on, straining to better impress her with his wide-ranging travels, painting each new scene with more and more incredible, spectacular strokes, as if daring her to keep pretending that she was captivated by the mud flats outside her window coloring the landscape in a stupor-inducing gray.

Despite her caution, Madeline was secretly enjoying the brassy American's boasts, knowing how they would have offended the fusspots back home in Kingston. She was even prepared to acknowledge his budding gifts as a poet when her perceived cold shoulder finally conquered his patience and the G.I. lowered his sights from Virgilian portraits of the Italian countryside to earthier exploits.

"After V-day those bald French girls treated us like they hadn't had a man in a hundred years. Left us brothers feeling like supermen." Peters paused for a peek but when she went right on staring at the stultifying scenery as if she hadn't heard a word, he continued undeterred. "It was like we had rescued lost innocents and we were their deliverers from evil. The only color they saw was the green in our uniforms so we never let on that a day before we'd been shoveling shit and sorting through limbs and dead bodies. For those half-starved women the worst was over, but I'll tell you this— if the whiskey hadn't been five bucks a shot, half of us would still be over there." The black private grew solemn. "It changes you—that taste of what it's like to be on top after you've spent your life afraid of how low a man can get. It hardens you inside—" the soldier stopped with a bitter look that abruptly brightened, "but you know what, Mrs. Gardner? I'm happy to be back. Given my pick of all those liberated dames, I'd still go for a regular down-home girl— even if she wasn't as fine as you."

At last, she quietly turned him a look, but from the way his shoulders sank, it was not the look he'd been hoping for.

Their train squealed to a welcome stop and Peters was back on his feet, infused with fresh inspiration. "Hey! you ever had a Royal Majesty?"

Madeline cast him a scowl that said, 'what now?'

"Aw, c'mon now, you can't keep givin' a jive-talkin' superman that face—"

Her thin grin suggesting the wounded plea had succeeded, Peters grabbed it like a life line. "Now, you jus' set yer purdy self right here!" he commanded. "I'll be back quicker than a Dadeville duck on a June-bug!"

The private went hopping out to the aisle and Madeline was hoping she would not regret letting down her guard when she heard the trill of high-pitched voices coming closer. Peering down through her window, she saw a pack of barefoot children crowding the tracks holding up sticks hung with strings of sorry-looking shrimp and roasted peanuts. A familiar ache jolted her heart as she recognized the stunting effects of childhood hunger.

"One Royal Majesty for a Nubian queen!"

Before she could find her wits, Peters had plopped half of a gigantic watermelon smack in her lap.

"Taste that beauty and tell me it ain't almost as sweet as you." Skinning her his row of gleaming teeth, he passed her the spoon he said he had snitched from a porter's serving tray.

Madeline stared at the red-fleshed boulder crushing her thighs, too stunned to speak.

Peters shook two of his knuckles next to his ear. "Thumped that sucker just like my momma taught me, so I guarantee you it's ripe."

Hiding her horror, she clutched at the thought that the soldier was playing a prank to get even until she saw that he was watching her with rapt anticipation. Emerson had warned her that Southerners were very touchy about observing local etiquette. If presenting your traveling companion with a slab of fruit weighing close to a stone was considered a courteous gesture, she had no gracious way out.

"Go on, take a taste!" Peters coaxed her. "You won't get one like that in New Orleans."

Deciding it would do her less harm to be polite, she attacked the giant melon and scraped up a tiny slip. "Mm, you're right, it is delicious." She had to admit, the juicy red flesh was like honey. "Aren't you having any?"

"Nah," he said, waving a hand in contempt. "Growing up I ate so much melon I can't stand to swallow no more. Anyway, it wouldn't look right, me slurping a watermelon when I'm in uniform."

Well, that's just fine and dandy, Madeline thought crossly. It's beneath you to eat this vulgar fruit, but my good linen skirt doesn't rate consideration. "You know, Private Peters—" she broached innocently.

"Friends call me Mundy," he cut in to insist, flashing his big white grin.

"Mundy," she obliged him, smiling sweetly, "you know, it's awfully warm and this lovely melon is awfully sweet— you think you might get me a glass of water?"

"Why, it would be my pleasure!"

"Perhaps with some ice—? If they'll let you have it—"

"Don't you fret that pretty head. I learned to handle myself over in Europe. Whatever it is, you can count on Mundy!" he promised, straightening for a sharp salute before marching out with a confident grin threatening to stretch all the way to New Orleans.

When she was sure he was safely away, Madeline wriggled up from her seat and heaved the heavy melon through the open window. Smoothing her linen skirt, she sat back down with a satisfied smile hearing the giddy high-pitched shrieks as her Royal Majesty landed on earth, as if ordered from heaven.

I could not decide what pained me more as we left the Res Café to find our car—the fact that my parents had gone back to their sniping or that my stomach was bloated with Santa Anna nut pie. After devouring Connie's offered slice, I had ducked into the restroom, so I missed the dust-up with the stooge playing Zorro. My mother had accused him of charging us double and now she was fit to be tied because my father had gotten tired of arguing and settled on paying the jacked-up bill and skipping the tip.

"You stiffed the poor waiter who probably makes peanuts. He isn't the one making colored folks pay double."

"Then he should complain or work someplace else. It's not as if they treat their Spanish speaking customers any differently."

"You don't know that, Emerson. This is San Antonio, not Birmingham."

"Oh—and you do."

"Yes, I *do* know. A minute ago you said you were done with begging. The man looks at you hard and you bow on bended knee."

"I want to get where we're going. You heard him, he was about to call the police."

"I wish he had," my mother declared as he opened her car door. "It's not right, Emerson, and you know it."

My dad let it drop, and although I welcomed the end of their spat, I dared not remind him that he had forgotten to ask the Angells if they had room for our luggage. It wasn't that I was worried about being able to sleep, I was worried that if I did manage to sleep sitting up the entire eight hours to New Orleans my legs would be in such pins and needles they would hurt like crazy and maybe never recover. I was willing to bet my mother had not forgotten, but I knew she thought this whole thing was screwy because she had reminded my dad three times that he was half-blind in one eye and hated driving at night. The problem she had was that the pair of matching red suitcases taking up half of our Valiant's back seat belonged to her and she was fed up with my father telling her that she should have listened to him and shipped them ahead along with the bulk of our clothes and furniture. So for the sake of my legs and world peace, I decided the smart thing to do was to stay awake as long as I could and keep wiggling my toes.

As I stretched out as far as I could, it struck me that my father had taken a picture of me in his head the day I convinced him I was old enough to walk two miles to school and then forgotten that kids keep on growing. His flicker of surprise the first time he realized I was using the damper pedal on our piano was nothing compared to the look on his face when my mother announced that I needed a full-size violin. 'Already? That can't be right, he's only nine.' I was afraid he was going to say that we could not afford it until my mother told him she had saved enough from her dressmaking and we could trade in my three-quarters. If I'd had half the sense that I have now, I would not have chosen that moment to remind him that I was also big enough for the bicycle he had promised to buy me for my birthday. 'We'll buy you a new violin but you're not getting a bicycle. There's too much traffic. You could fall and break your arm. It's too risky if you plan to be a musician.' 'Dad, I'll be careful—cross my heart and hope to die!' Okay, that wasn't too bright. Words matter.

That probably killed my chance for a bicycle but I did take back my oath never to speak to Benedict Arnold again. When I got through whining that my father was a stingy-no-good-double-crosser my mother gently explained that the son of one of his classmates had recently been struck and killed while riding his bicycle. Just my luck, the kid was ten. 'He's scared, son. Your father would never forgive himself if something happened to you.' That put a stop to my fuss. I just hoped he wouldn't still be scared when I turned eleven.

It reminded me again that kids are dupes. To three-year-old eyes the world is a great big Easter egg filled with presents—like fireflies or the perfect pattern on a turtle's shell. Even a threat, like crackling thunder, or the wet kiss of an enormous leaping dog, once the first rush of fear is over, becomes a thing of wonder. Happy children are the easiest to deceive because we don't waste time pondering things we don't understand. How was I to know why someone left a dead cat hanging on the front door of our house the week we moved in? Or why we came home from church a day later to find it ransacked, my stamp collection stolen along with the toy cash register holding my two-year savings of dimes and nickels. Since none of it made sense, that night I had my very first nightmare. I remember my father reading me the Twenty-third Psalm and my mother assuring me there was nothing to be afraid of because there were no tigers in L.A. and even if there were, she and my dad would protect me. I must have believed her, since I had forgotten about it all until we landed in Las Cruces, all except my utter bewilderment that someone would want to smash my pet turtle's beautiful shell.

Perhaps it had all been so easy for me to forget because these awesome gifts kept showing up in my life, the girl next door being the best among them. It didn't matter that she was twelve and I was three, Shayla had greeted me the day we moved in as if I were her long-lost kid brother. Once I discovered she could keep me in a head lock with just one arm and swing me around in the air so high I thought I was flying, I was prepared to follow her anywhere. The world's second great wonder was my beautiful Aunt Gwen who overcame my disappointment at starting lessons on the piano instead of the violin. I remember sitting at the keyboard beside her feeling like a prince because of how regal she looked with her arms bent like a queen and her back held perfectly straight. I was so in love that after I started kindergarten I would slip out of bed and be at the piano by five every morning. I obeyed my father and tried to play softly, but I'm pretty sure those two early practice hours, Monday thru Friday, were why Shayla's dad put up that concrete wall between our houses.

Looking back on it now, I would have to say that, apart from getting the chicken pox and a bout of pneumonia, I made it through early childhood remarkably unscathed. Little did my six-year-old self realize how quickly our new neighborhood was changing or that my happy days with Shayla and my adored Aunt Gwen were already numbered.

Traveling the streets beneath an otherworldly slate sky, Emerson often felt as if he was struggling against excess gravity, but the more he saw of the Crescent City, the more he understood the genius of its comforts, like midday bourbon and a funeral band making the sun rise again. In a town where much of the freed South's torn body and soul had taken refuge, there was always time for that second cup of chicory or to sit and ponder some visionary's garish old colossus, the building's facade carved with sphinxes overseeing crocodiles, storks and peacocks there to fend off dangerous dreams. Less fitting were the boulevards' cheery red trolleys in a place that hid its demons and dark intrigue with zany inventions, and yet the people with their blending hues and colorful clothes were as familiar to a boy from Kingston as their weakness for putting warm milk in their coffee. Only years later, after surviving the North's frozen cities, would he appreciate just how close he had been to Africa.

While the South's gravity-burdened pace could feel sluggish even to a Jamaican, the war had galvanized his classmates' ambitions. The Sisters of the Blessed Sacrament had founded the college to uplift the sons of America's enslaved and dispossessed and now, as proof of their success, the once inadmissable were no longer satisfied with being invisible. For a thirty-six-year-old under-graduate, the impatience of youth was inspiring, but he was even more gratified when the dean, upon reviewing Emerson's qualifications, agreed that an accelerated two-year course would amply satisfy his degree requirements.

His narrow windowless room was less encouraging but it was only a mile from campus and the rent did not tax his budget. His unforced charm had soon endeared him to Hortense Walker who jealously guarded his need to study in peace and complete the year with perfect grades, despite his offense against her culinary pride.

"Now you tell me—just how am I s'posed to go about feeding you?" Hortense griped the day he arrived and had gone on griping ever after. He had offered to prepare his own meals but Hortense Walker considered a man scrabbling around inside her kitchen an affront to God, the order of the universe, and her precious good name. "I only put up with you because you're a college gentleman," she would grumble, half-hiding her smile, "but I'll have you know you're the first man in creation to turn down my chicken and biscuits."

"Some beans or one of your tasty omelets would do just fine, Mrs. Walker."

"See, that's what I just can't figger. You'll eat the egg, so what you got against the bird?"

"Not a thing, but I don't see those eggs start running when they spot you with that cleaver in your hand."

Though Emerson enjoyed their easy banter, the pressure he was under to succeed at his studies made for a lonely existence. He had been of two minds when Maddy wrote to say she was coming. Even though money would be tight without her income, he missed his wife dearly, and could tell from her letter that his mother was doing her best to make her life miserable. On the other hand, Maddy was accustomed to a spacious home with a lawn and a flowering garden and the Walkers owned what in New Orleans parlance was called a shotgun. One of a long identical row built by freedmen in the 1870s, it had a pointed gable at the entry and four rooms in line so that with all the doors open you could stand in front and shoot a bullet clear through to the back. Some argued the term was a corruption of sho-gon, Yoruban for God's house, and not, as more than a few wary-eyed wives suggested, a good setup for getting a bead on a two-timing husband. So while he was not that concerned by the thought of Maddy gunning him down, it did mean the only way out to the Walkers' yard was through his bedroom. It was also the only way in when his landlady decided to bar her front door.

Hortense was crestfallen when Emerson told her he was moving come summer.

"Aw, Doctor," she beseeched him, using the honorific she employed when bragging about her high-class boarder, "you'll set the neighbors thinkin' I couldn't take care of you proper. I'll only charge for the little extra feeding—and I'll cook your greens in nothing but butter—you have my word as a Christian."

"It's not that, Mrs. Walker. I can't have your husband stumbling through my room in the middle of night when my wife's in bed with me." Lem Walker was a wiry, fifty-four-year-old dyspeptic destined to die with a liver as rough as a corn cob.

The landlady crooked an arm against her hip. "I'm tired of that drunkard shaming me. Let the old buzzard sleep out in the yard, like I told you. That'll sober him up."

"You know that won't work. Lem will just pound on the door and keep all of us up."

"That man ain't gonna cost me another good tenant," she muttered, grabbing her cleaver. "I'll put the fear of God in him, don't you worry!" When she promised not to bolt the front door and keep her husband in line, Emerson considered the expense of moving and decided to risk it.

"I know this is not my place," he chanced discreetly, "but it may be that Lem craves you more than he craves that bottle. Men hate to admit this—after being kicked around all week, once in a while a man just wants a little soothing."

He knew it was a stretch, but Hortense Walker had the hands and build of a middle-weight boxer and he feared, watching her hack the large cabbage in half with a single stroke, that Lem's next drunken late-night appearance would end in carnage. So he was heartened when the fifty-year-old battle-ax loosened her jaw and simpered with an echo of herself twenty years ago.

"You think I've been a little hard?" she wondered in a tiny whisper. "You know what, Doctor? You're right!" She puffed up her body, her craggy face proud. "Folks shouldn't go crucifying my Lem for having a few drinks on a Friday night. At least *my* man doesn't go chasing blowzy women!"

For the first time since he had moved in with the Walkers, Emerson was able to sleep undisturbed on three consecutive Friday nights. By the fourth week, poor Lem was a wreck.

"Doctor," he sputtered, detaining Emerson the next morning after breakfast when his wife left for the backyard's washing shed, "something terrible's come over that woman. They say it can happen to females her age. You reckon she needs to see one of them head-shrinkers?"

"Head-shrinkers?"

Lem licked his lips with a haunted look. "You know, mind doctors and such."

"A psychiatrist? Not from what I see—lately your wife's been as cheerful as I've seen her. Got a fine energy about her."

"That's the doggone problem!" Lem bawled, pressing his head between his fists. "At the start I didn't mind her hustling me home to take off my boots and let me relax while she poured me a drink. Now, I can't finish my whiskey before she's hauling and pulling me into the bed. She don't even wait for me to be the man no more. Doc, the woman done drained me dry. I can't take it!"

"Maybe you should try eating more," Emerson teased, harking back to Friday night when Hortense had insisted on stuffing Lem with enough alligator sausage and peach cobbler to halt Sherman's army.

"Very funny," Lem grumbled, scowling at his leftover breakfast. "I can barely stomach the sight of them grits." He bent down and rolled up one of his pants legs. "See that?" he said, pointing to a patch of shiny scar-tissue so translucent for a second Emerson thought it was bone peeking through the skin on Lem's ankle. "That's from acid." He rolled down the pants cuff then yanked off his undershirt to bare his chest. A long pink line crossed from his clavicle clear down to his navel. "I got that when a tank overflowed and I slipped off the catwalk—broke both kneecaps as a bonus. Don't get me wrong, I care about her, Doc," he contended, his scarred hands wringing the shirt in exasperation. "Womenfolk ain't never satisfied. They jaw at you 'til your ears won't stop buzzin' and you can't stand the sight of 'em. They figger they know you inside out but they don't know nuthin'. Thirty years sweatin' blood inside a foundry puts age on a man. I gots to ease the pain just to keep on truckin'."

"Try aspirin. That hard liquor will kill you."

Lem's graying head wagged. "What's the difference? If that woman keeps poppin' my nuts, I'll be dead in a year. Ain't there some kinda medicine—a tranquilizer, maybe—you could get her to take? Just to settle her down a piece? She'll listen to you."

"Sorry, Lem, there's not a drug in the world that will solve your problem." Emerson smiled as he suddenly saw Winters waiting with hopeful eyes for his weekly packet. "If you want my advice, talk things over with your wife. Find that happy medium."

Lem slipped the undershirt back on and got up from the table with a grunt. "Thanks a heap, Doc."

Emerson feared he had made an enemy, but before long Lem went back to being his tolerable taciturn self and far less stressed. Hortense, however, grew more and more prickly.

"You could have told me you weren't coming home for supper," she muttered when he came into the kitchen excited about the surprise invitation.

"You know I would have—I only found out this minute—"

"And you jumped at the chance for a fancy meal. I suppose you must be tired of my plain home cooking." Hortense Walker sought out appreciation like a sponge soaking up water.

"Now, you know that's not true. Look how fat I've gotten on your buttermilk pancakes." He rested a pleading hand on her shoulder. "You understand, don't you? It's not every day a fellow gets invited to dine with his favorite professors."

She brushed his hand from her shoulder. "Those professors know you don't eat nuthin'? 'Cause your wife'll be here tomorrow and I'm here racking my brain trying to think of what to feed her."

"Oh, don't bother going to any big trouble. Maddy won't be expecting anything fussy."

"Of course. Lord knows I'm not refined enough to know good hospitality."

Emerson gabbled to make amends and Hortense let him grovel for almost a minute before her hard look cracked with a moth-eaten grin. "Go on—get out of my kitchen! Just make sure to dress yourself nice and proper. Those professors won't cotton to seeing some raggedy-tailed negro show up in their quarter."

Still in his cream linen jacket and burgundy tie despite the humidity, Emerson was in a high-stepping mood as he headed for the St. Charles streetcar. Not since his all-nighters with Mason Jans had he enjoyed such a stimulating evening. His hosts had warmed to him instantly when he interrupted their apologies to say that he too had given up eating meat. He had come prepared to be politely circumspect and been astonished to find himself discussing Egyptian freemasonry and its influence on the metaphysical themes in Mozart's Magic Flute as opposed to the Christian mysticism of Wagner's Parsifal—with two nuns, no less! He had to hand it to America's Catholic philanthropists, at least when it came to hiring professors, they did not seem frightened by free-thinkers. His only regret was that when the subject turned to non-violent disobedience, the late hour had kept him from defending his position. He would have argued that Socrates had consciously resisted and not passively submitted since his death itself had proved the law was unjust.

He was so consumed with reviewing the many points he wished he had made, he did not notice the dark sedan until it stopped and two white men jumped out and blocked his path.

"Where you comin' from, boy?"

He was about to run when he glimpsed their badges.

"Sorry, officers," he gasped, feeling the thuds in his chest start to slow. "I didn't know you were the police."

It was a moonless night and the streetlight was too dim for him to make out their expressions.

"Boy, I asked you a question. Where ya comin' from this time of night?"

Emerson stiffened at being barked at like a child. He was about to ask what law he had broken when the baton struck his cheek.

"Answer the question, nigger!"

While he paused, clutching for the words his fright had scattered, the cop swung again, striking him flush across his jaw.

"Speak, boy!"

Emerson rushed his hand to the burning pain and felt the

swelling. "I'm on my way home from visiting with my professors—they share a garden cottage on Liberty."

"What's their names—these *professors*?"

"Sister Brenda and Sister Esperanza."

The cops glanced at each other in quiet amusement.

"Musta been right cozy—two nuns and a nigger."

The officer tittered and a dark savage rage rumbled up from an unknown corner in Emerson's psyche.

"Their last names, boy!"

As the throbbing from broken blood vessels seemed to explode the side of his face, he pictured the injured Prince thrashing on the dumb-cell floor. "I can't recall their surnames," he mumbled, wincing from the burn spreading across his jaw. "You'll have to ask the university."

"University? Kinda long in the tooth for a college boy, ain't you, nigger?" Emerson's assailant strode in close. "Sounds like some bull to me. We'd better haul this one in."

Before he could protest, Emerson found himself cuffed then stuffed in the back of the unmarked sedan with a bludgeon to the ribs for good measure. While his batterer drove, the second cop smirked at him over his shoulder. "Make it easy on yourself, boy—we both know you don't belong in this neighborhood. Some bluenose pin your numbers, or are you one them ignorant Georgia freelancers tryin' to dish snowflakes on the sly?"

From where Emerson sat, he could have been speaking Urdu.

"Naw, the jungle-bunnies know better than to try and sling that trash up here," the driver sneered, "they're not *that* stupid ..."

"Oh, Andy, I ain't sure you're right about that," his partner drawled, aping a popular radio comic. "Most niggers I know are so dumb they can throw themselves to the ground and end up missin'."

The one good thing about learning to sleep sitting up was that I could stir from a doze and no one would be the wiser. So when I woke up and heard my parents' bickering, I perked up my ears and stayed still as a mummy.

"Most prodigies never make it. If he's lucky, he'll end up playing pop standards in some dingy café."

"Admit it, Emerson. You're just disappointed that his talent is in music."

"Rubbish. Talent is not enough for us. His best bet comes from a good education."

"He could stay in L.A. and get a good education."

"Really? What was the use of having him transfer—just to skip another grade? The one teacher who showed our son any interest sat him in the back of her class and let him write stories all day. When I was his age I was starting Greek and Latin."

"Oh, what a tragedy—he's almost ten and not learning dead languages."

"Now you're just being obtuse. Even their better schools can't retain good teachers. Isn't that why you jumped to join that blue ribbon commission? And what good did it do, besides getting the governor's name in the papers? Those on top aren't going to pay to level the field. The more of our children they're forced to teach, the worse these schools will get."

"We could have sent him to private school—"

"The good ones won't take him. And even if one of them did *and* they lowered the fees to where we could afford them, he'd just have one more stripe against him. At least back home, once he passes his exams, he'll be on a government scholarship right along with his peers. He won't have to hate himself for being different."

"—he can hate us instead for destroying his career."

"There you go again, misusing our son. Our so-called backward island must have some decent teachers, seeing how you keep boasting about Mason's son getting into Juilliard."

"Yes, but on the piano. Who will teach him the violin? Your dear Miss Leguerre from her studio in hell?"

I must have flinched because my father said, 'shush!' and they both clammed up. I had heard about teachers from hell: they drooled and rapped your knuckles with a ruler and made you spend a year playing nothing but scales, so I sure as hell didn't want one. I'd already had a close shave when I was six, and my Aunt Gwen left for a trip across Africa. The old woman she recommended wasn't really mean, but she had two ferocious-looking cats and her house was like a cave, dark and musty-smelling. The last straw came when I started to play and she put a cushion under my feet so I could depress the pedals. I stopped in tears four bars in, hearing the notes all run into an ugly muddle. She saw things my way and took back her cushion, but on the drive home I put my foot down. No way was I studying with someone who had plainly gone deaf.

Luckily, my parents wanted to visit Anu's health food store. My mom must have told her about my trauma because she squeezed me an extra carrot juice and said she knew a pianist from Hungary who could teach me. One of the first things I remember Anu saying when I met her was that she drank a lot of carrot juice because it helped her to see more clearly, so I went home relieved, feeling I could trust her. I reckoned someone who had come here from Hungary and ended up working for the Lawrence Welk Show probably still had his hearing.

Aunt Gwen forgave me for nixing her choice when she returned from Africa six months later and heard the progress I had made under Mr. Batori. His low-key approach suited me just fine, even if he had me playing Joplin and Anderson when I was still in the thrall of Bach and Beethoven. Of all my teachers, I would miss his lessons the most.

Unlike Mr. Batori, who seemed tired of what Shayla's dad called 'long-haired' music, Mr. Rosenblum brought his passion for the great composers with him from Europe. A renowned conductor back in Russia, like Anu and Mr. Batori he had come to L.A. after the end of the Second World War. He also had no children, which could explain why the first thing he did was start two youth orchestras. I'll never forget when I was finally good enough to play in his junior orchestra and he smiled as I sat in the back of the second violins and said, 'welcome! Now we'll hear something!' Had Mrs. Bernard greeted me like that when I joined her second grade class, I might not have spent the entire day too scared to ask if I could go to the bathroom.

I'm still ashamed that I had been such a chicken. It wasn't as if Mrs. Bernard was hard of hearing or had attack cats guarding her desk. In fact, once she realized where the smell was coming from she let me stand in the closet until my mom came with clean pants. I never had another accident, but whenever I glimpsed her eyes dart my way my knees would start shaking. I used to think there was something about me that made her skin crawl, but after a while I realized I was not the only boy in class who felt that way, because Mrs. Bernard never smiled.

The man who started the whole darned thing never smiled either. He had shown up at my old school out of the blue wearing a short-sleeved white shirt and a skinny black tie with a silver clip. I remember being fascinated by the plastic holder with five mechanical pencils in his left shirt pocket after Mrs. Calhoun escorted me to the empty classroom, then patted my shoulder before she left, explaining that the man at the desk was here to give me a test. He never spoke, except to say 'begin' and 'stop,' but I never thought he was mean, just all business. Kids can read whole books on grown-ups' faces.

Now that I was about to change schools again, this time in a whole other country, I wondered if my new teachers would be old and going deaf or just plain mean. I doubted they would scare me as much now that I was older, but I worried that their classes were going to be hell if the kids there could all speak Latin.

Something about the way the row of hump-backed cars sat packed in side by side in front of the terminal brought back to Madeline's mind a color photograph of bulbous sea-lions sunning on a white sand beach in California. Her imagining felt doubly strange, as she was far from relaxed and the sky overhead was gloomy; plus her feet were beginning to ache and she felt like a big easy mark standing alone, keeping half an eye on her bags while she searched every dark male face that came within sight. Her anxiety rushed to its peak and stayed there when she caught the stooped black porter frowning at her from under a rusted signpost warning travelers to be on the lookout for thieves and loose women. What on earth was she supposed to do now?

"Your majesty? Lost on your lonesome?"

Madeline felt her panic recede as Mundy Peters struggled towards her bearing a second duffel bag and his big provocative grin. She started to return his smile then cringed, recalling her earlier subterfuge. As she had hoped, it had taken the dauntless private over fifteen minutes to wangle those ice cubes from the whites-only dining car but she doubted he really believed she'd managed to polish off half of a twenty-pound watermelon.

Peters set down his cumbersome bags with an empathetic look. "How come you're out here like Little Bo Peep? Your husband forget you?"

"Of course not!" she retorted, then realizing she sounded ungracious, explained that she would have called from inside the station but the home where he lived did not have a phone. "This is really not like him."

"If you say so," the private grinned. "A buddy of mine was supposed to meet me, but it looks like he follows C.P. time as well."

"C.P. time?"

The big G.I. chuckled. "Colored people's tempo; never right on the beat, 'cause we're tired of being hustled."

"Don't tell me— the extra bag belongs to your friend."

"Now, aren't you the prettiest detective this side of the F.B.I.? Yep, he snuck off to sweet-talk some gal and I'm the sucker. Speaking of which—" Peters peered at her deeply, "you never told me what you did with the rind—"

While her estimation of Mundy Peters had gone up since his lascivious whistle, her impression remained that he had come home eager to test his newfound skill as a lady-killer. So while his resourcefulness made her want to confess, she was leery of ceding him the high ground. "These train porters are most accommodating—" she deflected obliquely, "now, if you'll excuse me, I must see about finding a cab."

"Here's a thought! Why don't we share one?"

"No, I don't think so—"

"Oh, c'mon, what's the harm? I'm headed close to your husband's campus. I doubt he'd want you braving these shady streets on your lonesome."

Madeline thought about the sign warning about loose women.

Taxi drivers could be tricky to deal with and it wouldn't hurt to be with someone who knew his way around. "What about your friend?"

"He knows where I live. Anyway, that Negro needs to buy himself a watch!" Peters flashed her a wink. "Maybe your husband should get one too."

Hortense Walker was outside on her porch as their taxi arrived. She glowered down through the passenger window. "You Mrs. Gardner?"

Madeline quickly withdrew her arm after Mundy raced to open her door and tried to help her out of the cab. "Yes, I'm Madeline— you must be Mrs. Walker—"

The landlady's eyes crimped suspiciously. "Who's that soldier fella with you? Your husband never mentioned havin' kin in New Orleans—"

"Edmund Peters, engineer, U.S. Army!" he announced with a crisp salute. Then, still on a high from the ringing cheers and passing carte blanche of Liberated Europe, he fibbed cheekily, "Ma'am, wouldn't you know it? Mrs. Gardner and I got to talkin' on the train—turns out there's a middling chance we're second cousins."

"Say what?"

Hortense's hands-on-hips pose brought the G.I. back to where he was and served to warn them both that they were trifling with a sturdy Protestant who understood how a woman's good looks could lead to wantonness.

Chastened, Mundy Peters pressed his hat to his chest. "I'm Miss Jamesie's grandnephew, born right 'round the corner on Fremont."

Hortense stood unmoved. "Is that so? Then you'd best be gettin' along. I need to speak with Mrs. Gardner in private."

Only the night Adrianna slit her wrist had Madeline known the chill grip of unalloyed terror. The war had shown her that the germs of tribe could infect normal people with implacable cruelty, and as inspired as she was by the possibilities in this expansive new country, she knew that Americans could be deeply tribal. So while she tried out benign explanations to keep her mind from drawing terrible pictures, she was grateful when Mrs. Walker came back with some warm chamomile tea and sounded cool-headed. Yes, Emerson was missing. Yes, it was the South, but it was not the time to let loose of her wits. She was about to ask if Hortense had thought to ring the university, then shrank, remembering the Walkers did not have a phone. She was contemplating whether to try and find her way to Emerson's campus when she shot up from her chair and spilled her cup, startled by hope and the knock at the door. It was Mundy Peters. In her haste, she had left her makeup bag inside the cab.

When Hortense finished explaining about the professors' dinner invitation, Mundy promptly took charge. "Don't you fret, Mrs. Gardner. I'll help you find him."

"Hold on there, Private!" Mrs. Walker commanded. "I'm not letting the Doctor's wife traipse through town like a strumpet. You just settle on down while I make myself respectable."

Madeline was not sure why the three of them ended up riding the streetcar after crossing Emerson's deserted campus twice, searching for the one person the private was 'one hundred and one percent' certain would help them. Hortense Walker's immobile expression as she sat mute between them only enlarged her confusion. Fear would have crushed her spirit beyond its limit had Mundy not kept softly repeating that she could trust him. She needed to believe him. Everything was going to be fine.

"I don't see why you suddenly want my opinion—you're the one who decided to hit the road and trust your luck." My mom's sharp hiss felt like showering ice. "I swear if we didn't need gas you wouldn't even stop to let your son ease his bladder—not that you'd care if I told you my back is killing me."

"Are you serious? Complain is all you've done from the start."

I wasn't sure if I'd been dreaming, or if my parents had been arguing non-stop since I woke up briefly on our way through Houston. They were keeping it down so as not to disturb me, and as I drifted in and out of sleep, their squabbling had merged with the hum of the Valiant's engine, reaching me vaguely like the drone from Beethoven's Pastoral Symphony. Awakened to the reality that not only were they able to sustain this insane split between the Father and the Holy Spirit, the reminder that I was the one who got it started left my insides shivering like the strings in the fourth movement's violent storm.

Our Valiant swerved wildly back to the median and I wondered why my dad decided to take his foot off the gas and leave us coasting. My mom sucked her teeth and Delroy must have shared our confusion because he flashed his high beams for us to pull over. The lead sky hung low with devouring clouds disclosing a slim hope of daybreak on the horizon. As we sat speechless on the side of the vacant highway, I had the sense that we had zoomed far off course and were marooned inside our spaceship on a cold uninhabitable planet. I was sure we were doomed. Then, all at once, I was back on earth seeing Captain Angell slowly appear through the desert mist, hunched with hands thrust deep inside his pockets.

"You missed the turn off," he said, leaning into my father's open window then nodding across to my mother who responded with an 'I-told-him-so' shrug.

"That's my husband, Captain. Never deviate—come hell or high water!"

"Tell you what—why don't you drive for a while?"

To my surprise, she reacted peacefully.

"Of course, Emerson. All you had to do was ask ..."

Delroy checked his watch then suggested switching after we doubled back to the turn-off. "What you folks need is a good strong pot of hot coffee and maybe a pile of flapjacks soaked in syrup," he added, shooting me a grin.

As he hunched his way back to his station wagon, I felt grateful that we were traveling with a war pilot. Although the captain could stir up the same queasy feeling haunting my insides, especially when he started talking rough to his wife, at least he knew where he was going and, unlike my dad, when he blew his top he never stayed steamed for long. The jury was out about the gun hiding inside his ankle holster.

The off-the-track service station was attached to a hole-in-the-wall called Dunderhead's Doggie Joint. The grown-ups got their gas and coffee but I lost out on those flapjacks. Flapjacks need cooking and the joint's attendant, a pudgy redhead who looked thirteen, tops, explained that the cook was his uncle and his uncle was the mechanic and mechanics never work before seven-thirty. He offered to warm me up a hot dog which I thought was pretty friendly but I settled for a stale jelly doughnut. As we paid the kid slipped me an extra doughnut, saying it was on the house to make up for the flapjacks. He gave me this long puppy-dog look, like he was sad to see us go. It was weird, but I didn't blame him. He was all by himself, and there was nothing around for miles.

The kid's lost look reminded me of the one friend I made at my new school before I blew it. Teddy and I both used to rush out to the playground at recess hoping to play kickball, but there were only five on a side and no matter how soon we got there, we never got picked, so the two of us would end up playing tetherball. When that got boring, Teddy asked if I played chess. I said no, so he offered to teach me. After a month I could give him a challenge, but Teddy still won. Afraid that I wasn't having much fun, he asked if I had any baseball cards I wanted to trade. Teddy was a huge San Francisco Giants fan. When I said I didn't really like baseball and would rather play chess, Teddy looked shocked. 'Not even Willie Mays?' I just shrugged, ashamed to admit that I didn't know who Willie Mays was.

Teddy and I would still turn up at recess, hoping for a chance to play. Finally, one day, the third grade class was away on a field trip and since just enough boys had shown up to make a team the Rossolinis had no choice but to pick us. The Rossolini brothers were the best athletes at school and were in the Boy Scouts, so they were always the ones put in charge of the ball and made captains. I ended up kicking the winning home run but poor Teddy never got on base. He was my friend, so I lied and told him it was just bad luck, but it was obvious that kickball was not his game. The next day I got picked right away and I guessed from the look on Teddy's face he was worried that he'd have no one to play with at recess. Teddy came a few more times after that, then stopped showing up altogether. We were not in the same class, so in my excitement at being picked for every game I never gave it any thought until much later when I saw Teddy crossing the schoolyard with his legs in braces. I asked if he wanted to play chess at recess but Teddy shook his head, saying he'd rather sit by himself and read. When I asked if he was sure, Teddy looked me dead in the eye and said yes. Even thinking about it now, it makes me feel rotten.

While the kid at the Doggie Joint walked with me out to our car bragging about how far Mickey Mantle could hit a baseball, the grown-ups decided to pair back up by sex, reason number one being my dad was plum exhausted and number two (which I pretty much surmised), he and Delroy hated talking to their wives almost as much as they despised listening to the radio. To be diplomatic I went with Connie and my mother.

Big surprise, the moment we hit the road they were gabbing a mile a minute and never even checked what was on the radio. It wasn't that my dad and Delroy hadn't shot the breeze some when they were together, but with Connie and my mother it was like the words had been backed up in their pipes and they could finally run the faucet full blast. Not that it bothered me all that much. The only ones on the radio that early were evangelicals shouting about the blood of Jesus and being washed white as snow once the godless cities get wiped from the earth by the Wrath of the Lamb. L.A. had never seemed so terrifying as it did on that long drive through Texas.

The scenery was as drab and depressing as the weather, so even Connie's chirruping did not keep me from nodding off. I came to after another catnap and saw that the clouds had darkened and started to sweat, the steady drops thickening the closer we got to New Orleans, so that after a while it felt as if we were plowing through thick gray soup. Lying still, my ears tuned in to Connie's voice when it sounded hoarse, like she'd been crying.

"—what else could I do?"

"I don't know, but I couldn't have done it—not that Emerson would ever want me to."

"Of course he wouldn't. No man wants to, but he was Delroy's commanding officer. And it only happened that one time—"

"Be glad your husband showed up. Otherwise who knows what else that no-good dog would have tried."

Connie sagged in her seat with a sigh. "That's always been my problem—from before I was even grown—it's the way God made me. I don't go looking for it. That shouldn't mean I got to dress like a frump and cover myself in a muumuu."

"What about Delroy? How was he supposed to feel?"

"When your husband brings his C.O. home then it ain't five minutes before he's jumping up saying he's got to run to the store, what's that tell you? This is 1940s Alabama we're talkin'! White folks didn't come visiting—much less an officer all the way from Montgomery—just to chew the fat with a colored cadet? Please—" Connie snorted. "That man's eyes were making a meal of my bones from the first day he saw me. I didn't have this extra meat on me yet, so I went down real easy. I knew Delroy would give his right arm to join the corps. He wanted to fly! And there I was, facing the man making the decision—pass or fail. If you failed, it was all over—your plans, your dreams, everything. You were back to being nothin'. No second chances. What else *could* I think? I did it for the man I loved, and for twenty years I've been paying for it."

The hurt in her voice made me shiver, like the time a sad look came over Anu's face and she got all choked up after a customer asked if she had ever been married or had any kids.

Connie went back to blubbering and my mother sat rock still behind the wheel, her gaze on the slip of road not shrouded in fog. We must have covered ten solemn miles before she turned and cupped her hand on Connie's shoulder. Her eyes seemed to hold a question she was not sure how to phrase, and when I saw her peek at me in the rear-view mirror I figured she was just as mixed up about the whole thing as me. For a second I thought she would let it out, but instead she gave Connie's shoulder another squeeze and peered ahead through the fog as the three of us listened to the windshield-wipers' steady faint clacks.

Emerson crept to the edge of the plank-bed farthest from the open toilet viscid with cigarette butts and feces. The detectives had grabbed the limelight as they shoved him inside the precinct, boasting that they had bagged one of 'them biggity college coons.' Not satisfied with their fellow officers' sardonic claps, they let their imaginations run wild, concocting lurid fantasies featuring 'two hard-up nuns and a pet monkey.' When the desk sergeant finally mastered his cackles to ask what Emerson was in for, they said it was a toss-up between attempted burglary and resisting arrest, depending on which one required less paperwork.

Stripped of his shoelaces, belt and tie, he had been led to his cell by the station's baby-faced rookie who blushed as a second round of raunchy wisecracks trailed them halfway down the hall. Stepping out after locking him inside, he had Emerson place his hands through the iron bars whispering as he removed the shackles that, once the detectives were gone, he would let him back out to make a phone call.

The rookie left and Emerson checked his sore puffed jaw then winced as the entire left side of his face felt as if it had been cauterized by fire. As he tasted the warm blood inside his cheek, gagging as it tickled his throat, he thought about Madeline arriving tomorrow and started to choke on his helpless rage. Overcome, he contorted his mouth and cursed his fate with a soundless cry.

'Answer the question, nigger.' The demand had confounded him, like a shiv to the gut. What *was* he doing here? He had never felt especially burdened by his race. Growing up he could count on the quality of his speech and apparel to shield him from the abuse required to keep the less fortunate from confusing an empire's law with justice. Spurred by Montesquieu and Locke to trust Thomas Jefferson, he had listened with open ears to successive presidents proclaim that America's republican ideals were the answer to a belligerent world. Tonight her policemen had shown him that the quaking prayer, 'there, but for the grace of God, go I,' haunted her smug white heart like a tolling bell. So as his sore jaw throbbed and he feared for his wife, wishing she had never left home, the question lingered—what *was* a sentient black man doing here?

When the rookie returned and quietly released him as promised, he strained to think of who he could phone at this time of night. He recalled having read somewhere that Sister Brenda's last name was McCloskey, but when he inquired the operator said her number was not listed. Unable to think of anyone else to try, he resigned himself to being locked up overnight and ringing the dean's office at eight the next morning. He clung to his hopes through a sleepless night only to see his day of deliverance annulled as the new cop on duty refused to let him out to make his call.

"Watch your mouth, nigger," he warned when Emerson let loose his exasperation and yelled in his face, "or I'll make sure it ain't no use in front of the judge. You catch my drift, *college boy*?"

The officer snickered and sauntered off, stroking his bludgeon, leaving Emerson to stare helplessly out of a sinkhole that apparently had no bottom. Unable to scream and too angry to weep, he collapsed on the hardwood slab, convulsed with laughter until his swollen jaw and cracked ribs protested. He wondered what the Prince would say if he could see him now, caught in that ruthless spider's cunning web. Rejecting his worst fears, he reminded himself that as bad as things looked, he was not a poor epileptic. Someone was bound to miss him before the judge could order him to slave on a chain gang. At least he damn-well hoped so.

"Looks like you're sprung, boy."

Emerson glanced up from the corner where he'd retreated to guard his nose from the noxious toilet.

"You're one lucky nigger," the cop observed with a sour grunt as he unlocked the bars.

Seeing his beloved waiting safely at the sergeant's desk, Emerson nearly fell to his knees. Though the precinct house was dim and dingy, her presence had never been more radiant. He rushed to embrace her, then stopped as he spotted Hortense Walker and the prepossessing soldier looming beside her.

"There you are, my poor darling!" his wife exclaimed with a theatrical lovingness that seemed an ill fit to Madeline's character. "You've had us all so worried!"

Before he could make sense of her greeting, the desk sergeant chided him. "You shoulda told us you was British," he said in a bantering Irish brogue. "We coulda cleared up this pother from the start."

The trial which threatened to doom him to the bowels of hell abruptly dissolved into a farce. He was about to retort that he had not realized that foreigners were exempt from groundless arrest when Madeline read his thoughts and jumped in before he could speak.

"We're still learning our way around your country, Sergeant," she rushed to explain, her tone, like her demeanor, naive and pleasing. "I promise, from now on I shall see to it he never sets a foot outside our house without his passport."

The Irishman grinned beneath the red-veined nose that dogged his looks like a fire-plug. "Ye've roped yerself a right smart lass, boyo. Best leave her to do the thinkin' in the fam'ly."

Emerson waited until the four of them were safely on the street to ask how they had found him. Revealing the astuteness of a seasoned diplomat, Hortense headed off Mundy before he could vaunt his role in the rescue. "We reckoned the precinct nearest your professors was where to start inquiring. Private Peters is from the neighborhood and was kind enough to escort us."

Mundy's hurt glance across to Madeline undid her effort. Emerson gave the soldier a cold once over, pausing to frown at the G.I. insignia. "Are all American privates this obliging to strangers— or only to married women in distress?"

Madeline gasped; Emerson was almost never sarcastic. "What's come over you?" she berated him. "Private Peters and I made our acquaintance on the train from Biloxi. He's been enormously kind and completely honorable. Frankly, without Mundy's help I don't know what I would have done."

Ashamed for having thoughtlessly unleashed his anger, Emerson drew a calming breath. "Forgive me, soldier—I've had a trying night. She's right. I should be thanking you."

"Think nothing of it," Mundy insisted, though a grain of hurt remained in his tone. "As you saw for yourself—in the U.S. of A., we save our kindness for strangers."

"And you have been *more* than kind, Private Peters," Madeline underlined, ignoring Hortense's disapproval. "You've gone out of your way and we're grateful."

"I'm surprised you didn't drop your bags at your auntie's instead of dragging them back with you."

Mundy smiled at Mrs. Walker's skepticism. "My aunt's was still a ways off when I realized Mrs. Gardner had forgotten her bag. I figured better get it to her then than who knows when? So I had the cabbie turn us around."

"And we're lucky that you did. Aren't we, Emerson?" Madeline suggested.

"Very lucky," he responded dryly.

Embarrassed by his tone, Madeline turned her appeal to Hortense Walker. "Would it be all right if Mundy stayed for tea? I think it's the least I should do, but I wouldn't want to impose—"

"Humph, impose?" her landlady scoffed. "The Doctor can barely carry himself and you want me to give the poor man some tea—? He had us too worried to eat. I'm not about to let a Good Samaritan just go-on his ways and leave my house hungry!" She aimed Mundy Peters a piercing eye. "You ain't one of them Hindu pacifics are you?

'No, ma'am.'

"You eat chicken and biscuits?"

"Yes'm."

"Good. It's been one hell of a day, so y'all just simmer on down. When we get home I want you all to sit and get acquainted proper while I fix us some vittles."

"And I'll help—" Madeline offered.

"In a pig's eye," Hortense contradicted her firmly.

Smiling, Emerson aimed the soldier a cautioning shrug and Mundy relaxed with a big, white grin and dared no argument.

I roused with a start when Connie gave an earsplitting sneeze and promptly got the hiccups. My first thought as I curled back up was that the three of us were sure to catch colds. With the windows rolled up so the only unused air came through four thin slits, breathing inside the vinyl-upholstered station wagon felt like trying to draw oxygen from toxic steam.

"Try relaxing your diaphragm," my mother suggested, "that usually helps."

Connie hiccuped three more times then stopped. "Hey—that works!"

"Good. Now finish what you were telling me before he wakes up."

Realizing I had them fooled, I closed my eyes and did not move.

"Delroy never said a word when he came back with that liquor and saw me on my knees. Got the ice from our kitchen and poured the man a drink like it was nothing. It eats at me to this day but Delroy still won't talk about it." Connie drew a loud deep breath and unburdened herself with a sigh. "That's how I know I let him down bad. What was I s'posed to do? I was eighteen, dumb as a board and scared out of my mind. I'd never been alone with a white man before. At first I was relieved he hadn't jumped on top of me— then the bastard unbuttoned his pants—I think, *eventually*, we would have gotten past it—but that vile man just *had* to throw it back in our face after they gave Delroy his medal. It hadn't been enough to humiliate us, he had to drive a stake through our marriage."

"Why would someone be that cruel?"

"I think he was mad at himself for wanting me—it shamed him—coveting what Delroy had. Niggers don't deserve silver stars and pretty young wives. Mostly he was mad because after the war his buddies found out he'd done us a favor."

"A *favor?*"

"Yes, a favor. Cadets were not supposed to be married. I don't know who ratted us out, but one way or another Delroy's C.O. found out that we'd eloped as teenagers. I was sixteen, sheltered and sick of being told what good girls could and couldn't do. Delroy was tall, good-looking and smart so it didn't take much of a shove for me to fall for the idea of being married to a pilot. I knew what I was doing when that white man told me to get down on my knees: I was helping the man that I loved. I wanted Delroy to get his chance, a chance to do what he'd dreamt of doing since he was a boy growing up in some no-hope town in Missoura." Connie's voice thinned to a mournful whisper. "And he's never forgiven me."

My mom's tentative tone filled with sympathy. "Is that why you never had children?"

Curious, I popped one eye open in time to see my mother pass Connie a tissue.

"Delroy turned hard after we left Alabama," she bemoaned through her snuffles. "Once in a blue moon, when the stress got too much, we'd be like a couple of stray dogs in heat, but the man I married hasn't made love to me in sixteen years."

She started to cry, and I must have budged, because my mother alertly changed the subject to how much she was looking forward to seeing old friends in New Orleans. It sounded like she had enjoyed exciting times living with a woman called Aunt Jamesie in Faubourg Tremé. Seems the woman had been a Storyville institution (whatever that means), having earned her reputation back in the days when big wheels were made out of men's small vices. According to my mother, Aunt Jamesie's old mansion on Claibourne Avenue had seen more things than would fit in a tabloid-writer's dreams and kept them quiet. What never kept quiet were its walls on a Monday night.

Her five-bedroom boarding house had gained its fame thanks to Aunt Jamesie's soft spot for hard-up musicians. Her dead husband, 'Toothpick' James, had made a fortune selling moonshine from the grooves of their slick-toned horns and she never forgot it. As a result, even though every musician within striking distance of Faubourg Tremé was known to show up for the weekly jam sessions, she could rarely count on more than one or two paying regulars. Not that it mattered. As far as Aunt Jamesie was concerned, the only love in the world came from music and she wasn't shy about letting everyone know she came by it double—because, you see, her grandpa Souchon's second cousin had married a first cousin once removed on Great-Aunt Lila's father's side and his third cousin just happened to be a fellow named Louis Armstrong. Leastways, that was the story Aunt Jamesie told when you met her.

Connie ventured that house must have been swinging come Mardi Gras, but my mom told her, no, that was the one time the place was dead as a tomb. If some broken-down cornet player did drop by the week before Fat Tuesday, it was only to mooch a hot meal then catch some z's before the next all-nighter downtown. If a band musician wasn't working during Carnival, he might as well let the pawnshop sell his horn because he couldn't blow popcorn. So while Aunt Jamesie kept her stew pots simmering with sweet potato soup and jambalaya, she no longer got wound up and worn down by Mardi Gras like she did back when she was up till dawn pouring

Toothpick's bootleg, sweetening lips and shaking her hips while the band had the jammed joint jumpin' to the Sugar Town Strut.

Hearing my mother brag about all the famous musicians she'd met, I couldn't wait to meet this legend, who sounded like the closest thing to a Negro film star or a character plucked from Tom Sawyer's wild imagination. My chance came sooner than I expected, as an hour later we had parked both cars in front of Claibourne Avenue's rambling tree-shaded relic. We had just gotten settled in the living room when my troubles started.

"So you're the talented little fella your momma's so proud of! Come give Aunt Jamesie a hug!"

She had greeted the five of us with a smile that warmed me on sight, and while accepting hugs from people I had only just met was more acceptable than kisses, it was not a practice I was disposed to tolerate. So I surprised both myself and my parents when I violated my principles and crossed to where she sat with her arms outstretched and granted her a brief cuddle. I was even more surprised that although Aunt Jamesie was extremely large she wasn't flabby and her skin smelled fruit sweet, like dear Mrs. Walters, which was saying something, because Mrs. Walters was in her sixties and my mother said that Aunt Jamesie had to be close to her eighties.

Even though she never made it to my list of adopted aunts, Mrs. Walters was the person I most liked to stay with when my mother needed a place to drop me on short notice. I was heartbroken when the government made her move to make room for the freeway that split our new neighborhood in two. Not only did Mrs. Walters have a baby grand piano that put our old upright to shame, her backyard had two guava trees and one with lemons, which meant I could count on getting a glass of fresh lemonade and a slice of buttered bread slathered in her homemade preserves. So it seemed only right when I found out that Aunt Jamesie had a lemon tree out in her garden, seeing that she had a Steinway grand in the middle of her living room.

I figured the music in her voice, and the fact that she still had all her teeth, were the reasons I had let my guard down. Having gambled that a quick hug would do me no permanent harm, I was pulling away to recover my dignity when, instead of releasing me, Aunt Jamesie drew me up onto her lap and left me staring straight down her fur-trimmed robe to her sagging bosom. I nearly passed out.

"I'd ask you play me a little something, but I'm afraid the old girl needs new hammers and I know you piano players hate nothing more than sticky keys." She gave a rumbling laugh, like a tuba-player using vibrato, and clasped me tight as I tried to pull free, afraid she was crazy enough to try and kiss me. "Neva mine, boo" she cooed, feeling me squirm as my eyes fled from her breasts, "you're right, it's too hot for a snuggle. Maybe when I'm up in the hereafter, tappin' my feet with St. Peter, you young-uns will figure out what to do about our vexing climate down South."

She wasn't kidding. It was barely past seven and already my clothes felt clammy. Even when L.A. was covered in fog, the air never felt this heavy. Then again, it had been a long time since anyone dared treat me like I was four years old. I bolted up from her lap as she gave another rumbling chuckle and mercifully turned her attention to Delroy and Connie.

"Now, you just make yourselves to home while Maddy helps me whip up a little *bon gou*." She shot my father a look, "I won't bother askin' Doctor Gardner—you folks eat bacon and eggs?"

When Delroy smiled and said sure do, but she shouldn't go to any extra trouble, she shushed him with a wag of her finger. "What trouble? You're friends of Emerson and Maddy, that makes you like family. Besides, ain't no strangers cross the door at Aunt Jamesie's!"

Although I was pretty sure Aunt Jamesie had a screw loose, I was starting to like her.

Riding over the old woman's token protest, Connie joined my mother to help in the kitchen and Delroy and my father went to stretch out on the room's catty-cornered pink sofas and snatch some shut-eye. I was eager for breakfast, having passed on a second stale doughnut, but Aunt Jamesie was too unpredictable for me to risk hanging around her kitchen. As I thought of something to do in the meantime, I remembered thinking as we arrived at the mansion's tall iron gates that Toothpick James must have really been something. The old house had clearly seen better days, but any place with that many gabled windows and fenced in balconies must have been built for a prince or a duke. I had never been inside a home this big and creepy and the snoop in me decided to see if there were any clues still lying around from whatever went on back in the days my mother said nobody ever talked about.

The first thing that grabbed my attention was that the living-room doors were carved with birds that made me think of the ground doves I used to see roaming in Echo Park. Flipping the switch in the foyer, my eyes blinked towards the sparkling fixture high in the center. It was about two-feet wide and rimmed with fake candles that seemed to be dripping glass tears. With the lights on I could see that the papered walls were faded and and starting to peel and up near the ceiling there were pockmarks from missing paint and plaster, which somehow made sense since it was hard to picture Aunt Jamesie climbing an eighteen foot ladder to fix them.

I was heading for the mahogany staircase to prowl upstairs when I noticed the hall's impressive display of black and white photographs. I zeroed in on the largest one, lording over the center; it featured a man on a flowered float, like the ones I had seen at the Rose Bowl Parade. He reminded me of someone I knew, but it was hard to be sure, as he was dressed in a floppy straw hat topped with feathers and a long grass skirt like the ones bug-eyed cannibals wear chasing white men on television. His face was blackened and shiny and his lips looked almost grotesque, painted like slabs of white blubber. As I stared at the startling clown-face, it took me a while to realize that the man tagged with the sign 'King of the Zulus' was none other than the great Louis Armstrong. I recognized his likeness from one of my father's albums and remembered thinking that, unlike the players in Mr. Rosenblum's youth orchestra who made their trumpets squeal and shout, his sound was like a rich voice singing, which struck me as weird, because when I heard him try to sing on TV it reminded me of the time I misplaced the needle on my record-player and it went skidding across the vinyl. Why people ask a man who can make a trumpet sound like that to sing beats me, unless they're the type that get a kick out of hearing someone scratch up a perfectly good record.

There were other faces on the wall that looked vaguely familiar and a couple were even signed. I moved in for a closer look and a glossy photo grabbed my attention. It was a studio portrait of a girl around the same age as Shayla. She had wavy black hair like my mother and was dressed in a flowing white gown, posed at a grand piano with her left arm resting parallel above the keys, her serious eyes fixed on the camera. I stood there in awe, stunned to be staring at my own Aunt Gwen. I was amazed by how young and winsome she looked, then suddenly felt sad. Not only was I never going to see Shayla again, I was leaving my beloved Aunt Gwen and everything that seemed so vital about the world, like Annette Funicello.

I ordered myself to shake out of it and return to the mission. On a hunch, I put off checking upstairs and went to peek behind the foyer's chiming grandfather clock. When that proved fruitless, I checked the alcove in back of the staircase, but again found no sign of a secret panel. Applying my Nancy Drew Art of Deduction, I reasoned that even if there was no hidden passageway or old skeletons stashed in a walled-in closet, a place this big and decrepit had to be haunted. With that unshakable logic, I started upstairs and nearly jumped out of my skin when the staircase creaked with a groan that sounded one hundred percent human. I wasn't totally convinced there were actual ghosts, but discretion being the better part of valor, I aborted the mission and hightailed it back to the living room.

Madeline had been nervous about mentioning that she loved to sing, but she screwed up her courage and asked Hortense Walker if she could audition for her excellent church choir. Although she felt liberated here in New Orleans, she missed nursing and wanted a greater sense of purpose than tending to Emerson's clothes and taking Sunday care packages to a few neighborhood shut-ins. She had been pleased when Hortense introduced her to the choirmaster, then made anxious when her landlady sang her praises. The choir was packed with voices who could just as easily embellish a staid English anthem as belt out body-swaying, hand-slapping gospel a capella, a feat which astonished her seeing that Hortense Walker referred to jazz as 'that junkie music.'

"There's a real gift to be coaxed from that voice, Mrs. Gardner. You should take such God-given talent more seriously."

She had been so focused on her pitch it took a moment for the verdict to register. "Honestly? You really think so?"

"I never lie when it comes to music."

Feeling the moist hand press hers, Madeline peered into the benevolent amber-brown eyes, praying to find sincerity. Juan Ferrier was the parish's prized boy-genius, so for his eminence to praise her talent felt like the answer to a dream. What she was too new to know was that the conk-haired wunderkind with his swoon-inducing profile inspired far more than the musical ardor of the female congregants. Only in Madeline Gardner's artless mind was Juan Ferrier merely the Liberty Street African Methodist Episcopal Church's brilliant young choirmaster. Feeling flushed, she failed to retrieve her hand.

"You mean I made it? I'm in the choir?"

"Oh, I mean much more than that," Juan assured her, stroking her hand with his long graceful fingers. "I'm talking about pursuing a career."

A second passed while she worried he was poking fun. "You can't mean that, Mr. Ferrier," she said warily, retracting her hand. "Your choir has far richer voices than mine."

"Not richer, just bigger." The moist hand climbed to her arm and gave it a squeeze. "Think of your voice as an excellent wine; it needs time and care to develop." He paused to let her bask in his golden looks while he disarmed her defenses. "Mrs. Gardner, I mean Madeline—" he quickly amended, "you don't mind if I call you Madeline?"

She flushed inside and said 'no.'

"I realize this seems ambitious but it's 1947 and the color line cannot last forever. But there's no rush. We artists are still just buds on the vine in our twenties."

Vanity alone was not what stopped her from correcting him. She wanted no fresh scars for being thirty-three and childless; so when Hortense Walker suggested, with no shortage of acrimony, that, at least for her it was not too late, she decided to encourage her friendly new southern acquaintances to judge her to be as young as they wished. "That's almost too much for me to imagine, Mr. Ferrier." Her flattered cheeks were burning, but since she had made it safely through her twenties, she was not completely undressed from her senses.

"Let me do the imagining," the music director replied, turning more businesslike, "all you need to do now is focus while I guide your training."

"That sounds wonderful— but I'll never have the voice to match a Sister Tharpe or Mahalia—"

Juan stopped her with stomach-rippling laughter. "Heavens no! I wasn't suggesting you sing gospel. What I'm proposing is along the line of Camilla Williams. Classical."

"Oh—"

"But yes, it will take time—the voice is still raw." He searched her face. "If you're willing to do the work, I'm here for you."

Madeline wavered as he held her with his golden-eyed gaze, looking as sure of his prowess as young Apollo. She sensed he knew the secret that urged her to sing; the need to affirm there was more to her than a pretty face, that jealous stares did not make living easy. What she responded to in Juan Ferrier's look was its message that in this promising, confusing place called America, colored aspirations had to be grand to survive or hope's spark would quickly wither and die. So she stilled her heart and met Apollo's eyes. "I'd be willing," she said, her eagerness stopped short by her second thought, "but I'm only in New Orleans for a year. I'd need to discuss it with my husband—"

Ferrier smiled, clasping her hand. "I understand, but don't be discouraged. With that lyric voice it shouldn't take us long."

A mix of joy and trepidation had her spinning as she left the choir room. She had never tasted liquor, not even the wine Miss Dora wanted banned from her wedding, but the way her legs were shaking she feared she would stumble, drunk from her own excitement: a musical wizard just said she had talent!

Her husband was not impressed. "Camilla Williams? He told you that?"

"Can you believe it?"

"Frankly I can't."

"For crying out loud, Emerson! At least you could try and sound happy for me."

"How can I when my wife comes in bubbling like a besotted teenager? The boy is what—twenty-three, tops?"

"Juan Ferrier is not some *boy*—he's had his music performed in Carnegie Hall *and* Europe!"

"That's all good and well, but you're a married woman, not some brainless ingenue to be led down the garden path. Anyway, I'll have finished my studies in a year so the offer is moot."

Madeline sat on the boarding-room's narrow spring bed and waited for her temper to boil down to a simmer. Her urge was to bite Emerson's head off, but Mrs. Walker was home and the last thing she wanted was for the fussbudget to hear them arguing. Hortense had brought up the episode at the police station at least three times and made plain that, not only was she irked that Madeline had won Emerson's instant release by waving her British passport, but also because she had allowed Mundy Peters to call on her twice while her husband was away on campus. Having found his visits to be both unerringly respectful and a charming break from Hortense's judgmental chatter, she decided that, contrary to what she had always been told, not every man with a pleasing compliment is a sexual predator.

Once she had calmed, her fantasy was able to accommodate Emerson's viewpoint. To him, Juan Ferrier was Mozart's Don Giovanni and she was his cherished Donna Anna. A part of her was pleased by his protectiveness for it meant that, despite her fallow womb, he did still love her. Even before he left for college she had been intimidated by Emerson's knowledge, and worried that as a doctor's wife she would feel lost in more erudite circles. Although he never seemed to care when she excused herself once the conversation turned to metaphysical poets or the abuse of Eastern conceptions in German expressionism, she feared her disinterest in such irrelevant matters would set her enemies back whispering that poor Doc deserved better. At least, if she did manage to sing on stage and even once send an audience wild, her husband would not look at her and see more disappointment.

"So you don't want me taking lessons?" Her dejected look shifted to the maplewood bureau to search his face in its mirror.

"What will it cost me?" he mumbled, glancing away.

"Nothing. Juan says he's willing to coach me for free."

Emerson snorted. "For free? Oh, then I know he wants something."

"How would you know what Juan wants?" she snapped, slinging herself backwards onto their bed. "This isn't hopeless little Jamaica. Sure, they've got a line that's tough to cross—but it's a big country with millions like us. Here, you pull for one, you're pulling for all. Folks don't tear each other down, they help each other."

"And I'm sure young Juan will help himself while he's at it."

Madeline knit her arms across her chest and aimed her indignance at the ceiling. "You're impossible! Well, I'm not a child. I don't need your permission."

"Fine, do as you like—who can stop you?"

"It would be nice to have a husband willing to support me."

"Support you?" Emerson sent a tired look around the windowless room scarcely larger than his cell at the station. "That's why I'm here—so you can brag that you married a doctor."

Madeline launched at him fiercely, but kept her snarl to a whisper. "Don't you dare put that burden on me! You're the one who always dreamed about becoming a doctor. I sacrificed to get you this far, and I'll keep on sacrificing, because that's the deal I made when I married you!"

I forgave Aunt Jamesie her early transgressions the minute I tasted one of her hot beignets. The way she hopped up and down from the table it was hard to believe she was pushing her eighties. Happily, age demanded respect, so my parents barely put up a fight when she insisted on frying me a second batch and sprinkling on extra powdered sugar. Since our relationship was now on a hugging basis, I felt entitled to ask the question that had been bugging me all through breakfast.

"Aunt Jamesie?"

"Yes, boo?"

"Why is my Aunt Gwen's picture on your wall?"

Before she could answer, a gravelly voice boomed, "good morning, fellow travelers!"

"It's about time you stirred!" Aunt Jamesie scolded, as my mother bounced up from her seat like a giddy teenager.

"Mundy Peters! We didn't know you'd be here!"

"C'mon now, Miss Madeline! You know I'd swim the breadth of the Mississippi to see the world-champion melon eater!"

I glared at the tall black man embracing my mother, annoyed by his big, rasping voice and gleaming-white teeth and the fact that he had bumped me off my question. I glanced at my father but he did not seem to care, which I found perplexing, seeing that he was the only man I'd ever seen hug my mother, and as far as I could remember, even that had been only once. There was definitely something odd that happened to people at Aunt Jamesie's.

"Now y'all pipe down!" Aunt Jamesie commanded when my mother started gabbing to the Angells about how she met 'this dauntless rascal' and Mundy Peters tried to defend himself. "Boy, quit your alibiing and say hello to our miracle baby!"

The sweet dough in my mouth turned sour. Figures. Just when you think it's time to forgive and forget, grown-ups make the same mistake all over again. Baby? Well, this time I would go down fighting. No way was that big lug getting a hug. Luckily, it turned out the guy was not crazy.

"Hey there, my man!" Mundy exclaimed, apparently surprised that with all his drooling over my mother, he had failed to see me. "So you're Maddy's long awaited package. Edmund Peters—pleased to meet you!" He stretched to greet me like a gentleman, so I said 'likewise' and shook his hand. Sanity restored.

Aunt Jamesie turned to me, grinning. "So, you were asking me why I had Gwennie's picture up on my wall. Your godmother is my grandniece, and Mundy here is her first cousin once removed. So you see? We're all family."

Okay, now things were starting to make more sense. I just wished my parents had warned me.

The women got up to fix Mundy's breakfast and he sat down next to my father and addressed me across the table. "Cousin Gwen tells me you're quite a little musician." The way he said it, I wasn't sure if it was a compliment or if he was making fun of me. "You should have heard her in her day. Your godmother was something special."

"I wish she hadn't given it up, seeing how much she put into it," Aunt Jamesie called out above the fried dough sizzling on her stove.

"You can only take so much frustration," my mother observed, coming back from the kitchen with a pot of fresh-brewed coffee. "Back then poor Gwen had two strikes against her—being colored and being a woman."

"As if now is any different," my father muttered, halting her hand from refilling his cup.

"I told Gwennie she should have dumped that long-haired stuff for jazz," Mundy grumbled. "Didn't do the Hawk no harm. In fact, it freed him."

Delroy nodded. "Music is music. But I can't take much classical. Too darn dreary."

Dreary? Had he never listened to Beethoven? I was about to put in my two cents then thought about Louis Armstrong dressed up like a Zulu and decided that until I got a handle on these people's habits it was better to keep my mouth shut.

"The only women in jazz I know of are singers or strippers," Aunt Jamesie announced as she followed Connie back in from the kitchen. "Not that stripping is the worst thing a woman is forced to do," she added, sucking her teeth. "Anyway, our Gwen wasn't cut out for that lifestyle—hopping from town to town, struggling to make ends meet, hoping for that big break." She set a plate of warm beignets on the table. "Can you picture Miss Prim and Proper playing some black and tan joint while her drummer's in the back room thumbing smack up his nose? Please. My grandniece comes from the respectable side of the family."

"You mean the *light* side of the family," said Mundy.

Delroy laughed. "Yup, we know you New Orleans folk *love* making that *café-au-lait.*"

"You ain't lying," Aunt Jamesie chuckled. "But sneakin' in the back door don't mean you come out respectable."

Mundy said something about a paper bag test that I found more than a little bit nuts and all of a sudden the discussion turned hot over what did or did not constitute being respectable with Connie and my mother taking up positions contrary to Mundy and Delroy and Aunt Jamesie jumping between either side. None of it made much sense to me, especially when my mother shouted down Delroy for saying she was the only one here light enough to pass as respectable in dear old Dixie. My dad, who had hardly said a word, finally cooled things off saying that he was upset to see the streets with all that piled up garbage and abandoned homes. "This neighborhood was never on top but it had its charms. Now it's like a slum that's lost hope."

"Taxation without representation," Delroy proclaimed. "This is the result."

Mundy shook his head, gulping a piece of bacon. "Can't reap gold from turnips. The war over in Europe changed everything. Sure, times were hard before that, but hard times have a way of bringing folks together. Some even start looking past color. The war stopped all that. You know who paid the price to stop Mr. Hitler? The working man."

Delroy was incredulous. "How you reckon?"

"You know how many Red Russians died in that war? Thirty million. Think about that for a minute," Mundy whispered. "That would be like wiping out almost a quarter of the U.S. population. I'm not saying they had a perfect system, but you don't come out the same after something like that."

Delroy still didn't buy it. "The commies ain't the solution. Our problem is the Man don't want us getting up off our knees and have to start calling us Mister and Missus, like he had to with the Jews and I-talians. He wants his slaves back."

"I'm not sayin' no different. I'm sayin', just like George Washington's boys needed the French, we're gonna need help. That's why there's a movement!" Mundy's words blared abruptly, like artillery fire. "Dammit, they owe us! We put our asses on the line for this country. I don't care what it takes. I ain't never going back!"

I sat listening to my heart thump as the grown-ups just sat there, like they were staring at ghosts. Finally Aunt Jamesie quipped that she was too old to pick cotton and too thickheaded to learn, but a chance to vote without having to figure out how in the devil she was supposed to 'write forwards, backwards' would suit her nicely. My mother laughed about how it took real cunning to come up with questions that had no right answers adding, "it's a shame the mockery these diehard confederates are willing to make of this democracy." Connie muttered, 'Amen, sister!' and everyone nodded, except my father, who'd sniggered when my mom said 'democracy.' He had pretty much withdrawn from the whole conversation, which did not surprise me. He always got quiet when my mother started talking politics, which happened a lot last year when she was constantly complaining about having to deal with the city council and the parent-teacher committee. When it came to politics, I had a hunch that whatever he wanted to say was not something he wanted me to hear.

My mother's disposition abruptly more positive, she beamed across at Mundy. "I was so moved when you wrote and told me you were registering folks to vote. You're being awfully brave. How does your wife feel about it?"

Peters was as tall as Delroy Angell and twice as thick, so it surprised me to see him shrink.

"Dorothy worries about our kids—you know—if something happens. I told her it's because of our kids that we're doing it. She ain't too pleased, but she'll stand by me."

My mother sent my dad a sidelong glance. "Good for her! I hope one day I'll get to meet your whole family."

"Too bad y'all got a boat to catch," Aunt Jamesie lamented. "Dorothy will be down here next month. She promised to ride with me for that civil rights march up in Washington."

Delroy looked as if breakfast had upset his stomach. "Don't tell me you buy that Martin King turn-the-other-cheek foolery!"

"Oh, knock it off, Delroy!" Connie barked and everyone froze. I realized then I had never heard Connie raise her voice. It must have shocked her too, because she straightaway went back to sounding like her soft, sweet self. "Excuse my husband, Aunt

Jamesie. Delroy busts a spleen whenever someone brings up Reverend King. I think it's wonderful what he's doing. Mundy's right that it's worth the sacrifice. If we can all just keep it together, the young folks will change this country."

Delroy looked like a dog waiting to be punished. "Beg pardon, Miss Jamesie. That was not fittin' of me—"

"Oh, quit yer grovelin'!" the old woman growled. "I've dealt with enough scoundrels who'd as soon cut you as look at you to get my nose out of joint because a man speaks his mind. Maybe one day when I'm up there doin' the hoochie-coochie for St. Peter, I'll look down at this same old mess and say, Jamesie you were a right old fool. But even fools got a right to dream."

Emerson was in better spirits as he left campus and headed home. He had been wary about pointing out the errors in his textbook, but after a stare of surprise, the biochemistry professor had agreed to consider his proofs and seemed genuinely appreciative. While he felt more sure of himself now that Madeline was here, he decided after his run-in with New Orleans' finest to ask Mundy Peters to list the neighborhoods he should make sure and stay clear of. Unlike last Christmas, when being away from his wife had worn on him to the point where it was hard to focus on his studies, he was looking forward to the holidays. It was a comfort seeing her there every night, waiting to greet him with the same bright-eyed impatience, so after thinking it over, he was pleased with himself for pretending not to have heard that Madeline was taking lessons with Juan Ferrier in secret.

He might not have felt so smug had he known why Hortense Walker gave him that loaded look when she mentioned it. He might have noticed that the warmth she had shown his wife in the summer had turned glacial since before Thanksgiving. Although he could sense that something had changed, he attributed it to the fact that Hortense had taken advantage of Madeline's offer to help with the household chores to work half-days at the Canal Street fish market. Were it not for his high-minded self-confidence, he might have been more in tune with the way coarser minds run and realized that he was married to a creole beauty who looked ten years his junior and, compared to Juan Ferrier, he was nothing to look at. For women like Hortense Walker, such pairings simply did not add up in a world where black was never beautiful and long-haired Eve was in league with the serpent. As for Lem, what better reason could a worn-down dried-up grunt have for rushing home after work than the chance for some charming company while the wife was out boning flounder.

Emerson's first inkling of trouble was finding the shotgun's front door open. He raced through the Walkers' empty bedroom and straight out to the yard where Lem was pacing in circles, arms crossed above his head, mewling that they had done nothing wrong. Before he could ask what in God's name had happened, his wife came dashing across the yard with Hortense hot on her heels, hoisting her cleaver. Time seemed to slow as he watched Madeline stumble an instant before the blade ripped the yellow cotton blouse, exposing her cut shoulder. He yelled 'stop!' just as she spun away from a second vicious swipe and lunged for her attacker's knees.

The dental bridge flew out of Hortense's mouth as she fell on her rump and lost hold of the cleaver. Cat-quick, Madeline pounced. Snatching fistfuls of hair, she was about to slam Hortense's head on the ground when Emerson rushed in to drag her off. He was still struggling to hold her back when Lem came staggering up, babbling about needles and thread. He ignored him and clutched up his wife as she stretched, trying to claw Hortense's eyes out. "Come, we need to stop that bleeding." He was amazed to hear his voice sound calm considering the vise grabbing his chest as he held her close and felt her tremble when she slumped against him.

He turned to steer them inside and Hortense paused from searching the grass for her dentures to bellow after Madeline from her hands and knees. "Succubus! Jezebel! Get thy devil self out of my house!"

Lem had his head in his hands, blubbering incoherently about his pants until Hortense silenced him with a look charged with mayhem. "As for you, Lem Walker—we'll see what's left of you when I'm done whuppin' your shameless behind."

Emerson eased his shaken wife onto their bed and freed her gingerly from the blood soaked blouse. Her body no longer trembled, but her blank look showed that she was in shock as he pressed a cloth to her wounded shoulder. As he waited for the bleeding to slow, he heard Hortense out in the yard cursing at Lem who was nobly barring her way, braving her wrath. He was grateful and surprised that the man had found the strength and presence of mind to make her cool off outside and felt the tightness in his chest subside as the blood-flow slowed enough for him to assess the extent of Maddy's injury. The cleaver had sliced four inches of flesh, breaking several minor blood vessels, but thankfully missed her axillary artery; though deeper than he could have hoped, at worst, she had suffered only mild neurapraxia.

Madeline winced and bit her lip as he daubed the gash with iodine from his first-aid bag in the bureau drawer. "I knew there was a reason I married a pharmacist," she joked, as he prepared a bandage. "Good thing you got home when you did, or one of us would be lying out there dead."

"What in the world went on with the two of you?" he asked, tenderly dressing the gash on her shoulder.

Madeline was about to throw up her arms then stopped with a grimace. "The woman needs her head checked. She cornered me out in the washroom, screaming how dare I come in her house and bait her husband." Madeline jeered disdainfully. "Can you imagine? Me chasing after that scrawny old drunk? I wanted to say, woman, you're either joking or out of your mind until she started quoting Scriptures about the harlot's lips dripping honey. That's when I ducked and ran out of there quick! She was just waiting for me to turn and confront her so she could slash my face."

Emerson slung a comforting arm lightly around her waist. "What do you think put that crazy idea in her head?" he asked, then paused when Lem knocked on their half-open door and peeked inside. He looked pale and dead sober.

"It's safe now," he whispered. "Sorry about all this. I didn't figure on her getting home so early."

Madeline grew incensed. "What does your wife getting home early have to do with anything?"

Lem lowered his head and flashed her a meek look. "I only imposed on you because Hortense don't much hanker to it now that her eyesight's goin' and I heard you tellin' her that a little sewing helps you relax." When Madeline kept staring at him hard, he shifted his penitence to Emerson. "Your wife was right gracious about it. She told me to just leave them on the bed and she'd hem for me when she was done with her washing."

"That's what got Hortense so upset she wanted to filet my wife? You asking her to mend your pants?"

Lem confessed that was just the half of it. "Hortense is not a vicious person. Sometimes your cup just overflows. Today her supervisor told her he had to let her go. Seems he thought she was taking too long to bone one fish. She was already seeing red when she came in and saw my trousers out on your bed. And to make things worse the heat had me drawing a sweat, so I was in the kitchen cooling off in my drawers. That's when she came stompin' in haulin' her grievance, shoutin' about us carryin' on behind her back. I couldn't sneak a word in edgewise before she tossed the pants in my face and ran out with that cleaver."

Emerson could not decide if it was shame or hatred Hortense was hiding, but she gave no reaction when he announced that they would be leaving as soon as they could find new lodgings. It seemed best for all concerned, although Lem kept begging them to stay. 'Don't mind Hortense. She'll come around. She knows you did nothing wrong!'

For Maddy, the embarassing ordeal was too much. For weeks afterwards she hardly slept but, as Emerson came to suspect, it was not due to the pain in her shoulder. When he pressed her, she finally explained that Juan Ferrier had taken it as an insult when she told him they would no longer be attending church.

"He told me I needed to thicken my skin if I expect to have a singing career. That fitting in someplace new is never easy." She moaned, her head bowed from shame. "I had to just stand there. I couldn't tell him why—"

What she failed to add was that from well before Thanksgiving several women in her choir had begun to openly resent the attention she was getting from their revered director. Nor did she share the fact that the bread pudding she had struggled to prepare for the pre-Christmas party had been left untouched after Hortense Walker made a point of testing the middle with her finger then lamenting that it was a pity such a pretty pudding turned out to be so dry, or that after today's rehearsal Juan Ferrier had pulled her aside to ask if it was true that she was secretly seeing an amorous G.I. As a result, Emerson was left scrambling after he returned late from the library to find her packing their belongings, swearing she would not spend one more night under that back-stabbing harridan's roof.

Aunt Jamesie thought it made more sense for the Angells to spend the night and leave refreshed in the morning, but Delroy wanted to get to Tuscaloosa by evening as he had an appointment up in Montgomery the following day. "Well, if you're dead set on doing more driving, you're not setting foot out of this house before you dodo."

"She means they should get some sleep," my mother explained while I picked my jaw back up from the floor.

So, I'd been right the first time. The old woman *did* have a screw loose!

The Angells were promptly hustled upstairs to bed and after Mundy finished eating, he asked my dad if he could talk with him privately. My mother wanted me to help with the dishes but Aunt Jamesie was quick to save me. "Oh, let my poor boo be. The child needs to stretch his legs after y'all had him cramped in that car all night. Anyway, now that your husband's not around, you can fill me in on what that busy head of yours has been up to the last fifteen years."

Screw loose or not, Aunt Jamesie was a-okay with me.

With the reigning power now a dependable ally, I shored up my nerve and resumed the hunt, reminding myself that while old mansions definitely had secrets, ghosts were only in books and on TV. Sure enough, the stairs did not creak, maybe because I raced up them two at a time. The Angells had been tucked in the west-most bedroom, so I turned east at the top of the stairs and listened for voices. I stuck my ear against the faded oak door at the end then held my breath and tested the knob—open! The light was dim, so I got on my hands and knees and scouted the floor for shoes, in case someone was inside sleeping. All clear—I was in!

Not wanting to flip on the light and attract attention, I parted the curtains and let in more of the sunlight filtering through the garden's leafy trees. There were half-filled packing cartons ranged around the brass-framed bed with an open box sitting out on the covers. From the looks of it, either someone had gathered up a bunch of old stuff to throw out, or was in the middle of moving. I almost shouted and gave myself away. Holy Smokes! Pay-dirt!

Fingers quivering, I reached for the hilt sticking out from the box and felt the smoothed wood grip. A rush of blood thumped to my skull as I drew the dagger from its gem-studded sheath and saw the double-edged blade nearly as long as my forearm. It could have belonged to Jim Bowie himself—it had to be at least a hundred years old! The black dagger felt deadly gripped in my hand—and scarily heavy.

I swiped it through the air like a sword and pretended I was Robin Hood fighting my way into Nottingham Castle. When I'd saved Maid Marion and had enough playacting, I slipped the long knife back in its scabbard and saw there was a stuffed manila envelope lying beneath it. More curious than ever, I undid the flap on the unsealed back. Inside were a bunch of old newspaper and magazine clippings gone yellow with age. Most seemed to be short write-ups about some dead musician, and I recognized the name of a banjo player from his signed photo hanging on the wall downstairs. I was about to put them all back when I saw that one of the notices had been underlined: The body of Manny 'Toothpick' James, reported to be one of the wealthiest negroes in the New Orleans underworld, was found in the woods near Natchez, Mississippi. The sheriff could not confirm the cause of death.

I stuffed it quickly back inside the envelope along with the others thinking, my mom wasn't kidding—Aunt Jamesie *had* been married to a gangster! I felt guilty snooping through her things, but if that old tarnished Bowie knife had belonged to her husband, these cartons promised treasures no kid could resist.

I dove back in hoping for another great find and pulled out a small rectangular case like the ones for eyeglasses. Inside were a pair of old copper coins, each around the size of a fifty-cent piece. The first one showed a shackled man on his knees with his arms stretched up to heaven inside lettering too worn for me to make out the words. The second was of a woman, also on her knees, encircled by the partially rubbed out question, 'AM I NO- A —MAN & – SISTER?' On its back it said 'LIBERTY 1838' and was ringed with the faint inscription I was pretty sure spelled, 'UNITED STATES OF AMERICA.'

I put back the coins wondering if they had been used like actual money and remembered what Delroy had said about people like us being traded like cattle to make men like Bowie rich. My inner detective telling me all this stuff was somehow related, I dug further down and found a bunch of postcards tied inside a thick rubber band buried near the bottom. I was still staring at the one on top when I heard my mom and Aunt Jamesie out in the hall. My pounding chest felt ready to crack hearing their voices coming closer.

"Child, I wouldn't stand for it either, but you know that's not Emerson. He's feeling the strain. These are soul-testing times."

"It's not just his anger, Aunt Jamesie. Things were looking bright for me in California. I don't want to give that all up to go back and start over. He says *I'm* the one being selfish."

"Honey, once a man latches on to a notion, he's like a starving dog and his bone. You could knock him in the head with a two by four and he wouldn't give it up."

The blood was thudding in my ears too loudly for me to judge how close they were to the door. I thought about hiding under the bed, but before I could budge, in walked Aunt Jamesie with my mother right behind her.

"So, this is where you'd gotten to! Did Aunt Jamesie give you permission to go through her things?"

I panicked and dropped the postcard. Disaster had struck the last time my mother used that tone.

"You leave boo be!" Aunt Jamesie ordered. "If there's something he shouldn't have found, then I shouldn't have left it lying around." She smiled and tossed me a wink. "Besides, there ain't no secrets between us."

The color drained from my mother's face and Aunt Jamesie clapped a hand to her mouth as she followed her eyes. I thought my chest would explode.

"I'm going to brain that Mundy!" Aunt Jamesie declared, picking the postcard up from the floor. "He's been helping me sort through all the junk I let pile up inside this old house. You'd think a grown man would have sense enough to know what needs hiding."

My mother turned on me as if she had not heard her. "Son, get over here right now! You and I need to talk."

Her tight voice trembled, but I couldn't tell if she was angry or scared. Probably because I had never heard her sound scared.

"Don't you go distressing my boo," Aunt Jamesie told her gently. "No need making a mountain over it."

"If Emerson finds out—"

"Oh, shush! You're still just wound up from what y'all have been facing. You go catch up on some sleep and leave this to Aunt Jamesie. Go on—shoo! I'll talk to the boy."

My mother started to give in, then stalled. "You sure? It's the last thing I need—"

"Now, Maddy, I *said* don't fret. You go on along and get some rest." My trusty defender smiled down at me again. "Boo and I are going to work it all out."

When my mother was gone, Aunt Jamesie put the postcard back with the others and shoved the box aside to make room on the bed. She sat down and told me to come sit on her lap. Seeing she may have just saved my hide from a whipping, I didn't put up a fuss. Settling me on her massive thighs, she asked how I felt seeing that postcard. I said it made me want to throw up. I wanted to ask how could anyone smile looking at something like that, much less want to put it on a postcard, but I was too upset wondering where it came from and why she had all those creepy postcards in the first place. She must have read my mind because she asked if I'd ever been so upset that I couldn't sleep. I told her yes, when I was little and had a nightmare that my pet turtle was being crushed in the jaws of a tiger. She rocked me on her lap and asked if I had ever been hurt real bad.

I said once, when I fell on the playground and the cut went clear to the bone. She pointed to the shiny scar on my knee the size of a nickel and asked if that was it. 'Do you ever admire it?' I thought it was a pretty strange question—it wasn't like watching a man get hung from a tree was something to gloat about—but seeing that I owed Aunt Jamesie big-time, even if she was a bit touched in the head, I shrugged and said, 'maybe sometimes—in a way, I guess—' She wanted to know if I'd ever laughed when I was really afraid. I said no, that would be stupid. She chuckled and said she had seen grown men laugh when they were scared. I told her the white people laughing did not look scared to me and she said that some nightmares can scare good folks stupid. I looked at her and asked why she kept all those pictures if she thought they were dumb and she smiled and said that, when I got to be as old as she was, I would understand that the most hurtful things in life are the things we try to overcome but can never forget.

Emerson hated to admit it but Mundy Peters had been their savior once again. The former soldier was back in town, hopping mad and spitting nails after he and his buddy had wandered from Hattiesburg to Kalamazoo and failed to get accepted to any of the government's new training programs meant to help returning G.I.s. The minute he learned why Madeline was desperate to move, he had them pack their bags and follow him to his great-aunt's home on Claibourne Avenue. The sixty-year-old ex-Parisian Garden hoofer had received them at one in the afternoon dressed in a leopard-print robe and high-heeled slippers. After a round of extended hugs, Madeline made a flustered attempt to explain how they had come to be homeless. The five-foot-ten languid fireball cut her short to say that, while she believed in God, she was not a good Christian, but if Mundy thought his friends were able to forgive minor sins, they could stay as long as they liked. When Emerson inquired about the rent, the woman who insisted they call her Aunt Jamesie had stopped him with the flat of her raised hand, saying she never discussed business before her breakfast, so what could she fix them to eat?

Mundy Peters had grinned ear to ear the whole time while Madeline stood in speechless relief.

Aunt Jamesie's New Year's Eve shindig proved to be an eye-opening though misleading introduction to what 1948 had in store for the immigrant couple. For two unworldly Jamaicans raised in Bible-abiding homes, an evening spent among old Storyville musicians was like discovering Paris in Henry Miller's *Tropic of Cancer*. It had taken them hours to acclimatize to the lingo and had Mundy not been there to translate, they might never have grasped why a *hep cat* couldn't *get down* without a *hard hitter*, or how a Tenderloin legend who started out playing *gutbuckets* for a *buck and a bit* a night, rose to pulling a couple of *Cees* each week from the hottest *jukes* before the moral crusaders and their tin-eared do-gooders set him back to where a month that fetched sixty *clams* was a month to splurge on some Cuban *hooch* and a *henhouse trim*.

By three in the morning, the band had thrown in the towel, tired of their snowy-haired drummer dragging the beat trying to eyeball-dally Aunt Jamesie. Too sloshed to be bothered, she swung her big hips past the skin-beater's glances and tried to get her new housemates to 'loosen up and live a little.' Emerson deftly evaded the frothy bottle of champagne asking how it was she had gotten to know so many top-notch musicians.

"Honey, if my dead husband hadn't grown up with a bunch of the fellas you see here he would never have shoved his way to the top. Manny had bigger ambitions than hawking bootleg for the rest of his life and he figured out quick that to strike it rich he needed the best black musicians just as sure as they needed him." She took a swig from her bottle then waved it tipsily around the room. "What y'all seen here tonight ain't half what I knew before we all got sunk by that damned Depression. Those who still had the gusto to blow left to shuffle between St. Louey and Chi*cah*go, but trust me—" she burbled an inch from Emerson's face, "their hearts stayed right here in New Orleans."

As the year unfolded and vagabond musicians kept showing up at Aunt Jamesie's, listening to the big house ring with impromptu sessions, Madeline realized how much she missed singing. Juan Ferrier had put aside his injured pride and urged her to continue, but she did not think it proper for him to have gone on teaching her for free when she was no longer part of his choir. She had held off approaching Emerson after his jubilation at India finally shaking free crashed into despair when Gandhi was murdered. She had never shared his belief that the demise of the British Empire would usher in a less violent, more tolerant world, but she was hurt when he chose to deal with his disillusionment by staying out late every night tutoring classmates. She put on a face not wanting to show that she was feeling neglected, and resisted asking him to pay for her singing lessons, knowing they might need every penny to get him through medical school. So rather than sit home all day moping, she decided to look for a part-time job.

Emerson quickly vetoed her idea. "I don't care that you used to work in the worst parts of Kingston. You haven't got a clue. A woman out alone in this town is asking for trouble."

"Baloney! I saw a woman walking out on her own when I went shopping with Aunt Jamesie, and would you believe it? —she looked perfectly fine."

"Make fun as much as you like. You're not getting a job and that's final."

"Really? We'll see about that!"

Despite the newspapers' encouraging list of job offerings, trying to land one was downright dispiriting. After searching for a week, the only place willing to hire her had been a stationery store she spotted with a Help Wanted sign in the window. The visored proprietor sat at one of the dim room's two large desks separated by a standing lamp and a four-foot-tall mother-in-law tongue. There was not a card nor envelope in sight. Told her job entailed answering the phone and writing down numbers, she put two and two together and walked straight back out.

She hated being dictated to, but when she just managed to twist free from a zoot-suited masher trying to sweet-talk her into an alley, she remembered the sign at the depot and realized Emerson was right; she had not been here long enough to be wandering alone across the city. It disappointed her that, for all its refreshing liberties, a web of taboos and implicit constraints added to the cost of its indulgences. New Orleans had jazz, which meant it disguised riddles inside its syncopated rhythms and dared the greenhorns to figure things out. Humbled, she turned to Aunt Jamesie.

"Sorry, *ma chérie*. Unless you think your husband won't mind you scrubbing toilets, you'll have a tough time finding work in this town. I have an old sewing machine, if you're handy with needle and thread, but I can't say I'll be much help getting you customers. Most of the folks I know are either too old or too broke to be ordering new clothes."

That's when it hit her. The musicians she'd met were already champing at the bit for the start of Mardi Gras. And what was every fun-loving soul in town eager to have in time for Carnival? A costume!

Aunt Jamesie grinned. "Now you're getting the swing."

By the third week in January, she had cornered enough of Mundy's friends and Emerson's classmates to pin down three orders. She was out selecting fabrics when she felt the soreness, and it was not in her damaged shoulder. The midwife was almost sure, but Madeline stayed wary and hurried home to view herself in the mirror. Contemplating the uneasy woman facing her stark-naked, she watched as she prayerfully raised her hands and cupped her breasts, discovering them so sublimely full and tender, but only able to sense one deep ache at a time, did not feel the tears she saw streaming down her cheeks. At last! *At last!* she could weep, praise Jesus! and Dr. Joseph's incredible hands. See that, Little Miss Big Head? God did not curse you to be a failure.

She earned twenty six dollars and forty cents for the pirate's vest and bandana, the grass skirt and the harlequin outfit, but confirmed of her hopes, she forgot about her singing lessons and spent the rest of Epiphany learning to knit. Fat Tuesday arrived and the big parade streamed right up Claibourne Avenue, its lusty krewes, first white, then black, advancing like time-traveling swing-bands invading Rome on a pagan feast day. Mundy Peters had realized his childhood dream to march with the Zulus and proud Aunt Jamesie waved from her gate, stately and sequined like a burlesque queen as he filed by in his grass skirt and beads, tossing coins to the clamorous imploring crowd with his face greased black and his lips chalked white.

The expectant couple observed it all from their bedroom's upstairs balcony, leading Emerson to say that he had never seen such a maniacal display and Madeline to rue that it was sad not being able to enjoy such fun.

Not since her preschool days playing with Charlie Chaplin had she felt so complete. After a rough start, her life in New Orleans was playing out as a cautiously-wished-for bequest. She had been both surprised and a little put off when Aunt Jamesie responded by fussing over her like an anxious mother hen. In her more peaceful frame of mind, she welcomed Lent's drop in excess, content to sit and knit in the garden as the tides of roaming musicians ebbed and the sun came closer. How could she not be content now that spring was in the air and Life was giving her so much to look forward to? With Emerson set to graduate, the timing was perfect! Not only had her calculations made her certain that, come summer, she would be blessed with a son, it meant she would be back on her feet before Emerson went off to medical school. But as those gloomy church ladies back home loved to say, 'Man proposes and God disposes.' Perhaps from the strain of his mother's excitement or an impatience to please, the child failed to follow his tidy schedule and started kicking in May.

She drew on her well of experience and stayed calm, reassuring her fretful husband and soothing Aunt Jamesie who seemed on the verge of a nervous breakdown. On the mad dash to the hospital, she strained her lungs with long, deep breaths, slowed her contractions through gritted teeth and defied the pain. The valiant child struggled and after great effort, finally emerged to receive his paeans. But sadly, his whole heart was never in it. In Latin, such a condition is known as *ductus arteriosus*, and at the start of one's life it is perfectly normal. A romantic would say it was wrong that before you've lost your first love, or even been kissed, there can be a gaping hole in your heart, but from the moment you are born, there it is, right between your aorta and pulmonary artery, and either you close it or you end up breathing blood. That's a big challenge when you're tiny and still weary from fighting to live before your time.

The sallow visage, framed in her somber habit, was a blur

behind Madeline's harsh tears. "I'm so sorry, Mrs. Gardner. The sisters and I did all that we could."

The sun was back full blast as we set off from New Orleans the following morning. Aunt Jamesie did not smile when I hugged her goodbye. I knew she wasn't happy about us leaving, but there was a whole lot more to it than that. No one seemed to have had much to say the previous afternoon, so I'd been surprised that Delroy and Connie had changed their minds and stayed for dinner when Mundy was forced to leave on account of an emergency. There had been homemade buttermilk biscuits and my favorite vegetable patties, so even though it felt wrong to have my usual appetite, I made sure to be polite and praise Aunt Jamesie's cooking, only for her to laugh and say, 'thank you, boo, but your mother made them fritters. Us regular old carnivores are stuck with my jambalaya.' The Angells laughed and said it was perfectly fine with them, but it was the last time anyone felt like laughing.

Everyone's mood had turned so glum, I actually wished I was back on Aunt Jamesie's lap listening to more of the amazing stories she'd shared after packing away those terrible postcards. Turned out her husband was nicknamed 'Toothpick' for that long pointed dagger I had found so intriguing. When he started making serious dough selling moonshine from his milk-wagon, Manny bought it from a repentant patroller and kept it holstered inside his jacket. Word was he could drop a gunslinger at twenty paces before he could draw a bead and pull the trigger. After making me swear not to tell my parents, Aunt Jamesie confessed that her husband had been forced to kill a man, that in those days it was do or die, but that even though it was self-defense, Manny always regretted it. She told me that after they opened their snazzy café, he put his knife away for good. He hung on to his gun, but only to threaten, as he never kept it loaded. When I suggested that was dumb she shook her head and said, 'no, boo, my Manny wasn't dumb, but there were twenty years between us and by the time we met, like most men who made themselves something out of nothing, he had made a wagonload of enemies. He knew that, one way or another, he was getting close to that call from St. Peter, and he didn't want anyone hunting his wife for revenge.' She said he had made her promise that, no matter how it happened, she wasn't to cramp her nature and forget all their good times together. I asked her if Manny was one of the men hanging from a tree in those awful postcards and she hugged me tight with a misty look but didn't answer.

Mundy Peters had been in the kitchen talking on the telephone when I wandered back downstairs after Aunt Jamesie said she needed to freshen up before it was time to start making dinner. With my parents and the Angells still upstairs resting, I thought about exploring the garden but changed my mind when I saw it was raining. I could not stop thinking about Aunt Jamesie's stories from back in the teens and twenties, wondering if she was one of those grown-ups who love to exaggerate, or if it really was true that some of the richest men in New Orleans would offer her rubies and pearls just to boogie-woogie, that she used to babysit Louis Armstrong, who was mad for her red beans and rice, and that the reason he played such a sweet trumpet was because, from the time he was a tyke, the other showgirls took to calling him their little Dippermouth and would brush his lips with kisses. The photo display on her wall told me that at least half of it was probably on the level. Still, it was hard to believe that musicians as famous as Satchmo and Nat King Cole used to stay in this creaky old house because none of the hotels downtown would take them in. The craziness of it all left me thinking there must be some parallel world where my parents and their friends used to go before I was born; a world a lot more colorful than the one I knew, but somewhere no one dared to show on TV—it was almost as if someone in charge had decided that anyone who stayed there too long became untouchable.

"Good for you, boo! A boy who loves to read is bound to go places."

Aunt Jamesie had given me a great big smile when she came down fully dressed and saw me sitting alone in the living room, finishing my book on Hannibal. I told her, yes, please, when she offered to make me a glass of her slow-sugar lemonade. Now that we were buddies, I decided Aunt Jamesie wasn't crazy, just lonely, and lonely people needed hugs. I knew that, because after outgrowing all three of my invisible playmates, I had felt lonely myself. That lousy day also turned out to be the last time I got to play with Shayla. She had me trapped in her bedroom closet and was tickling me to tears when her father heard me gasping between squeals of laughter and sent me home. I was miserable that whole week until my dad gave me hug and explained what growing winsome meant. I was relieved to know it had not been my fault—life was simply not as fair as I thought it was.

I was still mourning Hannibal's defeat and the Romans' decision to banish him from Carthage, when Aunt Jamesie cried out, "Dear God!" Her shriek must have carried upstairs because my parents and the Angells were all racing downstairs seconds after I closed my book and rushed for the kitchen. Mundy had his arm around her trying to hush Aunt Jamesie's sobs when my father ordered me upstairs to take a nap.

"But I'm not sleepy!"

"Then go read a book."

"I just finished it."

"Son, please—there are some serious matters the grown-ups need to discuss—"

Much like my mother when she caught me with those postcards, he didn't seem angry as much as distressed.

Mundy thought I should stay. "Some of the kids they turned those hoses on were younger than your son."

I had no idea what he was talking about, but I was disappointed to hear Delroy side with my father. "I've got to agree with Emerson on this one. We shouldn't be letting little kids fight our battles."

My mother began to put a word in, then made up her face when Aunt Jamesie rode over her and settled the matter. "Emerson is his father, he gets to decide. Boo, you go on upstairs, like Daddy told you. There's a book you can read up in the room we were in. It's called *Black Boy*. You and I can talk about this later."

Seeing that the odds were stacked against me, I sulked upstairs. Normally I would have been eager to plunge into a new book, but I was dying to know about this world where children my age fought battles to help grown-ups. The kitchen was in the opposite wing from the room with the boxes, so I ducked left at the top of the stairs and crept back across the hall, listening for voices. When they seemed the loudest just outside an upstairs bathroom, I slipped inside and hunkered by the heating vent.

From what I could piece together, the big upset had to do with a friend of Mundy's who had disappeared out in Mississippi farm country. "The president needs to be protecting our people," Connie moaned. "It's not that easy," my mother protested. "You know how things work in Washington. President Kennedy is doing as much as they'll let him." Someone gave a snort—I was pretty sure it was my father—and after an exchange I couldn't decipher, Delroy said the president would do better helping folks find jobs than leaving their future to the goodwill of a Delta politician. "That's fine to say," Mundy retorted, "but the wise and the cynical never done nothin' for nobody. We earned the right to vote." That must have gotten Delroy's goat because all of sudden his voice rang out loud and clear. "Go on then—be a hero! But you won't see those reverends preaching forbearance in their three-hundred-dollar suits out there risking their black behinds. White folks gonna hate us till the day they die. Just accept it." That sent the grown ups all shouting at once until Aunt Jamesie nearly busted my eardrums whistling through her teeth. "Quit yer barkin'! This ain't the time to be jumpin' on soap-boxes!"

I was making a mental note to have her teach me how to whistle like that when I heard Mundy snap, "forget it! I'd stay and show you my side of it but I need to meet with my people."

There was a lot of mumbling and from the little I was able to pick out, it sounded as if Delroy and my father were walking Mundy out to his car, apologizing and urging him to be careful, while Connie and my mother stayed in the kitchen consoling Aunt Jamesie. Disappointed and just as confused as when the argument first started, I figured I might as well try the book she recommended since I had nothing better to do. I was forty pages deep when I realized my mother was calling for me to wash my hands and come to dinner.

I had gotten so absorbed with Richard's story I could not wait for supper to end so I could devour the remaining three hundred pages. I was almost to a hundred when my eyes let me down and kept closing. I had dropped off when my mother came to say it was time to brush my teeth. I asked if I could read in bed, but as expected, the answer was no. I was too groggy to put up a fight, and my mother had barely finished tucking me in before I was deep in dreamland.

Dripping sweat by the bucket, I was perched in a buckboard wagon crossing the desert when Sheriff Gomez came galloping on his powerful black horse at the head of a posse. He pointed his big .45 at my head and said he had no choice but to take me in. I pleaded that I had not done anything wrong and could see his deputy swinging a rope, like a cowboy fixing to lasso a steer. I was about to pull the long black dagger from inside my jacket when someone snuck up from behind and grabbed me in a bear-hug. As I struggled to wrestle free, the redhead from the Amity Motel, sneered down at me, whispering, 'eenie, meenie, mynie mo ... ' She was snapping her gum, laughing hysterically as she started to tickle me, when, zap! I was sitting on stage at a nine-foot grand piano. My body tingled as I spotted Shayla smiling at me from the audience but, as I began to play, the piano went rolling away on its casters. I picked up my stool to follow it and each time I started to play, the piano went wheeling away. I lunged to grab it and something hard, like a baseball bat, crushed my back, knocking me flat. I was lying on the ground smashed to a pulp when Aunt Jamesie pulled me into her arms and nodded towards the TV. Rubbing my eyes, I stared in disbelief as I slowly conceded that the person on the screen with her skin smeared black and her lips swelled white was my mother, dressed in a bikini top and short grass skirt, dancing a calypso with Louis Armstrong.

I forget how the bizarre dream ended, but I awoke before dawn, eager to get back to *Black Boy* and see what happened next. I knew I would never make it to the end before we left, but I was obsessed with learning how Richard made it through such constant abuse. I was about to find out if I got my wish and he had summoned up the courage to tell his grandmother the truth when Aunt Jamesie noticed my light on and whispered for me to join her downstairs in the kitchen.

"So, what do you think of *Black Boy*?"

I stopped and thought her question over, far from sure I knew the answer. "Is Richard *Black Boy*?"

"You're a smart boy. What do you think?"

"No. I think that's what everyone else thinks."

Aunt Jamesie looked pleased and said I could keep her copy and read it on our trip. I was so elated, I felt I had to do something to thank her. Seeing the grown-ups begin drifting downstairs, I decided to see if enough of the piano keys were working to play her *Heart and Soul* or the *Boogie Woogie*, but when I opened the lid the entire action was missing.

After breakfast, as everyone gathered to say good-bye, Aunt Jamesie's eyes were filled with water. I knew how she felt, so I hugged her tight and did not flinch when she cried and kissed my cheek.

The flat, frozen ground stretched white beyond the limits of his vision reminded Emerson of the lines that had brought him here.

Dear Applicant, we regret to inform you ... Those seven cold words typed seventeen times onto seventeen cold white sheets of paper had begun the lines that shifted the ground which led to the end of what had brought him to America. His wife had been slow to comprehend.

"What do you mean, none will take you?"

He stood penitently as she struggled to sit up higher in bed. Imprudent optimism had its consequences, no matter how worthy the motives. The love of his life had suffered enough, so he had kept the rejecting letters, hiding one after the other as they arrived. "They turned me down. I wasn't admitted."

"Don't joke with me, Emerson! I'm in no mood for it."

He hung his head. "I'm not joking."

"They *all* turned you down? Even the ones up North? I don't believe it!"

Emerson spread the seventeen rejections across her bed. "We made all their deadlines but they had already filled the seat. See for yourself."

"One?" she cried, her disbelieving eyes wide as she started skimming through each letter. "That's it? That's all they'll accept in a year? Just *one?*"

"One seems to be the colored allotment. Or zero."

"And our two? What excuse did *they* give?"

"There are only two colored medical schools in the entire country. They felt they had to give priority to those who'll be practicing here. Seeing what happened to us, I can't fault them. Those nuns are saints, not surgeons."

Madeline reared up in a fury. "Must you always be so damned understanding? If that's what they wanted to hear, you should have told them you were staying when they interviewed you!"

"What—worm in on a lie?"

"Oh, for the love of God!" she lurched up to throttle him, then sank, clutching her belly.

He rushed to hold her until she recaptured her breath, trying not to see the dark half-moons that had shown up lately beneath her eyes like tiny graveyards. "They know our history," he said patiently when she pushed him away. "Do you think it would have impressed them to know I was willing to put my ambition ahead of our people?"

"Our people? They're *all* our people!" She snatched up a handful of letters and crushed them in her fist. "See these?" she cried, shaking the wad under his nose. "That's the line—white on one side, trash on the other!" She tossed the crumpled sheets angrily into the air and they fluttered to the floor like crippled doves. "That's what giving up now makes of our sacrifice. A pile of trash!"

"I never said I was giving up. Have faith."

"Fine. Have faith." Madeline winced and collapsed onto her pillow. "But for God's sake, Emerson, learn to fight!"

It was for her sake he found himself in a place someone born and raised in the tropics could only perceive as Earth's wintry end. Like grieving Parsifal in search of atonement, he had roamed to where the sky was so pale it shivered. "Oh, Canada," he moped, lumbering through the blizzard, "December is not the month to greet thee!"

As he slogged through the freezing snow, fearing for his fingers and toes, he wondered if Maddy would credit his grit as much as his gamble if she could see him now. He had ventured to this place at a time when living things seemed destined to expire inside a cerement of frigid cotton because it held the grail that would redeem their pursuit. Assuming his records were in order, he had been promised a seat in medical school for the semester starting the third week in January. The challenge now was to survive until then.

He had taken his landlord's advice and bought himself fur-lined boots, but the rented space heater did little to allay the tooth-chattering cold. Bedtime found him curled like a fetus, his distressed hands and feet vying for the rubber hot water bottle before it turned cold. And just when he had discovered the warm salvation of double-layer socks, flannel underwear and a pair of twill pajamas, he awoke to find his skin erupting with painful blotches from an apparent allergy to untreated wool.

Watching a chain of frosted cars swish by, their headlights glowing yellow through the falling snow like cats' eyes, he forgave himself a rush of self-pity. In two more days it would be Christmas. He thought about his better half, warm in New Orleans, maybe putting the finishing touches to an eggplant casserole, or baking her peerless fruit cake for Aunt Jamesie's traditional midnight feast, and here he was, plodding shin-deep in snow, about to get frostbite.

A bulky Mercury Coupe pulled over and stopped close beside him. "Can I offer you a lift, friend?" The car's snow-dusted window rolled lower, revealing a benign pink face. Emerson's shoulders let go of their tension as the kind male voice sounded appealing, but he was not about to take chances. "No, I'm almost there. Thanks all the same."

"Got someplace to go on Christmas?"

The question unnerved him and he was about to hurry along when he glimpsed the cleric's collar. The benign gaze was on his jacket as he shivered with his hands pressed deep inside its pockets.

"I see you're new to our parts. You're welcome to join us for Christmas, brother." Wind-swept flecks of snow clung to the pastor's brow and eyelashes as he reached to offer up his card through the open car window. "That's the address. Any family up here with you?"

Emerson shook his head.

"Then it's settled!" The parson's face brightened as he brushed off the snow stuck to his lashes. "Service starts at eleven. I can promise you a fair-to-middling sermon and a first rate meal."

As he held the card in his gloveless hand, Emerson felt a blood-stirring tingle reaching clear to what he was almost sure were his toes. "That's very kind of you, sir!"

"Don't mention it—and it's Pastor Julian," the Good Samaritan corrected him. "Come early. I want you to have one of the best seats in the house."

He watched as the parson drove off without asking for his name, too elated by the thought of not having to spend Christmas alone with a tin of baked beans to make much of it. Then he remembered that, after buying his boots and paying the deposit for his landlord's heater and hot plate, he was left with the grand sum of three dollars and eighty-three cents until Maddy's draft arrived. Afraid it would look crude to show up at the pastor's home empty-handed, he walked back to his room, groping for a way to save face.

The slumbering town was blazing white as the sun returned in time for Christmas morning. The storm had scrubbed the cheerless sky blue and, with most citizens still happily snowbound, the frosted streets sparkled in the peaceful silence. Passing the ice-capped homes decked with pine-cones and holly, he pictured the early goings on inside: parents pulled from the warmth of their beds, half-asleep as they sat and sipped some warmed-over coffee, children breathlessly unwrapping their presents, praying with fingers crossed that Santa had overlooked their transgressions. Visualizing one of the holiday's ubiquitous fantasies, he brooded about his lost son and his sweetheart abiding at a distance. As he often did at this time of the year, he thought about the innocent man he had failed to save and wondered again if hope was a gift or a broken promise.

He was pondering how much of one's life was set by the stars when a commotion of clanging bells saw his languid pace hastened by a converging throng rushing to outpace the cold. Sighting the typical white spire, he was relieved to see that the church was not overly imposing. Worldly presumptions tended to increase in line with the size of the congregation, so in spite of what the pastor had said, he was keen not to offend by choosing the wrong pew to sit in. He had barely removed his hat when a firm hand grasped his elbow.

"Welcome, brother."

He turned but saw no one there, then realized when the voice chirped 'Merry Christmas!' that he was being greeted by a waist-high elf in a dark green tunic and red and white striped stockings. "Why, thank you, brother, and a Merry Christmas to you!"

His response drew a half-hidden grin. "Good. You're here nice and early. Pastor Julian will be pleased," said the elf, who kept a firm hold on Emerson's elbow and ushered him up the center aisle to the frontmost pew to the accompaniment of softly tinkling bells.

"I'd rather not be this far up. I am only a guest."

"Exactly," nodded the elf. "Relax, brother. It's Christmas— you'll see why." With that, his escort hurried off to more jingling bells which Emerson now realized were sewn on to the elf's pointy-toed slippers.

The hairs on his neck began to crawl as he sat up front by himself and felt the curious eyes of the incoming faithful. He braved a glance at the pew filling in behind him and was met with a broadside of gleaming teeth. He grinned back, stuck half-turned and feeling foolish, grateful when he was able to turn and stand as the organ trumpeted the introduction to *Adeste Fideles*. He had started to feel less conspicuous when the lessons and carols ended and Pastor Julian mounted the pulpit to deliver the Message.

Merry Christmas!

Merry Christmas!

Glorious day, is it not? The sun beaming on us from Heaven— God's whole saved world a magnificent shining white, free from the stain of sin! So, my brothers and sisters—when you woke and saw this glorious morning did you take a moment to count your blessings—or were you in a hurry to look under that tree and count up your presents?

Timid laughter.

Did you remember? Or were you distracted thinking about all that fine rich food simmering on the stove for when you skedaddle on home after service? Mmm, I can smell the turkey and stuffing from here!

Cautious titters.

But suppose I told you that instead you'd been invited to dine with our Lord? Would you be the one who cried to Jesus, 'happy the man who shall sit at the feast in the kingdom of God!'? Or would you shrug to yourself and say, 'gee, the Lord already gave me everything I wanted for Christmas...' Folks—do you see where I'm heading? —are you grateful, knowing you've been chosen, or are you satisfied just knowing that you've been blessed?

Eight hundred eyes blinked and the minister aimed his forefinger at Emerson who suddenly felt as if he was watching himself from a lonely distance.

As you can see, the Lord has sent us a visitor. Stand up, brother, and tell us your name.

Taken aback, he faltered to his feet, unsure if his mind was in charge of his body. A frog caught his throat and he struggled to mumble his name.

Speak up, brother, so your friends in the back can hear you!

He was about to obey but the minister nodded knowingly with his beneficent smile and continued.

Yes, welcome, Brother! Friends, you see—? The Lord sheds His Light in mysterious ways! You all are wondering—what brought this stranger to be among us on such a glorious day? Not what, my friends, the answer is Who! Who else but God? God whose love knows our needs before our asking, so that when we forget—as we all do—He sends us a reminder. He comes and sits among us—just another poor sinner alone on Christmas—no family, no presents waiting to be opened, no splendid table with all those tempting treats I know you ladies have been busy concocting to ruin our waistlines. Pastor Julian paused for the anticipated chuckles. *There he was—shivering out in that terrible storm—no gloves, no warm coat—not even a scarf to wrap his throat—just that cheap jacket you see on his back. My guess is a few of you saw him on that corner and drove right on by—got to get that shopping done, in case we're snowed in on Christmas! So what do you think Jesus is telling us with his visit on this His day of all days? —did He not say, if anyone—ANYONE—thirsts let him come to me—?* The pastor's sharpening voice grew fervent and he stretched his open arms down towards Emerson, as if to lift him straight up to the pulpit. *Turn your back on Him and all those blessings—the ham, the goose, the mincemeat pie—the magical toys the children pleaded for—maybe that mink stole the little wife had her eye on—All those wonderful gifts will be taken away! For it shall be given even unto the crippled and the blind and the lame!*

When the minister had finished using Matthew, Luke and John to browbeat them, it was time for Communion. Emerson was about to dig for the dollar he had reserved for the collection when he heard the faintly tinkling bells and felt the firm hand restrain him. With the relentless eyes again boring into his back, the elf guided him to stand and accept the Holy Sacrament. After he had returned to his pew to pray while the pastor finished ministering Jesus' body and blood he considered escaping right after the benediction before the curious eyes were upon him, but decided that would be too ungracious. He would not have managed it anyway, as the organist was still improvising the postlude of *Hark! the Herald Angels Sing* when what seemed to be nearly half of the congregation came mobbing his pew.

It took him a moment to make sense of the gabbling confusion and realize that some were pressing him to come home with them for Christmas dinner, while others were feverishly trying to jam dollars into his pockets, saying he must buy himself a good winter coat and warm mittens. It took him over fifteen minutes to convince them that his straits were only temporary and persuade them to take back their money. He thanked each of them profusely for their generous gestures, then swelled with shame when, in place of their excited smiles, one by one, they all wished him a distraught Merry Christmas and staggered away, plainly wondering how their kindest thoughts had failed them.

I was baffled reading *Black Boy*. Everybody was out to kick him in the teeth. Huck Finn may have been an outcast, but at least most people were willing to let him be. Even Richard's own family seemed to hate him. I just did not understand it.

Cramped from sitting for almost an hour, I had moved to lie on the floor with my legs across the luggage in back of the driver's seat. My parents must have thought I had fallen asleep because they started talking in hushed voices. My father was not happy with Aunt Jamesie.

"He found them by accident? Why does she save them?"

"Her memory's not what it was. She meant to get rid of them. I knew I shouldn't have told you. You always overreact."

"Overreact? You saw the book she gave him to read. Did she also forget that he's nine years old?"

"He's almost ten. Anyway, what are you so afraid of?"

"Afraid of? What are we supposed to tell him when he starts asking questions? That black boys are only in the South? That there are no more lynchings?"

"Shh, you're going to wake him! The poor woman's going through a lot. Mundy wants her to come live with him in Mississippi but she'll be dead in a year if she has to leave that old house. Now, with that poor man Mundy persuaded to help register folks gone missing, she's worried sick."

"Can't fault her for that. The last thing they needed was Mundy's name in the papers."

"You can't hide from injustice. Mundy's not one to cut and run."

"And I am—is that what you're saying?"

"He didn't fold his hands when they barred him from college. He joined the movement."

"Fine for him. It's his country."

"Like it or not, it's our country too."

"Hardly." My dad grunted, then changed the subject. "By the way—did Connie ever mention why Delroy wanted to come back to Alabama?"

"She said it was so they could finally reconcile with her parents. Why do you ask?"

"He wanted to know if in Jamaica a man was allowed to kill to defend his honor."

"What?"

"He said it's sanctioned in the Bible."

"Oh, good Lord."

"I reminded him it's the twentieth century—no judge is going to care what it says in Leviticus. I thought he was putting one over—you know Delroy—but he was dead serious. He said, if lawmakers can use the Bible to justify Jim Crow, he can use it to defend his honor."

"Men and their injured manhood," my mother whispered. "Poor Connie—"

"You sound like you know something about it—"

"If you don't know, one can only imagine—"

"Dad? Who is Jim Crow?"

My parents snapped their necks towards each other, stunned as I poised the question and they realized I had heard every word.

"Jim Crow isn't a person—well, he was a person—a long time ago. Son, it's complicated—"

When my dad seemed about to give up my mom jumped in. "It's what they call the law in these southern parts. It divides people by skin color. It's backward and hateful, but people like Mundy are going to change it."

That explained why Richard got so jittery around white folks and why he and his friend hated themselves for making those white men happy and agreeing to knock each other's brains out. It probably left them feeling as lowdown as I did back in Las Cruces, except I no longer gave a hoot how those motel receptionists saw me.

Disgusted, I closed the book and sat up to gaze out the window, glad to see we were away from the long gray coast of endless mud flats. My eyes grew wide as we rounded a sign marked Protected Area and entered into a man-made wilderness where deer and migrant birds welcomed the return of slash leaf pine and loblolly. The light retreated as we pressed deeper inside the forest and I shuddered at the spooky look of the trees and their fatal shadows.

My mom gave a shiver. "Emerson, I pray you know where you're going!"

Blackened cotton-fields like churned up battlegrounds offered scary glimpses through the woodland breaks. Mutilated bodies loomed inside my head like warning ghosts as it dawned on me that ours was the only car on the gloomy gravel-fringed road.

"I'm following Mundy's directions," my father growled.

"Are you sure you're remembering right? You should have written them down."

Their squabbling was squelched by the advancing roar of a V-8 engine. I peered through our Valiant's rear window and saw a red pickup gaining on us at a reckless speed. It pressed right on our tail and my father quickly pulled off to the graveled shoulder. The pickup truck raced on by, kicking up dust, and the two shirtless punks perched on its sidewalls flipped us the bird. My dad relaxed and quietly counted to ten before he checked the road in his rearview mirror and carefully continued. We were close to the edge of the forest when we saw the truck finish a lurching three point turn and come barreling back.

"Lord, not now," my father muttered.

"I want to go back to civilization," my mother moaned, then we both cried, "look out!"

The red pickup was speeding straight at us. My dad jerked the wheel and my heart was in my mouth when we promptly went skidding. We fishtailed a full one-eighty as the pickup roared on by, its four white teenagers doubled in stitches seeing our Valiant left slanting across a ditch like a dinghy with its prow on the pier and its stern in the water. My father called to me frantically as he rushed to lift the suitcases that had fallen on top of me when I slammed against the front seat and onto the floor. As he helped me out of our tilting car, the pickup slowed as it passed us again and the punks in back waved, singing, 'so-long, niggers!' to the tune of *Goodnight Ladies*.

"Congratulations," my mother sneered, her handkerchief clamped to her forehead as she climbed from the ditch and saw my father straining to reach inside the glove compartment. "You've got us stranded in the sticks of Mississippi."

"Can you ease up for just one minute?" he shouted, as he maneuvered to extract the map and unfolded it across the car-hood. "I can't hear myself think!"

"Fine. You think while I bleed."

My conscience quaked as she took the cloth from her face and exposed a cherry-sized bruise.

My dad rushed to comfort her.

"Don't touch me!"

"Why are you being impossible?"

"I'm fine."

"You're bleeding."

"A lot *you* care—"

I wept inside but I was pretty much shockproof by now. In a world where people bring snacks to a hanging, a rift between the Father and the Holy Spirit seemed more and more possible. I was depressed, worrying where this trip through hell would lead us, when a lean old man in overalls and a floppy hat came ambling up on his mule. My gut gave a jitter as his look reminded me of the white men smiling in that awful postcard.

"Here's a pretty pickle!"

The band on his wrist dazzled my eyes as he slipped off his mule and sauntered towards us. He stopped and stroked his stubbled gray chin, assessing our angled Valiant.

"Now, that'll jar your preserves. You folks prefer drivin' backwards?"

My mom rejected his crack. "Far from it, sir! Some young hoodlums ran us off the road."

"Run ya off, huh—" The old man echoed, as if judging the facts to his own satisfaction. "Can't say it ain't likely." His face looked like wrinkled red leather as he fanned himself with his hat and thought things over. "Y'all sit tight—I'll be back."

"That mean you'll call the service station?" my father asked hopefully, but the old man got back on his mule and didn't answer.

Half-turning as he started away, the old man waved and again the flashing bracelet blinded my eyes. "I'm down the road a piece. Best you folks stay inside yer buggy."

My dad tried to nudge my mother to do like he said, but she wasn't having it.

"A little late to be worried about the mess you've dragged us into," she said acidly, unsnagging the hem of her dress from some clinging underbrush.

Tired of listening to my parents yap about whose fault it was *this* time, I went to sit in the car and pick up the story from where I left off. Now that I knew that Jim Crow was the law down south it made sense that a black boy would avoid crossing white folks, but it was still hard to believe that he could get in trouble simply for reading. I was excited because in this chapter Richard and I were both learning some of the same new words and was also amazed that a nineteen-year-old who loved books had never heard of Mark Twain. He did know one word I had not come across until this trip and I was promising to look for *Prejudices* by H. L. Mencken when the thought was blasted out of my head by the growl of heavy machinery. Bolting out of the car, I saw the old man returning on top of a rumbling tractor.

"Ain't no tow truck servin' these parts that I know of," he said matter-of-factly, taking a nimble hopstep as his feet hit the ground. "Hope this works, cause if it don't, y'all be stuck here all night."

"You're being awfully considerate, mister—?"

"Roebottom's the name, but plain Roe serves just fine," the farmer replied and my father introduced us by our first names and again tried to thank him. "Looky here, Emerson," Roe said bluntly, testing a long, thick rope with a big iron hook on its end, "just 'cause folks ain't friends don't mean they can't be friendly. If I was in a fix, I'd like to think you'd do the same."

Roe fastened the hook to the Valiant's undercarriage and latched the front bumper to a V-shaped leather harness linked with chain then tied it to the rope which was slipped around and knotted to the back of the tractor. The old man faced me with a gleam in his eye.

"Can you drive Pappy's car?"

I looked stupidly down at my feet, thinking, can't he see my legs won't reach the pedals?

"You can steer, can't ye?"

That sounded better. Sure thing! I reckoned.

"Good!" he said, giving me the thumbs up. "I need you to steer us right while Mammy and Pap give her a good ole shove once I signal. That'll help get past any drag from inertia," he explained, taking the chance to give me a quick science lesson and confirm his credentials before instructing my parents. "If y'all feel a slip, jus' keep pushin'! You ain't slippin' far tied to this big dandy," he assured them, tipping his head towards his tractor.

It took me a couple of fearful swivels to get the Valiant to budge, but after that I steadied my grip on the wheel and kept her lined up straight. We were back on the road in sixty seconds.

"Can I give you something for your time?" my father asked, taking out his wallet.

The old man's bracelet blazed hot-white. "You can keep yer money. Ain't no price on my scruples."

My mom stopped brushing the dust from her hair and rushed to smooth Roe's feathers. "We wouldn't presume to afford your kindness, sir. But there must be some way to show our appreciation."

"Y'all wanna do me a favor?" Roe snapped, tossing the coiled-up rope on the floor of the tractor's cab. "Git on just as fast you can git, and don't say zip about it to a dad-blame soul."

"But why?"

"Why?" the old man spat at his feet to show what he thought of the question. "Because some folks are just born ornery. Folks'll be what they will be—no need agitatin' 'em!" Mr. Roebottom seemed to have quickly mastered his temper because as he swung back towards me the sly twinkle again shone in his eye. "I thought you said you couldn't drive? You tell your Pap he best teach you to work them gears before you strip 'em."

"It's a push-button automatic," I explained, glad for the chance to boost my image and show I wasn't totally ignorant about driving.

"Now don't that figger!" the old man chuckled. "Well then, you ain't got no excuses!"

My father cut in. "Can you tell me if I'm on the road to Dobbins? It's up near Runningside—"

"Runningside? You're on the wrong road if you're headed to Runningside. You need to go back about four, five miles and take the first right fork you come to. That'll take you out by Runningside."

"I was looking for a fork in the road," said my father, "but I never saw one."

"It ain't much of a road. More like a cow path, so you gotta look sharp. Take it slow and you'll make it. Just keep watch on that oil pan. It's pro'ly had a pretty good lickin' ..."

I was mesmerized by the old man's bracelet and done with being shy. "Excuse me," I said, boldly tugging Roe's sleeve as he settled on top of his tractor. "What does that say?" I pointed to the silver band's inscription.

He gave the bracelet a quizzical look. "To be truthful, boy, I don't rightly recall. My mother-in-law gave it to me back on our wedding day—my wife's half Creek, so I reckon it means something special to an Injun."

"Oh," I said softly, intrigued and let down at the very same time. Again the bracelet glistened as the old farmer rumbled off on his tractor, never once looking back.

"Mm-mm-mm. Frame that picture." Aunt Jamesie watched as Madeline hesitated on the stairs ahead of her niece's prodding. "Honey, you'll be the belle of the ball!"

Madeline posed in the high-cut, off-the-shoulder gown and made a face. "Are all the women in your family born bullies? Your niece refuses to leave me in peace."

The Tenderloin hoofer turned dowager rebuked her bluntly. "Listen, child. The Lord didn't give you those looks to keep to yourself. A little socializing is just the thing to get you back among the living."

"It doesn't feel right with poor Emerson all alone up in Canada." Madeline gazed at her gown. "I was waiting to wear this when we celebrated his acceptance."

"So you'll just have to get busy and make another one for when the good news comes. It shouldn't take long."

"Great idea, Auntie! Maybe I'll stick around to help."

Madeline's shoulders relaxed, embracing Gwendolyn's offer. She had always focused on the happier aspects of life but this was more than even a colored woman born poor should be forced to bear: the weight of mourning a child she had prayed for so long and so intensely, knowing it was because the one hospital willing to take her had no surgeon on call. And then, just as she was starting to believe her spirit would heal, having to confront the chance that, despite his gifts and all they had been through, her husband might never become a doctor. That cup would be bitter, knowing that not once had she questioned her commitment. It had not helped that, after feeling the stubborn spark in her soul flicker out as she watched them bury her sweet blue baby, she had been granted neither the time nor space to exhaust her anger with God. When she tried withdrawing to the solace of her bedroom, again came Aunt Jamesie bursting inside, fussing for her to come down and eat right this minute when she had neither the taste for food nor the energy to chew. So the despot's niece showing up when she did had not only provided a timely distraction, it may have spared her from losing her mind.

Everyone was struck by the resemblance—Aunt Jamesie insisted that they could pass for sisters—but the future best friends had not spent much time together until the New Year's Eve party when Madeline dealt with her misgivings by glueing herself to Gwendolyn's side. When Aunt Jamesie's eggnog began putting too much of the spry back in some of her Storyville old-timers, her niece seemed to equally welcome having a steady companion. Free to enjoy themselves, by two a.m. the new friends were practically giddy, joking and laughing in each other's arms as Madeline stuck her palm against more rum-puckered lips hunting a New Year's kiss and Gwendolyn slapped away another woozy grope for her 'bootieful keyhole.' After the last sloshed reveler had been shoved out the door and Gwen came to help her out of her gown, Madeline brooded over how different the night would have been had her life gone to plan.

"Chin up, girl," Gwen scolded. "Your husband's not dead. Neither's your fight."

At moments like that it seemed that they had known each other forever, but it was Gwen's talent at the piano that gradually lifted Madeline out of her funk. Day after day, she would lie upstairs in bed, soaking in Schumann's *Scenes from Childhood*. As dark reveries led her back through unformed memories, she would feel the clamp clench her throat then a sudden release stirred by the tender strains of a Chopin Nocturne. Over time the murky flashes receded along with her haunting fear of choking as the musical part of her brain delighted in Gwendolyn's touch. Her breath no longer burdened, she roused her waned resilience eager to know how it was that Aunt Jamesie's niece had become such a brilliant pianist.

"I was a star in my childhood." Gwen's deadpan reply bore a harshness at odds with her sensitive nature. "I must have been seven or eight when my teacher started taking me to perform for our colored elite. You should have seen me with my hair in curls sitting at the keyboard in my white lace dress with my skinny legs dangling in those long white stockings. By the time my feet could touch the floor I was giving a recital in some fabulous mansion almost every other week. Sometimes for just eight or nine people, sometimes in a ballroom packed with close to a hundred. But that was a long time ago. Before everything could be immortalized on the gramophone."

"That's a crying shame," Madeline groused. "Records are fine but a gramophone doesn't come close to matching live musicians."

"I agree, but it's always right there in the parlor and men don't feel pressured to prove they're cultured the way most women do. Once they realized their wives were happy to be the first to get the latest from Caruso or W.C. Handy while their husbands played poker, the Sunday afternoon salon passed out of fashion."

"Is that what discouraged you from pursuing a career?"

Gwen chuckled. "Are you kidding? Just the opposite. I was seventeen and pretty sure of myself, especially after two of my old patrons sponsored me so I could study up in New York. I graduated at twenty ready to make a big splash. My teachers had told me that to have any chance of a concert career I would need a good agent so I went to audition for one of the top impresarios. He turned me down before I played a note. I'll never forget what he told me: 'You may have made a name for yourself in New Orleans, but to the rest of the world a Negro pianist is a passing curiosity, like a computing chimpanzee or a midget harpist. At any rate, single young women aren't fit for the concert circuit. You're a nice-looking girl. Find yourself a well-off husband, make handsome babies, and if you feel the need, try to attract a few good students.' I stormed out of there swearing that before I got married or resorted to teaching I had to know how much of myself that loved making music I could stand to lose. I took a job as a church pianist and gave small recitals, mostly in Brooklyn and the proceeds mostly went to charity. After fifteen years I realized I had lost my need for applause."

Madeline was not convinced. "I've listened to you practice for hours. You put your whole heart in it. Why work so hard if you no longer want to perform?"

"A performer has to play what her audience wants to hear. I just want to play what I love."

Her friend's resignation, pained and deeply wistful, struck at Madeline's core. "I don't believe you."

"You will," Gwen whispered, her features drawn until a sudden thought made her smile. "Listen—why don't you come back with me to Brooklyn? I know you're bored with being here alone and not working. The city's desperate for nurses, and it's a lot closer to Ontario."

"You mean it? I've always dreamt of seeing New York!"

Brooklyn was being finely powdered white as the fast friends arrived from New Orleans. The minute they were out of the station, Madeline turned up her mouth and stuck out her tongue like a hungry fledgling, impatient to taste the delicate falling snow. Feeling the snowflakes spray delightfully across her face, she reveled in the brisk winter air sending her blood to warm her cheeks and make them tingle. She had been warned, from long before she ever imagined making it here, that New York was the modern Babel, but as those first days passed and she made her way around the city, it struck her that, if Satan thrived on idleness, a place where the trains ran all night and everyone did everything at breakneck speed could not possibly find the time to be wicked. There had certainly been nothing sinful about her first experience in Carnegie Hall, even if Heifetz's virtuosity bordered on the supernatural.

"Gwen, you fantastic friend, that was some performance," she exclaimed still dazed and on her feet after the fourth and final encore ended in another thunderous standing ovation. What an amazing violinist! Thank you for this incredible evening."

"The evening's not over, darling. Some friends I've been wanting you to meet are waiting for us outside the hall. We're all dying to hear this blind pianist everyone's raving about."

Madeline checked her watch. "Now? Why it's past eleven!"

"You're so lovely," Gwen laughed, pinching her cheek. "Darling, the night's just beginning—and the club's right nearby on Fifty-second Street. Oh, don't give me that look! I saw you out of your shell at my aunt's New Year's Eve party."

Maddy's discomfort increased as Gwen picked out her friends among the crowd still loitering outside the hall. One looked barely her height, the other extravagantly tall. Seeing that both were male and one was white, she flushed in panic. You're married, she reminded herself and thought of Emerson shivering as he tried to study in his drafty room. She was about to beg off when the two apparent opposites pressed through to greet them.

"Maddy, I'd like you to meet Cyrus, and this is Joe. Joe and I met at Juilliard."

Cyrus gazed at Madeline from his sky-scraping height. "Are you also a musician? If you are, I shall dare not make a peep all night." The goliath's teeth gleamed, a striking contrast with his unalloyed black skin.

"No, I'm Gwen's plain friend."

Cyrus peered down at her closely. "Why don't I believe you?"

"You mustn't. Maddy is a very talented singer. Sorry, dear," Gwen chuckled, "you won't get one past Cyrus."

A short walk later, Madeline found herself trapped at a small round table coughing up smoke, tucked tight between Joe and Gwen who shouted in the crouching waitress's ear to ask for two Shirley Temples. Despite the noisy chatter, there was an air of anticipation enveloping the room, and the packed-in audience instantly fell silent seeing the rangy figure being guided to the piano. The escort left and the pianist bowed stiffly to the smattering of cautious applause, then quietly sat and started to play. With the first staggering flourish Madeline forgot about the smoke and heat-shedding bodies and was back in heaven, her jaded spirit revived by the spell of a fleet-fingered alchemist whose soulful phrases implied there could be bliss in being blue.

"I see why this city never sleeps—there's too much to miss!" She was still replaying the evening as they made it back to Gwen's apartment from the subway not long after three a.m. Her upbringing whispered that this was wrong—anywhere with nights this thrilling had to be wicked. "I like your friends. What a pair the two of them make."

Gwen kicked off her shoes and stretched her legs on the couch. "That's better! I couldn't wait to get those darned things off. Joe is the one who introduced me to Cyrus. Joe's a marvelous pianist. He could have had an impressive concert career, but decided he'd rather play jazz. Scandalized his parents. It's funny. We're like mirror opposites."

Madeline lifted her friend's stockinged feet and sat down to massage them. "I can see he likes you. Too bad he's so short—"

"—and so white." Gwen chortled. "We're just good friends but I've always admired Joe. He's one of those people who'd quicker suffer than betray his principles. Joe could be famous by now, but he refuses to play for segregated audiences." She paused, then turned to better see Maddy's face. "What did you think of Cyrus?"

"The man mountain? He seems very intense."

Gwen's face lit with a grin. "I know. We met when Cyrus came to speak at Joe's Transcendental Fellowship Center. Joe says he's what they call an adept."

Madeline stopped rubbing Gwen's feet and watched her in interest. "Really? I remember Emerson talking to my brother about adepts back in Jamaica." She shook her head in reflection. "The two of them would jaw about Gandhi and Eastern philosophy till the cows came home … but aren't adepts what most people consider to be fakes—like psychics?"

"Heavens, no! It's not like ouija boards or that mystic mumbo-jumbo. It's spiritual. It's about developing insight and why certain people have a gift for healing." Gwen pulled her legs from Madeline's lap and sat up uncomfortably. "I'm not explaining it very well. You'll have to ask Cyrus. It's very liberating but the whole thing's still pretty new to me."

"Aha!" Madeline exclaimed. "Now I know what else was behind tonight! Is it serious? You and Cyrus?"

Gwen laughed. "So, *you're* the psychic! We've known each other barely three months and you can read me like a book. Cyrus proposed a week before Thanksgiving. That's why I left to spend the holidays in New Orleans. I wanted a clear head before I gave him my answer. So what do you think? Can a stubborn woman set in her ways marry happily close to her forties?"

"Why not, if he can read minds and is not too old for you to train properly." Madeline reached a hand to her friend seeing her slump. "Dear, I'm kidding! Two city sophisticates are sure to be copacetic." She hugged Gwen tight then held her at arm's length. "But you better hope he's adept at massaging feet. As big as he is, you'll be living in those high-heeled shoes just to stay in touch."

"They don't tend to tarry on Christmas," Pastor Julian bemoaned. Having exchanged the black robe for a tailored suit, the minister with his manicured nails and finely-coiffed gray hair gave the impression of a man doing his best not to feel diminished by the specter of old age.

"I'm afraid I may have sped them on their way," Emerson explained, seeing the pastor's disappointment at finding him waiting alone in the narthex. "I had to turn down several dinner invitations."

"Oh good. It's difficult to know if one is making an impact."

Emerson laughed, recalling how swiftly he had been surrounded. "Oh, you definitely made an impact. I was offered enough for a full-length coat, six scarves and a dozen mittens."

The minister smiled back warmly. "All in the Christmas spirit, no doubt."

"No doubt."

Their ensuing conversation centered on Emerson's surname as Pastor Julian could not restrain himself from joking twice on the short walk to the rectory that he had clearly been sent to plant the seeds of goodwill.

The Julian home was an unattached red-brick cottage with white trim moldings. A coned pine wreath dappled with snow encircled the tarnished brass clapper on the unlocked front door. Inside, the flames from a crackling log fire sent Emerson's revived blood racing to his numbed extremities. Centered on the fireplace mantel was a large open bible on a white ceramic pedestal shaped like two upturned palms. Across the room five pink and blue painted copper fish were arrayed on the wall by size, large to small. The room was dark and densely furnished and Emerson was surprised to see a ceiling-high fir tree adorned with bowed scarlet ribbons and tiny lit candles.

"You'll need a sturdier coat than this if you expect to outlast our winters," said Pastor Julian, as he took Emerson's jacket.

"I came here from New Orleans somewhat precipitously. It's not nearly this cold."

"I'm sure it's hot year-round in Voodoo Land," the reverend quipped, then called inside. "Dear—I'm back. Come greet our guest!"

A flushed fiftyish woman came in looking harried yet softly demure in a puff-shouldered purple dress mostly hidden by a yellow apron. She glanced at Emerson warming his hands by the fire and gave a slightly perturbed smile upon being introduced as Mrs. Julian. "Merry Christmas to you, young man! Please—make yourself to home—" She turned her husband an anxious look. "Father, I'm afraid the ham isn't quite ready."

The mention of ham sliced Emerson's conscience as he realized he had failed to warn the pastor about his meat-free diet. With Mrs Julian's efforts vividly plain on her ruddy perspiring face it would be boorish to bring it up now. Reminded of what else he had forgotten, he asked for his jacket, dug inside the pocket and found the long stemmed white rose happily intact in its cellophane wrapping. "May this modest flower mark a new fellowship," he proposed, presenting it to his hostess.

The minister's benign gaze sharpened. "This doesn't have anything to do with voodoo, does it?"

"Don't be silly, Father!" his wife admonished him, accepting the rose. "Why, I think it's a lovely gesture. My, that's a posh looking suit!" she exclaimed abruptly. "Was it a gift?"

Interpreting it as her attempt to skip over the awkward moment, Emerson shrugged. "You could say that," he answered ambiguously.

Satisfied that the rose was not a threat to his home, Pastor Julian directed his guest to one of the two large wing chairs while his wife scurried back inside her kitchen. "I'm glad to hear our congregants rallied to help you. They never remember until Christmas and by then it's too late. Of course, we don't have many of you up here—not like New Orleans ... Normally I wouldn't have been out driving with a fierce storm brewing, but I've been having this annoying problem with my hip—yes, our Master does work in mysterious ways," the pastor murmured to himself, then went on to describe the good works his church was doing in Africa. As he spoke he seemed to grow steadily more self-contented, his cheeks aglow as if warmed by his reflections.

While Emerson listened passively, growing more and more bewildered, the minister explained in teleological detail why famines are visited upon the poor. When his guest showed no sign of endorsing his immanent theories he turned his sights on Emerson's island.

"So, what's it like where you come from? Are there many Christians?"

"Most certainly," Emerson declared, disguising his amusement. "We are particularly receptive to the idea of a world without toil." He ran on quickly when the pastor failed to see his humor. "Our island has all the main Protestant denominations, and our fair share of Catholics, so I'd say we have just about every path to the next life covered. It's the here and now that finds us lacking. Our faith could benefit from a bit more science."

"Faith always comes first," Pastor Julian insisted. "Of course, there are those who think it's a tragic burden—trying to save the unsaved. I remind them God is Love and we are still our brother's keepers!" he avowed and Emerson was relieved to hear his wife ring the bell for dinner.

The table was set for a feast. Arrayed around a glass bowl of water with floating red and pink carnations sat an immense baked ham, a casserole with leeks and scalloped potatoes, butter-mashed turnips, a platter of sliced beets with wedges of lemon, a basket of fresh-baked rolls, an array of condiments, and atop each plate a cup of lemon sherbet topped with a single green grape.

After the minister finished a pleading grace that wandered forlornly from Addis Ababa to Poto-Poto before ending gratefully in the Canadian province, Emerson complimented his wife on her elegant presentation then tackled his sherbet, apologizing to his stomach for its pending test.

"I hope you're not disappointed that we're not having turkey," Mrs. Julian apologized.

"Nonsense, June. Emerson is from the West Indies!" Pastor Julian set to carving the gleaming shank trimmed with maraschino cherries set inside yellow wheels of glazed pineapple. "Probably likes nothing better than a nice, thick slice of ham—right, brother?"

"Actually, a tiny sliver will do. It looks delicious, but I'm not a big eater—doctors ascribe it to a lack of enzymes." Emerson prayed the desperate excuse would not offend.

The pastor stared at his chubby-faced guest. "Something's been filling you up by the looks of it!"

"I eat a lot of bread and butter—it's filling and cheap."

The word cheap worked its magic.

"It's all right, June dear," Pastor Julian said consolingly when his wife sat looking as if she had suffered a crippling blow. "I remember what my uncle told me about his time in the Congo," he explained, setting a slightly smaller ham slice on Emerson's plate. "He said the biggest mistake we Christians can make is believing you can lift up the degraded overnight. Don't feel badly about it, my dear. He's wise to go easy on our fattier food."

Emerson steered the conversation away from his diet while silently blessing the ham about to pass his lips. "I take it your uncle was also a minister?"

"Indeed. Spent years of his life in the bush. He must have converted close to a thousand—I don't rightly know what to call them—Congo-men? Of course, they'd insist on mixing in their old idolatries. My uncle said he had a dickens of a time convincing them that it's blasphemous to worship trees. He finally gave it up and became a diamond trader."

The minister continued to speculate as to why God's Spirit had such difficulty reviving the darker continents. Through it all, his wife uttered not a word. Emerson could not decide whether it stemmed from shyness or discomfort. When she offered him a chunk of plum pudding and he promptly accepted, she broke her silence to ask about his wife.

"She sounds lovely. You have no children?"

"None so far," he answered glumly.

"I'm so sorry! Father and I have two boys—of course they're grown now with their own families." Her voice drifted sadly. "No more visiting the old folks for Christmas—I'd go to them, but I could not very well leave the pastor here all alone."

Her husband beamed at her appreciatively. "Quite true, my dear. I'd be lost without your talents in the kitchen."

"That I know," she muttered faintly. "Is your wife a good cook, Emerson?"

"When she has a mind to—I'd say so, yes."

She smiled shrewdly seeing him finish the last of his pudding. "I see you have a sweet tooth. Well, I hope she didn't spoil you too much or your stay here will be most unhappy."

The tasty pudding had gone down easily but Emerson was glad when the pastor had them bow their heads while he thanked the Lord for their bountiful repast. His stomach had lost its patience for digesting muscle years ago and was threatening to get even by having him throw it up on the Julians' carpet. Mercifully, his hosts were not eager to detain him.

"Lovely to meet you too, Mrs. Julian—yes, of course, thank you, *June*," he said when she corrected him and handed him a package with leftover pudding and several ham slices. "I won't forget your kindness," he said, squeezing both their hands in turn after slipping on his coat.

"Think nothing of it—God speed!" said Pastor Julian, shutting the door quickly against the cold the moment Emerson had stepped outside.

He had barely made it back to his room before the ham and creamed potatoes disappeared down the sink behind thick gobs of plum pudding. Evening found him stumbling back and forth to the bathroom, wishing he were dead. When his stomach juices finally settled, his twitchy skin was covered in goosebumps as he had forgotten to feed the metered gas heater. Lighting the room's small two-burner stove, he heated a pot of water along with some milk. When he had finished sipping the cup of warm milk, he filled the hot water bottle and took the edge from his sheets before crawling into bed with Goethe's Faust. Morning saw him quick to exchange the packet of pudding and ham for his landlord's tomato juice and bicarbonate of soda while the remains of his day were spent huddled by the heater, munching dry toast and telling himself that, no matter how cold and bleak a northern winter, he would see it through for Madeline.

The arrival of her draft the following day brought reviving warmth. Snug in his new sheepskin coat and fur-lined gloves, he left the clothing store girded to brave the freezing outdoors and search for a holiday gift on sale. After finding one to his liking at the neighborhood drugstore, he ordered a grilled cheese sandwich at the eat-in counter then asked the pharmacist for some aspirin tablets and a bottle of milk of magnesia before heading back to his room, hoping to wring inspiration from the German's philosophical masterwork. Perhaps because his very first reading had come the day he learned that his father was never coming home and his mother came close to blinding his eye, he had always sympathized with the hero's struggle. He wanted to believe that, like Faust, he would be saved in the end, but alone in his musty room's gloom the old demons returned as he read the poem's bittersweet Dedication. He feared life's mournful repetition. If he was to find the strength not to despair of his calling, then the cheer of Sunday morning communion could not come too soon.

He arrived during the organ prelude and seeing no sign of the solicitous elf, slipped quietly into a row in back. Unlike Christmas, when scarcely a free seat could be seen, the church was still only half full as he stood for the opening hymn. He was at first relieved and then disappointed that no one stopped to greet him or join his pew. The congregation seemed dispirited, the few looks aimed his way more curious than engaging. Crediting the lethargy to holiday overindulgence, as the service ended he decided to take the first step and greet one of the members who had begged to buy him mittens. He approached the familiar face and was about to say hello when the man shrank back. His ears crimson, the congregant turned to murmur in the ear of the fur-draped woman in the pew beside him. Seemingly annoyed at being drawn from her conversation, she cast Emerson a frosted look then looped a hand inside her husband's elbow and with a hasty good-bye to her friends, firmly dragged him away.

Bemused, he left to speak with some of the others he saw gathered some distance away, thinking they'd be pleased to see him snuggled inside his new winter clothing. But as they spotted him heading their way, they each stared past his shoulder then continued talking, pretending not to see him. Thinking either his memory for faces was poor or he had broken some unspoken rule, he halted to make sense of this strange behavior and spied the pastor in the center aisle counseling an attentive young couple.

"Pastor Julian, good morning!" he said happily.

The couple cast him startled looks turned to awkward smiles before thanking the pastor, promising to consult him soon again then scurrying off.

"I've brought you a real present this time!" Emerson proudly revealed the gift he had concealed at his side.

The minister gave it a glance, then pulled him aside. "What are you doing here?" he hissed, hardly moving his lips.

"I enjoyed your Christmas service … I was thinking of joining the church."

"You what!?"

"I realize I'm not Presbyterian, but you've all been so kind and generous—"

"It's out of the question." Pastor Julian's abrupt demeanor was glacial. "We were pleased to have you with us for Christmas—but becoming a member—that would simply make everyone uncomfortable, yourself most of all. Surely, you understand—"

Emerson needed no more enlightenment. He thanked the minister for his candor, tucked the shiny wrapped box with the snow globe and its three wise kings back under his arm, and left the church.

My father was worried about the bump on my mother's forehead, but she insisted it was only a scratch, and besides when did her feelings ever matter? We both knew she was using it as a reminder—that was how rotten things had gotten. Now that I reflect on what had been inconceivable just a few days before, I realize the war between my parents should not have hit me out of the blue. Their differences were obvious once I started to pay attention—all I had to do was look at their friends. My dad only got really talkative around Anu and Cyrus Helger; both were important members of the Fellowship, extremely health conscious, and rarely spoke above mezzo piano. On the other hand, apart from my Aunt Gwen, Happy from Havana was my mom's most frequent companion, and the only woman I knew who wore slacks. And if Anu's calm makeup seemed to suit a gentle adagio, Happy's tongue was set at allegro, its dynamic range stuck between forte and fortissimo. I liked Happy a lot. She was fun to be around and had won a permanent place in my heart when she managed to convince my father to let me go with her and her daughter to Disneyland. Happy could be pretty persuasive. The one thing I hated about Happy from Havana was her habit of calling my mother *mami*.

On our careen into the ditch one of the Valiant's wheels had picked up a stone and I could see my mother flinch at each click. She never complained, but I got the feeling she was biding her time. Finally my dad stopped at the side of the road and she promptly flipped on the radio. Out popped Bobby crooning *Blue on Blue* and a sad look came over her face as she watched my dad stomp out to inspect the tires then storm back inside. My heart skipped a beat seeing him raise his fist to slam the steering wheel until he caught sight of my mother's eyes and abruptly pushed 'Drive.'

The annoying thunks persisted as we made it to the fork and saw why we had missed it the first time. Less than a road, it was more like an expanded horse trail some explorer had cut through the forest. Again the tall trees closed in above our heads, cloaking the byway in darkness, and for an instant I imagined us as plucky pioneers, like those wholesome families on TV headed west in their covered wagons to start life fresh in the wilderness.

The radio buzzed with static and my mother clicked off the

dial, fresh out of patience. "This is where he lives? I hope to God you don't get us stuck way out here!"

"Relax. We're almost there."

"Don't tell me to relax! We're wandering in the backwoods of Mississippi and you expect me to relax?"

I breathed easier as we made it through the forest to some open farmland. Spotting an old log cabin in the middle of an untilled field, my mind had us near the end of my made-up pioneer movie for a minute. My mom switched the radio back on, and Bobby's heartbreak faded into *It's My Party.* My dad glared at me in the rear view mirror when, out of boredom, I started bouncing to Lesley Gore's catchy beat. He was reaching for the dial when the trapped stone clunked as our Valiant rocked with a jarring thump and changed his mind. I got the message and stopped bouncing. My butt was numb from being stuck in the same position, but I really didn't need to be jumping up and down while we were bumping across ten-inch potholes.

We had been rocking and rolling along for about another ten minutes when the trail took a downward slope and we found ourselves veering east on a dried up riverbed lined on both sides with thistle stalks blooming fuzzy white and purple flowers. A tract of decrepit bungalows loomed on the northern rise beyond a spaced row of tar paper shacks. The whole place looked sad and forgotten, like some western ghost town ditched by ruined fortune-seekers.

An animal squealed in the distance and, out of nowhere, a gang of half-naked little rascals came racing after our car along with two of the skinniest dogs I had ever seen. The way the whites of their eyes fixed wide as they spotted me made me think of the opening of Black Boy when Richard watches his mother's broom catch on fire. Their rigid looks turned suspicious when we turned to mount the slope and my father stopped the car to ask for directions.

"Can one of you tell me which house belongs to Dr. Cheever?"

The children stared at us silently, pawing the ground with their toes, as if my dad was speaking a foreign language. For a second I thought the mud-stained bungalows behind them were hovering magically above the ground, then realized they were all set on broad concrete slabs. From the grooves fanning out on the earth beneath them, it appeared that heavy rains sent water streaming through here like funneled rapids. My dad asked again and the tallest boy, who was thin as a rail and looked a year or two younger than me, frowned and said, "ain't no doctor in these parts, sah."

My father pressed him but the boy stood dumb. "You sure? Heavyset gentleman, very dark skin?"

Meanwhile the rest of the brats were gazing at me through the back seat window like I was some rare prized creature people kept in their fish tanks.

"When was the last time you two were in touch?" my mother stuck in, taking distasteful stock of the settlement. "He's probably moved."

Her comment seemed to light a bulb in my father's head. He grinned at the awkward black boy. "He likes to whistle while he walks."

The boy's face lit up. "Oh, you mean the crazy blind man!" He pointed towards the ridge. "Last house up."

"Crazy blind man?" muttered my mother after my dad had thanked the boy for his help and continued up the rise with the kids and dogs again chasing our tail before dropping back, one by one, and ceding the race.

The bungalow's front door was open, so after knocking twice without an answer my father decided we might as well go on inside. We were two steps in when a powerful smell sent me staggering. I held my nose expecting to see a room strewn with garbage but, to my surprise, the place looked reasonably clean. A frayed loveseat with lumpy cushions sat alongside a pinewood table holding a huge hurricane lamp while two straw-bottomed chairs sat by a beaten up mattress piled high with books. The cracked walls were bare save for a placard that said *Keep Smiling* and a color photograph of President Kennedy beside a lampoon drawing of a glamorous sad-eyed blond. The bubble over her head read: *I know his heart is mine.*

As the three of us crept deeper inside like nervous burglars, a dusky-voiced blues singer pleaded with his lover from somewhere out back.

"Cheever?" my father hollered, so loud I jumped.

The singer went mute and a large muscular woman came

wandering in behind the stench that had me stopping my breath.

"Sorry, sugah," she said, glancing my way then down at her splattered apron, "there ain't no dainty way to clean chitlins." In the hall's spare light her smooth black skin looked almost blue. She gave my parents a long fierce look, like the ones I'd seen on the children. "Can I help you folks?"

"We're old friends of Dr. Cheever," my dad explained.

The woman's tight mouth loosened and she wiped her hands on the messy towel slung across her left shoulder. "I'm Marilee. Pleased to meet you." She briefly touched her matted black hair. "Excuse my appearance, we weren't expectin' company. Cheeve couldn't hear y'all with that radio of his blastin'. His ears ain't too sharp these days anyways."

My father looked distressed. "He only told me he had to suspend his practice, not that they had left him blind. How has he been handling it?"

"The God's honest truth? Not too well. Not since his mama died." Marilee's mellow drawl was rich, like melted fudge. "Y'all come on back. Cheeve's gonna be as tickled as an old gray dog at Christmas."

My father yelled, "Cheeve, you old miscreant!" as we entered the yard and sent two startled chickens flapping. A stocky black man wearing dark green glasses whistled through his teeth and limped up, propelling himself with his cane.

"Bless my soul, if it isn't the great Emerson Gardner himself! When you wrote to say you'd try and stop my way I didn't believe you."

My dad chuckled as they warmly embraced. "You always were a hard man to convince."

Marilee excused herself to attend to her chitlins and Cheever seemed to size up my mother from behind his dark glasses. "I can't see to read but I can still make out shapes. I'd say you cut as fine a figure as ever, Mrs. Gardner. How has this peripatetic husband of yours been treating you?"

"As well as can be expected," she retorted stiffly.

"So there's room for improvement!" he chortled before turning my way. "And this is your son. Mighty proud to meet you! He won't tell you, but your daddy is the one who got this dumb cluck into medical school."

"Pure fiction. Don't listen to him," my father protested and now the whole yard filled with the stink. I clapped a hand to my nose to breathe through my mouth.

The blind man grinned. "City boy, huh? You folks need some water," he announced abruptly, hearing my mother start to gag. "You all go on inside while I fetch Marilee. It should be tolerable with the door closed."

The three of us escaped back into the house and my mother had me sit with her on the sofa. She whispered to ask if I was hungry when our host came hobbling in whistling a Negro spiritual I knew but could not name. My hand still cupped across my nose, I shook my head to say no while my father helped the doctor into the chair beside him.

"Finest water in Mississippi," Dr. Cheever boasted, as Marilee showed up carrying a tray with four filled glasses. "My pappy boxed these underground springs himself, God rest his soul."

Marilee smiled at me and said if she had known what day we were coming she'd have made some lemonade. My father told her not to worry, this was just a doctor's visit and she and Dr. Cheever both laughed.

"You didn't tell me your mother had passed," my father rebuked him as Marilee again left for her outdoor kitchen. "Why stay on now that she's gone?"

"You said it yourself—it's home."

With the bungalow doors shut front and back and the sun beating down, the air inside had grown stifling. My mother pressed her cool glass to the discolored knot on her forehead. "You're happy, living like this? With no indoor plumbing? No electricity?"

Dr. Cheever skinned his teeth. "I see just fine in the dark. All those years I spent striving, I was asleep. It all had to be taken out of my hands for me to wake up and see the real ugliness of it. That's why my mama would never budge—she said her soul would rest easier if she died among people who cared about her. Folks think I'm touched in the head, but the thing is, Mrs. Gardner, I feel safe here. I can please myself."

"They know about Birmingham?" asked my father.

"Doubt it—leastways, they never heard it from me. No need scaring my poor mama when she was suffering in bed."

An amazing idea bloomed in my head. Dr. Cheever was just like Richard in *Black Boy!*

"I always thought I'd get back my sight, but cocky scientists are a lot like preachers; they know there's no easier fool to skin than a believer. This old place is all I have left. I'm just grateful Marilee sticks by me."

My mother looked astonished. "She's your wife?"

The blind doctor grinned. "Not in the eyes of men—but I reckon that's how the Good Lord sees it."

Madeline had been worried about applying through an agency. Her goal was to start working as soon as possible and she had been warned that it could take months to get a green card. But after describing her training and experience, she had been cleared for a job at Brooklyn's largest hospital in less than three weeks. Her self-worth seemed to be easing back on track until she realized her supervisor had relegated her to giving sponge-baths and emptying bedpans. After a week she'd had enough of being treated like a maid.

"You do realize, Nurse Mauger, that I am a pediatric nurse certified by the Royal College of Medicine. I'm certainly capable of drawing blood and administering medications."

The ward supervisor, an anorexic Scots-Irish matron known in private and without affection as The Maugerwoman, peered down the long descent of her nose as if viewing a sample of sputum. "They may think you're qualified to perform brain surgery where you come from—on my floor you'll need to meet my standards."

"Meaning?"

"*Meaning*—there are some who hire for this hospital who think any little birdbrain will do, so long as she sports nice ankles and smiles prettily for the doctors."

"I see—except that where I come from," Madeline retorted

pointedly, "nurses have no time to smile, even if there were doctors for us to smile at."

The matron's face cracked with a chain-smoker's discolored grin. "You know what, Gardner? I think I like you! But I can't make exceptions. You'll need to strut your stuff on paper."

"You mean a written exam—"

"You *are* quick!"

"Will it earn me more money?"

The supervisor chuckled. "You bet, but it could take a year to make it official."

"A whole year?" Madeline smiled, catching on to her game, "that's disappointing!"

Nurse Mauger bent across the station counter to confide in a hush. "Here's the thing ... I'm shorthanded on the graveyard shift. You think you could manage the floor on your own for a week or two?"

Madeline gazed down half of the long corridor with its gray linoleum floor and calculated that at two to a room there had to be close to fifty beds on this wing alone. "All on my own?"

"Well, if you don't think you can handle it ... "

"Just for a fortnight?"

"My other nurse is out on leave. You'd be helping me out of a jam."

"Fine. I'll do it. How big is my raise?"

Nurse Mauger gave a raspish chuckle that sounded like a novice driver stripping his gears. "I can try and swing fifteen, but you'll probably have to settle for ten—"

"—percent?"

"Yes, percent."

"And it's permanent?"

"I'll put in the paperwork if you show me you can manage it." The supervisor returned her attention to the notes on her desk. "Now go bring me my charts after you've monitored those temperatures!" she growled and Madeline dashed off, suppressing her grin.

As it turned out, running the night shift did not carry the kind of autonomy she had been led to expect. While the demands of the job lived up to its billing, Nurse Mauger had failed to mention she would be reporting to a barrel-hipped Swede known in medical circles as Our Lady Macbeth. As is often the case when strong personalities bisect, Nurses Lindstrom and Gardner contracted an instant mutual loathing. Hospital wards tend to be as transparent as insular towns and patients with nothing but time on their hands make keen observers. The nightly blur of Madeline's white-stockinged feet had won the heart of one insomniac in particular.

"Slow down, my Jamaican flower, or you'll shed all your lovely petals!"

Madeline had stormed through the open door to her patient's room wagging her finger. "Now see here, Mr. Collingsworth," she chided the sixty-year-old, "I've told you twice to stop reading and turn off that light. You need your rest."

"How can anyone sleep with you galloping up and down the hallway?"

"Go on with you—I'm wearing soft-soled shoes. You could not possibly hear me."

Smiling, the large Trinidadian lowered his glasses. "Who told you we need sounds in order to hear? Ludwig van Beethoven composed his greatest works when he was stone deaf—"

"Oh, be still," she shut him up sternly. "Since you're awake, I'll punish you now." She took away his book and ordered the diplomat to lie on his side. When he gave her an injured look then complied, she waited to see his burnt-caramel frame relax, then plunged in the needle.

"Nurse Gardner, your gossamer touch is sublime," he gushed as she swabbed the pinprick on his bottom. "I can't tell you the torments I suffer at the hand of Our Lady Macbeth."

"Then you'd best behave, or I'll have her doing this tomorrow," she warned him affectionately, leaning across the bed to turn off his reading light.

"Too late. I'm leaving."

Madeline stopped in surprise. "Tomorrow? Malaria is not to be taken lightly. I doubt the doctors are ready to release you."

"That may be, but I'm ready to leave. Before I go I must ask you—" he gently paused, "have you demanded to know why our

Lady of Inverness has you running the entire floor while she lolls on her caboose thumbing through magazines?"

She had grown fond of Vincent Collingsworth who lightened her nights with his wit and erudition, but she worried that, in taking her fellow West Indian into her confidence, she may have shared more about her colleagues than she should have. "Not to worry," she assured him carelessly. "Things are always difficult when you're new, but nothing I can't handle."

"I admire your integrity, Nurse Gardner, so I hope you'll pardon a little advice from a ripe old hand. Speak kindly, but remind these Americans that it is about to be the 1950s; there are no more slaves and masters. If they know what you cannot tolerate, they'll be more inclined to respect you."

Although the diplomat's words would stay with her, Madeline's instincts urged her to accept the supervisor's challenge. If Nurse Mauger was putting her to the test, she would prefer to end up dead on her feet than allow Lady Macbeth to see her defeated. And after not working for over a year, not only did she still have the energy to do the job, the warrior in her enjoyed it. Nurse Lindstrom's greeting the following night was particularly sour.

"Here, he left this for you."

Madeline took the envelope the chunky Swede shoved in her face and straightaway noticed the tiny tell-tale bumps suggesting it had been sloppily resealed. "Somebody opened this!"

"Are you accusing me?"

"I don't know, Nurse Lindstrom—is your name somebody?"

The ice-blue gaze sparkled with enmity. "Use that tone with me again, and I'll see your perky black backside tossed from this hospital."

"I'm sorry," Madeline apologized, torn between heeding the diplomat's advice and preserving her job, "I didn't mean for it to sound as if I was accusing you. Do you happen to know who Mr. Collingsworth left this with?"

"No idea, sorry ..."

Madeline bit down on her lip as Lindstrom self-consciously dodged her look and hurried off. She would bet her last dollar that the woman had stolen the money Vincent had left her and there was

not a damn thing she could do about it. On the bright side, her trial
with Lady Macbeth was almost over.

"Congrats, Gardner," announced Nurse Mauger. "You're the
first newbie to make it through two whole weeks. The good news is
you'll get your raise, but they're keeping you on the graveyard shift."

Madeline thanked her, groaning inside. Vincent had clearly
seen how the play would unfold, but she would swallow her spit
until the time came to draw the line on Nurse Lindstrom and her
sticky fingers. It did not help that the diplomat's replacement turned
out to be a caviling housewife terrified that life was passing her by.

"Nurse Gardner, fifty isn't all that old any more—don't you
think I'm too young to be doing this?"

Within an hour of her admittance, the woman had asked her
that question three different times. She had tried to be reassuring,
telling her sweetly that nothing was going to go wrong—yes, her life
would go on, until she realized Mrs. Pettigrew's anxiety stemmed
less from the risk of undergoing major surgery than being left to her
own company. Like clockwork, every fifteen minutes she would
press Madeline's button—could you bring me a glass of water?—I
don't like this pillow—be a dear and rub my back, won't you? I still
can't fall asleep—you think you could let me have another sedative?
You can have the whole damn bottle, Madeline thought
uncharitably, answering yet another three a.m. summons.

And the whole time the woman had her rushing to and fro,
Nurse Lindstrom had not budged off her rump. By the second night,
Madeline was convinced Mrs. Pettigrew was either chucking her
pills or immune to barbiturates. That she was being asked to
comfort a mother of three moping about an elective hysterectomy
only made more tangible her own simmering resentment. She
started taking an extra while to respond after her light went on for a
seventh time until she was confronted by the untapped power
residing in the lungs of a neglected suburban housewife in the throes
of a mid-life crisis. So before Mrs. Pettigrew's howls woke every
patient on the wing, she went dashing and her fleet, soft-soled feet
promptly went flying.

"Dad, what are chitlins?" The question had been on my mind ever since our visit with Dr. Cheever. When he was slow to reply, my mother shifted towards me from her seat.

"They're made from a hog's intestines. The dish is more popular here in the South."

That explained the smell. It was the part about them being popular that had me stumped.

"But aren't intestines the bowels?"

"You're correct, son."

I sat up feeling encouraged hearing my dad sound impressed. He had worn a hang-dog look ever since saying good-bye to his friend and I saw this as my chance to repair some of the damage between us.

"So why would people eat them?" I knew what having a b.m. meant in our house.

He caught my eyes in his rear view mirror. "You remember the talk we had with Delroy about people in the South owning slaves? Well, back in those days, the masters would give their slaves the parts of the animal they didn't eat, like the ears and the snout and the entrails, which is another name for the intestines. Since it was either that or starve, the slaves figured ways to make those unwanted parts edible. Some made their chitlins tasty enough to be hailed as a delicacy, but the reason most people still eat them is because they're poor and entrails are cheap."

"Is Dr. Cheever poor?"

My parents sat mute as though each was hoping the other would answer first. My dad seemed to grasp that, after reading *Black Boy* and seeing all those scrawny kids stuck in that crummy settlement, I had started to realize that being poor was a terrible thing. He told me Dr. Cheever had grown up with next to nothing but he had worked very hard and become a prominent surgeon.

"Why did he go blind?"

My question seemed to hang in the air and in the silence I realized our back wheel was finally free of that pestering stone. I leaned up against the front seat awaiting his answer.

"He lost his sight two years ago when his house was destroyed. He's still adjusting but he'll be fine. He has dealt with hardship before."

Something kept me from asking how Dr. Cheever's home got destroyed, exactly what I am still not sure. Perhaps it was the look on my father's face when he saw that his friend was really blind. It was the same drained look I had seen on Anu when someone asked if she had any children. Or maybe the fact that I was seeing the world with clearer eyes made me able to figure out the very things my parents were not willing to tell me.

Before this trip, I'd had no idea there were these fences, like rules kids did not see and crossed at their peril; how someone could grab you and hang you from a tree, just for the fun of it, or blow up your house and leave you blind, and unless you were ready to fight, all you could do was keep quiet and stay on your side. What made it so perplexing was that I could not imagine Mrs. Calhoun and my Aunt Gwen being on opposite sides. If it was just my color that mattered so much, what made Justin Ito and me all that different? And if the law said people with different colors cannot eat or sleep together, how could Richard have lived with his grandmother if his grandmother's skin looked white? None of it made any sense.

All that I knew was lost, as practically overnight my happy childhood had vanished like a dream. Then suddenly, remembering what Anu had said, I took heart; no matter how bad things seemed, the ones I loved would always be with me.

Once he read Gwen's telegram, the choice had been made.

"Emerson? What on earth? Why aren't you in Canada?"

He had debated with himself the entire trip—should he tell her right off or get around to it later? There was no way around it. One more commitment was about to be broken, but he could no longer shoulder everyone's desperate expectations. For most of the winter his reason had been winning, wrestling loneliness into shame and his libido into contrition, then April arrived with her days as dark and cold as ever.

If he wasn't sure she would simply call him a quitter, he would have told her how his experience with Pastor Julian left him wondering if the student beside him saw a deserving classmate or a fraud. One especially thoughtful professor had fed his paranoia, taking pains during a lecture on psychosocial development to gaze his way and explain with great sympathy that what made the Negro Question so insoluble was the fact that the black African had contributed zero to civilization. At the time, he had been suffering from walking pneumonia and felt too weak to correct him, but as the semester wore on and he was forced to face his classmates' soft-eyed looks, he agonized over why he had not spoken up. Was it because he feared being laughed at if he explained that ancient Nubians were among the precursors of what is now called enlightened medical practice, or because he no longer trusted his own knowledge? Feeling more diminished by each token gesture, he was ready to erupt at the next thoughtless Canadian kindness. So when word of Maddy's accident arrived, he grabbed the excuse to avoid the spring's predictable new virus and threw in the towel.

He began to hand over the single red rose then stopped short seeing the two extravagant bouquets on her bedside table. "Sorry, I could only bring you my heart—"

"Oh, those—" Madeline gave the flamboyant floral arrangements an offhand glance and mutely accepted the offered rose. "The gigantic one is from Gwen and her new beau—you must meet Cyrus—you two are sure to hit it off. The dahlias are from Mrs. Pettigrew. She's very sweet but hopelessly neurotic." She nodded approvingly at the sheepskin coat. "I'm glad you finally bought yourself some proper winter clothes. Now tell me about Canada. How are your classes at university?"

He squeezed his fedora, still damp from the day's freezing rain. "I'm not going back."

"What do you mean you're not going back?"

"We can't keep imposing on Gwen. I'm staying to take care of you."

"Like hell you will! I'll be up and about in no time."

He frowned at her indulgently. "Maddy, you have a compression fracture and a herniated disc. The doctors want you off your feet for at least three weeks."

"I'm going to strangle that Gwendolyn Bilodeau!" Madeline

whacked the mattress with her fist. "I told her not to worry you."

Emerson braced himself to withstand the coming storm. "It's not just that—I can't take it. I can't face another winter—shivering morning, noon and night—living on tea and boiled cabbage. I can't bear us being apart for three more years."

"Then I'll come and join you! I can work just as easily up there."

He bowed his head and toyed with his hat. "No, I've decided. The Grail is clearly not meant for me. I cannot turn endeavor into penance and pretend it's virtue. I'm sorry."

He stood meekly while his wife set her tongue upon him with all the righteous outrage she had imbibed from her mother. He said not a word as she accused him of being too cowardly for his high-flown ideals, that he was quick to wilt at the slightest adversity and, most unforgivably, he was betraying the talent God gave him. But her vehemence fell on deaf ears. He had come knowing full well that she expected him to give in, for she had made the mistake of believing that their inner fires burned with the same ferocious certainty.

When he felt she had purged enough of her hurt to hear him out, he shared the rest of what he had planned. "There are other ways to serve the medical profession. I have decided to pursue a master's degree in biochemistry here in New York."

Madeline stopped and observed him closely, as if searching his heart, then after a thin, slightly puzzled smile, murmured, "well, why didn't you say so—"

He could not tell if she meant it as a rebuke, but when she motioned him close and stroked his cheek, he dared hope from her look that, given time, she would heal enough to forgive him.

Time was not as salutary when it came to her spine. The slipped disk in her back had begun pressing a nerve that made her cry out at the barest movement. Weeks after her fall she was still flat on her back in the hospital, confounding her doctors, distressing her husband, and threatening to climb the walls from boredom. The orthopedist thought they should consider surgery.

"I'll be candid with you, Mr. Gardner. I can't guarantee your wife won't end up in a wheelchair."

Madeline was dead set against it.

"No! I'm not going under anyone's knife! Emerson, I'll be fine. I'm sure of it."

Having seen how her face would contort after some small careless move, he was not convinced. It tore at him seeing her endure such constant agony, but he also recognized that spinal surgery was an extremely risky procedure. When he tried polling the hospital doctors they seemed equally divided until one of the first-year interns suggested trying a certain new wonder drug.

Though he firmly believed in mysteries, Emerson was not a firm believer in miracles, so he was not prepared to say the cortisone shots were the reason he arrived in her room the following day to find his wife on her feet, fully dressed, ready to be released. Reason suggested that after five weeks of natural healing and physical therapy, her last stumbling block had been finding a way through her memorized pain. Cortisone miracle or not, he sought out the intern and showered him with grateful praise, hoping, as he recalled his own trial under Midas Coombs, that the assertive young applicant had not just earned the spite of his astounded advisers.

For her part, Madeline could not wait to return to work so she kept to herself the fact that, while the injections had brought decisive relief, she was not pain free. The nurses were all eager to have her back, Our Lady Macbeth in particular, having been reminded how taxing the job actually was, but her doctors had not been fooled and insisted she take six weeks off to fully recover. She had protested, viewing all that time dawdling at home as a luxury she could not afford, until they assured her she would be receiving her usual salary. Apparently, Nurse Mauger confided, the administration greatly appreciated her not threatening a lawsuit over the janitor's failure to mark off the wet linoleum floor he had just finished mopping.

She had grown so accustomed to living with pain she scarcely noticed when another sharp twinge crimped her spine. More distressing was trying to predict her store in life now that her husband had thrown away his last best chance. She thought about her mother's lifelong pretense and whether it had been easier to endure than being slandered as a marriage-wrecker. It made her wonder if love commanded duty, and whether duty alone could foster love. Not wanting the anger inside her to boil into bitterness, she kept her thoughts positive and set her heart on finding them an apartment. Although the one they ended up renting was smaller than she had hoped and got minimal sunlight, her disappointment was greatly outweighed by the fact that her best friend lived in easy walking distance.

By June, the sudden clenches had finally dissipated as the fragrant heat of early summer aroused parts of her body she had only been aware of while she was pregnant. Emerson resisted her at first, wary of re-injuring her back, but his reticence only intensified a desire to feel him inside her. The new urge seemed strange because, as determined as she had been to bear his child, she had never looked forward to their lovemaking. Having counseled her daughters that intercourse was a wifely concession begotten by Eve, Miss Dora would say her fall into lust proved the power of the Big Apple's temptations, but living with Gwen, who would rather attend a concert or a lecture at the Spiritual Center than see a Broadway play or the latest hit movie, had felt downright prudish after her time at Aunt Jamesie's. The truth was, it had been years since she had enjoyed the privacy she needed in order to relax in bed with her husband. Even when they were alone at home in Jamaica, her brain had been too pressured about conceiving to become immersed in the moment. Now she could sigh and moan, even bawl out her frustrations like some jilted heroine in one of her sister's cheap erotic novels, but she never did. She was too impressed by the toughness of New York and its long summer days that let even pure girls stay out late to play and made Emerson's every loving exertion expressively tender. It helped that her back had made him so cautious, for it left her free to take charge and see if two distinct bodies able to fuse in one ecstatic motion could ride over their troubles. By September the air felt as heavy as it had always been, yet so much lighter. Her pains forgotten, she was ready to face the future, cheered to find her strength and hopes refreshed.

My gut was making hungry noises as we pulled up to the first gas station after Mobile Bay. As I would later discover, the sleepy-looking spot was called Spanish Fort and was the site of the last major battle in the War Between the States. The station itself, an unpainted slate-roofed shack boasting a single ancient pump, looked as if it dated almost from Lee's surrender. Inside the open garage, a rusted propane tank stood by a long black hose hanging looped on the wall alongside several used tires.

My father looked skittish as he stepped out to ask the attendant if he would mind checking our Valiant's undercarriage. The mechanic, a rangy fellow with straggly brown hair flowing out from under his cap, chuckled and said, "shirr thang, that's what I'm paid for." As he left to fetch his dolly, I noticed that he walked with his shoulders hunched, as if toting some immovable load.

My mother had been nursing her bruise and had not said a word for the last half hour. I felt bad, knowing she had to be as hungry as I was since it was almost two and we'd been living on raisins and sunflower seeds since seven that morning. I was hoping the fact that she had not been complaining meant she decided my father was right to take the old farmer's advice and keep driving till we were back on the interstate. If there was one thing this trip was teaching me, it was that there were some things worth kicking up a fuss about, and some that were not.

The mechanic reappeared from under the chassis and assured my dad that our little side trip into a Mississippi ditch had caused no real damage beyond a puny dent on the muffler, which he had 'tightened up right proper.' Seeing our luggage piled in the back, he asked where we were headed. "Ain't that the berries!" he cried when my father explained that we were on our way to Miami to board a ship bound for the Caribbean Isles. "Vacation?"

"Nope," my mother snapped. "It's a one-way trip."

"Good on yah—" the attendant replied, uncertain how to size up her answer, "though they say the weather's darn near perfect in California. Either way, you're smart not to be tarryin' 'round here—the climate's not that hospitable—if you catch my drift. Gee, thanks—" he blurted when my father handed him three dollars, "that's mighty big of you! Sure you won't take me along—? They say

I got me a half-n-half cousin down in Barbados."

My dad laughed along then asked if there was somewhere nearby that might serve us something to eat. After taking what my growling stomach took for an eternity, the mechanic replied that there was a place with decent grub down in Loxley, but we'd be better off waiting until we reached Pensacola.

"Just keep on over to Eastside and y'all will be fine. So long as the traffic ain't crazy, you should be there in about an hour."

My father thanked him again and climbed back into the driver's seat. His look was pleading as he turned to my mother. "What do you say? You think you can make it that long?"

She let the handkerchief fall into her lap and I was glad to see the lump on her forehead looked smaller and that she was no longer bleeding. "You have the wheel. I'm just here for the ride."

The hurt in her voice made me sad. Where had our 'all for one and one for all' motto gone? And if it was really gone for good, on what side did I belong? Or was I on my own?

The wedding of Gwendolyn and Cyrus the following June was the climax of what would prove a transformative year for the Gardners. Madeline had earned her certification and, thanks to The Maugerwoman's helpful persistence, had gotten her raise and was back working days. Even Nurse Lindstrom had been among the staff waiting to greet her, laughing along when they toasted her return with sip-cups of glucose and water and christened her Slippy. Emerson, meanwhile, had completed both semesters at university and begun work on his thesis. As Madeline predicted, he had been delighted with Cyrus Helger, and quickly wrote to tell Mason that he had made friends with a theosophist. The wedding itself was a marriage of temperance and cross-cultural splendor. The nuptials had been a pearl of Christian simplicity, while the banquet, held in an opulent, sculpture-filled temple, featured neither flesh nor wine, but left in the hands of a Chinese epicure, the Helgers' guests were treated to a feast fit for the vegan gods of Pythagoras.

Back home after the reception, Madeline acknowledged she was smitten.

"I adore this city! Why don't we stay?"

Emerson looked doubtful. "Dr. Joseph had the society sponsor me because he thought I could help our country. I owe it to him to go home."

"That's ridiculous! They did it because the government cheated you out of that scholarship. You graduated top of your class. It's not your fault you'll never be a doctor."

"Maybe it *is* my fault. You said yourself, I should have stuck things out in Canada."

"Fine. If it bruises your conscience that much, let's just pay back the money."

"With what?"

"We can sell our house back home. Or we can borrow against it and pay off the loan once we're both working." When he was slow to answer, Madeline finished slipping out of her maid-of-honor gown and sat close beside him.

"There are so many more chances for us here. Do you really want to go home a failure?"

"So that's what concerns you? You're afraid people will think that you married a failure?"

"You're the one saying it, not me!"

Emerson shifted away, stung by the potency of his temper. He had spent his life learning to discipline his passions, to channel destructive emotions into pursuing good, and here he was, unable to escape the demons born of resentment. No matter what he said or did, he would suffer, knowing that between him and the woman he loved stood the irredeemable fact that he had fallen short. If ever so briefly he had sensed it in her eyes or in the hollow of her voice, through all her miseries—the failures to conceive, the loss of her sister, the terrible moment she learned the baby had died followed by the gnawing of self-contempt as she resigned herself to never giving birth again—not once, even in the face of those painful rejections, had she blamed her unhappiness on him. That she never put into words the feelings he had glimpsed did not mean there was peace in understanding. It was almost too unbearable for him to accept that, even though he adored her still, their marriage had been diminished. For love does not easily concede that what will be, will be; it punishes the heart that fails to make real a loved one's dreams.

And so it was decided. They would stay in New York and become United States citizens to improve their prospects for work and someday adopting a child. Freed from her fear of returning home to her consummate humiliation and the recapitulation of poor Little Miss Big Head, Madeline set to reordering her life. Vincent Collingsworth's advice smoldering in the back of her mind, she bit her tongue during Nurse Mauger's weekly dressing-down dished out with indifference to the guilty and innocent. She smiled prettily to her doctors and patients alike, less to worm into their good graces, so much as to sustain her new positive outlook and focus away from her pinching back. It was far from easy, as the pressed nerve was keen to remind her when that time of the month was approaching, but as a product of Miss Dora's rigorous training, she understood that pain was part and parcel of what women were expected to suffer.

She noticed that her colored invalids were the quickest to see through her smile, shaking their wise gray heads when she said she was fine, and trying not to burden her with their entire weight when she came to ease them onto their bedpans. By contrast, her white patients would either unconsciously tense and shrink from her touch, forcing her use all her strength to shift them, or go limp, as if her slender frame could bear not only their weight, but the weight of their troubles. Sometimes, when bitterness or the odor of death overwhelmed them, they would curse her and demand to know why she was smiling. If she was feeling vindictive, she would tell them it was because she was happy.

And it was partly true. She had fallen hard for the restless city that epitomized America's world-beating swagger. Fifth Avenue's extravagant fashions fevered her sleep as did the brilliant madness of Times Square at midnight and the joyful delirium overrunning the Great White Way on New Year's Day. She loved this place packed with scruffy migrated talent free to hustle across an island where bankers played the role of kings and concrete visions grew taller by the day, where young prophets came to suffer and sing sad songs for those who knew what suffering was and set their sights on the moon. For a Kingston misfit who had seen so many great hopes wither and die, nothing seemed that far out in nineteen fifties New York.

Though Emerson was impressed by its 'can-do' spirit, he sensed that driving all that fitful energy was the fear of being judged. He glimpsed it in the darting eyes of the Polish bellboy gulping a sandwich grabbed from the Automat and the Italian waiter's hesitation when Cyrus Helger invited him to lunch in Manhattan. He heard it in the deli-owner's halting English and the Irish cop's bark as he spooked a tiny black boy. For all its newness, the city was as hidebound as New Orleans, its luxuriant towers built on the same old complexes. Difference was, if you wanted to make it here, you hunted your pleasures in the dark of night and never got seen putting cream in your coffee.

He and Maddy had been introduced to uptown-after-hours by Gwen's friend Joe. Harlem, he said, is where America goes to make peace with its soul. The night they joined Joe at Minton's Playhouse had been a revelation. Billed as music for the literate, Emerson had come expecting the blue reflections of Muddy Waters, or even better, the mercurial wit of New York's swing-time aristocrats. Instead, the five-piece band had him hearing the Prince's screams as his life was beaten out of him. The cacophony was apocalyptic; screeching phrases rushing in waves, the horns' brass fury deconstructing melody to simulate the honking insanity of the daily rat race. Jazz was too modest a term for this feverish exorcism: it was Nietzsche shaking his fist at Paul; Douglass calling out the mendacity of liberty bought with bondage; it was Aimé Césaire excoriating Europe's civilized bigotry; it mocked, it howled, it snarled and it wailed; it shook Beethoven out of his grave to renounce Napoleon, once more, with feeling; it was Sojourner Truth pounding her mighty chest, making husbands and slave-masters quail in their boots. This was not music to entertain; this was passion boiled from the blood of four murderous centuries intent to rip Rome's transported web of greed and deceit. At the end, he and Madeline were grateful the onslaught was over. The dissonance asked too much of their fragile contentment.

Emerson was not any happier the following day when his wife came home flushed with excitement.

"I want to take another stab at singing. Joe thinks I have what it takes."

"Joe is a dreamer."

"Thanks."

"I wasn't commenting on your ability."

"No? Then what, Emerson—I shouldn't even try?"

"Joe's a crusader. We can't keep chasing what's not meant to be."

"Maybe this time it is! I didn't know Joe would be there when I stopped by Gwennie's. She pressed me to sing and he was honestly impressed. Emerson, today I had to help lift a four hundred pound patient. I don't know how much longer my back can take it. Joe is a superb musician. I think he knows what he's talking about."

"Joe plays in beatnik dens and lounge bars. That's not the milieu I want for my wife."

"He's not talking about having me sing jazz. He agrees with Juan. He thinks I have the voice to sing opera."

Emerson stared at her, dumbstruck, his thoughts in a fog. Finally recovered, he asked if they could talk about it when his mind was not preoccupied with completing his thesis. She told him fine, but she intended to accept Joe's offer to coach her on the operatic repertoire. He rang Joe the very next day.

"Why are you feeding fantasies to my wife?" He did not think Joe was out to bed his wife, as he suspected had been the case with Juan Ferrier. Joe was far more dangerous. "You know what I'm talking about. How many colored singers have you heard at the Metropolitan Opera?"

Joe said that was the point. Someone had to try and Maddy has a beautiful voice with exceptional high notes.

"Joe, I'm asking you as a friend—don't make her part of your noble experiment. She's endured enough disappointment."

Joe finally agreed to be frank with her about the realities, then adding to Emerson's annoyance, claimed that ultimately it was Maddy's decision.

He broached the subject with her again that evening. Before he could explain why he had sounded so hesitant, she looked him square in the eye and told him to put it out of his mind and focus on his thesis. She had not sounded at all resentful, so he was surprised when Gwendolyn Helger drew him aside the next time they met and asked how he could be so unfeeling.

"Come now, Gwen. You, of all people, must know it's impossible what Joe has in mind. I don't want Maddy getting her hopes up and ending up crushed."

Gwen considered him with pity. "You poor sensible scientists. You think what hurts most is on the surface."

Our stop at Bob's Good Eats in East Pensacola had proved both educational and a gut-releasing gift. Not only did the sight of an indoor bathroom appear as a blessing from heaven, my stomach was so grateful I would have sworn to God Himself that Bob's macaroni and cheese baked in a pie crust was the finest dish in the whole wide world. It completely erased the brutal memory of my encounter with chitlins and as I dug into some sweet potato pie, I felt so at home I almost thought that I was back in L.A. perched at the counter in Anu's health food store.

I had always felt that Anu and I shared a secret we never spoke about and no one suspected. I never knew how old she was, except that she was older than my mother. From we met I had been captivated by Anu's hair, the thickest, shiniest black hair I had ever seen, but for a reason I only understood years later, it always struck me as being unusual. Not that it was easy to tell where Anu came from just going by looks. To me, her face was a beautiful dark orange moon that glowed pure kindness. Her 'golden boy' was what she called me. Back when my legs were too short to manage it, Anu would lift me onto one of the metal-framed high stools and, without me asking, pour me some of her fresh-squeezed carrot juice in a cone-shaped paper cup set inside a stainless steel holder. I never got tired of drinking Anu's carrot juice and neither did she, which, now that I think of it, might partly explain how she got her complexion.

I must have been four or five when I heard that customer ask about her family and saw the blood drain from Anu's face. I hated to see her that sad, so after thinking it over I suggested that once I was bigger, if she liked, the two of us could be married. (Like most small children accustomed to being doted on, I thought highly of myself.) As she replied, Anu's look gave me my first faint sense of what it means to bear untouchable sorrow. "Thank you, sweet boy, but I have a husband." She reached across the counter and placed her palm against my heart. "You can't see him because he's always right there inside me." Her answer would puzzle me for years until I learned that Anu had escaped from Europe during the war but her husband and son had been captured and killed.

It was only after we finished eating and my parents stayed to chat that I realized this was the first restaurant I had ever been in and not seen a single white face. The place that looked packed when we wandered in had mostly emptied out and Bob had come to join us while we finished dessert. He had been plainly excited when he heard we were traveling from 'way out west' and was eager to boast about his hometown. We learned that Aztecs and African slaves were among Pensacola's first settlers and that after the great warrior Geronimo surrendered, he and several Apache families had been brought here to do heavy labor and also serve as a tourist attraction. Bob claimed that before the Jim Crow laws took over, Pensacola had been run by his own granddaddy and other well-to-do colored folks. He bragged that back then the town had become so successful it was advertised as an example of Negro government by none other than Booker T. Washington.

My stomach content, I began to feel sleepy and lost track of what they were saying, but before we left Bob must have touched on a sensitive subject because my parents started jawing at each other the second we were back in the car. Although I couldn't quite follow my father's argument as the words 'sop,' 'smokescreen' and 'de facto' were all new to me, it appeared he did not share Bob's view on a law that made it wrong for schools in Pensacola to do what they were doing in Los Angeles. My mother, on the other hand, sounded pretty annoyed by what he was saying and kept insisting that the law was not a fig-leaf (whatever that means) and that anyone with a lick of sense knew that the Supreme Court ruling had been long overdue. That's when my dad lost his temper and had me shaking in my sneakers even though I knew they were both too worked up to notice. He told her she was kidding herself if she thought people in this country would somehow suddenly become color blind. To which my mother replied that thank goodness there were men like Bob and Mundy willing to fight for their rights because if it was left to people like him, we would still be stuck riding in the back of the bus, crying 'massa.'

When she tossed her head, convinced she had won the point, I prayed that was the end of it, but my father was not about to let her have the last word on this one. "That only shows you don't know the first thing about human nature—or Booker T. Washington!"

The instant silence was thick. Though I still lacked the crucial pieces to make out the puzzle, I was beginning see that while some of my parents' differences did revolve around me, there were a lot more issues between them. I had blamed myself for sparking the battle, but it was clear to me now that this war had long been coming. It did not make me feel any better. It seemed loony that two people who shared the same bed, ate the same food, and loved the same child could see the same things so differently. I knew from reading *Black Boy* that a kid can have good reasons to hate his upbringing, but apart from resenting the fact that my father was afraid to let me have a bicycle, until two days ago there had been nothing about my home life to make me wish I'd been born to another family. In fact, my dad had punished me only once, and that was only because my mother told him to. Happily, my wits had kept me from laughing and letting him catch on that it didn't hurt one bit.

Now that I had seen our Trinity's dangerous fault lines, I wondered what would have happened if my mother had lost back in Las Cruces. Would we have slept out in the desert? What if Sheriff Gomez had not been so understanding? Or a white man? Would we still be in jail? It dawned on me that while she was busy demanding our rights, these had been the questions troubling my father. And the fact that they troubled him still was what stoked my mother's anger.

"Maddy, we're going to be late—you can fix your face in the cab!"

Madeline quickly erased another skewed stroke of her eyebrow-pencil. She hated hearing Emerson pretend to be oh-so-cool. He was right that it was an extravagance, but there was no other option except the back of a bus, and there was no way her spine or her pride was going to tolerate that for seventy-two hours. If he was set on leaving New York, she was leaving it in style.

She had cared enough not to remind him that while he was the one making the decision she was the one with the primary income. It was not as if they could not afford it. As she fully expected, Dr. Joseph had returned the bank check, then written her back to say that he blamed himself for discounting the American reality and she should try and convince Emerson that, while he was right to be disappointed, he had not let anyone down. It took her some time and effort, but she managed to persuade him that Dr. Joseph was being sincere. Still, the quizzical look he gave her said that he doubted even she believed that everyone who knew them appreciated just how much they had sacrificed.

Although she had been blindsided by her husband's abrupt decision, she was not surprised that he wanted to leave, even if he was too embarrassed to admit his real reason. It amazed her that after three years living in this climate, her husband still could not abide the cold. At the first brisk October wind he would grumble like a bear without a cave to skulk in through winter. She had laughed out loud when she saw how he wrapped up to confront November: after starting with the prerequisite long underwear, he would tuck his shirt and tie inside his trousers then button on a heavy cardigan before cramming his arms inside the suit jacket and swaddling his resulting bulk in a full-length wool coat, the polished wing-tips protecting his feet nestled safe inside shin-high rubber galoshes. And that even on a snow-free day well above freezing. Now that she pictured it—with those stout limbs and big brown head atop that fuzzy-haired torso, he did have a rather ursine look. No wonder the poor dear despises the cold, she joked to Gwen, in his last life he was Winnie-the-Pooh!

So it did not surprise her that Emerson had relished Cy

Helger's suggestion that they join him and Gwen out West. It was the autumn of '52, a year since he'd earned his postgraduate degree, and while there had been several promises, so far the only firm to call him back had him shuttling samples to and from hospitals and college laboratories across all five buroughs. Which meant, with winter on its way, he could look forward to trudging the ice-slicked city streets hoping not to slip and break his neck, then sloshing home through melting slush ankle-deep for the bountiful reward of thirty dollars a week. It would mean good-bye to Carnegie Hall and her covert lessons with Joe, but after reflecting on the hazards she faced at work and how much she already missed her best friend, Madeline was all in for the plan: it was California, here we come!

As their taxi stopped at the curb of the airport terminal, she was glad she had chosen to wear her pricey new gabardine suit and matching powder-blue pumps. Emerson had scoffed, saying it was silly to doll herself up just to sit cramped inside a smokey tin crate for eight and half hours, but scanning her fellow passengers she started to gloat. Every one of them could have been on the way to an auspicious conference or special event. And the good thing about wearing a suit, she enlightened her un-fashion-conscious husband as they settled inside the plane's frosty cabin, is that once we touch down in sunny Los Angeles the jacket becomes a stylish accessory.

She had gripped Emerson's hand with such force through take-off it was a wonder she had not broken one of his fingers. At each heart-stopping plunge up to and beyond their regrettably short layover in Chicago she would clutch his arm and feel the tension he was hiding beneath his smug grin at seeing her show weakness. She had cast envious glances at their swivel-hipped hostess stalking the aisles in her snug navy suit wondering how she managed to keep her balance on those thin stilettos. And as they bounced inside another death-evoking air pocket she was tempted to ask their placid attendant for one of the cocktails she was doling out liberally but decided against it. More than knowing that Emerson was bound to disapprove, she had tried a few tiny sips of champagne only twice and she worried that while a drink might settle her nerves, it would be humiliating if it upset her stomach.

By the time they landed in Los Angeles, she was so spent from anxiety they were halfway down the mobile stairs to the tarmac before she realized she had forgotten to take off her jacket and fold it stylishly across her arm. She checked the observation deck and sure enough, there was Gwen right in front at the rail, swinging her arms trying to draw their attention. They had left New York with its early morning November nip and arrived in time to greet L.A.'s afternoon heat near its peak, but even though she was boiling inside her smart powder-blue suit, as she wiggled a dainty gloved hand up towards the excited, waving crowd, she felt for one brief, heady moment like a movie star.

The drive from the airport in the Helgers' new pink Cadillac convertible prolonged the fantasy that she was living in the pages of those celebrity magazines which boredom had led her to devour during her weeks of immobility. She reached for Emerson's hand, and for the first time in far too long, sensed him at peace as he smiled at her loving gesture and gently squeezed her fingers in return. As if tuned to her fancy, Cyrus decided to veer off for a quick jaunt through Beverly Hills. More than the fabulous homes, it was the intense blue sky above the smooth green grass and the towering palms, the sun's familiar warmth kissing her cheek bringing memories of mangoes and slow cane sugar to the heady perfume of roses and the smell of the ocean that dared her to hope that, after all the pain and heartbreak, they had finally found home.

As we left Pensacola and my parents retreated to nurse their latest wounds, I returned to my book, wanting no part in disrupting the truce. When I first started reading *Black Boy*, I did not think he and I had much in common, but after all I had seen I began to see poor Richard differently. We both were oddballs who loved to read and let our imaginations run wild and neither of us had time for childish games because somehow, early on, we both had set our sights on a career that no one, apart from our mothers, thought was permitted for boys like us.

What impressed me most about Richard was that even though he often went hungry, unlike his friends who were happy to steal, stealing never occurred to him. His strength of character reminded me of the day I was on my way home from school and ran into two boys I knew vaguely from the neighborhood. They wanted me to go with them to the corner store, proposing that if we put all our pennies together, instead of each of us buying a lollipop or an atomic fireball, we could split a chocolate bar. While two of us stood in the aisle counting to see if we had enough for a jumbo with peanuts, the other boy snatched a giant bag of M&M's and whispered for me to hide it inside my jacket. I was stunned, but from the casual way the two of them were going about it I realized they had stolen from the store before and simply picked me to be the possible fall guy. When I froze and shook my head no, the boy shrugged and slipped the candy inside his shirt and made his escape while his accomplice gave the owner a penny for his Tootsie Roll. As I pictured myself being hauled off in handcuffs vainly pleading my innocence, I could not wait to get out of there, but something told me I had better not run.

I remember thinking I had done something noble by refusing to accept my share of the loot, but reading *Black Boy*, I began to appreciate what made Richard exceptional. The day we stole from that store the weather had been unusually cold for L.A. but at the time it never dawned on me that I was the only one wearing a jacket. I had never been tempted to steal because I had never shivered walking home from school or gone to bed hungry. How long would I have held to my principles had we driven halfway across Florida and not found some place willing to feed us? What if we lost all our money? Or were robbed? Would my parents let me starve? As these notions mounted, I grew more and more troubled. My father liked to quote 'to thine own self be true' but what are the rules when you're deemed an untouchable? Should I be like Delroy Angell and carry a gun? And if I do that in order to survive, does it mean I should be ready to kill? Does being the wrong color make you an outcast or simply an outlaw?

As a child raised in the Fellowship who loved his mother, I never had trouble imagining myself as an idea born of the Holy Spirit's infinite consciousness. That sense of being part of a boundless universe dreamt up by a loving God was nurtured in all the children of Fellowship members who came in every color, from a range of countries and widely varied backgrounds. What I understood now was that people like Anu, through years of meditation and sheer strength of will, had learned to cocoon themselves from the world I discovered in Las Cruces. Perhaps if they had explained to us kids that some grown-ups hate others in order to hide their own fear, I might not have tortured myself trying to understand why people I had never met thought I was scum.

The sign on the Interstate announced that we were nearing Ponce de Leon and I recognized the name of the conquistador who supposedly discovered Florida while searching for the Fountain of Youth. I wondered who had put that nutty idea in his head and if, as he lay dying from a native's poisoned arrow, he blamed his father or the Holy Spirit.

As much as he enjoyed the Helgers' company and living in their glass-walled home with its bird's-eye view of the city, Emerson was impatient to find a place of his own. He had long sensed that Cyrus Helger was not hurting for money, and now that the Fellowship had moved its headquarters out west, Cy's lectures on Eastern Philosophy and Astral Meditation had made him something of a celebrity guru to several of the Golden State's wealthiest families. In line with the Center's teachings, Cyrus refused to counsel them for money, but he was not above accepting their gifts, which explained the new Cadillac and the interest-free mortgage on a palatial bungalow in the Hollywood Hills. Gwen had begged them to stay through Easter but he feared that the longer they perched in such rarified surroundings, the harder Maddy would feel the comedown. Adding shame to his mounting anxieties, the Helgers' lofty address left him dependent on Gwen to chauffeur him down the long winding canyon roads and across Los Angeles while he searched for employment. So after the calendar turned to February and a job in medicine had still not materialized, he thanked his friends for their hospitality and moved with his wife to a garage apartment just west of the city center.

"I know it's small, but we can't keep depleting our savings."

"So let me go back to nursing."

"I don't want you working."

"And I don't want you hauling crates for a dollar-twenty an hour!"

"It's just for the time being. The job's from two to ten, so I can still do interviews."

"Emerson, really, I'm not an invalid."

"No. And that's final."

He ended up straining his back his second week on the job. He managed to avoid lifting the heavier cartons for the rest of the day, but by the end of the shift he was in so much discomfort the twenty minute walk home took him close to an hour. He had mentioned Maddy's bad fall in a letter to Mason and remembered her brother responding that they should try chiropractic treatments. He had read about Palmer's theories on spinal subluxation and they fit with his own opinion that a person's overall health relied on a well-functioning nervous system. Maddy had laughed in his face when he brought up the notion, but since he dared not tell her how he had hurt himself, he decided to turn his latest adversity into opportunity.

He waited until she had gone for her early morning walk the following day before crawling out of bed and struggling into his clothes. The aspirin had helped, but by the time he limped from the bus to the chiropractor's office the pain was almost unbearable. The practitioner turned out to be a dour Midwesterner whose manner, like his marginally furnished office, betrayed a strong affection for thrift. But after answering all of Emerson's questions with terse precision, Dr. Philemon showed that what he lacked in eloquence he made up for with a remarkably sensitive pair of hands. As Emerson strolled off to work, much relieved and in jubilant spirits, he was more determined than ever that Maddy should brave a treatment.

Try as he might, he could not convince her, but he did earn a kiss and a hug at the end of the week when he came home to announce that he had quit the warehouse and found other work. His self-esteem was wallowing in his wife's rare embrace until she asked what the job entailed and he told her.

"A dishwasher?" Maddy cried, dropping her arms. "You're excited about getting work washing dishes?"

"It's a lot less demanding and the pay is nearly twice what I was making. There is one drawback—" he took a reflexive step backwards, "it means working nights and weekends."

His wife was flabbergasted. "Washing dishes? We left New York so my husband could work as a domestic?"

He wrapped his arm around her sinking shoulders. "Trust me, it's just for now. I never told you—but when Cyrus wrote to entice us out to California he had just finished our astrological charts. He says our aspects here look very positive. Things are going to turn our way."

"Now see here, Emerson," she warned, squirming free from his clutch, "I'm glad we joined the Fellowship, but you know I'm not totally sold on that rigamarole about planetary influences. I've gone along with you this far, now I'm telling you straight—I won't sit here and fold my hands if you're still washing dishes come the summer."

He smiled and caressed her cheek sensing it was not the time to try and explain that all the trials they had been through had already been written. He was even more sure of it after his follow-up visit with Dr. Philemon. Cy Helger was right. It was not that he had wasted the last six years on some futile chase—the stars had guided him through all his privations so that he could learn that curing was not the same as healing, that just as a brokered peace did not stop the next calamitous war, medicine's new profusion of synthetic miracles did not allow for the patience needed to probe beyond the symptoms and address the cause. He had left the chiropractor's office a man possessed, sure that the ancients had granted him the answer to his long and frustrating quest.

Madeline had been both perturbed and gratified by the change in her husband. It would soon be summer and, despite having failed to land a single interview, he continued to be cheerful. She would have been climbing the walls or already defied him and applied for a job had Gwen not taken to showing up unannounced to take her for a spin in her fancy pink Cadillac while Emerson was out washing dishes. She had always worried that there was a guileless complacency to the man she had married, that his penchant for passive resistance made him soft. When on one of their long weekend drives she confessed to being afraid that after so many letdowns her husband had lost his ambition, her best friend chuckled. "Gosh sakes, Maddy, give the poor man time. He has barely been here six months and you think he should be running Johnson and Johnson!"

Madeline felt it ungrateful to mention how cut off she felt in the sprawling city that seemed the size of a continent as she tried to find her way around without rapid transit. It took constant effort to keep from bemoaning the fact that they had rented their three bedroom home in Kingston to pay for an apartment the size of her walk-in closet, or that Friday and Saturday nights found her alone without a gramophone, straining to hear Renata Tebaldi sing *Vissi d'arte* through the static on her dime-store radio. For her grateful side, it meant those intimate moments in bed with her husband felt even more precious. They were both naturally reserved, so under the day-to-day stresses of work, finding that spark of romance had sometimes taken more effort than either could muster. That all changed in California. Not only did Emerson come home every day and clasp her with purpose, the tenderness he had shown after she hurt her back had bloomed into a quivering desire that entered her with arousing slowness, restraining its need until she relaxed and gradually matched his speed to blend their merging cries that reached deep and brought peace.

During those months, Gwen's attentions told her that her best friend knew, without her saying it, that she missed the freedom and bustle of New York. If Gwen's plan was to make her fall in love with the Golden State's more languid attractions, it worked like a charm. And if the infatuation had begun on her ride through Beverly Hills, their overnight trips to Big Sur and Cambria had completed the seduction. Californians seemed to share her enchantment, sporting a breezy, self-possessed air as if they had earned their return to Eden and were now immune to the rest of humanity's mundane struggles. If there were pockets of misery filled with the less fortunate, she did not see them. Her only qualm since they first arrived had been induced by the earthquake that seemed out to demolish L.A. in time for Thanksgiving. It happened near sunset and she would never forget how the walls had bowed towards her, threatening that at any instant they could cave in and crush her. She had never felt the earth shift beneath her, so she had been astounded by her landlord's nonchalance. 'Oh that,' he said with a dismissive smile when she asked how he had managed. 'That wasn't but a jiggle. You should've felt the one last August.'

His nonchalance reminded her of one particularly splendid afternoon, strolling with Gwen through Venice Beach, and seeing a shaggy-haired young couple, their pale skin toasted to a golden sheen, suddenly halt right in front of them for a long passionate kiss. She had recoiled at their vulgar display until she realized their casualness was part of the spell. Glorious sunshine, shielding mountains, a placid ocean promising pleasant temperatures and congenial weather, these were gifts to be grasped with the innocence of children, undisturbed by moral twitches and impotent tremors.

"There's been some mistake—our secretary is in charge of hiring the janitors."

Emerson managed not to flinch at being waved off after a glance. He checked the nameplate on the wood-paneled office's desk and felt his heart's hammer-beats slow when it matched the one in his letter. "Dr. Mulholland? I'm Emerson Gardner—" He waited for the scientist to close his mouth and collect himself. "You scheduled me for an interview this morning."

Mulholland frowned at Emerson's outstretched hand and ignored it, gesturing for him to be seated. Taking time to gather his thoughts, the bespectacled scientist absently fingered the resume sitting on his desk. "So, you're Emerson Gardner—" he murmured, retaining the look of a rambling zoologist astonished to be facing a kind of mammal he could not identify. He peered at the curriculum vitae and shook his head. "Am I reading this correctly? Bachelor of Science degrees in biology and pharmacology and a Master's in biochemistry? No wonder Dr. Peel sounded so excited." Gray eyes as cold as a fencer's blade peered up through the black horn-rimmed glasses and trained on Emerson's face. "Pity you left out the most important part—"

The hammer-beats returned and increased their pace. "Did I? What part was that?"

"Oh, I think we both know the part I'm referring to—" Mulholland's lips curled as he stood to hand back the resume. "You're overqualified. I'm sure someone like you with those credentials will be happier in a position more suited."

Emerson left the interview in a haze of rage and desperation. Just when he thought that fate had him on the right path he ended up chasing his future down another blind alley. Cyrus had led him to believe that Californians tended to be free spirits, less cramped by convention than most Americans, but Mulholland's attitude had been as cynical as the detectives who manhandled him down in New Orleans. At least back east his interviewers concealed their discomfort with his race behind a pose of sympathy or respectful indifference. Now what was he going to do? With the end of June approaching, he was faced with having to choose between pulling up stakes and heading home broke, or bearing the shame of seeing his wife back at work just to help him put food on the table.

"It's not the end of the world," she said lightly. "This is not Jamaica. No one's going to criticize you."

"You don't understand. I came out here thinking things would be different. It's as bad as down South."

"No it's *not.* You're just angry and I don't blame you."

He was about to explain that he was not so much angry as near his wits' end when Madeline put off consoling him to answer the telephone. "It's for you," she said, her hopeful look intrigued as she passed him the receiver.

"Mr. Gardner?"

"Yes, speaking."

"I'm Dr. Peel from the Institute for Holistic Medicine and Research. I was curious as to why you turned us down."

"Turned you down?" Emerson gave his wife a mystified shrug seeing her eyes search his. "Not at all, Dr. Peel. Dr. Mulholland made it clear I was not what you were looking for."

"So it wasn't because the position only called for a Bachelor's?"

Emerson chuckled. "Not at all. I was attracted by the salary."

"I'm glad to hear that. Am I right that you know Anu Karela?"

He shot Madeline a hopeful look and felt his heartbeat start to race. "Yes, we met shortly after we arrived in Los Angeles. We belong to the same Fellowship."

"Anu and I are good friends. I was one of her health food store's first customers. She had mentioned that you applied for our position and spoke of you highly, so I was disappointed when I arrived today and they told me you had gone." Dr. Peel paused then continued hopefully, "—if you're not offended, would you be willing to return and complete the interview? The fact that you earned your Master's should not be a drawback."

Emerson took care not to sound too excited. "I'd be happy to, Doctor, but I don't believe my advanced degree is what Dr. Mulholland objected to."

"Don't worry, Mr. Gardner. I'll speak to Dr. Mulholland. We're not rigid and it's a sizable institute. Shall we say nine o'clock tomorrow morning?"

Emerson gave his wife a dazed look as he hung up the phone. "Can you believe it?" he whispered. "I think I got the job."

Serendipity. Madeline was delighted to have learned the word now that the future had turned promising as gold. Her life in California was truly beginning to feel as if it had been conjured by a wish-fulfilling genie drawn from a Mesopotamian fairy tale. As bitter memories vanished inside good fortune, it was as if she had awakened from a long fevered sleep and discovered she had never lost hope. Such was the strength of her faith, she had picked up its clues even before reality confirmed them. Why else, she asked, would Anu have been so quick to engage them and then remember a comment Emerson had made in passing? What other reason explained why out of all the people who shopped at Mr. Ramiro's grocery she found herself inexplicably drawn to Mrs. Walters? How could she have known that the sprightly fifty-eight year old was a nurse from Panama with a deceased Jamaican husband? Serendipity.

More unexpectedly, it was Emerson who had led her to see that this was not the luck in some game of chance, or what Aunt Jamesie prayed for playing the numbers; it was not the one in a million fluke that bookies and insurance agents all hedged against, or what the duped sought in tea leaves or a crystal ball. Sure, they had come to L.A. of their own free will, but as with all things, what is meant to be resides in the stars and the motion of planets, in the gravity of time and the inscrutable whims of God who loved Mahalakshmi before He knew Adam.

Her belief regrounded in hope, she felt the closeness of the Holy Spirit she recalled from her early wrestles with Death. This time there would be no tears, no hopeless dash to find a doctor, no anger to burn into depression unmoved by soft words and sorrowful hands. Life had been awaiting her in California, and she was sure, down to the fraction of an hour, that under a year short of her fortieth birthday, the grown-up girl they all pitied as poor Little Miss Big Head would finally give her husband a son.

He had worried the whole time she was gone. The way she breezed through pregnancy and childbirth had left them both more than half believing she had been cured by the magic of prayer, or as his skepticism preferred to put it, positive thinking. But magic, like sunny optimism, is more illusory than durable, and lifting a fifteen-month-old from his crib is not as easy as cuddling a newborn. With rest and the faithful attentions of Gwen and dear Mrs. Walters, she had been back on her feet by the summer, mooning over her son, pain free as a convict granted clemency. Then two weeks before mother and child were due to leave for The Miraculous Triumphant Return, the fickle nerve in her lumbar plexus made her scream as she bent to put on her shoes.

Willpower can be a frightening thing. Madeline had refused to let him cancel the tickets, try as he might to remind her that, even if she could dress herself without weeping, she would be traveling alone with a twenty pound toddler. "Poppycock!" she growled, baring her teeth. "My son has been walking on his own from he turned ten months." And since he was left with no option short of tying her down, his heart and soul had flown off to Jamaica, leaving him a nervous wreck until the end of September when Mason wrote to say that his wife and child were doing just fine.

He had gone to speak with Dr. Philemon the day after she left. As much as he felt indebted to Dr. Peel, the Institute's reliance on animal testing offended his moral instincts. Though some of its work promised significant benefits to humans, the carnage was staggering—over two hundred mice, eighty white rats, twelve rabbits, two guinea pigs and a nine-year-old basset hound all indifferently sacrificed—and that was just in his first two months on the job. Even now, two years later, the moment he arrived and saw those doomed creatures crammed in their cages, his conscience battered him.

He was not looking forward to explaining himself to Madeline. In her eyes, he would always be 'Doc'—the gifted healer God put on this earth to practice medicine. As she was quick to inform their new friends, rolling her eyes around their tiny garage apartment, had this country lived up to its promise, Emerson would have been a doctor by now, end of discussion. The fact that the Institute paid fairly well had cooled her indignation at seeing him settle for being a mere lab assistant. Now that they were happy together and starting afresh, how was he to tell her he could not spend his life inducing tumors in rabbits or feeling a beating heart panic inside its fur as he pressed tobacco tar inside a hamster's trembling nostrils? He could try appealing to her scruples, but knowing Madeline, she was sure to respond as if the universe was now on course for disaster. He thought about sharing his torments in a letter then decided it was better to wait and face the music when she returned in December. With luck, The Victorious Homecoming would still have her tripping the light fantastic.

"Wonderful—you want to give up medicine to become a quack." Emerson could not have hurt her more had he confessed to sleeping with another woman.

"You do realize your reaction is the definition of prejudice."

"So sorry—will you also be studying chicken entrails and

sticking dolls with pins?" Madeline's acid glare could bore through skin.

"Chiropractic is a proven therapy and a lot less risky than surgery—or those cortisone shots you've been taking. Ask Mason, since you no longer respect my opinion."

Hearing her brother's name, she pictured teenaged Dora big with child and wondered if, like a broken record, her daughters were damned to replay her disappointments. Her eyes turned to the photograph above the fake fireplace. The studio portrait showed Madeline seated with Emerson standing beside her holding their five-month-old and looking as proud as Tenzing Norgay atop Mt. Everest. It was her most treasured possession, except that her smile had turned crooked, marred by a hairline fracture the frame had suffered during the latest aftershock. Seeing how practiced she had become at smiling through pain, she wondered if she cast omens aside too easily.

She had ignored the twinges that seized her spine without warning because, throughout her pregnancy, she had focused on the day she would prove the know-nothings wrong. Not her childhood illness, not her love for climbing trees, not her years riding bicycles—none of it had left her sterile. Now all those jealous moral guardians who despised her for marrying Doc and made it their mission to slime her name would be the ones left with mud on their faces. Aunt Jamesie had proclaimed it a miracle, which was exactly the word that dribbled from Mildred's lips when she showed up with her grandson. She had managed to grin and not show all her teeth watching her twenty-month-old bedazzle his grandmothers by singing *The Happy Wanderer*, then reciting the Twenty-third Psalm perfectly, just as she had drilled him.

But while the scars from her barren years were soothed by old acquaintances' warm baths of praise, the oil in their smiles reminded her she was the daughter of a fallen woman. That she had managed to birth a son did nothing to change the fact that she had staked her liberation on her husband's ambitions. So while pride would have her deny that her value rested entirely on Doc succeeding, Mildred's parting shot made sure she could not. "Did you hear—? Coombs Pharmacy is opening a second new store uptown. His daughter sure made good use of her inheritance. Now *that's* a smart woman."

Convinced a fortuitous conjunction of circumstances had made the choice for him, he ignored his wife's objections and enrolled to study nights at the Chiropractic College. Madeline had responded to his treachery by placing an impenetrable wall of ice in the middle of their bed to condition him to life after intercourse. After a month of nightly cold showers and less frequent if futile attempts to breach the frosty barrier, he had started to doubt there was a viable path to reconciliation when, by luck, he ran into Nurse Walters.

"It's the darndest thing," she said. "For Sale signs have been springing up across my neighborhood ever since I moved in. Makes me wish I had waited to buy—might have gotten me a better deal."

Taking the hint, he leapt for his chance. "Darling—" he whispered, bracing to greet her chill, "Dr. Peel just promised me a raise. I believe it's time we found you a house—"

Warmed by her excited smile, he did not think it wise to risk his escape from perdition by mentioning that the potential raise came out of a raging dispute at work. Drs. Peel and Mulholland's rumored nomination for a Nobel Prize had earned the tobacco industry's anxious attention. Should they be willing to help disprove that smoking caused cancer, the cigarette-makers were prepared to hand them an offer no scientist with serious ambition could casually refuse. The problem was Drs. Peel and Mulholland had set out to prove the exact opposite.

The industry's proposal had split the Institute into two opposing camps. Put simply, Mulholland wanted the four million dollars and Peel did not. With the board members evenly divided, they decided to compromise. They took the money. The windfall would go to PROBE, the Institute's newly conceived department for Pathological Radiology, Oncology and Biochemistry Experimentals to be headed by Dr. Mulholland.

Emerson was preparing to inject an albino mouse with methylcholanthrene when Dr. Peel showed up in the lab.

"Tell me, Gardner. Has Mulholland approached you about joining his team?"

Emerson looked askance. "I wouldn't expect him to. He barely speaks to me."

"He's busy bribing away my best technicians," Dr. Peel complained, his broad pate furrowed. "He's got the funds but I was hoping you'd stick with me."

"I appreciate what you've done for me, Dr. Peel. No need to ask."

"Capital! That tickles me pink!"

It took Emerson a moment to realize the laconic, lumbering scientist was taking one of his clumsy stabs at humor.

The bald Canadian smiled with open relief. "I intend to put you in for a raise. I've slipped down the totem-pole, but I will do my best."

The raise lay stuck in the zygote stage but thanks to the owner's rush to sell and a loan from Cyrus he had kept his promise. The thaw was complete when he showed up after work in a 1947 Studebaker with the keys to the two-bedroom tile-roofed stucco house Madeline had fallen in love with. "Emerson, you trickster! Why didn't you tell me you were spending all those late nights learning to drive!" Nurse Walters would later claim that the night the Gardners moved in half the neighborhood had trembled. Neither of the happy new homeowners frolicking up in the clouds paid any mind to what actually caused it.

Satisfied with her modest new home thanks to its full-sized den and eat-in kitchen, Madeline was too wrapped up playing the doting mother to dwell on the fact that her husband was away night and day. Since the Lord had finally answered her prayers, she had reordered her world to rotate around her son. She had prayed he would be musical and not tone deaf, like her mother, so she praised Him again listening to her toddler belt out *Frère Jacques* and remembering the intense look that came over his face when her nephew perched him on his knees at the keyboard back in Jamaica. When Emerson put her off each time she asked him to buy a piano, she called on Gwen, who was more than happy to take her godson so she could work afternoons at the neighborhood bakery. She had been on the job no more than a week when Gwen returned with her son, her exuberance bursting.

"Maddy darling, I'm afraid you've got a serious talent on your hands."

She needed no more encouragement. The old upright was tuned and sitting in her den within two months. Following Gwen's instructions, she would play a major scale, announcing each note, then ask her three-year-old to name each one as she repeated them at random. When he got them all right, she gave a week's notice at the bakery, bought a manual on beginner's piano, a children's workbook on music theory, three packets of number two pencils and a binder of manuscript paper. If only that miserable old Gloria Leguerre had lived to see her now!

Emerson had felt like a child on the night before Christmas as he planned his surprise. Not only had Dr. Peel kept his word, the director had arranged for his long-due raise to be retroactive. As he presented the two thousand dollar check at his new local bank, the teller paused to look him up and down as if he had worn a sports coat to a black tie dinner before informing him it would take three days for the funds to clear. Assured he could access the money by Friday noon, he returned to the furniture store and promised to bring the four hundred dollar balance in cash in time for Saturday delivery.

He could hardly wait to see Maddy's face when the van arrived with the double-leaf mahogany table and six silk-upholstered mahogany chairs she had been pining for since the day she had spotted them in the store's show window. He was not so simple as to think that an expensive dining-room set would see her accept being married to a chiropractor, but she might lay off accusing him of turning into a self-absorbed, misanthropic cheapskate.

He left work early to beat the lunch-hour crush and was pleased when he arrived and found the bank almost empty. So he was surprised as he took the withdrawal slip out of his smock to feel two men behind him sidle up close. They began talking loud, in the sporting manner Hortense Walker disparaged as 'niggerish,' when one of them abruptly shouted, "hey, Doc!" He turned, thinking it was someone he knew from Jamaica, then saw that their faces were both shining black—blacker than any he had ever seen. As he stalled in surprise, the one who had shouted waved a handkerchief in front of his face as if swatting at a fly. He tried pulling away feeling the grab on his lab-coat and the sweet-smelling cloth press his nose as a strong hand clasped him by his neck. And the whole time the pair kept right on laughing, as if the three of them were buddies having a lark.

The teller with the platinum dye job he had spoken to on Monday, ordered him to please step forward. His eyes beginning to tear, his mind was flashing replays of his assault by those plainclothes detectives. He thought about yelling for help then decided it was safer to stay calm. He leaned in closer to the platinum blond tipping his head with his eyes opened wide, hoping to induce her to press the alarm. Instead, she gave him a nervous look and asked if he was all right. He was still struggling to warn her when one of the men pushed in and took over.

"Stay cool," he muttered, "you're doing fine."

"Now you've done it. We're lost in the godforsaken Panhandle."

As it had been since the battle in Las Cruces, my mother could not pass up a chance to stick it to my father. This time it *was* my fault. I should have spoken up back in Tallahassee, but how was I supposed to know you had to be white to use the bathroom in a public park in Florida? I had always pictured the Sunshine State as being pretty much like California: lots of oranges, white sand and bikinis. You just don't expect a place that sets up billboards inviting people to come and lay on the beach and turn brown to be scared of actual brown folks. Thankfully, my father ignored her jab and talked to me patiently.

"I can either pull off into those woods, or you'll have to hold it a little longer. Your choice."

My bowels hurt like crazy, but even if my mom hadn't said we were risking big trouble straying from the highway, no way was I dropping my pants out there in the open. So I told him I'd hold it.

"Instead of driving us around in circles, maybe you should have told that deputy to do his duty. Laws are meant to be followed."

That did it.

"Will you make up your mind?" my dad shouted. "That deputy is probably in the Klan."

"The situation was completely different. It was a public place and there was no colored facility. We had witnesses."

My father grunted like he'd taken another punch to the gut, but it was sheer exasperation. "And you think *I'm* the one who's naive!"

Seeing that I was the one who stirred up this latest round, I decided it was time I sacrificed. "Dad, I guess I could go behind those trees—"

"You sure?"

"Yes."

"I'll go with you," he said, pulling our Valiant off to the side and cutting the engine.

I was about to say I'd go by myself when I heard church bells ringing from somewhere off in the woods. I was out of the car in a flash as I would swear they were chiming *Beautiful Dreamer.* "Dad, can you hear that? Those church bells are ringing a song from Looney Tunes! Don't you think that's a little weird?"

As he came to stand beside me, the bells grew faint so it took him a moment to catch what I meant. "You're right, son. That does seem an odd choice for a church. Maybe there's something about those chimes on one of the maps."

Excited by the thought of an adventure, I forgot about the poop pressing my intestines. "You think we can find them?"

My mother leaned across the steering wheel to catch my eye through the driver-side window. "I don't think that's a good idea. We could end up even more lost than we are."

"Madeline, please! I know where we are." My father pointed to a spot on the map he had stretched across the car-hood. "How about that—there's a Stephen Foster museum in White Springs. I bet that's where those bells are coming from. It looks about three miles north from the interstate, probably less than half that from here."

"Emerson, be sensible. Mundy and Delroy both warned you about this stretch. We shouldn't go wandering about out here."

Strains of *Swannee River* chimed through the thick green trees and for a moment it seemed that the whole world was peaceful and still.

"Please, Mom? It would be educational!" That one always worked on my parents. Besides, what grown-up would dare say no to a kid begging to visit a museum? Looking back on it now, I realized that by barring me from using that outdoor toilet, the deputy had done me a big favor: he gave me a chance to see a working carillon belfry up close. Chiming through the forest, the ninety-six tubular bells had sounded practically ancient but, as it turned out, they were almost brand new. My first thought, seeing the carillon's massive brick tower, was that it belonged in a city beside a grand cathedral and not off in the woods in the middle of nowhere, yet those homey Stephen Foster melodies seemed to suit the rustic surroundings perfectly.

The minute I saw all the instruments the museum had on display I was bursting with questions. The curator, an old white-haired gentleman with a hitch in his step that suggested his right leg was a bit shorter than his left looked keen to oblige a kid with my enthusiasm. I was disappointed when he told me that the instruments were all too priceless to ever be played so I sadly turned away and pointed instead to the museum's blacked-face images from the so-called minstrel days. When I asked why they were all trying to look like Louis Armstrong the old man patted my head and said, 'you are one bright little nigger!'

My mother promptly paled, but when my father cut in to explain that we were traveling from California, and desperate to find a bathroom, the curator took it upon himself to lead us to the lavatory, hitch-stepping his unhurried way past a line of hooded stares and terrified eyebrows.

We were barely back in the car when my mother unloaded. "You see, Emerson? That's what happens when you stand your ground."

I held my breath then let it go when my dad just turned his head and spoke not a word.

"No, Emerson isn't here—yes, he does usually brown bag it—no, it's definitely not like him—yes, I'm sure he would have said something—" Madeline kept her thoughts from running wild. There could be a perfectly good reason why Dr. Peel was calling to interrogate her at two o'clock on a Friday afternoon. Regrettably, as was the habit with doctors, he preferred asking questions to sharing information.

"Dr. Peel, would you mind telling me what's going on?"

"I'm sorry, Mrs. Gardner. I didn't mean to alarm you, but your husband took an early lunch and has not been seen nor heard from since he left. There's been a surge of interest in our research. You're quite sure he hasn't been offered other employment?"

"Quite sure, Dr. Peel. Emerson would have told me."

The scientist paused on the line. "This is troubling," he confided uncertainly. "When he shows up, would you please have him call me? I'm at the Institute till late."

As she slowly hung up the phone, Madeline made a mental note to ask Cyrus if there was something in her husband's astrological chart that made him prone to disappearing. The Helgers' number rang nine times before she remembered Gwen was taking Cyrus to the airport for his flight to Haiti. She started to dial Nurse Walters then realized she would have already left for her shift at the hospital. She tried the Chiropractic College and was told that Mr. Gardner was not there and no evening classes were scheduled on Fridays.

As a child she had noticed how much livelier her mother became when Mr. Jans was around. When she asked why he only visited them twice a month he had smiled and said, 'absence makes the heart grow fonder.' And it was true. After their long months apart, she would always forgive Emerson for not sharing her longing to 'cut a rug' like her jitterbug-crazy girlfriends or her taste for epic Hollywood movies full of glitter and bombast. It was enough that her husband was loyal and his touch was tender even if his highbrow discussions with Cyrus Helger left her bored and ignored. But as the hours passed and he was still God-knows-where, she began to wish that instead of marrying an egghead eager to retreat from the relevant world, she had married one of those uncomplicated, dissatisfied men who stayed out late drinking with his buddies, or sneaked to see some over-made-up floozy happy to stroke more than his dented ego. At least if she thought her husband was out enjoying some boorish tryst, she would not be fretting with her head in a spin, desperate for someone to call before she choked on the boulder compressing her larynx.

She thought about dialing the police, but they had sounded completely disinterested when she reported finding a dead cat hanging on her door and her new home ransacked. To be fair, nothing of great value had been stolen, and Shayla's family had gotten a similar reception and shrugged it off as the work of idle teenagers. But she kept going back to what Mundy Peters morbidly referred to as Emerson's 'gentle treatment' in New Orleans. She had expected law enforcement in sunny Los Angeles to be more civil until she read that fifty cops had gone on a drunken rampage and two years later not one had been charged despite putting their victims in the hospital. When she shared her disbelief that the city leaders would allow a scandal that big to go unpunished, it took Mr. Ramiro to clue her in. "Hurt L.A.'s image?" the elderly grocer had scoffed. "You got it backwards, *mijita*. They don't want the spics and niggers browning up Hollywood. Why do you think they keep recruiting these good-old southern boys? To keep us in our place. It's not a police force, it's an occupying army."

If Emerson was in trouble, she would deal with their army, but if Mr. Ramiro was right, it would help to have someone with clout standing beside her. When no one came to mind, she rang the Institute and asked for Dr. Peel. She could feel herself breathing again when the Canadian promptly called back and brushed off her apologies.

"Please, Mrs. Gardner—I quite understand. Our dear Anu feared she was having a stroke when her family disappeared from their train out of Bucharest. But don't torment yourself. This is not

Nazi-infested Europe."

Dr. Peel rang off, promising to alert the local precinct commanders and have his secretary join her in inquiring at the city hospitals. When she finally got through dialing them all, the day was done. She gave up and managed to clear her head enough to fix her son his supper. By the time she got hold of Gwen, her nerves were shot.

"Deep breaths, Maddy darling. I'll be right over!"

As she waited for Gwen to arrive, her son wanted to know why Daddy was not home in time for supper.

"Daddy is going to be late. He might not be home till after your bedtime."

"But it's Friday. He's supposed to bake us an upside-down cake."

Having grown wise as to why life had exposed all the broken hearts around her, she had sworn never to lie to her child. Seeing her four-year-old's trusting face, she prayed her words would turn out to be true. As Miss Dora had taught her, the most damning lies were often born of omissions.

It had been more than six hours since our lunch in Pensacola, but after our detour to see the carillon tower, my father seemed hellbent on reaching Miami without another stop to eat or sleep in the state of Florida. My mother had her ears pinned to the radio, trying to keep hold of a station boasting up-to-the-minute news. I guessed that something big must have happened because I had never seen her this agitated. But then nothing had been like usual from the day before this whole trip started.

I was still creeped out by Aunt Jamesie's postcard and the way the man's head bent sideways like he was really, really tired, even though I knew he was already dead when that picture was taken. If people living here still held picnics for things as awful as that, I could see why my dad was in such a hurry. No wonder Richard couldn't wait to move north. After reading *Black Boy*, I no longer had that queer feeling inside, but I was still steamed about that curator calling me 'a bright little nigger.' Old or young, no matter your color or you didn't know why, where Elan and I grew up talk like that earned you a kick in the shins—and if it ended at that, you could count yourself lucky. But the way the old man said it made me think something about me had aroused some peculiar affection, like I was some unusually intelligent pet he knew existed but never expected to come across. I wondered if a similar affection explained why those minstrel singers blackened their faces. Maybe in order to sing stuff like that you had to pretend you were Old Black Joe or Jim in Huckleberry Finn—or maybe Delroy Angell was right when he said that white folks loved making up sad black characters in order to hide from their sorry selves.

"It's Dr. Peel—they've found Emerson!" Madeline exulted, covering the receiver.

"Thank God!" Gwen whispered.

"No, that's fine, Dr. Peel. I'm here with a friend. We'll find our way there. I can't thank you enough!"

Madeline turned a stunned look towards her friend. "They found him wandering the desert near Barstow."

"Mercy! Was it a car accident?"

Madeline shook her head. "The police didn't say. He had no identification so it looks like they assumed he was either a hobo or a wetback snuck in from Mexico. He's been locked up in some San Bernardino jail since the middle of the afternoon."

Gwen threw her arms around her friend and held her close. "He's alive and safe, that's what counts. We can deal with the rest once we get him released."

The deputy's distracted smirk disclosed that he was secretly counting the brews his pals were going to buy him, calling him a bonafide liar when he told them how this fab convertible Cadillac pulled up to the jailhouse door around midnight and in came these two colored foxes pushing a coon-baby asleep in a stroller. The projection faded as Madeline kept up her barrage and he finally roused himself to answer. "How long? Can't say. He was in there when I got here. Has he eaten? That I don't know—he kept bugging me for water so I gave him some. What's the charge—? Hold yer horses, miss, I'm about to look. Says here, John Doe, booked for vagrancy and suspicion of entering the country illegally. Bail? I couldn't tell you—the sheriff can decide that when he gets in tomorrow—"

Having seen how the young deputy had blinked and licked his lips when they first showed up, Madeline sat patiently back in her chair, giving him time for an eyeful while she slowly crossed her legs. "Now what would the sheriff think if he came in and found you had kept us locked up here with you alone all night and not a word to a living soul?"

Alive to her play, Gwen leaned suggestively across the deputy's desk. "You know what they say about us fast colored gals—I could see the sheriff getting the wrong idea—"

Blushing, the deputy blinked then promptly rang the sheriff who was not at all pleased at being pulled from his wife. "Boy, just write the effin' summons and let the damn nigger go!"

Faint from hunger and heat-stroke, Emerson had needed both women's help to make it out to the car where he kissed his son, who remained blissfully asleep through it all, and promptly passed out. After the two hour drive back to Elmwood and father and son were tucked safely into their beds, Maddy wondered if her friend would mind sleeping over. "I can only offer you the couch, but I could use the company."

"Like you needed to ask," Gwen snorted.

It turned out neither of them could sleep more than a wink and after chatting over coffee they spent the rest of the morning trying to stay alert enough to keep a restless four-year-old quiet. It was noon before Emerson surfaced from his comatose state, though still in a trance. His faculties starting to pierce the fog after he finished slurping a bowl of split pea soup, he struggled to answer when Madeline asked how he had ended up wandering across the Mojave desert.

"I already told you—I don't know."

"Try!" she insisted.

"Easy, girl," Gwen whispered. "He might still be in shock."

Emerson gazed at her calmly. "It's fine. I'm feeling better with some food in me." He closed his eyes trying to summon back lost impressions, then slumped and gave up. "Sorry, I just can't remember. It's like someone lopped off the top of my head and stuffed it with cotton. All I recall is waking up face down on scorching sand with a skull-cracking headache."

"Maybe this will jog your memory." Madeline showed him his soiled lab coat. "How did those smudges get there? They're not from sand."

He absently fingered the coat, his strained look that of a man awaiting the promise of dawn. He closed his eyes and sat deep in thought for almost a minute before he spoke. His eyes still shut, he recalled a sweet, sickening smell and being hustled from cool into warming sunshine. Touching a hand to the back of his neck, he winced feeling the painful knob and remembered being shoved roughly into the back of a car. Then, as if the tide gate had been breached, it all came flooding back.

"There were two of them!" he exclaimed, staring at the sudden recollection as Maddy and Gwen watched him anxiously. "That's it!" he cried, snatching up the smock to reexamine it, "my brain must have dismissed it as a dream." He pointed to the coat's black smears. "Those bandits had their faces masked with shoe polish. It was a set-up!"

Darkness was spreading over our way like an omen as we exited the interstate. The low buildings with their panes glinting yellow, appeared to me as hunkered animals watching their prey pass safely by. My mother had given up trying to pull in the signal from Mississippi and in the gloaming, a voice more pleading and tender than nine-year-old ears could describe crooned *Our Day Will Come*.

"I hope you know what you're doing," she murmured, peering through the lamplight to the griminess encasing Jacksonville.

My father shot her a look and matched the grievance conveyed in her whisper. "Can you ever be satisfied? You complained that you were hungry. I'm trying to find somewhere you can sit and eat in peace."

Forced to choose, I would still end up siding with my mother, but ever since we visited with Dr. Cheever I had caught myself feeling sorry for my father. I had seen how shaken he was by what happened to his friend, but what had affected me most was the pain that came to his face seeing the disappointment in my mother's eyes as she sat not saying a word while the two of them talked about old times. It was the same hurt look he had the day I turned five and stopped letting him kiss me goodnight, saying men don't kiss, they shake hands. At that moment I realized how deeply he still loved my mother. I also realized that, even if the past could be undone, he no longer had the power to please her.

"Instead of wandering Lord knows where, why don't we stop and ask someone?"

"All right, fine, since you trust anyone's judgment more than mine."

"Now you're just being ridiculous."

The soulful voice floated inside. She sang for us not to cry—but to love and offer a smile.

"Dad, I need to pee—" I was ready to lie if lying would save our loving Trinity, but even then, I knew I was dreaming. There was no escaping the past, and I was tired of always worrying that I would say the wrong thing or react on instinct, tired of feeling as if I had to spend the rest of my life walking on eggshells, or balancing on a tightrope strung across a boiling tar pit. I was tired of seeing the simplest, stupidest things blow up into a battle.

Our purring Valiant started to slow and my dark mood lifted as I spotted the bright neon sign for a popular chain of diners. I was already planning my order when we pulled into the parking lot and saw the sign in the window: We Serve Whites Only.

A call from Dr. Peel made sure the vagrancy charge was dropped, but the bank continued to insist that Emerson had demanded the two thousand dollars in cash and then closed the weeks-old account himself. Convinced that the teller was in on the swindle, Madeline had gone with Emerson to speak with the manager who curtly informed them that Miss Fairclough was away on vacation. When she persisted, the bank manager had ordered them out of his office warning that if they intended to press their ludicrous claim they would be advised to find a good lawyer.

After the police came close to laughing them out of the station, Cy Helger had insisted they let him pay for a private investigator who took barely a day to discover there had been two other reports of customers being mugged then stripped of their entire accounts in the months since the bank opened branches in that part of the city. The retired Italian cop unfolded his hands. "You're good people— so I'm not gonna string you along. Trust me—there's nothing you can do—"

Madeline resented the anger on Emerson's face when she announced that she was joining the night shift at Nurse Walters' hospital. "No, I won't be neglecting our son. Now that he's started kindergarten I can sleep during the day. I'll worry about summer when it gets here. All you have to do is get me there and back. Oh, for heaven's sake—I'm not abandoning my family. I'll be home in time to make breakfast."

Though his rage had annoyed her, she could imagine how he trembled at the thought of his mother discovering that his wife was stinting on sleep to help provide for his child. But she only had to glance around their empty dining-room to tacitly imply that, if he expected to go on paying for chiropractic classes, they would need the extra money. She might have faced sterner resistance had he known the job would introduce her to Felicia Molina, the hospital's Cuban dietitian who insisted everyone call her 'Happy.'

Lively and loud, Happy had blown into the Gardners' lives like a level-five hurricane. Though the hospital had her listed as 'white,' in colored circles the talkative Cuban divorcee was considered 'high yellow,' while Madeline thought high octane described the speed at which words tumbled out of Happy Molina's mouth. Once she realized the nutritionist was, in fact, speaking English, she and Happy had become fast friends.

"Listen, *mami*," Happy nudged her for the umpteenth time, "it's a free country. You don't need *papi's* permission."

"I can't. It wouldn't feel right."

"*Porque?!* No. We go and leave *papi* at home. Why should you care if he says he's not gonna take you?"

Madeline smiled and for the umpteenth time said she'd think about it. Unable to put it out of her mind, she rang Gwen.

"Be careful, darling. Little escapades like that blow marriages apart, and your friend sounds like a real firecracker."

"You'd like her. Happy is nobody's pushover."

"I'm sure she's not," Gwen chuckled, "she's your friend. But you still have a husband."

Madeline sighed into the phone. "That's just it. Emerson won't even find the time for us to take in a concert—forget the movies. Here we are—practically in Hollywood! Maybe getting drugged then chucked in the desert is what turned my husband into a somber old misanthrope."

"Turned? Darling, your husband turned somber the day he was born!"

"That's where you're wrong, darling. The day we met I caught him lounging in his drugstore with a shameless little minx primping in his lap. Can you believe it?"

"Not in a million years," Gwen laughed.

Emerson noticed the tiny clouds of disenchantment beginning to dim the glow that bearing a son had returned to his beloved's face, but he saw them as the natural consequence of too much work and not enough sleep. When she suddenly proposed they take dancing lessons, he was sure that her outspoken new friend had been the instigator. Although her affectionate manner made Happy Molina tough to resist, much like his mother's fruitcake, he could only stomach the non-stop chatterbox in minute servings. Given her hatred for President Kennedy, he was surprised that she and Madeline were such good friends, but something told him that, like Joe and Juan Ferrier, Felicia Molina had gotten close to his wife hoping to remake her.

"Dancing lessons do sound like fun," he lied sweetly. In truth, he found the idea of learning the *cha-cha-chá* about as appealing as a visit to the proctologist. "I just don't know where either of us would find the time. We're burning the candle at both ends as it is."

"I knew you were going to say that! But it's not just for fun. Happy has met a lot of important musicians through her Cuban friends. She even knows Ricky Ricardo. Someone like that could be a big help to our son's career."

"Ricky Ricardo isn't real. He's a TV personality."

"Shows what you know. He's a real musician and that's his real band."

"I doubt it. Anyway, I thought you were grooming our son strictly for classical."

"Don't be a snob. Most jazz musicians have had classical training. Look at Joe—and Mr. Borati. Of course I'd prefer to see him in Carnegie Hall, but contacts are contacts."

He feared he had no way out until it turned out the class met on Saturday nights and he was able to remind her that Cyrus had asked him to lecture on satyagraha and self-reliance and he needed those evenings to prepare. "There'll be time once I'm finished with school and you're not out working nights, exhausting yourself."

"You know what's exhausting, Emerson?" Madeline huffed. "Being married to a perpetual student."

He had left it there, but misfortune earned him a lasting reprieve six weeks later.

"That's it. No more of this," he declared after he came to fetch her from work and found her hobbling. "I'll tie you to the bed if I have to!" he muttered, seeing his injured wife straining to hold back tears.

On the drive home he listened in quiet frustration as she confessed that she had wrenched her back helping a young new mother having an epileptic seizure. After coaxing his anxious son back into bed, assuring him Mom would be fine, he returned to the car and carried her inside to their bedroom. After helping her out of her nurse's uniform, he had her lie flat on her stomach. He judged that the pain must be truly severe because she tensed but offered no complaint as he worked on her spine. Within minutes, he felt her slowly relax, then go limp as she drifted off to sleep.

For a week he kept replaying the soft warm smile she gave him later that morning when she came slumping into the kitchen, struggling to tie on her robe, and found him at the table with their combed and dressed son munching scrambled eggs and toast. They had both agreed her nursing days were over, but when she bluntly refused to see Dr. Philemon, he told her that unless she was prepared to say that she had lost all faith in his good sense and abilities, she had to let him treat her himself.

"Fine," she gave in before adding cannily, "then how about this? I'll give you six weeks to convince me I haven't lost the man I married to worthless quackery."

When Emerson's skilled hands brought her unexpected, lasting relief, Madeline revised her latest setback into an actual blessing. Hoping to restore some of her lost income, she spent her final paycheck on a second-hand sewing machine and with the help of the Helgers' contacts landed several clients among Hollywood's aging, not quite famous actors thrilled to have their own personal dressmaker who could recast their image without forcing them to spend months eating beans from a can. She enjoyed hearing them boast to their friends that she never used patterns and watching them pale when she suggested a bolder fabric, as if they thought the way to impress was to conform exceptionably. Nothing topped the moment at that first full fitting when their trepidation changed to glee as they saw how with that discrete stripe of color their waxen profile no longer blended into the background. A gown for a special awards night was not only enough to fill her weeks as well as her pocketbook, it left her fantasizing about her latest creation inducing the envy of some glamorous star and making her the next Dior or Coco Chanel. Sadly, such orders were rare, so she made up the lean times selling cosmetics door-to-door so that her son could have the violin lessons he had long been begging for.

Her energy revived now that her back was pain free and she was no longer working nights, she joined the PTA at her son's new school and set about charming his principal in the hopes of providing him with a potent ally. Six months later she was elected to the district school board, and a year after that appointed to the governor's special advisory panel on education. In the meantime, she had set Gwen to hounding Mr. Borati until the piano teacher overcame his distaste for pushing young prodigies and agreed to let her seven-year-old audition to play on the radio.

Through some serendipitous celestial alignment, her life in California seemed committed to the very script she had dared to conceive. All doubts were forever removed when Mr. Rosenblum, the venerated Russian conductor, called to say he had heard the broadcast of her son's performance and thought it would do hearts and minds a world of good to see his talent featured with the city's youth orchestra.

She was still pinching herself as she called to tell Gwen. Gone was her pining to go dancing. She was riding high.

Mom had gotten that look in her eye, and it frightened me.

"No, Emerson, I won't just let it be. I'm hungry. I'm going inside."

It had not frightened me the day she confronted Miss Finch for checking 'poor' next to 'courtesy' on my report card after my spat with Justin Ito. I hadn't been scared watching her tangle with a six-foot sheriff in Las Cruces, but that look was in her eye before she taunted that waitress in Texas and it had taken five whole minutes for my legs to stop shaking after Delroy pulled out his gun and we ran for our lives.

She flipped on the Valiant's interior light to fix her face. "It makes more sense than driving around in circles."

As she clicked shut her compact and dabbed on fresh lipstick, my father bent across the seat to whisper in her ear. I stared through the diner's plate glass window at the people eating inside and acted like I wasn't focused on every word he said.

"You heard what they were saying on the radio. Things are getting heated. This is not the time or place."

"Relax. I won't insist that they serve us, but they should be polite enough to tell us somewhere that will."

With that she was out of the car, streaking for the entrance. I jumped out to follow, but my dad was on me in a flash. He had me by the arm about to drag me back when he glimpsed a man inside the window toss his napkin and jump up angrily from his table. "Okay, let's go in," he muttered, letting go of my arm. I snuck him a grin and, like magic, my dad stood two feet taller.

Inside, my mother had her feathers up going toe-to-toe with a man in a chef's white hat and apron. Were it not for his lack of gray hair I would have sworn it was Mr. Ramiro, my mom's favorite grocer back in L.A. He and the man with the angry red face turned to glare as we came inside.

His balled fists trembling, the man shifted his red-faced stare to where his wife sat looking as if a foul smell had just ruined her supper. "You'd think these outside agitators would have learned a thing or two! Now y'all look here—"

As he whirled to shout at my parents, I noticed that the other dozen-odd patrons had all stopped eating to watch, their faces gripped tight, like fresh conscripts poised for action.

"Please, I don't want no more trouble," Mr. Ramiro's look-alike pleaded.

This time my dad beat my mom to the punch. "We're not looking to start any trouble. We're just travelers looking for a decent place to eat."

"That's exactly what I was explaining," my mother stuck in, sharp as a knife.

The grocer's double looked ready to wet his pants. "And I told you, *por favor*, you can't be in here."

The angry diner stepped towards my father threatening to punch him. "You heard him, boy—git! Or does Jorge need help throwing out the garbage?"

My heart was pumping, but my dad held his ground, his hands steady as a gunfighter's. "It seems I was mistaken," he responded, his voice restrained and dignified, like that of a hero turned reluctant killer. "I had expected to be speaking with gentlemen. Come, my dear, since they can't help us, we're leaving."

I dared not look back as we headed out to our car and I felt my swelled chest bursting. Not only had my dad left the red-faced bully tongue-tied, he had defused my mother's temper. Still, it felt bizarre to be driving away flush with a sense of victory when we had accomplished nothing. But as the journey continued to teach me, when it comes to a fight, power lies in numbers, and even the mighty Hannibal knew when to retreat.

The mean looks on the diners' faces left me thinking that everyone in their alien world must feel under siege. Trying to imagine what it was like to always feel trapped, I thought about walls and why it was that grown-ups kept on building them. It wasn't as if nothing ever changes. Even the perfect girl I'd hoped to marry had changed. One day she was wrestling me in her shorts and sneakers and the next she was parading around in her pleated skirts and saddle shoes acting as if I didn't exist. Her betrayal makes me wonder why I never once considered marrying Cookie. Not only had Cookie been the first person to welcome us to the neighborhood, she turned four just months ahead of me and had the craziest magenta-red curls and the heart of a daredevil. I guess I never thought about Cookie that way because her mother was always quick to call her home when she'd sneak across our street to play, and we had not been friends for that long before her house burned down and her family left and never came back.

The fact that she still pops up in my head makes me think that even when walls were invisible, they stood like mountains, presenting the bold with an irresistible challenge. It seems to me that somewhere in that riddle lay the discrepancy between the Father and the Holy Spirit. Looking back on it now, I guess my father thought the risk was not worth what the walls kept hidden, while my mother was hellbent to scale them and see for herself. What I would never know was if breaching those walls would have made me a prince or a prisoner.

After we had roamed through half of Jacksonville, my father finally gave in and stopped to ask an elderly colored man leaning against a lamppost if he knew of a good place to eat. The old man frowned, giving our Valiant a blunt once-over. "California, huh?" he grunted, squinting at our license plate. "You folks be best off headin' on north a spell. Y'all can take your pick on the Avenue."

'The Avenue' turned out to be the main drag through an all-black neighborhood. It was going on eight on a Friday night and I grew excited seeing all the young people out strolling the sidewalks. Apart from the time we were coming back late from the Helgers and got stuck inside a mob of midnight hipsters drawn to the Sunset Strip's razzle-dazzle, I could count on two fingers the people I had ever seen out walking after dark. My first thought was that they were teenagers on their way to the movies or the local dance spot, except that they carried themselves with the same grim seriousness I had seen on my best friend Elan after his grandmother's funeral.

The old man had steered us true as the Avenue offered several restaurants to choose from. When my father voted for the chili parlor boasting 'home-style cooking to warm your heart' my mother shrugged as if to say, 'whatever.' I was happy to go along as my stomach burbled to remind me it could not care less.

The packed place was smaller and far less immaculate than Bob's Good Eats, but the fake brick walls held an earthy aroma that promised food cooked to comfort. My mother asked to see a menu and the woman who welcomed us smiled. "We never bothered printing menus seeing that half our customers find reading a strain. But don't you worry, sugah, Sam can tell you whatever you need to know."

After a booth came free and we had settled in one of the cozy wood stalls scarcely too large for the three of us, my father asked our waiter if he knew of a decent motel where we could spend the night. The waiter, who I assumed was Sam, snorted as if my father had asked him if he could fly us to the moon. "Sure thing. Just keep drivin' for a hundred miles—and then some—"

"He's joking—" my mother said.

Sam, a round-eyed tub of a man, heaved a sigh. "Wish I was, sweet lips. There used to be one halfway to St. Augustine, but the Klan blew it up a while back. Word is niggers were usin' it to hustle smack and knock boots with white prostitutes." Sam shrugged. "Who knows? Might have even been true—"

"So what do you suggest?" asked my mother, honing her stare that started at 'sweet-lips' and grew sharper at 'niggers.' "There's got to be someplace travelers stay."

"No disrespect, ma'am—" the man replied, "but this is Florida we're talkin' about. Even if one of us could rustle up the dough— who's gonna risk it on a colored motel? Hell, down here it's risky to open a bank account."

My dad gave Sam a thin smile. "Brother," he said in a folksy tone I had never heard him use before, "I know just what you mean. That's the thing about this land of the free. We're free to be marked wherever we go."

"Or *not* go—" A thread of gold sparkled from the waiter's teeth as he grinned at my mother. "I'm Sam, by the way," he said proudly after my dad extended him his hand, "in case you were wondering."

"Great to meet you, Sam," my father replied, as if he didn't already know.

The handshake must have bonded the two of them, because just as I was busy scraping the last morsel from my bowl of Lean Fridays Three Bean Chili, Sam came back with three big hunks of pecan pie. "On the house," he brightly announced. "Don't want you folks to leave here thinkin' we're so hard up we can't afford our guests some southern hospitality."

"That's right kind of you, Sam. We have been a little starved for common courtesy," my mother said tartly.

"I hear you, sister, but think nothin' of it. I'm not shy to brag that this humble place has been feedin' our family for three generations. We're like that new wristwatch they been sellin'—we take a lickin' and keep right on tickin'!"

After my father left a five dollar tip that almost matched the entire cost of our meal, Sam's friendly aw-shucks manner turned serious. "I wasn't being funny when I said y'all best keep on drivin'. There's a lotta goings-on like we ain't seen before. Folks who might take y'all in for a night are either too scared or they're plum full-up tendin' to those college kids down here organizin', stickin' their necks out. I'm grateful for what they're tryin' to do—" Sam paused and shook his head, "I just pray we make it through in one piece."

I did not know what goings-on Sam was talking about, but I suspected it had something to do with what my mother had heard on the radio and why all those teenagers were still out roaming in bunches, some of them giving us the keen-eye as we returned to our car. It felt like an episode from the *Twilight Zone* where the whole town gathers outside waiting for the Martians to land in their spaceship.

That the scene seemed so strange set me thinking about the way people down here said nigger instead of Negro, and if that explained something that happened in first grade that I had never forgotten. Most of the other kids had just started learning to read and Mrs. Calhoun had brought in one of those picture books showing different types of people and occupations. I remember seeing the picture of man in a suit and beneath him the word 'Caucasian.' The book also showed him dressed as a policeman, a fireman, a farmer and, finally, a doctor standing beside a female Caucasian in a nurse's uniform like my mother's. The next page pictured a man colored red in a rawhide outfit and feathered headdress and below him the word 'Indian.' Beside him was a black man dressed like a railroad porter labeled 'negro.' That did not strike me as fair, so I asked Mrs. Calhoun why Caucasian and Indian both started with capital letters and negro did not. To my surprise, she said the book was wrong and I was right. That's when I knew the two of us would see things eye to eye. What I never figured out was why someone as wise as Mrs. Calhoun showed up with that dumb book in the first place.

With incredulity that would rise to disgust, Emerson had watched as Dr. Mulholland and his lackeys broke faith with their sacred oaths to fatten their pockets. It had taken four years, but thanks to their tactics, PROBE had taken full charge of the Institute. Through a relentless public relations campaign backed by mountains of cash, the cigarette companies had not only persuaded the politicians that evidence could not be trusted, they were managing to turn the entire scientific process on its head. A flummoxed Dr. Peel found his groundbreaking proof that tobacco contained a harmful carcinogen suddenly being questioned by colleagues and friends who, like so many who seek to deceive themselves by projecting their own motives onto others, suggested that, sadly, the distinguished scientist had been seduced by fame and fortune.

With PROBE anxious to impress its growing pool of pharmaceutical partners, the Canadian was ordered to shift his focus from finding cancer's cause to testing cures, which revealed new symptoms to treat, which meant developing more drugs, and that, in turn, demanded even more tests and experiments. Although Emerson viewed his consequent pay raise as a partial salve for the scientist's conscience, he had waited to voice his qualms out of respect for his benefactor. Dr. Peel had implored him to stay and help turn the tide, but his mind was made up—the day he qualified as a chiropractor would be his last at the Institute.

It distressed him when his wife responded by again turning cold, refusing to credit his reasons. Since she could hardly deny that her back had improved immeasurably, she no longer referred to chiropractic treatment as useless quackery, but that did not stop her from claiming that this sudden contempt for his job was due to his new obsession. "Dishonest?" she scoffed when he complained that PROBE was willing to deceive the public if it meant bigger profits. "Have you forgotten what 'honest' childbirth was like before antibiotics? I don't. I had to bury those girls." She was even less impressed when he reminded her that the job had him doing unspeakable things to helpless animals.

"How can you be so morbid when you're helping to save people's lives?"

"Eviscerating innocent life does not make me a superior being."

"Poppy-show! Come join us on earth. You're not the Redeemer."

He ignored her sarcasm. "Why do we have to be torturing animals when we could be helping our bodies prevent disease naturally?"

"Now you sound like an indulgence peddler from the dark ages, or one of these bible thumpers who think it was God's will that made their children die from whooping cough."

He held his temper and tried to explain that he was not against science, he was against distorting methods to fashion results. He wanted her to see why outfits like PROBE were so dangerous, but he knew that in the distraught depths of her heart she was convinced it was just sour grapes. No matter what he said, she would always believe that his convictions had been hewn from his failures.

"What are you doing?" my mother demanded as our Valiant exited the pitch dark highway.

"It's late and my eyes need a rest," my father replied.

"Okay, I'll drive."

"No. It'll take another two to three hours to get to Miami and the last service station we passed was closed. I figured we could all use a nap."

My mother stared at him as if he'd gone crazy. "You want us to sleep out here?"

"There's no one around. It'll be fine."

"Give me the keys, Emerson."

"Didn't you hear what I just said? Our gas is down below an eighth of a tank."

"Then can we at least stop somewhere closer to civilization? I need to call Aunt Jamesie."

"It can wait."

"Suppose it's not safe?"

"We're safer way out here. Believe me."

I could swear I saw smoke coming out of my mother's ears but it was probably vapor from the stifling humidity. She stared out into the murky night and for a second I thought she was going to jump out and walk. Instead, she rolled down her window and shifted as far away from my dad as she could manage. I could tell she was very upset and from the way she had startled me awake shouting, "Jesus!" I was pretty sure it had to do with something she had heard on the radio.

"I don't believe you. Do you really think Booker T. Washington would criticize him for trying to break the color line?" Her scathing voice set off my alarm but my father kept his to a murmur.

"I never said that."

"You implied it."

"No I did not. I said he would deem it too great a sacrifice. Booker T. Washington wanted colored folks to build their own institutions."

"With what? The corns on their feet? You saw how the poor live down here. It's a disgrace for a country this rich." She peered nervously into the darkness outside her window, scouting the shadows for anything sinister. "The worst of it is, probably half of them are Old Massa's offspring. Somebody's got to stand up to these hypocrites."

My dad swivelled around to check and caught me with my ears wide open. "Can we talk about this later?"

"Fine. But once it's daylight we're finding a phone so I can call Aunt Jamesie."

Their tiff lost steam before it could turn into another drawn-out fight and I quietly praised God and my two crossed fingers. Once the drumming in my chest had ceased, I settled in my seat to try and sleep. That proved easier said than done, as the temperature inside our car had to be over eighty degrees and breathing Florida swamp air was like inhaling soggy cotton. I was starting to think my father had mapped out this whole southern trip to punish us. He knew that neither of us wanted to leave L.A. and the way I saw it, my mom and I both had pretty good reasons, but that had not a made a scrap of difference. I was hating the thought of us being stuck on his crummy little island then I remembered the day he brought a mango home and me thinking it was the most amazing thing I had ever tasted. How bad could it be if I got to eat fruits like that every day and live near my grandmothers and a host of cousins? Life's new possibilities were stopping me from feeling sorry for myself when a small bird flapped close by my ear. My skin started crawling as I saw that the bird was actually a giant insect. In a flash, the three of us were racing to roll up our windows, swatting bugs the size of dragonflies. Great! I grumbled inside, feeling one land on my neck, we were either going to suffocate or get stung to death.

"What now, Brave Leader?" my mother sneered, clapping her hands to squash an enormous mosquito.

"What can I say?" my father snapped back. "Put on some repellent and don't leave your window that open."

"Pardon me for wanting to breathe. Darn it all to hell!" she cried, slapping another gallinipper from her cheek. "I told you we should fly. Now look at the mess you've got us in."

"You do realize those airline tickets would have cost more than the car you're sitting in. Then what would you drive back home to impress your friends?"

She put off answering him to lean back across the seat and pass me the bug spray. "Here, son—make sure to keep it away from your eyes. Don't try blaming this whole disaster on me, Emerson Gardner." She returned to laying into him. "I'm not the one who thought it was worth throwing away everything we worked for to get wrapped up in this baloney they're calling Independence."

"I see—" he cut her off when she scoffed, "so to you, wanting our son to grow up in his own free country and get a proper education is baloney."

"No, what's baloney is thinking freedom is worth a dime when you're poor as a church mouse and stuck on a destitute island with a quaint profession people there have never heard of."

"You just delight in cutting me down! You have to go against everything I say because your Cuban *mamita* branded it inside your head that I'm keeping you down and wives deserve their own say so."

"Why not? It's our lives too. Just because our genitalia is different doesn't mean we shouldn't have a say."

"Aren't you modern! You want to have a say? How about having a say in a country that doesn't hold itself together with lies? How about saving your spit for the stooges shedding tears because Jamaica is no longer going to be run by callous nincompoops?"

"How about you stop nursing old wounds and put your family first for once!"

I wasn't sure what prompted the blow-up this time, but it shook me back to what would forever remain the very worst day of my life. The day I sorely wish I could change but could never forget. It was the day before we were due to begin our cross-country trip and my father wanted me to box up the junk in our garage. It was hot and the job was boring, so when he left to run an errand, I took the chance to slip away and see Elan one last time. I could not have been gone for more than an hour, but as I hurried back home I saw my dad waiting by the garage with his belt out. Before I could get a word in edgewise, the man who had never hurt me in his life, who soothed my tears when we found my pet turtle with his insides showing through his shattered shell, had me gripped by the neck, ready to tear off my hide when my mother shoved herself between us.

"You're not whipping my child! He has the right to tell his friends good-bye."

That's when he slapped her and my perfect childhood crumbled.

She jammed her nose right in his face. "Neither my mother nor my father ever laid hands on me, so don't you try it!"

The demon goading my dad's blind rage had also made him deaf and dumb because he swung at her again. She ducked his slap and punched him in the face. He tried clutching her in a bear hug but she crouched like a football lineman and put him on his back with a driving head butt. I watched, stricken with fright, as my loving parents wrestled across our backyard like drunken brawlers. The world was ending in front of my eyes but my brain refused to conceive it. I had to believe they were already calling it quits when my Aunt Gwen's Cadillac came rolling up our driveway. Guilty tears streaming past my cheeks, I ran to greet her and buried my terror inside her bosom.

"I'm not going."

"What are you talking about?"

"I'm not getting on that ship."

"For Christ's sake, Maddy. How many times do I have to say it? I'm sorry. I'm sorry I'm not the man you married. That man cannot exist in this country."

The look she gave him wavered between irritation and pity. "Why do you insist on dismissing all the good things? People all over this planet would jump for the chance to live here."

"Except the ones they brought. The ones who dug the ground—used until they turned into dust. The ones no one sees or gives a damn about—the ones who look like our son."

"Some ones, not all—"

"You think it's worth it, being the exception? What happens when he realizes none of those kids at his school will ever be his friends, and his own friends are either in jail or think he's a coward?"

"A coward? You're the one running home a failure. Open your eyes! The country is changing—these young people won't rest until they can dream like everyone else."

"By then we'll all be dead and gone—if that ever happens."

"It beats not trying. You think our son won't resent us for stymying his talent? Like it or not, this is his country."

"Yes, he was born here. That doesn't mean this country loves him. I won't let my son risk his life trying to be an American. I won't beat my breast over his dead body."

I don't know how we survived that night in the car out in the sticks between Jacksonville and Miami, but somehow we did. The mosquitoes had kept me awake so once we were back on the highway, free from their attacks and the smothering humidity, I had quickly fallen asleep. The crackling from the radio stirred me awake and my ears perked up hearing the newscaster report that fifty teenagers who had refused to leave the public library were being held in jail. I asked if he was talking about the ones we saw last night out in the street, but my dad said, no, they were talking about a sit-in back in Alabama.

"Those kids were arrested for wanting to use the library their parents' taxes help pay for," my mother clarified, shooting my father the same snide look he had gotten from Delroy Angell.

I had gotten so used to the world making no sense I did not even bother to ask her why. Instead, I thought about our happy times when I had just learned to read and she would take me to our neighborhood library where I discovered Charlotte the spider and Winnie-the-Pooh. I remembered being heartbroken when they tore down our branch just weeks after I came across the shelf of Nancy Drew detective stories. I only found out months later that it had been destroyed to make room for the freeway. It was probably just as well. I have learned enough since then to realize that, even if I knit all the clues together, no one cared—not when there were people walking around free who would kill a perfectly harmless turtle.

The sun was up as I saw the sign saying WELCOME TO MIAMI.

"You can drop me off at the bus station. I have my own money."

My speeding heart nearly fled from my chest. I had been half asleep when I thought I heard my father grunt and say, 'you are not going back.' Why was life suddenly so confusing? "Mom?" I cried, lurching for the front seat. "You're not coming with us?"

She was wiping off tears as she twisted to face me. "Your father won't tell you, but I will—they shot Mundy Peters."

"Is he dead?"

"We don't know. I'm going back to be with Aunt Jamesie."

"Can't I go with you?"

"Your father decided it's best that you go on with him."

Shockwaves of panic went blasting through my brain. Like Perry Mason, I needed an objection—quick! "But who will make me breakfast?"

She smiled, then glanced at my father. "Your dad can make breakfast—remember?"

"I know but—"

She put a gentle finger under my chin and lifted my face when I started to cry. "You're a big boy now. You have to be strong. Once things get settled, we'll be together again—I promise."

My old self was sure she was telling me the truth, but I really wasn't.

As the three of us stood outside the station to say good-bye, I went and clung to her with all of my strength. I could see my father hiding tears in his handkerchief as she stooped to hug me one last time. Hearing her whisper that I must never give up my dreams, it felt like she was setting us free. I tried not to cry watching my parents silently lock eyes as she stood to leave and picked up her matching red suitcases. As she turned and walked away, her back held firm and erect, I knew that, even before our journey had started, this was the way it was bound to end.

W. B. Garvey is the author of the award-winning historical novel, WHITE GOLD, companion to his critically acclaimed PANAMA FEVER: DIGGING DOWN GOLD MOUNTAIN. Garvey, whose writing has appeared in several publications including the *Killens Review of Arts & Letters*, is also a classically-trained violinist who has performed as soloist with renowned symphony orchestras and as a recitalist in major U.S. concert halls. He was born in Los Angeles to immigrant parents who moved the family back to Jamaica when he was nine years old. A graduate of the University of Southern California, Garvey has lived in Los Angeles, Kingston, London, and New York City. He now resides and writes in Phoenix, Arizona.

ALSO BY W. B. GARVEY

PANAMA FEVER: DIGGING DOWN GOLD MOUNTAIN

The electrifying saga of the machinists, masons, powder-gangs, cooks and mechanics who flocked to Panama in the late 19th century to work on the French effort to dig a sea-level canal. Crackling with action and adventure, it tells the story of two young men, Thomas Judah, the son of a wealthy merchant, and Byron Cooper, an orphan from a sugar plantation, as they seek their destinies and confront the catastrophes of earthquake, disease, political corruption and insurrection.

— Garvey's talent is strong and palpable. He writes with gusto of the many variants of hardship that keep the story rip-roaring from event to tragedy. *Jamaica Observer*

— Wickedly imaginative! ... It is a story of friendship, betrayal, greed, tragedy, human suffering and frailties, and hope, set among one of the greatest engineering undertakings of all time. *Jamaica Gleaner*

WHITE GOLD

It is the beginning of a new century and the eyes of the world are on Panama as the United States Army takes over the building of the Canal that will alter history and reshape the future. WHITE GOLD centers around William Roberson, an ambitious young railroad engineer from Jamaica determined to earn a better life, who finds himself caught between Winifred, his Jamaican wife who cannot abide life in Panama as Jim Crow laws are imposed by the Americans, and Isabella, the rebellious love of his life, who teaches him that there is more to life than duty and his beloved machines.

— Equally colorful and reminiscent of place and time ... an entertaining and educational sojourn to a time and place that changed history and the people who helped to do it. *African American Literature Book Club*

— Winner of the 2018 International AAHGS Book Award for Historical Fiction. *Afro-American Historical and Genealogical Society*

CPSIA information can be obtained
at www.ICGtesting.com
Printed in the USA
LVHW080024031121
702272LV00007B/62